THE
NIGHT
WE
BURNED

S. F. KOSA

sourcebooks
landmark

Published by Sourcebooks Landmark, an imprint of Sourcebooks
P.O. Box 4410, Naperville, Illinois 60567-4410
(630) 961-3900
sourcebooks.com

Library of Congress Cataloging-in-Publication Data

Names: Kosa, S. F., author.
Title: The night we burned : a novel / S.F. Kosa.
Description: Naperville, Illinois : Sourcebooks Landmark, [2021]
Identifiers: LCCN 2021002068 (print) | LCCN 2021002069 (ebook) |
   (trade paperback) | (epub)
Subjects: GSAFD: Mystery fiction. | Suspense fiction.
Classification: LCC PS3606.I5337 N54 2021 (print) | LCC PS3606.I5337
   (ebook) | DDC 813/.6--dc23
LC record available at https://lccn.loc.gov/2021002068
LC ebook record available at https://lccn.loc.gov/2021002069

Printed and bound in the United States of America.
SB 10 9 8 7 6 5 4 3 2 1

For Claudine. I am so grateful for your friendship.

CHAPTER ONE

Portland, Oregon
December 9, 1999

She'd survived another night on the street, but she wasn't sure how many more she could take. As the 20 bus roared to a halt a few feet away on East Burnside, hope lapped at her like a receding tide—a little weaker each time. The fifth bus since she'd dropped herself onto the curb, it ground to a halt in front of the graffitied thrift shop. After the third bus of the morning, she'd taken to letting the gritty water kicked up by its tires splash all over her shoes. Brown droplets sank into the sodden canvas of her stolen Keds and spread a renewed chill along the tops of her feet.

There was a smell to her weariness now: the low, flat, oniony funk of her own body, the acrid, iron backbone of scent wafting from the clothes she'd scrounged in St. Louis and hadn't taken off since, and the high, stinging note of gray bus exhaust. She wasn't sure which day it was; it didn't really matter anyway. And she wasn't sure what time it was because apparently the sun never came out in Portland this time of year.

A chubby girl in a trench coat carrying two Walmart bags stuffed full plodded down the bus's steps. At the bottom, she paused to secure her grip on her bags, twisting the loops around her fingers. She stepped out of the way with a murmured apology when she heard an annoyed sigh from behind her. A Black woman in a raincoat tromped down the stairs next, followed by a white, middle-aged man scowling at the sagging, gray sky.

As the man and woman turned in her direction, she tucked her damp hair behind her ears and shook the cup that bore her last two quarters, a Starbucks one she'd dug out of a garbage can, dried foam crust grubby on the rim. The woman in the raincoat sidestepped and kept walking, not even sparing her a glance.

It barely hurt anymore; she'd learned that people who had enough avoided making eye contact with those who didn't, people like her, as if even *seeing* her was too much to ask. Didn't mean she could afford to stop trying to be seen, though. She'd gotten kicked out of the Mercy Lamb shelter for fighting with that bitch who stole her socks, which meant no breakfast. It felt like her stomach was eating itself.

"Sir, I'd be grateful if you have any spare—" she began as the man approached.

"Five if we step off into that alley behind you," he said in a low voice, stopping directly in front of her. Stained khakis and Timberlands. He was already half-hard.

She stared down at her soggy shoes, frayed and knotted shoelaces. Shook her head.

It wasn't that she hadn't done it before, and that was the problem. A little chunk of her died every time, and she didn't have many vital pieces left.

"You're an ugly little bitch anyway," he muttered as he stalked by.

She lowered her head onto her knees and shivered. Gritted her teeth to keep from screaming. Maybe she could get hit by a car. Do something crazy. Mug someone, not that anyone would be intimidated, scrawny as she was. But if she could get hospitalized or arrested, maybe they'd give her something to eat. A place to sleep. God, she just wanted to sleep.

She flinched when someone brushed up against her. It was the girl with the bags, settling herself onto the curb. "I'm Eszter," she said. "What's your name?"

She turned her head. Looked at Eszter. Lowered her head onto her knees again. Then held her cup out and feebly shook it.

Eszter stayed quiet. Didn't move or fidget. Like she was perfectly comfortable sitting there in the cold and damp. "I really would like to know," she added after a few minutes.

"My name is Christy." It wasn't; she hadn't told anyone her real name since leaving home. Eszter didn't *seem* like a social worker—she actually didn't look any older than Christy—but Christy wasn't about to risk being sent back home.

"You look hungry, Christy," said Eszter. She dug in her purse, fake tan leather. Came up clutching a grease-spotted paper sack. "These were made this morning."

The smell hit, cinnamon sweet. Christy peeked inside. "Muffins?"

"Have one. They're really good. Morning glory."

Christy glanced at the outside of the bag. No logo. The muffins weren't wrapped. "You made them?"

"No—a friend of mine did." Eszter took the bag from her, reached inside, and pinched off a chunk of muffin. She popped it into her mouth and chewed. "Not poisoned or anything. See?" She offered the bag back to Christy.

"I didn't think they were poisonous," she muttered, retrieving a muffin for herself—nuts and raisins, not her favorite. But she'd eat headcheese and brussels sprouts at this point. The sugary burst on her tongue dropped her eyes shut.

"When was the last time you had a real meal?" Eszter asked.

Christy shrugged, her mouth still full. She wondered if Eszter was a volunteer, like for a church or some high school community service thing. Just looking for someone to help.

"How old are you?" Eszter asked.

"How old are *you?*" snapped Christy, shoving the rest of the muffin into her mouth.

"Eighteen," replied Eszter. "How long have you been on the street?"

Christy wrapped her arms around herself, running fingertips over the bumps of her ribs.

"Eight months for me," Eszter said quietly. "I left home when I was sixteen." She let out a dry laugh. "I actually thought it would be better."

She hadn't expected Eszter to be homeless, what with the freshly baked muffins—she'd have to find out which shelter doled them out. Christy nodded toward the Walmart bags, which looked like their owner: thin, pale skin stuffed to bursting. Clothes with tags still attached. "So you stole all that?"

Eszter shook her head. "Things are different now. I'm in a really good place. But I remember. I mean, it was only a year ago." She chuckled and looked around. "I think I once sat on this exact curb, actually. Have another muffin. There are three in there."

"I don't want to—"

"Go ahead," Eszter said, smiling. When she smiled, she was almost pretty, dirty-blond hair framing her moon of a face. "You need it more than I do."

Christy made short work of the last two muffins. They were more delicious with every bite, a buttery, soft crumb laced with warm spices. "Why are you being so nice to me?"

"You heard me say I was on the street, right? Where are you from? I can tell it's not Oregon."

"Midwest." It was more truth than she usually told.

"Really?" Eszter's hazel eyes were bright. "Me too! I stole money for a bus ticket. Mom had a stash in her drawer." Those shiny eyes rolled. "Probably hiding it from my stepdad. He was such a..." She shuddered.

Christy grunted. "I stole my mom's purse too." But it hadn't had anywhere near enough to pay for a bus ticket. She'd hitched. And learned what it took to make it across the country, little shards of her soul scattered from Chicago to St. Louis, Kansas City to Denver, Boise to Portland. "I left in July. Didn't bother to pack a coat." With a bitter laugh, she rubbed her hands along her arms, trying to raise some warmth. Her fingers were gray with the cold.

"Winters are the worst," said Eszter. "At least we're not in Chicago."

"I used to like winter. I liked the snow. Now I'm thinking I should head south."

"Why?"

"Why not?"

"I did that too," said Eszter. "I didn't even know how to tell I was in a good place until I'd already been there for a while, since I'd never been in a good place to begin with." Eszter bumped shoulders with Christy, strangely familiar, strangely...nice. For the first time in a long time, Christy didn't feel the need to flinch away. "You know what I'm saying?"

"Yeah." It was weird, sitting here on this curb, the cold gnawing at her ears and chin, her fingers and clammy, sockless feet, making a new friend. "So what happened? You just bought a bus ticket and came to Portland? Do you have family out here or something?"

"Yes," said Eszter. "A big, extended family. It just took me a while to find them." She turned to Christy. "And none of them are related to me."

Christy's eyes narrowed.

"We actually live just a few blocks away," said Eszter, jerking a thumb behind her. Then she patted the stuffed bags. "I was just out getting us some supplies."

Christy glanced at the Walmart bags. Shirts, sweats, packages of... tighty-whities? Fruit of the Loom. "Looks like you guys go through a lot of underpants."

Eszter pressed her lips together, obviously trying not to laugh. "Yeah, we do." She turned to Christy and said, "I'm wearing three pairs right now, actually."

Christy found herself giggling at the fake-somber confession. "Maybe I should try that. My butt is freezing." She eyed Eszter's attire, thick gray sweats stretched across generous thighs, newish-but-cheap-looking sneakers, a pink sweatshirt beneath that big trench. "Do you all dress alike?"

Eszter looked down at herself. "It's not like it's required or anything. We wanted to make sure everyone has something clean and nice to wear, and this stuff doesn't cost much. Whatever works." She pawed through one of the bags. "You look like you could use a change of clothes." The corners of her mouth twitched upward. "And maybe a few layers of underwear."

"I'm okay."

"You're soaked."

Christy felt squirmy all of a sudden. For a moment, she'd felt an easy camaraderie, but now she was back to feeling like a charity case. And sure, she'd been panhandling for days, but she'd liked it better when she'd felt like Eszter actually liked her. "I'll warm up once I start walking again. I'd better get going."

"To where?" Eszter asked. "You really have somewhere great to be?" She pointed at the cross street by the bus stop. "I live on Twenty-Ninth Avenue. Three blocks up. Come and hang out. Everyone's nice, I promise."

Christy scooted away. "It's a church, right? This whole thing?"

Eszter gave her a solemn look. "The last time I set foot in a church is when I was eleven. Holiday service. The whole family. It was, like, the only time we ever went. Me and my little brother, my mom, and Bob." She bit out his name like a curse. "And my brother, right in the middle of the singing, he needed to pee, so Mom had me take him. And then he wanted a snack, and we found a bunch of crackers and grape juice in this little room. I was so hungry—" She pulled her trench coat tighter around her, cheeks growing pink. "I was fat even then, and Mom hated it. Hated *me*. I don't think she'd let me eat anything that whole day." She sighed. "Anyway. Long story short, we got caught, and I got a beating that I will *never* forget." Her voice was shaking. "But I guess the good part about all of it was they never made me go to church again."

"That sucks," Christy murmured, wrapping her arms around her knees.

Eszter made a distressed noise and dug in her Walmart bag, coming up with a big black sweatshirt that she held out to Christy. "I can't stand to watch you shiver anymore. Please?"

Christy's first instinct was to refuse, but then she realized how stupid that was. It didn't matter why Eszter was being so nice—Christy badly needed another layer. She took the garment and pulled it over her damp flannel. "Thanks."

"But you're still afraid I'm a church person?" asked Eszter.

Christy watched a few cars go by. "I used to like going to church. My grandma took me and my little brother." She couldn't remember if her mom had ever gone; most days, she was closeted with her loser of the week and a bottle of Wild Turkey, and the only time she'd emerge was to yell at Christy for having the TV too loud or running the AC too long, using too much electricity. But Grammy had taken them to church every week for a while, and she'd always have them back to her place for ham and potatoes and green beans. "It was really nice."

"Does she know you're out here?" Eszter asked quietly.

"She's dead." Dropped right at her cash register at the dollar store where she'd worked for over ten years. "My mom called it a brain bleed." It had taken Grammy three weeks to die.

"I'm so sorry."

"That's why I never go to church anymore."

"Because it reminds you of your grandma?"

She shook her head as a familiar rage bubbled up. "Because it's all crap. They say prayer fixes stuff, right? I prayed every single day for Jesus to make her better." She'd smelled like pickles and peaches and Pall Malls. She'd had a raspy laugh and loved to rewatch *Seinfeld* episodes she'd recorded on her VCR. To Christy, she'd been the best person in the world. "And if Jesus even exists, he didn't listen. Didn't care."

"I don't blame you."

Christy looked up the street. The next 20 bus would come soon;

every half hour seemed to be the schedule. Already there was a skinny, old Asian man waiting for it, holding a wilting newspaper over his head, pathetic defense against the icy mist. Even in the new sweatshirt, she felt raw, oddly bare and exposed. But she wasn't sure if it was the weather or the conversation.

Eszter placed a hand on her arm. "You've been through a lot," she said. "Maybe more than I have, but I feel like I dealt with enough to get what you might be feeling. I've had to do things I didn't like just to survive. I've let people hurt me because I felt powerless, because I thought I was worthless and that no one cared. And even when I found people who did care, I didn't trust it at first." She smirked. "I'm thinking you know the lyrics to this song."

Christy sighed. Rubbed her face wearily. "By heart."

"I'm not trying to convert you or church you or whatever, okay? It's not like that. It's just that I'm in a good place now, and I got here because people cared enough to help me, and I'm trying to do the same here. That's it, I swear."

She seemed so earnest. So real. "Listen—*you* seem great," Christy said. "But..."

"You're worried about my friends?" Eszter laughed. "They are seriously the nicest people in the world, and we're all just trying to help each other. And if I hadn't found them, I'm pretty sure I would have died under the Burnside Bridge last winter. So there's that."

Christy chuckled weakly. She'd slept under that bridge one of her first nights in Portland.

"You could just come for dinner. But if you want, I think there's also an open cot." Eszter grinned. "And probably a few more of those muffins. Ladonna makes a few batches every day."

"It's just a house?" asked Christy.

Eszter nodded. "A pretty crowded one, but a lot of us were on the street once. We take care of one another."

"Okay, so, like, a *crack* house?"

"A crack house where we bake muffins? If you want to live with us, you have to be clean." Eszter pushed herself to her feet. "Come on. Now I just need you to look at it so you can see that it's not what you're picturing. And if it looks like a crack house or if you don't like the paint color, you can keep walking to whatever important appointment you've got happening next." She held up one of her bags and gave Christy a playful wink. "I'll even throw in a change of clothes and ten dollars for the trip."

Christy slowly stood up, her limbs stiff with cold. The arms of the sweatshirt hung past her fingertips and thighs, and still she was freezing. But her thoughts pulsed with hope. She poked her fingers into the Starbucks cup and pulled out her two quarters. Tucked them into the back pocket of her ratty jeans. Eszter looked soft and slow and serious, like she desperately wanted to do good. If the worst that could happen was ten dollars and a change of clothes, it was worth the time.

And she couldn't think of one thing she had left to lose.

"Okay," she said. "I'm game."

CHAPTER TWO

Seattle, Washington
December 9, present day

It's a little after seven when I sit down in front of my laptop with my coffee, but I've been awake since three, thrown from sleep by a scrum of crazy dreams, flooding culverts, wet earth, all the clouds on fire. It's a relief to see my screen blink to life, to open up Facebook and see that other people still exist and the world isn't falling apart—at least not literally. Outside my window, clumps of snow tumble down, melting before they even hit the ground. Running to work this morning is going to suck.

December is an unsettled month for me no matter where I am. I'd hoped this year would be different, but here we are. It always starts just after Thanksgiving: My sleep falls apart. I eat even less than I normally do, log more miles than usual. I'm relieved when the New Year arrives, solid evidence of the distance between me and the past. With two exceptions, there's nothing I want to revisit.

Eric is one of those exceptions. I log in to my account. Well. Not *my* account. Dora Rodriguez has a few professional listings but doesn't do social media.

Eric has so many friends that he hasn't noticed that two of them are Tammy Deering. He was in a play with her in fourth grade. He probably accepted my friend request without noticing the duplication, just saw the familiar name and brought me into the fold. The real Tammy hasn't noticed either, maybe because she's long since become Tammy Horton. Or maybe because the fake Tammy Deering has never actually posted or otherwise called attention to herself. Her profile pic is of a cute dog—a Pembroke Welsh corgi—just like the pet the real Tammy once brought to school dressed up as a little hot dog, something nine-year-old Eric talked about for weeks.

Fake Tammy only has six friends, four of whom are randos who also like corgis and one of whom is someone Eric went to college with who also has a corgi. Her name is Liza Coates, and she friend-requested me about a year ago. I accepted because it lends me an air of legitimacy, but she actually turned out to be a cool person who I chat with from time to time.

And the sixth friend is *him*.

Eric turned thirty-four in October and seems to be having a pretty good life, thank god. He's just posted pictures of his kids dressed up for a holiday party, in shorts and light jackets now that they live down in Texas. The boy, Nathan, just turned six, and the girl, Emma, is only three. Two fair-haired, cherub-cheeked bundles of nonstop energy—if Eric's posts are to be believed—who seem to be living a very different childhood from the one their father endured.

I drink in the pictures of my brother, my niece and nephew, and read all the comments from a few people I once knew and many I never did. I linger over an image of Eric and his wife with the children, their smiles huge as they pose in their matching superhero

Halloween costumes. He looks so, *so* happy. I know Facebook isn't necessarily the place where people go to present the naked reality of their lives, but I hope the pictures he posts are at the very least a truth in and of themselves. I want to believe that in that one moment, they really were as happy as they look. I stare at his face in an attempt to overwrite the memory of how it looked the last time I saw him: rounded with youth, stricken with the pain I caused.

He looks like he's gotten over it. And I'm glad.

His green dot appears, so I log out. I finish my coffee and scowl at the winter outside my window as the warm dopamine glow of my brother and his family fades, leaving me with my reality, lonely by necessity.

Remembering why I really hate December.

I never give myself more than thirty-eight minutes to run to work: four-point-four eight-minute miles plus a two-minute allowance for lights. Anything more and I force myself to make up the time. My weekday breakfast typically consists of this small victory: I haven't yet been late.

Today might be the first time in the four months I've had the job—the editorial meeting is at nine instead of nine thirty. The heavy sky spits wet globs of snow into my face as I power my way over the Montlake Bridge. The app that tracks my pace pipes its unflappable AI voice through my earbuds, interrupting the electronica that primes my steps: "Activity time: ten minutes. Distance: one point two miles." Damn.

I lengthen my stride, but the grinding ache in my back, the pain that first reared its head just after I moved to Seattle, begs me to take it easy. But I won't. I'm still two years from forty, way too young to feel this old, and I plan to run until I die.

It's saved me more than once.

My leggings are soaked through with puddle splash tossed by passing cars, and the melted snow has soaked through my beanie. If I don't hurry, I'll be walking into the conference room looking as pathetic as a cat that's just been tossed into a bathtub. I'm glad, in this moment, that I no longer work at a fashion magazine. The women at *Slice* judged like it was the Olympics, only the scores came in the curl of a glossy lip and the arch of a perfectly threaded eyebrow, too ephemeral for this fact-checker to pin down with precision.

Four minutes late, I arrive at the gym, where I have a membership only so I can stow my stuff and clean up before work. After a lightning-fast shower, I brush out my damp hair, peering at myself in the mirror and considering for the millionth time whether to get it dyed, if only to stop the lingering looks and prying questions about why on earth someone my age has completely white hair.

The questions I really hate are the joking ones about whether it's the result of some terrible scare. I always laugh. Of course not. It's genetic.

Someday, I'll answer truthfully.

I turn away from the mirror and yank my hair back into a ponytail. No time to blow-dry. No time for anything except a bit of powder and a swipe of mascara and tinted lip gloss. Valentina always starts the meeting on time.

I layer on my dry work clothes, gently pulling on fresh compression socks over the mottled, scarred skin of my calves. After hanging my gear in my locker, I shoulder my pack and bolt out of the locker room. Two minutes until the meeting.

As soon as the elevator doors open to the fourth floor of the office co-op that houses the *Hatchet*, the reason I uprooted my life in St. Louis and moved to Seattle, I'm out and jogging toward the conference room, already shivering. I pause only to grab my heavy cardigan and the bottle of ibuprofen from my cubicle.

Valentina, wearing black slacks and a pink cashmere sweater, her ebony hair cornrowed on one side and falling in tight ringlets down the other, meets me in the hallway. She opens the glass door to the conference room while giving me a thorough once-over. "Already popping vitamin I, and the day's barely begun. You okay, Dora?"

"Just a little sore." I enter the room and realize we're the first ones to arrive. "I was afraid I'd be late."

Valentina rolls her eyes. "Apparently, my journalists don't take *any* of their deadlines seriously." Her four-inch heels click on the faux wood floor as she stalks across the room to the watercooler. She fills a paper cup and sets it in front of me. Out of habit, I've attempted to place myself as far from the seat of power as possible—near the back of the room—but still, that power seems to find me. Some things never change, I guess.

"How far is the back-and-forth every day? Six miles?" Valentina picks up a plate of cookies from beside the watercooler and slides it across the table. "Fuel up."

I pretend not to see them as I type my password into the laptop. "Almost nine," I admit.

Valentina whistles. "You got a race coming up? I'm doing a 10K in Tacoma in two weeks. One of those holiday things for charity. They even give you a Santa hat. Interested?"

"I don't do races," I tell her, trying to keep my voice friendly, because I know she only means well. "I never have. It's not why I run."

Valentina lets out a quiet ho-ho-ho and gives me a poke in the shoulder. "Come on, Rodriguez. You could come as my elf—"

"I need to pitch first today," Miles announces as he bustles into the room and plops down where he always does, near the head of the table. I glance down at my fitness watch and see my heart rate go from sixty-two to almost eighty in about three seconds. His glasses are still half-fogged and he's a little out of breath. His tousled, black hair is flecked with melting snowflakes. He runs a hand through it and dries his palm on the leg of his dark-wash jeans. "It's gross out there." He looks me up and down. "You look as cold as I feel."

I pull my cardigan closer around my body. "I'm always cold."

"I think Kieran was complaining about that just the other day," he says with a smile.

"What?" Valentina's eyes narrow. "Mr. Connover, are you implying—"

He holds up his hands. "I just meant that Dora showed no mercy when it came to calling out all his dangling modifiers!"

"I was pretty brutal," I say, narrowing my eyes. "But he needs to learn at some point."

Miles laughs, and this time, I don't even bother to check the watch because I can *feel* my heart kicking against my ribs as if I'm midway up a hill.

"The almighty copy editor has spoken," he says. His palms drum the table as a few other members of the investigative team file into the room. "I really do need to go first," he says to Valentina. "It's time sensitive. And you're going to love it."

"We're reviewing stories in progress before pitches," Valentina says firmly.

Miles's eyes find mine again. "Valentina told me you're from Bend."

A hard shock courses through my body, instant and cold. I clear my throat. "Yeah?"

He leans forward. "Were you there when—"

"Miles," Valentina snaps. Upon seeing that she's silenced him, she lets Freya, her admin, start the meeting with a rundown of the stories already in the pipeline.

I take some notes, but I only speak up on the pieces that have already reached my inbox. On my first day, Valentina Jones swore up and down that copyediting and fact-checking for a twenty-four/seven outfit like the *Hatchet* would be the most intense experience I've ever had. I pretended to believe that could be true. In actuality, working with the concrete details of a story became my escape. Dealing with the facts that most consider white noise gives me a clear pathway—guidelines to follow. Tangible truth.

I try to limit my lies to myself, see.

Heidi's story on the bestiality scandal at the Westhampton equestrian club was inconsistent on the timeline of threatening emails sent by the would-be "horse lover," so I'm going through the timestamps and confirming the corrections with the club owner. Kieran's piece on the con man who stole a tech titan's identity to purchase drugs on a yacht in Bodega Bay is almost ready to go, save for date and name confirmations as well as numerous edits for passive voice. Kieran, only a year out of Northwestern, bristles a bit at the feedback until Miles tells him never to lose his "sophomore edge." He's quiet after that.

Of all the stuff I do at *Hatchet*, I enjoy the investigative team the most; the majority of my work week is taken up with short pieces: political news, pop culture, and vignettes gone viral that are considered click-worthy enough to merit positioning in the sidebar of the home page, interspersed with the curated, sponsored product promotion that helps keep us fiscally solvent. Only about six long-form pieces from the investigative team—subscription only, of course—come out every month, and those are meatier. Lurid stories occurring somewhere else, happening to someone else. My only job is to make sure the pieces are clear and corroborated. Real.

By the time stories in progress have wrapped and it's time to pitch, Miles looks ready to leap out of his seat. His manner, loose and joking, makes him seem younger, but he's one of the more senior journalists at *Hatchet*. He was at the *Seattle Times* for almost a decade until Valentina lured him away with a promise of more freedom to follow his interests. We work well together; the only time he's ever gotten snappish with me was when I suggested a few rewrites to address what Valentina calls "default whiteness" from his last piece on the racist hazing rituals at an exclusive prep school in Southern California. But after snarling at me in the lounge, he emailed a revision within an hour, then showed up at my desk with a "muffin of apology" from the bakery next door.

I kept the muffin on my desk the rest of the day, smiling every time I glanced at it. Then I quietly tucked it into my trash bin before I left to run home.

"I need to go to Oregon," Miles announces. "Tip came in this morning, and it's gold. Five nights ago, Bend authorities were called to a trailer park—one had gone up in flames. They found a guy inside."

Valentina arches one eyebrow. "Okay..."

Miles grins. "He wasn't *burned*. His body was in the bathtub. It had been covered in some sort of flame retardant."

Heidi sets down the massive chocolate chip cookie she's been making a project of for the last five minutes. "So he was dead but not from fire? Was it smoke inhalation?"

Miles shakes his head. "Stabbed." He pokes at his chest. "And police found some sort of rock in his mouth. That part was leaked online by someone at the medical examiner's office. Apparently, police aren't too happy about that, if my call to the chief just now is any indication."

"A rock in his mouth," I murmur.

"I *know*," says Miles, peering at me with an intensity that makes me reach for my bottle of ibuprofen. I dole out four pills into my palm and toss them back, trying not to think about how much they feel like little pebbles sliding down my throat.

Valentina is less affected. "Okay. Guy stabbed, killer wants him to be found intact, leaves a calling card, but sets the trailer on fire to cover his or her tracks. What's the angle here? We don't do local one-off murders unless there's a real hook. You think this is a serial thing?"

"I don't know yet," says Miles. "But that's not the angle." He looks down at his phone. "Guy's name was Arnold Moore. 'Arnie' to his friends."

It feels like the pills have lodged in my esophagus. I reach for my water and take a sip, reminding myself that it's a common name. A common nickname.

"Is that supposed to ring a bell?" asks Valentina.

Miles gestures around the room. "Anyone here remember the Oracles of Innocence massacre, or were you all in diapers then?

Dora, help me out. If you're from Bend, you have to know what I'm talking about."

"I don't think—" My voice breaks. I gulp at my water, which immediately heads down the wrong pipe. "Sorry," I say between coughs. I gesture for them to go on without me.

"Anyone?" Miles frowns. "This was a huge story at the time. I mean, I was studying abroad in Spain that semester, and it was even on the news *there*."

"I remember it," says Valentina. "Cult massacre. Big fire, something like thirty people died. Lots of speculation about whether the victims committed suicide on purpose or were part of some crazy sacrifice ritual and whether the fire was accidental or on purpose."

It almost feels as if I'm floating above the room, watching this unfold from outside my body. We can't really be talking about this. A haze of unreality limns the room, softening and blurring the edge of the table, the sharp line of Miles's profile, and the ferocious curiosity in his voice. As my ears start to ring, I try to focus on each word coming out of his mouth, parsing each phrase, mentally bracketing them with commas, dividing them from their meaning.

It doesn't make anything normal again.

"Right," Miles is saying. "A big *fire*. And the three adult survivors all went to jail—one was charged with second-degree murder because she actually barred the door to the meeting hall to keep anyone from escaping. And two other people, one man and one woman, were found guilty of involuntary manslaughter because they didn't try to help anyone get out. The three of them just let it burn, with all their fellow cult members inside. Twenty years ago *this month*. You know cult anniversaries, right? Brings out all the crazies. And this one's in less than a week. The fifteenth."

Oh my god. I can't breathe. My vision begins to swim.

"What does this have to do with the murder of Mr. Moore?" asks Valentina.

"He was one of the three survivors," Miles says, looking triumphant. "Tell me this isn't a major story. I dare you."

I shove away from the table and stand up. "Excuse me," I whisper as I rush to the door and stumble into the hall. I don't look up until I've safely made it into a bathroom stall, where I press my hands to the cool metal walls and do my best not to sink to the floor.

This can't be happening. I've worked too hard.

I whirl around and retch into the toilet, squeezing my eyes shut at the sight of the four orange pills sinking to the bottom of the bowl.

I've been running for twenty years, but my past has just caught up.

CHAPTER THREE

Portland, Oregon
December 9, 1999

The house was on a street clustered with other houses that looked just like it, nestled in a quiet neighborhood a few blocks and a world away from the trash-strewn avenue she'd prowled for the past week, trying to figure out how to eat, where to sleep, how to protect herself.

"Not bad, right?" Eszter asked as she marched up the walk and opened the front door.

Cinnamon. The scent wafted forth in a wave that made Christy's mouth water.

Eszter waved her inside and set down her bags. "Ladonna knows her stuff."

A Black woman with fluffy natural hair and a baby bump leaned out of the kitchen and waved a batter-coated wooden spoon at them. "Hi there," she said before turning to Eszter. "I need more eggs."

"She just got back. Somebody else can get them," said a blond pregnant woman sitting on the couch in the living room. She gestured to a few others who had been sitting near her. "Do you have a list of other things you need?"

"I've got it," said a muscular, dark-haired guy in the dining room, holding a spiral-bound notebook. He took dictation while Ladonna recited a few additional items, then tore the page out of the notebook and handed it to the woman in the living room.

"This is Octavia," Eszter said, gesturing at the blond pregnant woman. "Octavia, this is Christy."

Octavia grinned. "Are you hungry? You look hungry."

"I'm fine," said Christy.

"She ate three of Ladonna's muffins," Eszter said.

Octavia patted her basketball belly. "Me too," she replied. "I couldn't help myself." Her sheepish expression made Christy want to smile.

Eszter led Christy into the dining room, where several people were chatting as they chopped vegetables and kneaded dough at the long, wooden table. She pointed down the hallway. "How does a hot shower sound?"

If Christy could smell herself, that meant they could too. "Sounds okay."

Eszter took in her hesitant tone and gave her a playful poke in the arm. "Don't worry. The door locks."

Maybe she remembered what some of the shelters were like. Christy kept her eyes on the floor as she followed Eszter down a hall, past a few bedrooms full of neatly arranged cots and sleeping bags. The door to the room at the end of the hall was cracked open, slivers of movement drawing her eye.

Eszter smiled over her shoulder. "Meditation session," she whispered. "Have you ever tried it?"

Christy wanted to laugh. "Sure. That's what I was doing on the curb when you found me."

"I know, it sounds weird." She led Christy into a room with a big closet, clothes hanging from racks and folded on shelves. From down the hall, behind the closed door, came the sound of a man's voice, an insistent, low murmur. Another person—it sounded like a woman—moaned. "They're channeling," Eszter said as she set down her Walmart bags. "It's a powerful experience."

"Uh-huh." So far, she'd seen two pregnant ladies. Maybe it was less of a crack house and more of a—

"Oh my god," Eszter said with a snort. "I can almost hear your thoughts from here. They really are just doing deep meditation. And if you stay long enough, you can try it yourself. It's hard to focus on anything else when you're just trying to get through the day, but when your needs are met and you're freed from all that?" She shook her head. "You'd be surprised what you can do." She gestured at the clothes. "Pick out some stuff that fits. We've got everything here." She opened a few drawers of a large bureau against the wall. "Underwear, socks, bras. Take anything you need. It's all clean."

It looked like a mini thrift store. "Are you serious? Why would you guys—?"

"Because you're a human being who needs it. Not that complicated, really."

"This is unreal."

Eszter grinned. "It's totally real. And you don't have to be scared it'll disappear or be yanked out from under you—but it took me a long time to start believing that, so I don't blame you if you're the same."

Christy chuckled. "You literally just met me."

"Maybe the best friendships start with the little things—like a clean, dry pair of underwear." Eszter's eyes glinted with playfulness. "Or even three layers of them, if that's what it takes to keep your butt warm." She pointed to the door. "Bathroom's across the hall. If you need anything else, just call my name, okay? I'll be right there."

Clean was a strange feeling, one she'd never noticed before or thought much about. But now, her hair brushed, a faint soapy scent rising from her skin, her body her own and covered in clean clothes, Christy wondered how she ever experienced this without appreciating it. Before leaving the bathroom, she smiled into the mirror, then frowned. "You can leave whenever you want," she whispered to herself. "You know how to get out if you need to."

But as she opened the door and heard laughter and conversation from the living room, she rolled her eyes. These people seemed harmless. Like she always imagined a healthy family might act. Or just a big group of friends, just crashing, no stress. Not rich, but happy. The only question that remained was *why* they were being so nice to her.

"Christy!" Eszter greeted her at the end of the hallway, grabbing her hand and pulling her toward the dining room. "Come meet everyone! This is Arnie." She nodded at a lanky white guy with messy hair who was chopping celery at the end of the dining table. He looked up and gave her a shy smile. "And that's Gilgamesh." She pointed to the guy who had written down Ladonna's grocery list.

"Gil." He held up his notebook. "Resident list maker."

Eszter gazed at him fondly. "In other words, the one who makes sure we have all the supplies we need to feed and clothe so many people."

"Who I *also* keep track of," said Gil. "Speaking of..." He looked Christy up and down. "We should talk."

"What?" Christy took a step back, her movement arrested only when she stepped on Arnie's toe. "Sorry!"

"He just meant that he wants to get your details," said Eszter. "Only what you feel comfortable telling him, though."

Gil waggled his eyebrows at her. "But I'm a great listener, right?"

"That you are," Eszter murmured.

He waved a hand at Christy. "It's just an unofficial roster. Easier for keeping track, remembering birthdays, making sure we have enough for everyone. Think of me as the team's general manager."

"I'm not *on* the team," Christy said.

He smiled and resumed his list making, and Eszter returned her attention to the people at the table. "This is Marie." She put her hand on the shoulder of a plain-looking girl, close to Christy's age, who had been emptying peelings into a bin marked *compost*. "She joined us last week."

"Marie Heckender," said Marie as she offered her hand to shake. "Heck-*en*-der."

"Marie Heck-*en*-der," Christy said, hoping that was what this girl wanted to hear.

Marie grinned at her. "This place is amazing, right?"

"I...guess?"

"You don't have to pretend," said Eszter. "You haven't made any decisions or commitments, and there's no rush."

"Commitment to what?" asked Christy.

"Each other," Octavia said as she emerged from the kitchen, muffin in hand. "You'll see."

"And it'll change everything," Marie enthused.

Eszter shook her head. "She'll make up her own mind."

"When's Darius going to be done?" Marie asked Eszter.

"When he's done," said Octavia, wincing and putting a hand to her belly. "You know that clocks don't matter here."

Marie's face fell. "Right. I have to stop thinking like that. Hours and seconds." She looked at Christy. "Have you ever thought about how arbitrary all that is? When we were kids, we never worried about it. We never worried about anything."

"I did," said Christy.

Marie blinked. "Well, sure. I just meant that we weren't *aware*, you know?"

Christy felt like she'd been aware since the moment she was born, of how much she wished she could live with Grammy, of the smell of her mom's breath, Mom's boyfriends' breath, too many breaths, all breathing on *her*. The urge to say so was almost too much, but she didn't want to snap at all these strange, nice people.

Once again, Eszter saved the day. "We all had different experiences before we came to this place," she said to Marie. "What's important is that we're all here now. And that's how we save one another. It's how we grow our consciousness."

Marie's face was flushed now, but she merely nodded. From down the hall, a door opened and shut. The effect was the same on everyone in the room—Christy sensed the shift like an electric current humming through the air. A soft clicking sound reached her, and a second later, two people emerged from the corridor: a gaunt, elderly woman wearing a knit cap, sitting in a wheelchair pushed by a tall, bearded man with deeply tanned skin and broad shoulders. He was handsome for an older guy; Christy guessed he was in his forties maybe. These were the people she'd heard meditating, and now she felt really stupid, assuming they'd been up to something dirty. She shouldn't have been so quick to assume.

The bearded guy whispered something in the elderly woman's ear, and she nodded wearily. He straightened up and surveyed the people in the dining room. "Marie," he said. "Get Shirin a glass of water and help get her comfortable in one of the bedrooms. She needs to rest."

Marie shot to her feet. "Can I get you something, too, Darius? Do you want—"

"If you take care of Shirin, you're taking care of me," he said with a gentle smile.

Marie rushed over to Shirin, and the old woman patted Marie's hand as she pushed the wheelchair back down the hall. Christy spared them a glance before returning her focus to the man in front of her.

He was looking at her too. "Who is this?"

"Christy," Eszter said.

"You look like you're considering running right back out the door, Christy." He scowled at the people in the dining room. "Who made Christy feel unwelcome?"

"They've all been really nice!" Christy said quickly—just as she realized that the people at the table were all grinning.

"Come sit down," said Darius, grinning in return. "Tell us your story."

"I don't have one."

"We all have one," said Darius. "And they're all worth hearing." He gestured toward the couch, empty now that the others had gone out for additional supplies. Darius sat on a chair nearby with a teasing expression on his face. "Clear path to the door there. Only a few steps, and you'll have escaped."

"How can you tell?" Christy mumbled.

"I have a lot of experience with people in pain," he said. As soon as she opened her mouth to deny it, he shook his head. "No one's going to shame you for it."

She sat back. Tried to swallow the sudden lump in her throat. Looked out the window as a kid rode by on a bicycle, wearing a helmet. *His mom must really care about him.*

"Who have you lost?" he asked.

"My grandma," she said before she could think about it. "She's the only person who ever cared if I lived or died."

"Not your parents?"

She shook her head.

"You don't have to talk about it until you're ready," he said. "And right now, Christy, you are surrounded by people who care whether you live or die. Do you believe that?"

"I don't know," she whispered.

"It's okay. But if you stay here long enough, I promise you—you'll *know* it, right down to your bones. And it will change you forever."

"What," she said hoarsely, "is this place?"

Darius leaned his elbows on his knees. His blue eyes held her fast. "Do you believe we're all connected, Christy?"

"I don't know what that means."

"We're all human, right?" When she nodded, he continued. "We were all born, and we're all going to die someday." He waited for another nod, then said, "Between that emergence into the world and that departure, we're all here, and we feel, and we know."

She stopped nodding. "What I *know* is that I've had to take care of myself since I was a kid."

"What you know is exactly my point. You understand that something is wrong. Something's missing."

"Like food?"

"That's just a symptom of the larger disease, but yes. You know you're hungry. But in that case, you know how to fix it. You do whatever you can to fill your belly because you'll die if you don't. But what about your soul? Your consciousness? What happens when you don't feed *them*?"

"I haven't really had time to think about it."

"Most of us spend our whole lives not thinking about it," he said. "But some of us realize we can't afford that kind of ignorance."

"And some of us are just trying to afford our next meal," she snapped.

He nodded as if he approved. "You're absolutely right. Which is why, I'm guessing, the first thing that happened when you entered this house is that someone offered you something to eat. Or a place to rest." He tugged at the sleeve of the sweatshirt she'd donned, fresh from its package. "Or clean clothes. It's called Maslow's hierarchy. At the bottom are your basic needs: food, shelter. Then comes safety. And only after those needs are met can you start to think about love. Belonging. But even *that's* not at the very top; it's only a stepping-stone. The next one is esteem. Believing in yourself. And after that?" He smiled. "After that, you're approaching enlightenment. But first, those basic needs have to be met, or you can't think of anything else. So that's where we start. Where we go from there is up to you."

"We?"

He shrugged. "You're young, so you might think you can do everything on your own. That you're invincible. That you can figure everything out." He spread his arms and gave her a teasing smile. "When you're old like me, you realize that's all a lie. That no matter how much money you have—and trust me, I've had plenty—no matter how much education—and yes, I have that too—you still need some help along the way. So, yeah—*we*."

Christy shook her head. "But you said *we* like it included me, and that's what I'm asking. Why *me*? You have no idea—"

He held up a hand. "Who brought you here?"

"Eszter."

Darius smiled. "She spots the heart in people better than anyone I've ever met."

"She really does," said Octavia, coming up behind him and placing her hands on his shoulders. "But *you're* the one who spotted the heart in me."

"It was so beautiful, there was no missing it," he said, bringing one of her palms to his lips and laying a light kiss there. They were *together*, Christy realized. She wondered if Octavia's baby was his. She didn't want to jump to conclusions again, but there was a familiarity there, an obvious bond.

Octavia headed back into the dining room. Darius followed her with his gaze for a moment before returning his attention to Christy. "We're all here because we want the same thing, Christy. We want to connect with something deeper than all this distracting surface crud. We want to touch that deep consciousness and make it real for one another. If one person were missing, it wouldn't be the same. Which is why I'm so glad you're here, for however long you're here. You have a questioning mind."

Did she? And did it matter, if they let her sleep on one of those cots tonight? If they fed her another meal?

Darius watched her for a moment. Then he put his hand on her knee, a warm, steady weight. "You're safe here, Christy. Even if you don't know it yet, you're among friends. Rest. Eat. Get to know us.

Stay if you want; go if you feel like this isn't the place for you. But either way, I'm grateful to have met you."

He got up and headed back down the hall, leaving Christy blinking in his wake. Her heart was racing, and her eyes stung. She hadn't said much, but he'd left her feeling like she'd given a lot away. Somehow, though, it felt good. Like a burden lifted instead of a weight of expectation pushing her down.

She got to her feet. Everybody else was busy, happily chatting as they worked on the meal they were preparing. Suddenly, she wanted to be a part of that, if only for the evening.

"Hey, Eszter?" she called. "Do you guys need any help with dinner?"

CHAPTER FOUR

Seattle, Washington
December 9, present day

M y first instinct is to run. Pack up my entire apartment, empty the bank accounts, terminate the credit cards, get a burner phone. Head for Canada or Mexico or Brazil, I don't know. Anything to put miles between myself and dead Arnie Moore. Between me and what Miles might find if he goes after this story.

Then I realize how stupid I'm being. How paranoid. How pathetic. I know how to survive. I know how to keep moving forward, even when guilt threatens to crush me. I've built a good life, a little lonely but mine to control. Am I really going to run at the first sign of trouble?

I exit the bathroom stall, rinse my mouth, and smooth my hair. Stare at myself in the mirror and assess. The first thing I need to do is understand what I'm dealing with.

By the time I leave the bathroom, the editorial meeting is over. Valentina's in the conference room talking to Freya, but she looks up as I pass. "You okay, Dora?"

"Yeah—but I shouldn't take ibuprofen on an empty stomach. Did you approve Miles's story?"

Valentina nods before returning to her conversation with Freya, a nonchalant confirmation of all my worst fears. I head for the cubicles, my heart speeding as I catch sight of Miles's curls over the top of a partition. He's on the phone, his head bowed over his laptop. I slip into the conference room and retrieve my own computer. Then I veer toward my own cubicle as my nausea returns. I have to get control of myself and *think*.

I spend a half hour copyediting Heidi's latest piece on the heir to an East Coast fortune—a long-lost child who turned out to be an impostor. By the time I'm done, I can feel the ground beneath my feet again.

I have a few options for how to deal with this mess. I could bury my head in the sand and hope Miles won't figure out my involvement. I've covered my tracks. Severed any link I might have had to my past self. It's possible even Miles couldn't figure it out, but I've seen him when he gets a nose for a story—he's relentless. So the passive approach is risky.

I could go back to Valentina and do my best to stab Miles in the back. Last month, I heard her yelling at him for running up too many expenses for his SoCal story. She might be willing to clip his wings after a few well-timed comments about the costs of a treasure hunt. I've been present for more than one lecture about expense reports and ad blockers and subscription programs and the woes of internet business models in the age of recession. After years at the *Chicago Tribune*, Valentina managed to gather some backers and start *Hatchet* on a shoestring. Over ten years, she grew it into the fifty-person juggernaut it is today, but the margin has always been razor thin, and other online mags have been dropping like flies. There are two copy editors at *Hatchet*, and I'm the newest, out of my ninety-day probationary period just a month ago, so if our finances go south, I'll be the first to walk the plank. Maybe I don't want to remind her of that. And...she brought in Miles with the promise of latitude, and I'm just the new fact-checker, not the finance director.

My only remaining option is to try to get myself into a position where I can understand this. And maybe even control it. I glance over at Miles again. He's finally off the phone, so I head over there.

"Hey," I say when I reach his space. "I missed the end of your pitch."

He looks up from his laptop—the *Bend Bulletin* site is up on his screen, and the headline reads "Trailer Fire Leaves One Dead in 'Mysterious' Circumstances"—and his expression softens with concern and relief. "Are you okay? I couldn't tell if you were choking or if I just grossed you out. I thought you went home."

"Nah, I'm fine. I actually wanted to hear more about the story," I say, my toes curling in my shoes. "I was only a teenager when the massacre happened and totally caught up in my own life, but I do remember it—it was all anyone could talk about for months afterward. Do you really think it's connected to this one guy's murder, just because he's one of the survivors?"

"I know it is," he says, pushing his glasses up his nose. "That rock that was shoved into his mouth? It's connected to the cult. I looked it up—painted rocks were found all over that cult compound after the fire twenty years ago. The killer's sending a message."

I force a skeptical eyebrow raise, even though sharp prickles are blooming in my chest. "Are you sure it's not just part of the mobile home that burned down around him? A chunk of the ceiling or something could have fallen into his..." I trail off, my words shriveling as his mouth twists into a condescending smirk.

"I just talked to the morgue attendant," he informs me. "He's nervous as hell about losing his job, but he was freaked out enough to talk to me. That rock in Moore's mouth was *painted*. Blue, apparently. Had symbols on it and shit. That's no chunk of ceiling."

"Fine," I say, dread and memory dancing in my thoughts. "It was a painted rock. And let's say the killer put it there—what do you think motive is?"

He nods like he was waiting for me to ask. "I'd just about forgotten about the Oracles massacre until I got this tip, but then it all came back. All those people, trapped inside that temple or whatever, and the door was barred from the outside. We all know that part. But did you know a lot of them were stabbed? Like, some of them were dead even before the fire. It had to have been absolute mayhem in there."

It was. The scars on my legs tingle with memory. The guilt rises up, threatening to choke me. "I remember reading something like that," I mumble.

"I realized something when I looked the whole thing up, though." He turns back to his laptop and clicks another tab—this one is the Wikipedia page for the Oracles of Innocence. "Three adult survivors, right? Along with something like a dozen little kids, all of them really young, like toddlers and babies. But one of those three adults"—he squints at the screen and reads off bits and pieces—"Shari Redmond— she went by the name Ladonna, apparently—she was sentenced to nine years for manslaughter. But...here it is: Marie Heckender." He gives me a triumphant look. "She's the one who barred the door, and she was only sentenced to ten years. She gave investigators names of who was inside the building as part of the deal that got her a shorter sentence."

"That's helpful," I say in a strangled voice. I should have paid closer attention to the trials. But by the time they started, three years after the fire, I'd left the state, off to start a new life with a new name, desperate to leave all of it behind.

"She gave investigators *thirty-five* names," Miles continues, oblivious to the terror that is melting my brain. "But they were all cult names. Things like Darius—that was the leader—and Basir and Goli. Not birth names, which would have made it easier. In the end, only twenty-nine of those thirty-five names were matched up with remains. That leaves six bodies that must have been too charred to be identified or that belonged to people who were off the radar, no families or friends to notice they were gone."

"That's a tragedy, but I'm not getting how it connects to the Bend murder."

His brown eyes crinkle at the corners. "I think the key here is in the bad math."

"Bad...math?"

"Thirty-five names. Twenty-nine matches. But only *four* bodies were never identified. Not six. To me, this looks like a revenge killing, you know? The killer went to a lot of trouble to send a message. Could have been a family member of one of the victims. Or it could be Shari Redmond or Marie Heckender, one of the two other adult survivors. *Or* it could be one of the *unknown* survivors. The two who got out without anyone knowing. Those two might have a deep reason to kill."

Stomach roiling, I say, "You just took about five leaps of logic to get to that, Miles. Let's start with this—how do you even know there were only four charred bodies and not six? Wikipedia isn't exactly known for its accuracy—"

He opens the Kindle app on his phone, summons up a book I recognize immediately. *Utopia on Fire: The Oracles of Innocence Cult* by Siobhan Culpepper. The cover image is black with flames that lick at the white lettering. When it first came out eighteen years ago, I checked out a copy from the library in downtown Bend and pored over every word, every name, terrified. But the author chose to focus on Darius and his financial crimes, leaving the rest of us in shadow.

Still, it was the reason I chose to formally change my name. Just in case.

I give Miles a vague smile, even as a glance at my watch lets me know my heart rate is skittering toward 120. "Are you going to interview the author?"

"I would have, but she died last year of ovarian cancer. It gives me some jumping-off points, though. Apparently, the cult was based in Portland before they moved down to Bend. I'm wondering about who got left behind and if they might talk. It happens when cults make that leap to craziness—they shed members. Like when Jim Jones took his people to Guyana, some stayed in California. Turned out they were the lucky ones, right?"

"Right," I mumble. A lot of them melted into the woodwork, too embarrassed or scared to be linked to such a disastrous and crazy cult. And fortunately, the same thing happened with the Oracles. As far as I know, no one cooperated with Ms. Culpepper as she wrote the book, including the defendants who were still gearing up for trial as the manuscript was being rushed to press, which is why the information in it relies on public records. "It's been years, though, Miles. If no one's come forward—and if that author didn't find them—what makes you think any of them will give you information now?"

"I have my ways." His gaze is so intent. "This one's a mile deep, Dora. I can feel it. And..." He clicks over to a bookmarked page in the ebook. "I looked it up—it says only thirty-three bodies, four that were never identified. See? Bad math! What happened to the other two?"

"Maybe the fire just burned really hot, Miles. Didn't they have trouble getting an accurate victim count after Waco for that reason?"

His shoulders sag a bit. "Could be, but think about it—what if two people got out of that building? What if they've been underground all these years, just waiting to strike?"

A half-hysterical laugh escapes me. "Seriously?"

He rolls his eyes. "Fine, fine. Give me a few days, and we'll see. But I'm telling you—the Arnold Moore case is unbelievably weird, and my conversation with that morgue attendant just now confirmed it."

"Okay, I'll bite," I say, trying to sound blandly curious rather than utterly freaked out. "You got more details?"

He leans close, all conspiratorial. "Arnold Moore wasn't just stabbed in the heart—he had five stab wounds. And in very specific places."

I need a drink. "What do you mean, specific?"

"Well, think about this. If you're going to stab someone, how's that going to go?"

"No idea where to even start with that one," I say hoarsely.

"I mean, if you've got the advantage on someone, say, you're holding them down, you're going to stab in just one place, yeah? Like stab-stab-stab." He says this while jabbing his hand downward with each word.

"Okay." I slide a finger along the top of the partition, watch my frayed fingernail catch in a groove. "Stab-stab-stab."

"But if the person's fighting back, you stab wherever you can, right?" He squirms on his chair, waving his arms like he's fighting off an attacker. "You get the point."

"Literally," I mutter. "So which was it? Was Arnie—Arnold Moore— fighting back or not?"

Miles doesn't seem to notice my mistake. "We'll know more

when there's an official autopsy report, but my source told me that it doesn't look like old Arnold was struggling much at all," he says, scrolling through his phone. "No defensive wounds. Empty bottle of cheap gin found in the bathtub with him. He mighta been drunk out of his mind. My guy said he was practically pickled."

"But the stab wounds weren't all in one place, like they would be for a person who wasn't struggling," I say, guessing.

"You nailed it. He had stab wounds"—he squints down at a note page full of his scribbly handwriting—"in the lower-left quadrant, a few inches from his belly button, and one in the top right, and that one slipped between his ribs. But then there were two on the lower left side of his back..."

My heart is running like so long ago, when I was sure it would give out before I'd covered enough distance. "That's four. What about the fifth?" I manage to ask. *And please don't say it's in the—*

"Fifth one was in the throat," he concludes.

I could be working myself up over nothing. My memory could be wrong. It *must* be wrong.

"I think the killer was trying to send a message," he concludes. "A big, elaborate message. Rock, flame retardant, tub, specific stab wounds..."

"Why do you keep calling them 'specific'?"

"Because it looks like the killer marked the places he was going to stab *before* he stabbed them. With permanent marker. Morgue guy said he could see the faint outline of black marks around the wounds. Pretty weird, huh?"

"Yeah," I murmur. "Pretty weird."

"I'm going to try to track down the autopsy report for Stephen Millsap—that was Darius the cult leader's real name. DA's archive only goes back to 2018 on the web, and that's only press releases anyway. No details. I need to file a formal request." He pushes his dark hair off his forehead.

"Why would you need *his* autopsy report specifically?"

"Just a hunch. Wondering if there are any more similarities. Painted rock. Fire. And...premeditated stab wounds."

"A lot of people in that meeting hall died of stabbing, though," I say in a hollow voice.

He waggles his eyebrows. "Like I said, just a hunch. I got the all clear from Valentina to head down to Bend and do interviews with the police chief and ME, along with anyone else who's game. And maybe I should get *all* the autopsy reports." He taps a reminder into his phone, the air around him almost crackling with his energy. "And any records of who else was in that cult, from the very beginning all the way until the end. I'll put feelers out in Portland. Maybe there's some sort of support group? Maybe one of them is our killer or can point me to those two mystery people who escaped. I want to be the one to track them down."

"Wow," I say as my watch beeps, warning me of an irregular, frantic heart rhythm. "That's a lot of work." But then, defiant hope sparks in me, bright as a flame. "Need some help?"

He sits back. "Really? I thought Valentina was really piling the work on you. I heard the whole litany during stories in progress."

"Nothing I can't handle. I'm a bit of a workaholic."

"Yeah, Valentina was urging some of us to try to get you out for happy hour or something." He gives me a coy look. "I'd be game."

I wave the maybe-kinda-sorta invitation away, even though the thought sparks a rebellious kind of want inside me. A normal life, with friends and lovers. I've never had that—and if I want it at any point in the future, I'm going to have to fight for it. "I was thinking, actually...I mean, this happened in my hometown, and I've always been sort of interested in it." I glance down the hall, where Valentina sits in her glass-walled office, talking to the air with a Bluetooth bud in her ear. If I'm going to do this, I need to be all in. A fact-checker can do most of her work from her desk. But a journalist? "Honestly, one of the reasons I took this job was that it seemed like there might be...I don't know, potential to...write something?"

Miles tilts his head. "Really?"

Nope. "Yeah, really. Like, get out there and do some interviews or something? Find some leads? But if that's a stupid idea, it's fine. I'll still help—"

"I think it would be fun, actually," he says. Our eyes meet, and I feel his gaze all the way down to my toes. "I'm leaving tomorrow morning. And no one else is on this. Not yet, I mean, except for the *Bulletin*, but that's just basic—no way they have the budget for investigative; I'm guessing they're barely hanging on, and half that rag is advertising." He shakes his head, presumably at the creeping demise of local journalism. "So it's all mine. I'm talking to the police chief tomorrow." He picks up his phone again. Checks it. "Ben Ransom. Obviously pissed off, but still agreed to a little sit-down. You really want to come?"

Oh god. Am I really up to this? The last thing I want to do is be face-to-face with Ben Ransom again. He just so happens to be a friend of my "parents." He was early in his career, just a detective when I met him, and I spent my three years in Bend terrified he'd figure out exactly who I was.

"Maybe we can divide and conquer," I suggest. "My mom's a social worker; I swear she knows everyone in town, and she might have a few tips for who we should talk to. And I can gather records and do your background research, stuff like that?" I already know where I need to go first.

His brow furrows. "I don't think Valentina will spring for this, though. I'm planning to go for a week to gather all my material, and it's near the holidays and rates are higher, and—"

"It's okay," I say with a bright smile. "I'll stay with my folks."

As soon as he nods, I whirl around and find Valentina. She's skeptical at first, but in four months, I've beaten every deadline and taken on extra work without a single complaint, and I promise to keep doing that remotely while I help Miles. I enthuse over the story's potential even as my stomach churns. I plead with her for a chance to do some writing, even if I don't get a byline. I promise her that I won't expense a thing.

I can *do* this. I can manage it. There are only a few pieces of evidence tying me to what happened, and I can make sure Miles never gets his hands on any of it.

As soon as Valentina gives me the all clear, I shut myself into the empty conference room to call a woman I've barely spoken to for over ten years, the person I just described to Miles as my mom.

"Hi," I say when she answers. "It's Christy."

I don't sleep. A restless anxiety has me in its teeth. My suitcase sits across the room, packed for a week, seven days to save my own life. In a few hours, I leave for Bend.

I sit up in the dark and slide off my bed, wincing at the ache in my back. I pull the storage box from underneath and dig through neatly folded blankets until I find it. Every time I've moved in the last two decades, I've almost thrown it away. I've sat on different floors next to different beds, wearing different clothes and different haircuts, staring down at it and wondering if I should get rid of it. But I've kept it every time, telling myself it's good to have one tiny piece of proof that it really happened. Proof that I survived. Proof that I'm the one in control now.

But it's also a reminder of everything I did.

Miles is right about the bad math. But he's also wrong. There weren't two survivors, not in the end. There was only me.

Thinking of her, my chest aching, I pick up the meditation stone. My eyes close at a flash of memory: our clutched hands, laced fingers holding on, the stone nestled tightly in the tiny space between us. About the size of my palm, the stone is unexpectedly warm, as if it, too, harbors memories of approaching flames. As if it, too, knows exactly how it feels when they reach you.

I once believed this stone was the key to everything. I clung to it at night, keeping it under my pillow, hoping to channel visions up from the deep, the insightful words and perfect thoughts that might finally, finally prove my worth.

I really believed it might.

I trace my fingertip along the primitive symbols: a triangle for the great mountain, Damavand; two parallel, curved lines and two intersecting ones forming the shape of a beak; and a crest to symbolize the ancient bird Simurg. Signs of triumph and strength, they were meant to act as beacons. The rock itself, rigid and strong, was the touch point, amplifying the power, the connection, the clarity of whatever the deep consciousness was communicating.

If you believe in that kind of ridiculous, generic, new-agey, appropriating gobbledygook, that is. I heave myself to my feet and carry the stone into my bathroom. It's like approaching a high dive—hesitating is doom. I toss the rock into my wastebasket, where it lands silently amid crumpled tissues and threads of floss.

I can only hope getting rid of the rest of my past will be that easy.

CHAPTER FIVE

The Retreat, near Bend, Oregon
December 24, 1999

Before Christy put on the blindfold, she caught Arnie's eye. Stooped in the way of a guy used to hitting his head, he stood near the window, casting nervous glances through the crack in the curtains. "I see a fire through the trees."

"Quit trying to cheat," Christy said.

Eszter, their mentor for the initiation, had brought them to this dorm and instructed them to focus and prepare. Then she'd passed out the robes and blindfolds and told them to leave their street clothes in a pile to be taken back to Portland, where they could be washed and reused by whoever came to the house. Gil would be managing the place, now that the rest of them were living at the Retreat.

Now Eszter touched Christy's shoulder. "Curiosity isn't the same thing as cheating."

Arnie pulled the black sleep mask down over his eyes. "How far is the walk?"

"This is the first part of a journey that will carry you through the rest of your life," said Eszter. "How far do you think it should be?"

Eszter sounded so peaceful, but she already knew what was coming—Darius had named her back in February. Over the past few weeks, Eszter had been Christy's rock. Her *friend*. She'd told Christy the whole story of how she became an Oracle, how she'd had to leave home because her stepfather wouldn't leave her alone, how she'd tolerated it for two years because she hadn't wanted to leave her little brother in that house, and how she'd finally felt like it was a choice between leaving and killing herself, even though leaving felt like a kind of death too. It had made Christy cry; she missed her own brother so much it was a physical pain in her chest. She was amazed at how much she and Eszter had in common, how Eszter knew what it was like to be used, to turn to the person who was supposed to protect you, your own mother, and have her be too absorbed in her own life to do a single thing. Eszter knew what it meant to survive. And she knew how it felt when someone really *saw* you, when someone actually seemed to care. Even though it had only been a few weeks, Christy realized now what a gift it was.

It had felt so normal, like being at a slumber party, cots scooted close, stories whispered in the dark as the women around them slept. Eszter had even confided her before name, and it had only seemed fair that Christy reciprocate. It felt oddly relieving, like she'd handed over a heavy weight. Before Christy pulled her blindfold down, she reached over and squeezed Eszter's hand.

Eszter squeezed back. "Darius invited you here for a reason. Trust it," she whispered.

Christy and Arnie and Marie stood in their bare feet, naked beneath their loose, handmade robes, blindfolds secured, waiting to step out into the frosty night. Arnie fidgeted next to her. As Gil drove them south from Portland that afternoon, he'd peppered them with all kinds of questions, just like he always did, only he didn't have his notebook with him for once. Eszter was right—he was a good listener. And maybe Eszter had opened the floodgates too. Christy had revealed more about herself than she ever had.

Even Arnie, usually quiet, had actually opened up a little. Before he'd gotten carsick, he'd told them that he'd been hooked on meth before the Oracles saved him. Just like Eszter found Christy, Darius himself had found Arnie under the Burnside Bridge on a frigid night last March, and he'd taken him to a diner for eggs and coffee. Then he'd taken him to the Portland house. Gave him chores to keep him busy, teaching him how he didn't need to tweak to feel good, that everything he needed was right there, with them. Now he was clean and ready for the next step, and he couldn't wait.

Christy touched her fingertips to the swath of black cloth and felt the domes of her own eyeballs beneath. The last few weeks were a dream she didn't want to wake up from. She wanted to appear as peaceful as Eszter, so everyone would know she belonged with them, but the dark had always made her nervous.

"Why do we have to be blindfolded?" asked Marie from somewhere behind her. She sounded so whiny and spoiled, but that figured. *Her* daddy had money, which Christy knew because Marie couldn't seem to stop bitching about how oppressive it had been and how she'd heard about this group from a friend and actually sought them out to get away from her family. As if that made her special. Christy suspected that the poor little rich girl was only doing all this—renouncing all material stuff, donating her bank account—to piss off her dad. Ever since they'd met two weeks ago, Christy had been waiting for someone to call Marie out for being there for all the wrong reasons, but it hadn't happened yet. Maybe tonight.

"We're going to run into a wall or something," Marie continued, making Christy want to punch her. "I don't see why this is necessary."

"It's necessary because they think it's necessary," Christy snapped. "It's not like anyone forced you to be here." She couldn't believe Darius had chosen Marie to come. But then again, some people were probably wondering why Darius had chosen Christy, so she shouldn't complain.

Eszter began to rub her back, murmuring for her to focus on her own journey. Christy shut her mouth, her cheeks burning. "I'm sorry," she whispered, poking at the blindfold again.

"It's scary to be deprived of the sense you depend on most to navigate in this world," Eszter replied. "It could make anyone feel on edge. But have your eyes served you well so far? They've led you to people and things that looked good but brought you nothing but pain." Eszter gave Christy's shoulder a gentle squeeze. "The blindfold helps you begin to see with more than just your eyes." She sounded so much more patient than Marie deserved, like Marie's attitude didn't bother her at all. "Both in this world and beyond."

Arnie coughed. Eszter guided Christy's hands to his shoulders. "You okay?" whispered Eszter, close to her ear.

"Yeah," she murmured, though she wished she'd eaten something earlier this afternoon when they'd arrived. When they'd gotten out of the van after the four-hour drive from Portland, a guy named Basir had been waiting outside the dining hall with fresh bread, hot and soft. Marie had scarfed a slice and Arnie had wolfed down three, but Christy had been too nervous to eat.

Now she felt a little faint, but maybe that was good. Maybe it made her more open, more able to approach the deep consciousness. As long as she didn't fall over or stumble. She wished she knew exactly what would be expected, what she'd have to do. At the Portland house, they meditated as a group every morning and evening, and though she'd found it boring and strange at first, it was kind of peaceful once she'd gotten used to it, though she still worried she wasn't doing it right. Tonight, she wanted to be poised, to convince the rest of them, and especially Darius, that he'd made a good choice. Gil had warned her that not everyone turned out to be a good fit.

She felt Marie's hands close over her shoulders. "Lucky," said Marie. "You get to be in the middle. Probably warmer."

"Maybe you should have worn a few extra layers of underpants," Christy said.

Eszter stifled a giggle and nudged Christy with her elbow. "I'm trying to be serious here," she whispered.

"Maybe I *should* have layered up," groused Marie, oblivious to their inside joke. "My ass is going to fr—"

"As I open this door," said Eszter abruptly, loud enough to shut Marie's mouth, "fix your mind on your life up until this point. Imagine it hanging off you like the deadweight it is. As you step over the threshold, shed it—your past, all that crap you came here with—so that you can be reborn. Feel yourself get lighter with each step toward the light. Arnie, put your hands on my shoulders. Let me lead you to your new life."

With a rush of frigid air, Arnie jerked into motion. Christy gripped his bony shoulders as Eszter led them outside. Pine needles pricked at the soles of her bare feet. The cold clamped onto her bones, and her teeth began to chatter. She was used to real winter; she was no stranger to chains on tires and waist-deep snowdrifts. But though Oregon was warmer, it was late December and she was barefoot, no gloves, collarbones exposed by the wide neck of her one-size-fits-all robe.

Arnie stopped abruptly, and she ran into his back. Marie stiffened behind her. "Are we there yet?" Marie whispered.

Arnie disappeared from beneath her hands, and Eszter murmured for her to be patient. Christy stood there, shivering while her eyes focused on a glow just on the other side of her blindfold.

"You're nervous, but you don't have to be," said a voice coming from only a few feet in front of her. This was the voice that had convinced her this was where she absolutely needed to be, and hearing it again made her heart drum. "Tonight is a celebration," said Darius. "You're being born all over again, this time as your true self."

She clasped her hands together and squeezed to discharge some of the jittery energy. She'd spent the last few weeks trying to find the angle of this too-good-to-be-true offer—and hadn't yet found one. Aside from Marie, everyone she'd met was nice—like, *really* nice. They'd treated her as if she were family, but not like the family Christy had before. Better.

Please let this be real.

"We already know you belong with us," Darius continued. "There are no silly high school cliques here, no dead-end jobs or mindless distractions, no abusive parents or boyfriends. There is only the deep consciousness, and our sole purpose is to help one another get closer to it. That's why we wear these silly robes!"

All around her, she heard a soft ripple of laughter.

Darius was chuckling too. "When I first received the wisdom of the robes, Gilgamesh thought I was insane."

"It's true," said Gil, his voice coming from somewhere to her right. "And I was like, dude, we are going to have to buy *a lot* of fabric."

The people all around them laughed again.

"The reason for the robes is to remove the needless distraction of worrying what you look like," said Darius. "Comparing yourself to others. Trying to stand out. That's not why we're here. We're here to reach enlightenment through connection to the deep consciousness. Your vanity doesn't matter here. Your fear and anxiety don't matter here. *Time* has no meaning here. The only thing that has meaning is your commitment to the journey. Sometimes the path is smooth. Sometimes it will tear at your bare feet, and only the strength of your conviction will carry you through. What matters now is that you make the choice to travel on this path with us. That choice is yours alone."

Hands closed around Christy's arms and guided her a few steps to the side. "On your knees," Darius said.

Christy's knee-jerk reaction was to refuse. It wasn't the first time someone had said that to her, and what came after always left her feeling empty and sick and awful. But then she reminded herself that no one here was going to hurt her, and she was supposed to be demonstrating her trust and purity of thought. So she obeyed, gingerly kneeling on the spongy ground. Everything here seemed covered with at least two inches of those darn pine needles. Her fingernails dug into the backs of her clasped hands.

"I have been fasting and meditating for the last day in preparation for your arrival," Darius said. "Waiting for the right names to come to me, the true names that you were always meant to have. Whether you accept that truth is up to you."

She angled her face toward the light, the crackling warmth of a fire nearby. She fought the urge to crawl closer to it. Instead, she remained still, waiting for her new *real* name. All the crap that had happened up until now, she would cast it off along with the name her mom liked to screech when she was eyeball deep in a bottle of

Jack. The one a few of Mom's boyfriends liked to whisper into the dark of Christy's room after Mom had passed out.

"You are Tadeas," Darius said quietly. He was on her left, speaking to Arnie. The liquid depth of his voice calmed the shivers for a moment. "You are a gift given by God. Do you accept this name as your own?"

"I do," said Arnie, except he wasn't Arnie anymore. *Tadeas*, she told herself. She wanted to call him by the right name from now on.

"Do you discard your old name and all that was attached to it—the mistakes, the lies, the pain, the toxic relationships, the indulgences and addictions—in order to embrace your true purpose?"

"Yes!" shouted Tadeas so enthusiastically that a few people around them giggled.

Even Darius sounded amused as he asked, "And do you accept that you are on a journey to touch the deep consciousness? Do you promise to devote yourself to that journey, body, soul, and mind?"

"I do," said Tadeas.

"Do you accept me as your guide along this road we are traveling together?"

"I do!"

"Welcome our newest oracle as a brother," said Darius.

"Welcome, Tadeas." The voices came from all around her, so many of them, solemn and steady. "Welcome to the Oracles of Innocence."

She'd imagined some sort of weird ritual, what with the naked-except-for-robes and the blindfolds and the fire. Eszter had said it was against the rules to reveal what the initiation entailed, so she'd been ready to endure a night in the wilderness or whatever hazing they dreamed up if it meant she could have a place to belong. Everyone was so nice that she'd figured it wouldn't be that bad—at least, not bad enough to make her crave another night at a shelter or another day hustling on Burnside, trying to forget she was alone, unseen, unloved...and pretty much always had been until a few weeks ago.

But it had just been a few questions! A few questions, and Tadeas was in the club.

She heard him getting to his feet and the percussion of congratulatory slaps on his back. She heard him laugh, strained as if he was also crying, and Eszter murmuring to him, saying that a release of emotion was natural.

Darius moved on to Marie, who was apparently on her right. He named her Fabia, which he said meant "lovely bean."

She could hear the what-the-hell in Fabia's voice as she accepted her name. But Fabia *was* kind of bean shaped. Stripped of her rich-girl clothes and wearing robes just like everyone else, she was nothing special, and maybe Darius knew that.

Christy bowed her head and told herself to keep a straight face. Fabia accepted her new name, answered all of Darius's questions, and was welcomed by the group.

Without warning, the blindfold slid up and off, and the world blazed into her vision again. She was kneeling in a clearing, in the middle of a bunch of people, maybe forty or so, most of whom she recognized from the Portland house, all friendly faces. They were all standing except for Shirin and Ziba, two skinny, old ladies sitting on lawn chairs near the stone-encircled fire. Everyone wore the same beige, homemade robes as the new initiates, though some had belted them with a length of twine. The jigsaw bark of ponderosa pines surrounded the group; the trees' high canopy offered them only a tiny patch of starry night above.

Octavia, her long, blond braid dangling down one shoulder, smiled at her as their eyes met. Gil stood at the edge of the group, his robe layered over the T-shirt and jeans he'd worn on the drive down—unlike the rest of them, Gil was driving back up to Portland in the morning. Christy had wondered why he wasn't going to live on the compound, but it had seemed nosy to ask.

Eszter was sweating near the fire, her gaze riveted on Darius. Ladonna and Kyra stood closer to the trees, both of them with hands on their pregnant bellies, which weren't quite as huge as Octavia's, but close.

A few other strangers stood in the clearing as well. She had no idea what they saw when they looked at her. A skinny dropout with wary eyes? A naive, young thing, a blank slate to scribble on? Or maybe, just maybe, a girl and nothing more. A little sister. A new friend.

She honestly couldn't tell. But after what she'd experienced the past few weeks, she felt hopeful.

When Darius stepped in front of her, she turned her face upward as if to receive a kiss of sunlight. Darius arched one eyebrow as he gave her a smile. "Are you ready, little one?"

She nodded, straightening her shoulders. She was nearly eighteen and hadn't been a child for a very long time, but she supposed he was old enough to be her dad. The absolute focus of his attention quickened her breath.

"You're eager for this new start," he said.

"Yes." She couldn't get there fast enough.

Darius touched her cheek. "Are you sure you're here for the right reasons?"

Food, shelter, safety, belonging, friendship? Her mouth opened, but the right answer wasn't there. If she said yes too quickly, did that actually mean no? And if she said no, did that mean they'd have Gil drive her back to Portland, just another worthless stray? "I think I am," she said, trying to make each syllable sound well considered and mature.

"This way of life isn't for everyone," he said. "I told you that."

He had, that first night at the house. Thirteen people crammed into the living room, Darius sitting on an ottoman and talking about how this life is just a skin over the veins of real existence, how you could tap into something deeper and live off that high, how you wouldn't need anything else ever again... She hadn't been sure she trusted it. But when he'd talked about *this* place, the Retreat, this special farm and compound meant only for those willing to absolutely devote themselves night and day to the journey, it sounded like a way to stop running, to stop chipping off pieces of her soul just so she could have something to eat and a place to sleep. This wasn't just a roof over her head and meals on the table; this was an actual family and a right way to be.

She hadn't ever been right. Not once in her life.

Octavia had come to her one morning about a week ago and told her that usually people weren't invited to the Retreat for months or even years, but now a bunch of them would be living there full-time, and Darius thought she had potential. She remembered the thrill of those words—he'd *seen* her. He'd looked at her like there was something special inside her.

Now he was questioning it for some reason. It made her chest feel like it was caving in.

"I'm here to find something more," she said. "I can't go back to what I had before now that I know the truth."

Once again, he sounded amused. "You've only caught a glimmer, like the fire you saw through your blindfold. To know the truth requires more."

"I'll do anything." The words tumbled out, more desperate than she'd intended. He hadn't questioned either of the other two initiates like this. He'd just let them in. And now quiet, hesitant Tadeas and whiny Fabia were staring at her as if a pair of horns had sprouted from her forehead.

Her face flashed hot with a familiar kind of shame. Then she looked over at Eszter, who gave her a reassuring nod, the lifeline she needed. Blinking away sudden tears and throwing back her shoulders, she looked up at Darius. "I'll do anything," she said in a clear, strong voice. "Anything you ask of me. I am *ready* for this."

His eyes were so dark. Piercing and inviting at the same time. "You're ready to be reborn?"

"*Yes.*"

"Like a butterfly," he said quietly, his thumb tracing a path along her cheek. "Your wings are going to spread, and everyone will see their beauty. Your real name is *Parvaneh*."

CHAPTER SIX

Bend, Oregon
December 10, present day

I park at the curb. The house looks familiar but different, same as a friend who ages visibly visit to visit, temporal snapshots that always make me keenly aware of weeks and hours and seconds, things I was trained to ignore until they became everything.

The blue paint is peeling in spots; the front gutter is rusting in places. Blades of gray-green grass poke up from the cracks in the driveway. But warm light glows from behind the curtains of the front window.

Twenty years ago, I saw this house for the first time. Martin and Hailey Rodriguez saved my life. They took me in and treated me like family. They gave me space and accepted my half-truths about the abusive family I'd run from. While the embers at the Oracles compound were still smoldering, while the bodies were still being recovered from the ashes, I watched the evening news with Hailey and Martin, acting as shocked as they were that the local cult had turned out to be even crazier than everyone thought. They gave me the new beginning I needed, and I've repaid them with a few texts and birthday cards, a lot of unanswered phone calls, and silence for years at a time.

I'm going to have to tell them about the name at some point, sooner rather than later. I'll have to come clean, about that one thing at least. I'm not sure how big of a deal it'll be; it could go either way. Hailey sounded weird on the phone, not that I blame her. This is a big ask. But everything between us since the moment we met has been that way, and she and Martin never seemed to hold it against me.

With a deep breath, I get out of my car, wincing at the pain in my back after six hours on the road. My suitcase, packed for a week, feels like it's filled with concrete. I pull it from my trunk as the pain snakes down my legs. My run tomorrow morning is going to be a bear; I can already tell. But I need it—I didn't move enough today, and despite the pain, I'm restless as a shaken soda.

I pull my roller bag along the walk and clumsily tug it up the two front steps to the little porch. The mat reads "Welcome! Did you bring snacks?" and it makes me smile. I ring the doorbell, and my heart begins to race. I have to remind myself of who I am, who I've always been, even though those two things are different. My details, my story, my memories. Sometimes it's hard to shuffle it all together into one deck.

The door opens, and Hailey greets me with wide eyes. Her white hair is pulled into a ponytail, and she's gained a few pounds. Her look of shock is one I'm familiar with, as are her first blurted words to me: "You're even thinner than the last time I saw you!"

"Hi, Hailey," I say. "It's really nice to see you."

She shakes off her surprise at my appearance and opens the door wider, allowing me to drag my suitcase inside. The air is laced with the scent of garlic and onions. My "adoptive" mother opens her arms to me, enfolds me in a hesitant, careful embrace. Like she thinks I might break. "It's been so long," she says, her voice tight with feeling.

"I'm sorry," I say. "I should have come down to visit as soon as I moved back to the West Coast."

"When I got your message that you were moving to Seattle, I was so excited, but after you said you were too busy to come down, Martin told me to give you some space. I've thought about you every day. But you never called!"

"I texted at Thanksgiving," I mutter sheepishly. "I really was busy."

She laughs. "I know I sound like a nag."

"It's nice to know one is missed," I say, letting her take my bag and roll it down the hall to my old room, where I spent three terrible, wonderful years climbing out of an emotional pit as deep as the Mariana Trench. I stand in the doorway and breathe. This is the place where I put myself back together, piece by jagged piece.

I might have missed a few shards.

"It looks the same."

"You didn't leave much behind," she says as she wheels my bag over to the closet.

The walls are eggshell white, the floor hardwood, the curtains blue. There's a picture of a rocky coastline and gray, choppy sea on the wall over the bed, which is covered with a quilt Hailey made herself. "Still busy at the hospital?" I ask.

"Oh, no, I started a private practice a year or so ago, and I've got a ridiculous wait list! I think the population's almost doubled since you moved away. Property value's up too. We're booming!" She looks around. "Do you want to unpack before lunch?"

"I'm not that hungry—"

She gives me a stern look. "Don't give me that. Martin's coming home from the plant and everything. And it's all vegan. I remember, you know."

I grimace. "Me too." How I gagged the first time she put a plate of steak in front of me. How I couldn't stand the smell of milk. "I appreciate it."

She squeezes my arm, frowns at the sight of her fingers, wrapped nearly all the way around my biceps. "Are you okay, Christy? I know this is a work trip, but—"

"I'm great. And I'll be out in a few minutes. I just need to let my colleague and my boss know I'm here."

As soon as she goes, I text Miles: I made it. Settling in.

He responds almost instantly. Thank god. So many leads that I'll need your help tracking everything down. Meet me for a drink tonight?

Sure—what time?

9 at Dogwood Cocktail Cabin?

I'll see you then.

I send Valentina a text letting her know I'm safe in Bend, and she tells me I've got three articles to copyedit by tomorrow at noon. I sigh and promise her it'll be done, but it means I'll have to get up before sunrise to run so I can spend the afternoon trying to figure out my game plan.

And making sure this thing stays far away from me.

With that thought, I head to the bathroom, wash my hands, and peer at myself in the mirror. Am I that different than I was? Hailey knew about my hair—we talked about it years ago. She gave me tips for makeup, since our hair was now the same color.

When I emerge from the bathroom, Martin is sitting at the breakfast bar. He's got serious hat hair and is wearing his coveralls, and I'm struck by how he, at least, hasn't changed much. "Hi," I say as he turns in my direction.

He slides off his stool and envelops me in a brief, gentle hug. "Welcome home," he says. His clothes carry the faint scent of bitter chemicals, and suddenly I remember the first time I experienced that scent, my skin clammy with sweat. *You look like you're runnin' from a ghost*, he'd said with a laugh.

He had no idea how right he was.

"Thanks," I whisper, guilt seeping into my chest, turning me cold. "How's life at the tire plant?"

"Well, I guess we're hiring," he says ruefully. "Hail told me you're in town to report on a suspicious death—that was one of my guys."

My stomach drops. "Oh. Wow. I didn't know. I'm sorry." And I can't tell if it's dangerous or helpful.

Hailey looks up from the pot she's stirring, steam billowing up to fog her glasses. "Arnie was such a nice man. Quiet, but you could just tell there was a sweetness under there, you know? He came to a few of the summer picnics, and we'd had him and his girlfriend over at Thanksgiving a few times, including just a few weeks ago."

Martin gives Hailey an affectionate look. "Always taking people in when they've got nowhere else to go."

"I know," I murmur, nearly drowning in relief. If I'd come down for Thanksgiving and ended up face-to-face with Arnie...

Martin reaches over and pats me on the shoulder. "Arnie worked for us for ten good years. The brass gave me crap for making the hire—someone figured out he'd served some time and why—but he was a solid worker. Never missed a day."

The table is set for three, and Hailey pulls the pot off the stove, her hands encased in holey, faded bear-paw oven mitts. She smiles when she sees me noticing them. "Remember when you gave these to me?"

"My first Christmas here," I say quietly.

"I think of you every time I put them on." She sets the pot on a fish-shaped trivet on the table, one I gave her my second Christmas with them. "What can I get you to drink?"

"Just water. I can get it."

"I guess you know where things are," Martin says gruffly, settling himself at the table. "We haven't rearranged in twenty years."

I grab myself a glass from the cabinet, fill it with water, and sink into the same seat I occupied at every meal for the three years I lived here. "You guys are really kind to let me stay."

Martin waves me away and settles in, letting Hailey shovel a generous portion of pasta primavera onto his plate. "So you're a reporter now?"

"No, still just a copy editor and fact-checker," I tell him. "I'm helping out the journalist who's working this story."

"Do you travel a lot?" asks Hailey as she holds out her hand for my plate.

"Almost never," I admit, nodding toward the serving spoon. "I ate a big snack on the way."

"Mm-hmm," she says, putting way too much food on my plate and handing it back to me.

"I'm still so impressed that you became an editor," Martin says. "Wow."

"A *copy* editor," I say. "A bit lower on the totem pole."

He fixes me with his pale-gray eyes. "When you came to us, you didn't even have a high school diploma."

Thanks to them, I moved away with my GED and a semester's worth of credits from Central Oregon Community College. "I've only had the job for a few months," I say. "The site is growing, but it's a pretty competitive industry..."

"Your boss must love you, willing to go the extra mile."

I shrug and push my food around the plate. "So how are you guys? I know I've been terrible about keeping in touch."

Their eyes meet across the table, and then Hailey turns to me. "Nothing much new," she says, glancing at the big, framed picture in the living room, a little girl with brown curls and a huge grin. "We funded one of those memorial benches on the River Trail in her honor, finally saved up enough money." She gives me a pained smile. "There's a playground nearby."

"She'd have turned forty this year," Martin says hoarsely.

"That's a wonderful way to remember her," I murmur. "But I know it's still painful."

The loss of their only daughter is a sorrow that shaped them long before they rescued me. It may have been *why* they rescued me. Why they helped me for so long. Why they would have kept on helping me if I'd let them.

And it tells me one thing: I can't tell them what I stole. Not today.

"So who's this journalist you're helping?" Hailey asks, her tone brightening.

"His name is Miles Connover," I tell them. "He was at the *Seattle Times* for years, so he knows his craft." It reminds me that I should have made sure he wasn't planning to go to the library this afternoon to check the archives. The thought of what he might find is enough to make me reach for my phone.

"You said you don't usually travel," Hailey says, looking pointedly at my hand holding my phone. I tuck it back into my pocket. A few more minutes won't kill me. "Why this time?"

I take a quick bite of my food to give myself a second to think. It's the first thing I've eaten today. "I've been meaning to get down here ever since I moved back, and this was my chance. Hey—you said Arnie had a girlfriend? Do you think she'd be willing to let me interview her?" Miles is so fixated on his whole "bad math" lead, and I desperately need to offer him a shiny, new object.

Martin rolls his eyes. "Her name's Gina," he says. "She's a piece of work."

Hailey gives Martin's arm a little slap. "Don't be like that. She really loved him."

"She's convinced he was killed because of the Oracles," Martin tells me. "Been spouting about it in our local Facebook group."

"Can you text me her contact info?" I ask, my heart kicking.

"Will do. Maybe it'll help her blow off some steam."

"If you have any other leads, let me know. I'd be really grateful."

"She should talk to Ben Ransom," Hailey says to Martin.

Martin sips his water and glances at me. "You remember him? About your height, with the crooked nose? Came to the block party each year, a few times with his uniform on?"

Hailey lets out a bark of laughter. "I forgot about that." She winks at me. "I think he wanted to look important."

"I think he mighta even had a little crush on you," Martin says to me with a smirk.

I force a smile. I always hated the way Ben looked at me. Like he wanted something but would never come out and say what it was. "I think Miles is already talking with him."

"I'm not sure he's too crazy about talking to the media," Hailey says gently. "He told me that someone leaked info to some reporter about Arnie's death report. He was not pleased. At all."

"Oh," I say. "Miles was probably the one it was leaked to, full disclosure." It's almost laughable that I, of all people, would use that phrase.

"Well, he's gonna have to field press requests, like it or not. We don't get a lot of murders around here. This is a big deal," Martin says, pushing his empty plate away. "Especially if Gina's right about the Oracles link."

"Yeah," I say, dread coiling in the pit of my stomach. "Especially then."

I sit on the bed, gazing down at the contact info for Arnold Moore's girlfriend. I've already texted Miles that I found her through my folks and that I'm going to reach out to see if she might have any useful info. Much to my relief, he quickly accepts my offer, telling me he's totally swamped. I dial her number, wincing at the metallic taste on my tongue.

"This is Gina," she answers in a raspy voice, like she smokes a pack a day. Or maybe like she's been crying for a week.

"Hi, Gina," I say, clearing my throat. "My name's Dora—I'm from the *Hatchet*. We're an online news magazine, and I'm calling about Arnold Moore."

I explain how we heard about Arnold's death and how he was an ex-member of the Oracles of Innocence.

That's when she perks up. "I was trying to tell Chief Ransom all about it! It's that cult for sure. I could tell he thought I was crazy."

"Why would he think that?"

She laughs. "Oh, honey. Why wouldn't he think that? Chief and I go *way* back. He breaks up my solstice UFO-watching party every single year, just to be an asshole."

"Ah. But you have information you think is useful to the investigation?"

"I *know* it's useful," she says. She's drinking something; the wet smack of her lips startles me just before she speaks again. "You see, Arnie told me stuff. About that night."

"The night of the fire on the compound?"

"Mm-hmm. I'd say I know more than anyone alive, but I guess that's not right."

My stomach drops—*please please please don't start talking about bad math.* "What do you mean?"

"Arnie never liked to talk about this stuff, see. He loved those people. Every single one of them. And he loved that place. You had to know him—he never would have hurt a fly. He should never have been in jail!"

"It sounds like you really loved him."

"He wasn't perfect—drank too much, for one, but who doesn't every once in a while, you know?" She pauses, and I hear the slosh of something near the phone, then a stifled belch. "He was too good for this world. And they took him."

Hope pokes its way to the surface of my mind, like a fragile pea tendril seeking the sun. "Who took him?"

She sighs, long and unsteady. Takes another swig. "It's all connected, you know? All coming back around. The visitors, the agents. You know."

"The visitors and the...agents?"

"No one believes in the visitors, but they're real. And those Oracles? I think some of them were the agents."

"I'm not following. Like, government agents?"

"No. I'm saying those three weren't the only ones *there* that night!" she barks. "See, Arnie knew all of them. And he didn't like to talk about all of it, but one night, he loosened up while we were watching the stars, and he told me: there weren't enough bodies."

Saliva pools on my tongue. "I'm sorry?"

"In that barn that burned. Arnie knew everyone on that compound. Every living soul. And they only pulled thirty-three bodies out of that place. Or maybe thirty-four? Something close to that."

Oh god. "But it was a fire. Everything burned. Isn't it possible—"

"That's what everyone says, but come on! They found everyone else, even those they couldn't identify, charred bodies, whatever. That's why Arnie never knew who exactly got out. But he'd narrowed it down to a few names."

"Which names?" I murmur, wishing I hadn't eaten anything earlier.

"Oh, I wrote it down somewhere a few days ago, just what I could remember. I'll find it for you. The six who were never identified. It's two of them who got out."

"That would be great," I choke out. Miles *cannot* be allowed to talk to this woman. Nutty as she is, she'll just confirm what he already suspects, which will make him more determined to figure it all out. I feel like I'm breathing in the smoke of that night, all over again. "And that's a really interesting theory, that someone escaped the fire, especially because the door was barred."

"Arnie told me it wasn't the only door!"

"But the other door was always locked," I blurt out.

"How do you know that?" she demands.

My watch chirps, warning me of an irregular heart rhythm. "I think I read it in that book about what happened?"

"Yeah, that lady had no idea," Gina grumbles. "I'm telling you, the visitors got a few out of that fire. And now they're agents, working for the aliens. They're coming for anyone who could out them to the rest of us. That's why they got Arnie."

My hope springs back to life. Martin *did* call her a piece of work. "I see."

"Are you gonna print what I'm saying in your paper?"

"We have a lot of other people to talk to," I say quickly. "If I'm authorized to get a full quote, you'll hear from me again. I'm just not sure which direction the story's taking right now."

"This is the direction," she yells. "This is the story! The agents are here, and they got Arnie!" She begins to sob. "They got him. And he never hurt anybody."

"Thank you for taking the time to speak to me. I'm so sorry for your loss."

I end the call and lean against the wall. My heart rate is nearly 130, and it's not because I just spent ten minutes talking to a grieving, unstable woman.

No.

It's because buried in all that crazy, she does know something. And if that something gets to Miles, it's one step closer to me.

I desperately need to find Miles another lead.

CHAPTER SEVEN

The Retreat
January 1, 2000

Parvaneh was spat from her sleep like a mouthful of sour milk, a spray of sharp exhaustion. Eszter was shaking her shoulders, her shadowed face round but for the nub of her chin. "Come on. We have to go," she whispered.

Down the hall, Parvaneh could hear whispers and the creak of plywood frames as women in other rooms climbed out of their beds.

"Octavia said we could sleep in—"

Eszter was still shaking her. "She's having the baby."

Parvaneh brushed off Eszter's hands and sat up. "How far is the nearest hospital?"

"Come on. Everybody has to help."

"Help with *what*? With the birth?" Parvaneh made a face.

Eszter was tying a tan cloth over her head, keeping her thick hair away from her face. She yanked Parvaneh's hair cloth off the hook on the wall and shoved it at her. "Maybe instead of worrying about yourself, you should focus your energy on the new soul the deep consciousness is sending into our care." Smoothing her palm over the pudgy swell of her belly, she gave Parvaneh an apologetic look. "I shouldn't have snapped at you. I was freaked out the first time too."

"Wait. The first time? How many have there been?"

"Since I got here, just two. Beetah had a little girl in May, and Goli had her boy in July."

Parvaneh glanced up the hall and lowered her voice. "Not to be nosy, but who knocked them up?" No one on the compound seemed to be coupled up, but there were a few pregnant women and several men around, some cuter than others, she supposed. "Were they pregnant when they joined?"

Eszter turned to her. "I never considered it my business, honestly."

Parvaneh narrowed her eyes. "Yeah right. You just don't want to gossip, but come on! I saw Ladonna walking in the woods with Vahid yesterday, and a couple times at dinner, I've seen Mir staring at Kyra like he wants to eat her alive, and I just wondered—"

Eszter pressed her lips together and gave Parvaneh a playful look of warning. "Later, okay? Unless you want to explain to Darius that you missed the birth because you were too busy asking about everyone's sex lives?"

Parvaneh snorted. "No thanks."

"Then let's go." Eszter pulled her meditation rock, rough edged and bright blue, from under her pillow and dropped it into the baggy pocket sewn into the front of her robe.

Parvaneh stared at the uneven outline of the stone resting on the lump of Eszter's gut, swallowing down the taste of envy. It was bitter, just as Darius had warned her it would be, when she'd asked when she could have a stone. He'd put his hand on her shoulder and asked, "Why do you want one?"

It had felt like another test, hers to fail. "I came here to touch the deep consciousness."

"Words are shells, Parvaneh. Our true intentions give them meaning. And right now, your words say to me 'gimme, gimme, gimme,' but I hear you offering nothing."

She'd felt the truth of his words in the hot sting in her eyes and the cold throb in her chest. "I'm trying," she had whispered.

He'd squeezed her shoulder. "That, I feel. Which means you're right where you're supposed to be." Then he'd warned her about the poison of envy. He'd said he could see that venom working in her soul.

Parvaneh had bowed her head so he couldn't see the defiance she had to muscle down. But he'd sensed it anyway. He'd tipped her chin up and pressed his thumb between her lips. The edge of his thumbnail scraped the roof of her mouth. Parvaneh gasped at the salty taste of his skin and the urge to reel backward just to have her body to herself again.

He'd pushed her against the wall. "Shh," he said quietly. "Understand the lesson I'm offering you. It'll come if you stop fighting."

After several long seconds, she forced herself to relax her face, her jaw, even though her heart still kicked insistently.

Darius smiled. "If you ever want to approach the deep consciousness, you have to submit yourself to it entirely. Some people, it takes a day. Others? *Years*, Parvaneh. As your guide, it's my job to know you. To understand how you fit into this body and when you're ready for the next step. Do you trust me to do that?"

She nodded, her tongue curling docile and slick against the bend of his knuckle.

He pulled his thumb out of her mouth. "Then don't ask when you get a meditation stone. When that time comes, it'll be obvious to everyone, and there will be no need to ask at all."

Fabia had gotten hers the very next day, after she'd fainted during the midnight session. Parvaneh's eyes had locked with Darius's as he'd lifted Fabia's limp body from the floor and held her against him. Parvaneh had felt something pull tight in her abdomen, a feeling she didn't recognize or like; it made her want to scream or cry or maybe run. And the next day, during afternoon session, when Parvaneh had showed up late with chapped, raw hands from doing the lunch dishes for the entire compound, he'd called Fabia up to the front of the meeting room and said he'd had a revelation the night before, of how Fabia was a perfect manifestation of *spiritus*. He'd explained that they were one body, united to reach the deep consciousness, and Fabia was their nerves or nerve endings or something like that.

Parvaneh had stared at Fabia's feet as she'd preened next to Darius, practically swooning against him as he presented her with the rock, painted forest green with black paint pressed into the carved markings. She simultaneously wanted to punch Fabia in her stupid face and collapse to the floor out of sheer exhaustion. Since she'd gotten her name, she'd thrown herself into the chores. It wasn't just that she wanted to prove she was worthy of being there: Darius had promised that work prepared the mind for the meditation sessions, and pure spirits—scrubbed clean of the worries that caked on and dried hard with laziness and spare time—could slip their physical boundaries and touch that vein of unadulterated *being* they were all reaching for. If that were really true, Parvaneh thought, curling her fingers against her palms and wincing as the movement pulled at the fissured skin at her knuckles, then she should be the one up there getting a rock, and Fabia should be in the dorms scrubbing toilets.

But no. Fabia had gotten the job Parvaneh had wanted—she got to spend all day playing with little kids—and still she whined at night, quietly, as they'd washed their faces and brushed their teeth in the large bathroom of the women's dorm, about how she hated changing diapers and wiping snotty noses. But in front of Darius, she was all duty and devotion, and there she was, getting her rock.

Tadeas had gotten his a few days later, and in typical Tadeas style, he'd fallen to the floor and kissed Darius's feet, nearly making Darius fall over with his slobbering-puppy love. Darius had hugged him, slapped him on the back, shaken him by the shoulders. Like he knew exactly what the guy needed. Unlike Fabia, Tadeas worked his ass off, milking the three cows, tending the twenty-odd pigs, shoveling their shit and pouring slop into their troughs, mentored by Kazem, whose tattoos peeked out from under the loose, mud-flecked sleeves of his robes, who cried every meditation session, and who hadn't said more than two words to Parvaneh since she'd been named.

It had made sense when Tadeas got his meditation stone. Parvaneh had told herself not to be jealous. Except now she was the only one on the compound who didn't have one. Well. The babies and toddlers didn't have them, she supposed. They had their own special nursery where all of them slept, tended by Octavia and Ladonna and a rotating cast of Oracles—including some of the men, maybe because they had fathered at least a few of the kids—who got to play with and cuddle them. Apparently, Darius didn't think Parvaneh was up to the job, so she got to scrub dishes and wipe tables and peel potatoes, while Basir, the bald cook who sounded like Tony Soprano, barked orders.

Parvaneh tied the tan cloth over her hair and slid her feet into clogs. She shivered as she gathered with a few of the others near the door, forcing her face into a placid, friendly smile that would tell everyone she was fine, she was serene, she was ready to help. She wished it were genuine; she hated being this fake person, this failure. She wanted her smile to be real, like Eszter's was. Like Octavia's was.

Behind her, Fabia was grumbling about the hour, how she'd been up meditating until two, how her back was hurting. Before Parvaneh could turn around and snarl at her, she heard Eszter murmuring comforting words, praising Fabia for her dedication and promising her there would be a reward for it, telling Fabia that her presence would be valuable at the birth.

Ladonna, her hair barely tamed by a tan headband and tufting out on either side of her face, her own huge belly taking up the space of another whole person, smiled in the dim light and said, "All right, girls. Do we have everyone?"

After everyone murmured their presence, all eight of them yawning and rubbing at their eyes, Ladonna shoved the door open and welcomed a blast of frigid air. The compound was lit by a dim, flickering, central light on its high metal pole and the glow of sunrise against the purple-black sky. Their clogs crunched through the fine crust of frost that had settled overnight. Parvaneh pulled her arms from her sleeves and shuffled along, hugging herself with her head bowed—until a scream brought it back up again. The sound had come from the place where they all spent every moment of free time.

"She's having a baby in the—?" Parvaneh began before being interrupted by Ladonna.

"She's been at it since three. Won't be long now."

"It took my mom two days to have me," said Fabia. "She loved to remind me of that, like I owed her something."

"It takes as long as it takes," said Eszter. "But this isn't Octavia's first delivery, and she told me her first was fast too."

Ladonna laughed. "Xerxes is always in a hurry. That little boy has never been slow a moment in his life."

Fabia groaned. "He never stops talking. 'I only have one mouth and one nose, so why do I have two eyes and two ears? Can I set dust on fire? Where do words come from? Can I have a baby when I grow up? Does the deep consciousness have a face? Is it a boy or a girl?' And that was just yesterday."

"Those are actually pretty good questions." Parvaneh winced at the faint sound of another scream and wished Ladonna would slow down—this vastly pregnant woman was marching them toward the source of the eerie wails like she was on a mission. "Especially for such a little kid."

"He's the oldest," Ladonna said. "The first baby we ever had on this compound. He's used to talking with adults."

"Yeah, I've seen him in the dining hall," said Parvaneh. Running around, stopping only to shovel a bite into his mouth before taking off again. "He's a cutie."

"He gets mad when I don't have the answers to his questions," said Fabia. "He kicked me when I couldn't tell him how many drops of water were in the ocean. And Octavia didn't even punish him."

"You're just as much his mother as she is," said Eszter as they reached the big double doors of the meeting hall. She paused with her fingers wrapped around the bracketed metal handle. "But you know that we don't punish children. They're closer to the deep consciousness than we are, and we should be listening to them, not inflicting on them the same wounds of our past."

"Makes sense to me," mumbled Parvaneh, remembering the

sting of backhanded slaps that came sudden and unexpected. She inhaled a big breath, readying herself as Eszter and Ladonna pulled the doors wide.

Unlike the rest of the buildings on the compound—which were single-story, prefab things almost like sheds, kept warm with generators and propane heaters—the meeting hall was more like a barn. Wide-planked wood floors, wooden walls, a catwalk and loft above the foyer. Windowless and candlelit, it was the only building on the compound that wasn't wired for electricity. Darius had declared it a sacred space, to be untouched by technology that was useful but sapped spiritual energy. The only exception to that was the electronic combination lock on the door that led to his private office space at the back of the building, behind the altar.

Despite the cold outside, the meeting hall was startlingly warm as they bundled inside and closed the doors again. The air was close and humid, like the inside of a mouth, and Parvaneh blinked up at the hazy curl of perfumed smoke rising from the incense burners at the edges of the cavernous room.

Like they always did when she entered this space, her nose itched and her head began to ache, but she didn't say a word about it out of fear it would be yet another black mark on her slate, yet another way she was not ready. She glanced over to see Eszter's hand dip into the pocket over her stomach. Fabia had her meditation stone cradled in her hands already. Ladonna and Kyra, both pregnant themselves, held their stones in one hand. Their other hands rested over their round bellies. Parvaneh slid her palm down the hollow of her own abdomen, wondering what it felt like to have another person growing inside such a small space.

She jerked at the sound of Octavia's groan from the front of the hall. Her gaze followed the sound right up to the altar, the place where Darius often lay and allowed them to put their hands on him, the place where they'd laid hands on old, gray-skinned Shirin last night. Parvaneh cringed at the memory of Shirin's face, her papery skin and dusky lips peeled back in pain as all of them touched her and meditated, stones clutched to their chests or pressed to her bony frame. Eszter had told her that Shirin had been diagnosed with bone cancer and was going to die soon, which meant that she was as close to the deep consciousness as a newborn. Ziba was the same, only a different kind of cancer. People that close to death could channel messages up from the deep consciousness for the rest of them because their souls were so close to joining it.

Now Octavia was on the altar, very much alive, naked and slick and trembling. Darius had his hands on either side of her head, his thumbs pressed to her sweaty temples. Her eyes were clamped shut, and her hands were clawed over the sides of the altar. Kazem stood between her legs, his solemn gaze riveted there, his hands on her knees. Tadeas held one of her hands but was facing the back wall like he couldn't bear to look at her, which might have been true. He puked at the drop of a hat.

Several of the other men—Mir, Parsa, Vahid, and a few whose names she was still learning—knelt behind Darius on the steps to the altar. Vahid was grasping Darius's heel, and the others had their hands on Vahid's back, always channeling the power and the spirit. Behind Kazem knelt Zana and Roya and Laleh, Goli and Beetah, and, to Parvaneh's shock, Shirin was there, too, gray faced and grim in her wheelchair, her skeletal fingers clutching at Beetah's shoulder as the younger woman held hands with the others and Goli clutched at Kazem's calf. His cheek twitched as she tightened her grip, fingernails digging in.

"Eszter, Fabia, Ladonna," Darius said without taking his eyes off Octavia's face. "At her shoulders." He instructed a few of the others to stand on either side of Octavia's legs. Within a few seconds, Parvaneh stood at the base of the steps alone. She shifted her weight from foot to foot, her skin hot and her head throbbing.

Octavia let out a whimper. "I'm too tired."

"She's close," Kazem said. "A few more pushes."

Darius lowered his face over Octavia's. "Focus on the consciousness, not the weakness of your body. Can you feel it? The new soul approaching?"

Octavia arched and screamed again. Parvaneh's eyes glazed over with tears. She had no idea what she was supposed to be doing. All the others seemed to know; they had their places, their stones, their roles. Even Fabia and Tadeas, who were as new as she was, had places of honor at Octavia's side.

"Parvaneh, stand by Kazem." His voice startled her out of her brooding. She rushed up the steps, nearly tripping headlong into the altar. The smell hit her, shit and blood and sweat. She glanced at the smeared mess on the altar between Octavia's legs and understood why Tadeas had his back turned.

"That is a gift from the deep consciousness—a new soul, a new pathway. Don't look away," Darius said firmly. He'd said it to Parvaneh, but Tadeas immediately turned to face Octavia again, focusing on the swell of her belly.

Everyone else was staring at Parvaneh, setting her teeth on edge. "Did you hear him?" Parvaneh snapped at all of them. "Don't look away."

Darius let out a bark of laughter that was cut short by a wrenching shriek from Octavia and a squelching sound from between her legs.

The tiny body slipped free with a rush of fluid. Parvaneh gasped as Kazem lifted the baby, a giant, pale raisin on a thick, greenish string, and plopped it onto Octavia's belly. She began to sob.

Parvaneh took in the fuzz between the baby's tiny shoulder blades and the swirl of dark hair on its head. She couldn't tell if it was breathing. It certainly wasn't crying. She swallowed, and this time, it didn't taste bitter. It tasted metallic—the taste of fear.

Kazem poked Parvaneh in the arm. "Take this." He handed her a pair of surgical scissors.

"But I don't—"

"Do exactly as I say." His voice was so deep. His eyes were calm. He explained what she needed to do.

"Will it hurt them?" she whispered.

Octavia laughed, weak and tired. "Nothing can hurt me right now."

Darius kissed her forehead. His hand was on the baby's back as the child let out its first complaining squawks. The others were meditating like their lives depended on it—Fabia was rocking back and forth, and Tadeas was chanting, "I feel it! I feel it! I feel it!"

Parvaneh felt nothing except the desire not to screw this up. She had been chosen to cut the baby's cord. This seemed important, and Darius had chosen her. If she did everything right, a stone had to be coming her way soon. Especially when Darius said, "This moment, we bring the new soul fully into our world and sever her connection to the deep consciousness with the understanding that she is a gift and a link to the core of being. I know all of you can feel that power pouring into you. Channel it into your stones."

The others clutched one another, clutched their stones, cried and murmured and swayed.

But Parvaneh had no rock. Instead, she had scissors.

The whole world shrank to that few inches of twisted greenish white and Kazem's rumbling, low words. "Between the clamps. Right there. Don't be afraid of it. Go ahead."

She grimaced as the blades sliced through the tissue, as the blood seeped from the severed ends. The baby girl began to cry in earnest, and Parvaneh blinked at the child's froggy face and gummy mouth.

A few seconds later, Kazem handed her a steel roasting pan full of blood and cord and something beet red and spongy. "Take it to the kitchen. Basir will be waiting."

The others were still in position. Meditating. Basking in the moment. Darius was whispering in Octavia's ear while she brought the baby girl to her breast. In their own little world. And Parvaneh... she was the errand girl, she realized. This wasn't a special purpose; it was the job of an outsider. She turned away quickly, nearly sloshing the contents of the pan down the steps of the altar.

Nostrils flaring at the iron-sharp smell, she made for the doors at the back of the meeting hall because the only other door was at the front and it led to Darius's private space. Still carrying the hope that her obedience would bring a meditation stone, she carefully shouldered one of the doors open, then nearly fell as it abruptly swung wide.

She staggered, blood splashing, coating her fingers. "Shit!"

"Isn't that a bad word?"

With a startled cry, she spun around and saw that the person who had pulled the door open only came up to her waist. With blond hair and huge, solemn eyes, he stared up at her.

"I guess it is," she admitted.

"Why did someone invent bad words if no one is allowed to say them?"

"Hi, Xerxes. It's nice to finally meet you."

He stood on his tiptoes, craning his neck. "What's in the pan?"

Parvaneh looked down at its contents and then held it a little higher. "I'm supposed to go to the kitchen." She *really* didn't want to know why.

"You'll have to wake up Basir," said the boy. "He's fast asleep. I went in there to get a snack and he didn't move." The child took a bite of a hunk of bread squished in his little hand.

Parvaneh snorted. "Stealing midnight snacks from the kitchen?"

"Everything here belongs to everyone, so that means it all belongs to me, and that means I'm not stealing," the boy said through a full mouth. He peeked around the edge of the door, and his expression softened from defiant to vulnerable in the shadows. "Is she okay?" he asked quietly. "I heard her crying."

"Oh! She's fine," Parvaneh said quickly, taking a few steps toward the mess hall, a double-wide trailer on the other side of the big clearing. She was acutely aware, no matter what everyone said about how they were all parents to the children, that Octavia was actually this child's mother. He fell into step next to her as she tromped across the clearing, his robe flapping around him, the too-long sleeves dangling over his hands.

"Are they talking to the deep consciousness? Did you hear its voice?" he asked as he kept pace with her.

"I—I'm not sure, actually."

"How can you not be sure? You heard it or you didn't."

"I might be kind of deaf," she said. "But I'm trying."

"I've never heard it, either," the boy replied. "Don't feel bad. What's your name?"

"Parvaneh."

"So it's your after name?"

"What do you mean?"

"Xerxes is the only name I have. But some people have more than one name." He gave her a once-over. "You look like you had another name."

She laughed. Fabia had been right—this kid was something, but in a good way. He reminded her a tiny bit of her younger brother, how his brain was always whirring. She wondered if he ever thought of her now, if he'd realized she wasn't coming back. "How can you tell I had another name?" she asked quickly, pushing down a pang of sadness.

"You look like how Izad looked when that black snake crawled out of a log and his eyes were like this." Xerxes looked up at her and made an exaggerated fearful face, his eyes popping and his mouth wide.

"I don't look like that!" Actually, maybe she did right now, carrying a pan full of bloody muck to the kitchen, of all places. "Not all the time at least."

"And it took you a second to remember what your name was just now."

"Shouldn't you be in bed?" she asked as they reached the mess hall door.

"I'm not sleepy."

"It's better if you're in bed now, though."

"Why?"

She gave her best Eszter-like answer, smiling as she thought of how her friend always seemed to have the perfect words for the moment. "Because all the adults are very busy with the birth of our new little soul. That's their job, and it's a big, hard one. But you have an important job too. You need to go to your bed and think good and loving thoughts, and in the morning, everything will be back to normal."

His brow furrowed. "If I think good and loving thoughts, will they come true?"

"Not always, but it doesn't hurt. And I think your thoughts might be pretty powerful right now. I think you could do a lot of good."

He seemed intrigued by the idea. "Okay. Then I'll see if it happens the way I want."

"Sounds good."

"Will you come play with me tomorrow? I'll tell you about my thoughts."

"I'd like that."

"Okay! Bye, Parvaneh. Ask Beetah to make you a new robe."

Parvaneh watched him scamper toward the children's dorm, bemused by the boy's strange mix of maturity and complete naivete. She looked down at the front of her robe. Her stomach clenched, and she gagged. Then she pushed the door to the mess hall open. "Basir!" she shouted.

"What?" came the reply. "What is it?" He poked his head out from the kitchen, flicking the lights on in the dining space. "Oh."

"It's a little girl," Parvaneh said as he came forward and took the pan from her.

"Ya think you spilled enough?" he snapped, looking from the front of her robe to the pan. "And it's already starting to clot!"

"What are you doing with it?"

"I have a great chili recipe." He rolled his eyes when she grimaced. "Ah, quit that. You won't know the difference from beef, and it's a way for all of us to have a little piece of the consciousness."

And Parvaneh had just shown she wasn't ready or worthy. Again. She swallowed back her disgust. "I'm sorry. I didn't understand."

He shooed her away. "Go change. You done good," he said gruffly. He pivoted and headed back to the kitchen, closing the door behind him.

Suddenly exhausted, Parvaneh sank onto one of the dining benches. Her robe was slowly going stiff in the cool air, her fingers sticky, her hair worming its way from the head covering and slipping into her eyes. She had no idea what time it was and little idea of what had happened over the past hours. But as she thought of the little boy with all his questions and the knowledge that he wanted to play with her tomorrow, she couldn't help but smile.

CHAPTER EIGHT

Bend, Oregon
December 10, present day

I spend the afternoon doing something I've avoided over the last eighteen years: I research the Oracles of Innocence. It's one of those keep-your-enemies-close kinds of exercises, rubbing up against memories that make my scarred legs tingle and my palms sweat. Miles is trying to track down the unaccounted-for victims, including the two possible unknown survivors. It's six people and only Oracle names to go by, but if I know Miles, that won't save me. So instead, I go in a different direction.

As excited as Miles is about those who might have survived the fire that night, there never were just three. What about all those *kids*?

I don't want to think about them. One in particular. But all of them are adults now, and implausible as it seems, one of them could have killed Arnold Moore. Are they still anonymous? Do they know who they are? Can I get Miles to bite?

After several fruitless searches, I hit the lottery. It's an article in the *Quest*, the newspaper of Reed College, and it begins with the headline "Fiery Beginnings: The Children of Darius."

On December 15, 2000, the Oracles of Innocence cult compound in Bend, Oregon, went up in flames, taking 35 souls with it. Three individuals, the only known adult survivors on the property that night, went to jail for crimes related to the deaths of their fellow cultists. There were other survivors of the catastrophe, though, and 20 years later, they are only just now realizing who they really are and where they came from.

I pause. Blow out a breath. I can feel the small, limp body in my arms, smoke-scented, flaxen hair tickling under my chin, the only softness in my world that night.

I squeeze my eyes shut and remind myself that this is what it takes to save my own life.

The night of the fire, as town and county firefighters waged a desperate battle with the flames, police officers discovered the children just before the blaze spread to their cabin. Twelve children, some only a few months old, others toddling around, just old enough to ask for their mothers, nearly all of whom, unbeknownst to them, were already dead.

That night, each of the youngsters was taken to St. Charles Hospital in Bend. Several were treated for smoke inhalation and dehydration. After that, social services took over, trying to find emergency foster homes. It could have been the end of the story. With their confidentiality protected and their last names unknown, with DNA still being collected from the charred corpses of their likely parents, these little ones began lives very different from those they had experienced from birth. But now all of them are in their third decade of life, and some of them have started to find one another.

The words hit me like a punch in the chest, and I read on as my heart pounds.

Somewhere on the internet, in a chat room that remains confidential to all but those invited in, the Children of Darius have formed a new family of their own, comprising individuals fathered by the cult's notorious leader, Stephen Millsap, a.k.a. Darius. Says one of the group's members, who asked to remain anonymous to protect his privacy, "My mom told me I was adopted when I was 16, and when I was 18, I told her I wanted to find my birth parents. That's when she told me who I was, and it hit me like a ton of bricks, knowing my parents were dead, that they were members of this cult." This kind of story is typical of a Children of Darius member, though feelings about the cult and its leader vary.

As the twentieth anniversary of the cult massacre nears, the group has grown to ten. The half siblings are hoping to convene in Bend sometime in December to reflect on the event that took their parents from them. There's only one problem. In the words of one member: "We don't have everyone yet."

A few children of Darius are still unaccounted for. It's possible these individuals are not aware of who they are or that they are but have no interest in joining. Technology may help uncover their identities, however. Some members found one another through use of modern forensic genealogy on sites such as GEDmatch, which was instrumental in helping discover the Golden State Killer in 2019. Others requested membership after scouring the dark corners of the internet to discover more about their own identity. Now, they are hoping to find their last remaining siblings to complete their family.

The story is full of rough edges, dramatics, vagueness, and a few errors—the author repeats the misconception that thirty-five bodies were found after the fire—but if what he's claiming is true and he's got a contact in that group, this is huge. It could totally change Miles's focus, taking it off the adult survivors and the whole "bad math" thing and placing it squarely on those grown-up kids who have banded together on the internet. Maybe even in person. Maybe even *right here in Bend.* It's a lead with a lot of loose ends, hidden identities, and a few kids left unknown. Perfect for keeping Miles busy.

I squint at the byline. Noah Perry. I click on his name. A senior at Reed, he's one of the editors of the school newspaper and has written and edited several other pieces over the last few years on things like the need for better vegan options in the school's cafeteria and a romantic relationship gone wrong between the student body president and vice president. There's a link to his email, and I go for it:

> Hello. I work for the *Hatchet,* and we're doing a story linked to the Oracles of Innocence. I just read your piece about the Children of Darius—really sophisticated work and great reporting! I was wondering if you'd be interested in talking to me about what you've discovered about this group. Please let me know if you're willing to talk!

I read it over a few times, upping the flattery and including a link to the *Hatchet* in case he hasn't heard of us. Small as we are, between Valentina and Miles, we're legit enough to draw applications from Northwestern and Columbia grads, so I would think a kid from Reed might be intrigued. After I send, I search for the other two adult survivors, but both Marie Heckender, a.k.a. Fabia, and Shari Redmond, a.k.a. Ladonna, prove elusive targets. I'm searching Portland newspapers when my email pings. It's Noah Perry.

> Hi, Ms. Rodriguez! Thanks so much for showing an interest in my work. I'm actually spending a few weeks in Bend now that I'm on break. Is your story

related to the Arnold Moore murder by any chance? I'd totally love to talk to you about the Children of Darius group, but for now, my sources have to remain confidential. Is that okay? I promised them that in return for their cooperation on my story. Let me know, and thanks again! I'm a big fan of the *Hatchet*!

This is even better than I thought. Confidential sources, a territorial but naive college journalist. He includes his phone number at the bottom, so I text him to introduce myself and let him know that I'm in Bend as well. I ask him if he wants to meet up at the Dogwood Cocktail Cabin at 8:30; it'll give me enough time to understand what I'm dealing with before I meet up with Miles. For the first time since this whole nightmare began, I feel some hope—if Miles is busy chasing sprawling leads, it might be enough to keep him off my trail.

I slip past a few smokers outside the Cocktail Cabin and pull the front door open, drawing a sharp breath between my teeth at the slice of pain in my wrist. A burst of frustration heats my chest as I rub the spot. The last thing I need is more aches and pains. Maybe it's the stress winding along my bones like barbed wire, squeezing tight.

Noah told me that he'll be wearing a black flannel and green T-shirt. From where I stand, a few guys might meet that description, but only one of them is staring at me from his position at the bar. Black hair, blue eyes, about the right age. He says something I can't hear, so I walk closer. "Noah? Hi."

His eyes dance over my face, my hair, and his brow furrows. He tilts his head and looks confused. Not an unusual reaction when I first meet people. Before they can cover it up, I get to see their confusion at the mismatch between my (relatively) unwrinkled skin and my white hair, which a lot of people assume I've dyed as a sort of fashion statement. He pulls it together after a second. "Dora?"

When I nod, he offers his hand to shake and gestures over to the bar. "I hope it's okay I brought a friend of mine." He sits down again and pats the back of a sandy-haired guy on his right, with a peach fuzz mustache and soft, round cheeks. He's hunched over a beer but looks over at us and nods. "This is Arman."

I wave and sit on Noah's left. "Do you both go to Reed?"

Noah shakes his head. "Arman is a local. I'm here to do a little research on the Oracles for another story, but it's great to have the chance to hang out with my buddy too. I was hoping to do some skiing at Mount Bachelor, but it's waaay too early in the season, so we'll do some hiking instead." He hands me a menu. "Can I buy you a drink?"

"I'll buy," I tell him. "You're doing me a favor, agreeing to meet like this." I climb onto the high barstool and settle in, wishing the seat had a back to support my aching body. I don't drink much, but right now, I'm feeling simultaneously stressed and buoyantly hopeful, so I might make an exception. And I think I read somewhere that ibuprofen and alcohol catalyze each other.

After a quick perusal of the menu, I order a drink called the Poco Loco and promise myself I'll drink it slowly. As I hand the menu back, I catch Noah staring at me from the corner of my eye. "Your hair is supercool," he says when I turn to him. "Reminds me of Rogue from the X-Men."

"Is that a good guy or a bad guy?"

"Both, kind of. She was raised as a villain and becomes a hero."

Unfortunately, I don't think that's my arc. "And she has white hair?"

"Just a streak. Anyway, it was cool of you to reach out. I didn't think anyone was interested in the story, seeing as it didn't actually involve any Reed students." He rolls his eyes.

"You're going to graduate in the fall?"

"Yeah. Finally." He does look a little older than I expected, like he took the circuitous route through school. "That piece was part of my senior project."

"How did you choose the topic?" I ask, having to raise my voice as someone turns up the music.

"Oh, I've been interested in cults since I first learned about them. I think I was in middle school?" He runs a hand through his hair, revealing much lighter roots. He's a cute guy, good-looking in a scruffy, lanky kind of way. His flannel is rolled up to his elbows, Oregon casual. There's a tattoo on his forearm, the infinity symbol. "I just got really fascinated by cult leaders, you know? The mind fuckery is unbelievable. Do you know much about cults?" he asks. "Like Jonestown? Jim Jones?"

I shake my head and focus on the drink that was just set in front of me. I hate the word *cult*. I hate how people react to it. Like anyone who joins a cult is a mindless idiot. But here's the thing, and I believe it with all my heart: no one ever joins a *cult*. Not on purpose. They hook up with nice people. They connect with the message of a strong leader. They feel like they belong when the rest of the world has stomped on them or turned them away. And that's why they stay. It's not like it's better on the outside, right?

Or maybe I'm just letting myself off the hook.

"The Peoples Temple," I say after taking a sip. It's spicy and sweet and would be all too easy to down in a few gulps. "I don't know much, but that one's pretty famous."

Noah nods. "Jonestown was probably the biggest cult massacre in history, by far. They were in California for years. Indiana before that. Then, as the authorities were closing in on old Jim, he took his followers down to this Promised Land in Guyana. Sounds nice, right?"

"There's always a dark side," I say.

"So true," Noah says. "I guess it wasn't the paradise they signed up for. But even with that, they stayed. And Jim started getting paranoid. Stocked up on guns. Cyanide. He had a whole plan for the apocalypse. But even as things got dark and scary, even as he started telling folks they might have to die for their faith, they *stayed*. Isn't that crazy? Almost no one left. No one said, 'Eff this, I'm not dying for this crazy-ass man,' and walked away. I've always wondered about that. Why didn't they leave?"

"Because it's not that simple," I mutter. I know that truth down to my bones.

"I guess," Noah says. He's got that pompous-college-student vibe, stuffed with facts but not much wisdom.

"Seems like you know your stuff. And the Oracles?"

"It seemed so similar but right here in Oregon: megalomaniac leader, people willing to die for him, and some of his victims weren't even identified after because they were basically strays, right? People who fell between the cracks."

"And kids," I remind him.

He grunts. "It's twisted, right? I've talked to some of them about how weird it is to find out your parents were crazy cultists. Talk about a mind fuck."

Arman glances over at us before waving over the bartender and ordering another beer. Noah chuckles. "Poor Arman probably gets tired of me talking about this. Hey," he says to the guy. "You want to change seats and talk to her?"

Arman shakes his head, but he gives me a nice smile. "I'm good with listening."

"You've actually talked to the members of this group?" I ask Noah. Miles is going to be here soon, and I need to get him to go for this.

Noah nods. "Mostly by email and text. Some are in college, one in the military. Trying to set out on their own. Some of them are pretty cagey, not that I blame them."

"Your article said the group was planning to get together," I say. "Are any of them in Bend now?"

Noah shrugs. "The whole get-together idea kind of fell apart. It's so near the holidays. People couldn't get away."

My hope shrivels a bit. "Do you think any of them would be willing to talk to us, maybe come forward?"

Noah glances over at Arman as he orders a plate of cheese fries. "I can certainly ask," he says as he turns back to me. "Since it's a bigger outlet, someone might bite. Keeping in mind that we're approaching the anniversary of their parents' fiery deaths, that is."

"Of course," I say quickly. "This must be a strange time for them."

Noah nods and sips his beer. "Super weird. And this murder? Arnold Moore? Wild, right? You obviously think it's connected to the cult. I certainly do."

"My colleague, Miles Connover, wants to establish that connection. There's some evidence to suggest it's related, but it's really not clear how."

Noah frowns. "You really think the Children of Darius are involved? I don't want to cause any trouble for these people."

"No!" I say quickly. "I'm not saying that." Even though I hope Miles will think so. "But it's a pretty interesting angle. A great way to develop a deeper understanding of what this kind of experience does to a person."

Noah looks down at me. His blue eyes are intense. "Nobody really seems to get it, right?"

I hold the eye contact. "It's hard to imagine, but we can try. It's a fascinating story."

Noah's gaze skips upward, focusing on something behind me.

"Hey," says Miles, pushing in next to me and flagging the bartender. "I figured I'd get a head start, but here you are." He grabs a menu and talks while reading. "How are your folks? Do I get to meet them? Do they have embarrassing pics of you from high school?"

I roll my eyes and give Noah an apologetic look. "They're fine, hopefully never, and no, they do not. Miles, I need to introduce you to someone."

His expression goes stiff for a second, and he raises his head. "I didn't think you were—"

"This is Noah," I tell him, leaning back so Noah can offer his hand. "He wrote a really fantastic article for his college newspaper about the kids who were found on the Oracles compound after the fire. I'll send it to you."

"Which school?" asks Miles as he shakes Noah's hand.

"Reed."

"Ah," says Miles. "That says it all."

Noah chuckles. "We get a lot of that. No, I'm not a druggie."

"But you have an interest in cults," he guesses.

Noah nods. "And Oregon is prime cult country. There was the Rajneeshpuram, the Ecclesia Athletic Association—they actually killed a girl there and abused dozens of kids—and then the Oracles of Innocence, which was the worst in terms of the body count. I mean, in the U.S., only Heaven's Gate is worse."

"Solar Temple," says Arman, leaning forward.

"That was in Canada, dude," Noah says. Then he introduces Arman to Miles.

Arman waves and leans back, treating his cheese fries to all his attention.

"What about Waco?" asks Miles without skipping a beat. "Didn't something like eighty people die there?"

"Seventy-six on the final day of the standoff," says Noah. "Six on the first day. But it's not clear if those were suicides, you know? A lot of them died in the fire on their compound."

"Like the Oracles," says Miles. "I don't think anyone knows for sure what happened in that building." Then he gets this little smile on his face. "Well. That might not be true actually."

Noah locks gazes with me for a moment before saying, "The Oracles are a twisted one for sure. And we *definitely* don't know the full story."

"Right," I say, leaning forward and giving Miles a hopeful look. "Like what happened to all the *kids* on the compound?" I gesture at Noah. "That's why I thought his story was so fascinating. It's been an unexplored angle until now."

"Uh-huh," says Miles, leaning back to talk directly to Noah. "The kids and maybe a few others who actually got out of the fire—that's a *totally* unexplored angle."

"That's a good point," says Noah. "With Jonestown, they could pretty much track any survivors who ran away. It was a remote part of South America—so the Americans were easy to spot, right? Bend's remote, too, but who's to say a few people didn't run? Including the night of the fire. I don't believe for a second no one got out." His eyes gleam as he looks back and forth between us. "I guarantee you some did."

"Whoa," says Miles. "That's my question exactly: Who got out? I guess you've done your homework."

My whole body goes cold. I can't freaking believe this. After all my work, are we really back to the whole bad-math thing? I want to scream.

Noah grins, revealing straight, white teeth. "I'd love to write for a place like the *Hatchet* after I graduate."

Miles laughs. "Is that so?"

"Don't laugh," Noah says. "I'm serious."

"I'm not laughing at you," Miles replies. "You sound a lot like I did twenty-odd years ago."

Now Noah looks hesitant, fiddling with a button on his flannel. "Are you guys interested in having an intern at all?"

"You got a résumé?" Miles says. He turns to me and sees my subtle head shake. "What?" he whispers.

"You want to move fast and keep this story to yourself?" I murmur in his ear. My heart rate is 132. If Noah turns out to be protective of the Oracle children and interested in the people who got out of the fire, he and Miles could be a great team, and I could be screwed. "Don't hire some college kid who'll brag about your every move on Insta or Snap or TikTok or whatever platform he's on."

"Ah. Good point." He turns back to Noah. "Let me think about it, okay? Give me your contact info, and I'll consult with legal regarding our intern policy." Noah gives Miles an eager nod in return, and they exchange contact info before Arman elbows his friend and the two head out.

I give Miles my prettiest smile, having temporarily stalled the situation. It's not that I want him to fail. It's not that I don't want him to win a Pulitzer. I just want to keep myself safe and sane and out of a cage, and this is going to be a tricky enough dance as it is. It might all come down to one detail, but I need to be the one finding them. Checking them. Doing what needs to be done to sift out the truth.

"Did you have a good interview with Chief Ransom this afternoon?" I ask Miles once they're gone.

"Guy's kind of a jerk. He has no imagination when it comes to this case. Completely dismissive of the Oracle connection." He takes a sip of his drink. "But I'm going to connect the dots for him." He looks over at me. "Headed to the library tomorrow. That might be a treasure trove. Archived articles from 2000—text is on the web, but pictures aren't."

My hand is shaking, so I put my glass down. "I can do that for you. Go deep in the local coverage at the time. Try to find you more leads."

His brown eyes narrow. "Yeah?"

I nod, caught off guard by the sudden intensity. "That's what I'm here for, right?"

After a moment, he nods. "Perfect. I want every relevant article, especially if there are any pictures of these people, names paired with faces. That's the key. I'm still trying to track down the six names that weren't paired with an actual corpse—"

"Maybe I can find that for you."

He shrugs. "Focus on those."

My stomach turns. "Anything else?"

"Access Portland papers from that time. Maybe we can find reference to people who stayed behind, maybe people Darius was friends with before he went off the deep end? He was from Portland. Made his money in the stock market and got out just before the '87 crash. Came home and voilà. Started a cult."

"As one does. Anything else?"

"Oh! Oh." He rubs at his temple. "Did you get ahold of Arnie's girlfriend? The chief mentioned her. Pretty obvious he thinks she's a crank, but you never know."

"I chatted with her this afternoon," I tell him. "The chief was right. She's a mess."

"But will she talk to me? Did old Arnie tell her anything about the Oracles?"

"She told me she already talked to the police about it."

"Right, but they might not be asking the right questions."

"She said she told them all she knew, and apparently, they didn't believe her."

"I might," says Miles.

"Do you believe in little green men called 'visitors,' who are recruiting human agents here on Earth to kill anyone who might tell the world about them?"

He stares at me, slack jawed. "Ah, crap."

I tell myself I'm doing Miles a favor. "She sounded like she was drunk, as in, she might have downed a fifth *as we were speaking*. My dad called her 'a piece of work,' and I can tell you right now she's not going to give you reliable info. I've done follow-ups with enough sources to know when one is full of it—and you can imagine what happens when you try to hang your hat on *that*."

"Yeah," says Miles, looking crestfallen. "I've gotten burned before." He throws back the rest of his drink and waves at the bartender. "It's not like we're hurting for leads, though."

I nod, relief flooding my veins, turning me soggy and loose. I didn't lie completely—I quoted Martin accurately. And she *did* blame aliens. She probably would have embarrassed us as a source. "We've got plenty to work with, and I'll be at the library in the afternoon to get more historic references. I have some stories to run through for Valentina before then."

"I should have known she wouldn't let up."

"She can't," I remind him. "She's got to keep everything running, and we only have two copy editors."

"And I've got one of them at my beck and call," he says, smiling again. "I guess I should remember how lucky I am to have you."

Guilt seeps through the mass in my chest, diluting the relief. "Don't ever forget it," I say.

CHAPTER NINE

The Retreat
May 7, 2000

B reakfast prep was done by sunrise, breakfast dishes by the time the golden ball of light filtered through the upper quarter of the dense canopy of the pines, and that was when Parvaneh could rub a little grease on her chapped hands and head to the meeting hall for morning meditation. It was already going on; Parvaneh and a few others were always late because of the nature of their chores. It always made Parvaneh worry she was being left out of something good.

As she exited the dining building, she listened to the shrieks of playing children, punctuated by the cries of an infant coming from the nursery dorm. She paused, unable to tell which baby it was—Kyra's girl, born three weeks ago; Ladonna's little boy, born two months ago; Octavia's little girl, Parisa, born on the first day of the New Year. So many babies to take care of—Parvaneh wondered if Xerxes got left on his own more often than not. She'd seen him wandering alone a few times, digging around in the woods. She'd only been able to play with him a few times. Meditation took up every moment not filled with work, but she didn't feel like a servant or anything. Most of the time, she actually felt happy, surrounded by friendly people, safe from the outside world, content, and busy. She fell into bed every night completely exhausted only to be roused by Eszter before sunrise to start the day's chores.

"Parvaneh!"

She turned to see Eszter jogging in her direction from the dorm. Her belly led the way, and when she reached Parvaneh's side, she put her hand on it, panting. "Headed to meditation?"

"Yep," Parvaneh said.

Eszter laughed. "Don't sound so excited."

Parvaneh returned her smile. "Hard to be *too* excited about something I apparently suck at."

"Oh, come on. It's not something you're graded on."

"Easy for you to say." Parvaneh pointed at the little lump of the meditation stone in the front pocket of Eszter's robe. "*You* got an A. Everyone else too—months ago! Everyone except me."

"I didn't realize it was stressing you out so much. Why didn't you say something?"

Parvaneh gave her a sidelong glance. "Seriously? It all seems so easy for you."

Eszter stopped in her tracks and tugged on Parvaneh's shawl, drawing her to a halt. "You can talk to me about this stuff, okay? A year ago, I couldn't figure out why I wasn't able to even sense the deep consciousness when everyone else seemed able to touch it so easily."

"What changed?"

She offered a ghost of a smile. "I put my trust in Darius. He invested in me."

"I know he does that," Parvaneh said. After the evening sessions, he often chose one person to work with individually. He'd never once chosen Parvaneh. She'd often wondered what he was getting up to with them so late at night, especially when it was a female Oracle like Zana or Eszter, but after her first stupid assumption about Darius's private session with Shirin, she'd figured it was better not to assume. "And it was helpful?"

Eszter bowed her head. "When I joined the Oracles, I thought it was a miracle. I thought this was the magical solution to all the crap I'd been through."

Parvaneh let out a dry laugh. "You mean it's not?" She sighed. "Don't get me wrong. I love it here. And I know people care about me. But I guess I thought the meditation thing would get easier, you know?"

Eszter drew her into a hug, the rock poking Parvaneh's flat belly through their robes. So close. "Receiving your name is only the start. It just means you're in the mix, that you've decided to do the hard work. Remember what Darius said about the whole thing sometimes feeling like crawling over broken glass?"

Parvaneh nodded against Eszter's shoulder. Her warmth felt good. She smelled like soap and milk and earth, maybe because one of her chores was to rise at four in the morning to milk cows. "I just wish Darius really saw how hard I'm trying. It's like he pays attention to everyone except me." She sighed. "It's hard not to be jealous of everyone."

Eszter squeezed her and let her go. "Darius loves all of us. You don't have to feel left out. Are you really worried about that?"

Parvaneh shrugged.

"You're not alone, Parvaneh. We all struggle with envy sometimes— just keep walking the path. It's worth it. I promise," she said, rubbing her belly. She'd been overweight to begin with, but in the last month, it seemed like she'd ballooned, hips straining against the seams of the robe. Wouldn't be long before she'd need Beetah to make her a bigger one.

Parvaneh watched Eszter. Listened to the swish of her palm over the fabric of her robe. "Are you pregnant?" she blurted out.

Eszter's face flushed. "That wasn't what I was talking ab—"

"But you *are*?"

Eszter nodded, looking down at her belly. "Am I showing already? I didn't think..."

Parvaneh felt her cheeks heat. She didn't want to tell Eszter that she just looked bigger all over. "You're glowing. How far along?"

"About ten weeks? Ladonna helped me figure it out. So that means I'll be due in December." She smiled. "It's an amazing feeling, knowing a life is growing inside you."

"Who's the father?"

Eszter blinked at her. "What do you mean?"

"You've been an Oracle for over a year," Parvaneh said. "I didn't know you were sleeping with anyone. Is it Kazem?" she whispered. He had a silent, rough charm to him. "But I've seen the way he and Zana look at each other," she continued, "so maybe not...?" She took in Eszter's red face, her teeth clamped over her lip. "What about Mir?" Short but muscular, Mir was a great storyteller and had a booming laugh. "Or—"

"What does 'father' even mean?" Eszter asked, not meeting her gaze. "The deep consciousness sends us a soul, and it doesn't matter which bodies offer up the building blocks of the shell that it will occupy. It doesn't matter whose body shelters it. Each of these souls belongs to all of us."

Parvaneh put her hands on her hips. "Come on. Whatever secret you've got, it stays with me. I'm a vault."

Eszter's gaze slid from side to side. "Fine. It's Gil, okay?" she said through clenched teeth. "Don't tell *anyone*."

Parvaneh opened her mouth, giddy questions on the tip of her tongue, but the door of the dining hall slammed shut with a bang, and Basir was striding toward them a moment later. "Why aren't you meditating?" he asked Parvaneh. "I turned you loose ten minutes ago." He glanced at Eszter and nodded, not questioning why *she* wasn't meditating.

"She offered to walk me to the meeting," Eszter said. "And I had a cramp, so she was staying with me until it passed."

"Oh," said Basir, his expression softening. "Take your time, then. I'll see you in the meditation space." He walked past them and entered the meeting hall.

"Are you sure the father isn't *Basir*?" Parvaneh asked, giggling.

Eszter closed her eyes, obviously trying not to laugh. "Stop it! We have to get in the right frame of mind!" She grabbed Parvaneh's hand as they reached the door, still smiling. "Becoming an Oracle doesn't save you. Staying does."

"Okay," Parvaneh whispered, shedding her laughter, girding herself. She could already smell the incense lacing the air. She remembered what Darius had told her in that moment with his thumb in her mouth, his body overwhelmingly close: he'd been using himself as a symbol of the deep consciousness, showing her that she had to stop fighting it. She wanted it so badly that it was a taste on her tongue, like yeast or salt, earthy and sharp.

With her head up, she inhaled the smoky-sweet incense fumes, held it in her lungs as long as she could. At the front of the room, about twenty Oracles sat close together, their hands on one another and on the channeler—the person whom Darius had deemed most connected to the consciousness for the session. It was Shirin, gray and gaunt, just as it was on most mornings. Ziba, the other elderly, sick Oracle, was usually the channeler during the evening sessions, when Darius himself didn't do the job—and when no one was giving birth, of course.

Shirin was curled on her side on a mattress on the floor, probably because it would have been too painful for her to be lifted onto the altar. Last night, Parvaneh had heard her screaming for Kazem, who came rushing in to bring her more pain medicine to douse the fire in her bones. Darius was at her side now, his fingers threaded into her brittle, white hair. Parvaneh had asked why the woman wasn't in the hospital; she certainly looked like she needed to be. But Octavia had only given her a quizzical look and said, "*This* is where she needs to be. She's eager for the embrace of the consciousness, just like we all are."

Shirin didn't look eager right now, though. She was trembling and moaning in apparent agony. But Darius held her head in his hands, and the others had their palms against her body, fingers curled around skinny limbs. Many of them had their meditation stones clenched in their other hands, occasionally bringing the rocks to their lips.

Basir was at Shirin's feet, and Eszter squeezed her voluptuous body between him and Fabia, who opened her eyes and gave Eszter an annoyed look. Parvaneh shoved down a kick of irritation. She knew she was supposed to love every person on this compound, and with some, especially Octavia and Eszter, it was easy. Darius, though intimidating, was steady and magnetic—she was scared but drawn in, always wanting more from him even as her heart raced and her fear made her want to run. Even the ones like Basir and Kazem, who were gruff or silent, weren't outright mean. No one else seemed to have her problem of despising Fabia, though—it was just one more thing Parvaneh needed to work on.

She edged behind Eszter, as there was little room anywhere else. The Oracles were crowded around Shirin, shoulder to shoulder, swaying like one giant, undulating organism. And Parvaneh had a part in it; she knew she did. She put her right hand on Eszter's back and closed her eyes, fisting her empty left hand. Behind her closed eyelids, her vision exploded with orange and brown, purple and black. She focused on the shapes, on the scents, on the sounds, trying to melt into all of it, trying to shed her own skin.

After a while, she sagged with frustration. Boredom. She wished there were a clock on the wall, then remembered it wouldn't tell her much; the session would be over when Darius said it was. Sometimes they lasted all day. Sometimes they ended quickly and everyone ran off to do their chores. Darius insisted that time was imposed by others to control them, and he taught them to deny its power...but Parvaneh couldn't help it. She felt as if they'd already been there for hours. She swore she could hear the happy cries of the children all the way from here. She wished she could breathe fresh air; her head was pounding. She squirmed, trying to get comfortable. Her left foot was asleep.

"You're not focusing," Fabia whispered.

She glared at Fabia, who had closed her eyes again. "Are *you*?"

"Parvaneh," Darius said quietly. "Fabia was trying to call you back to the moment. That was an opportunity for you, and you batted it away like a mosquito."

The reprimand had been delivered in a gentle enough voice, but to Parvaneh, it felt like a shout. A slap. A guarantee that a meditation stone was not in her near future. "I'm sorry," she said quickly. And then forced herself to add, "Fabia, thank you for trying to help me."

She closed her eyes so she didn't have to see Fabia's stupid, self-satisfied smile. She didn't believe for a second that Fabia had been doing anything other than trying to get her in trouble, but what mattered was how Darius saw things.

A warm hand took hold of her fist, pushed the fingers open. She opened her eyes to see that Eszter had reached behind her and pressed her meditation stone into Parvaneh's hand so that they were holding it between their two palms. Eszter laced her fingers with Parvaneh's and squeezed, making the rough edges of the stone dig into Parvaneh's skin. It gave her a sensation in the here and now, something to focus on. She imagined the stone was a cave and herself inside it, staring in wonder at the scatter of crystals all around her, lit by an unearthly light, growing brighter by the minute, warmer by the second. Her whole being pulsed with the wonder of it. This was it—this *had* to be it. The deep consciousness, glowing and infinite. Finally, finally, she was approaching it. Her eyes stung with tears. She clutched at Eszter's hand desperately and scooted closer, trying to tighten their connection. But in doing so, she knocked Eszter off balance, causing her to pitch forward.

Crack. A low, dull sound, followed by the old woman's hoarse screams. Everyone looked around wildly, their gazes landing on Eszter, whose left hand was still held tightly in Parvaneh's.

"I'm sorry," Eszter cried. "Oh, Shirin, I'm so sorry!"

"Basir, Tadeas, Zana, get Shirin back to her bed," said Darius. "Fabia, go fetch Kazem, and tell him to bring the medicine and a splint to Shirin's room." He stood up, grimacing. Like he felt every bit of agony right along with the gaunt, old woman at his feet, whose ankle and shin were already swelling and growing purple with blood.

"Oh my god," Parvaneh whispered. She watched in a daze as everyone else buzzed around Shirin, like they knew exactly what to do. Many left, striding up the aisle to the back as if they were on a mission. Basir and Tadeas and Zana, along with a few of the others, lifted Shirin's mattress.

Parvaneh tried to take the corner near her head, but Darius gently pushed her away. She stood helplessly as the others shuttled Shirin out of the meeting hall. Darius watched them go with an intense focus, as if he were willing strength into their muscles. A moment later, everyone had gone. Only she and Eszter remained. Darius turned to them. "Tell me what happened."

"It was me," Eszter said quickly. "I lost my balance. An accident."

"Leave," he said to her. He reached out and caressed her cheek, brushing away a tear. "You're lying to me, which saddens me more than you can possibly understand. You were trying to share your meditation stone with Parvaneh. I felt the change, like a static charge." His gaze traveled to where Shirin had lain, agonized and screaming. "Then came the shock."

"I only wanted to help," Eszter whispered.

"But you aren't ready to provide that kind of guidance, are you?"

Eszter shook her head, giving Parvaneh an apologetic glance before she trudged up the aisle and through the back door. Now Darius moved so he was face-to-face with Parvaneh. "You were trying to take what isn't yours. And in doing so, you disrupted our connection to the deep consciousness."

"I didn't mean to. She offered the stone to me, and—"

"Parvaneh, how could you? I'm not keeping a stone from you to be cruel. Why would I do that to my fellow Oracle? I'm doing it for your *protection*, to give you a chance to grow into readiness. You see the result when you're not ready. You see what happened just now."

Parvaneh nodded miserably. His heavy hands closed over her shoulders, and he pulled her against him. She stared at the hollow of his throat, saw the vitality beating beneath his skin. They were chest to chest. "Do you feel how we are connected?" he whispered.

She wasn't sure what he meant, but she nodded anyway.

"This is why we're here. To connect with one another. To reach for something deep inside one another. But we can do damage if we grasp for things before we know how to hold them, mentally and physically." His chuckle vibrated through her body. "Never pick a fruit before it's ripe. This is a lesson I myself have to learn each and every day. Patience."

"I'm trying. I didn't see the harm—"

"Is Eszter your guide here?"

"No."

"Who is?"

"You are."

"Not me. The deep consciousness. I am only its voice here." He looked down at her. "Why did you let her pull you away from my guidance? Am I not enough? Am I failing you somehow?"

She shook her head, her gaze flitting over his face. She didn't know where to put her eyes.

"Until you trust, you won't be ready to surrender." He pulled her hands up, placed them on his chest. "This is just the shell of me," he whispered. Then he put his hands on her waist, held on as she tensed. "And this is the shell of you. Inside of us, there are souls desperate to connect. The stones are one way of drawing your focus, allowing you to reach out. But don't attach too much to them. Because it's this that matters." He was pressed so tight against her. It made her want to cling and run and scream and laugh.

He let her go. "I need to rest," he said. "Please go help Basir with lunch." He walked to the front of the room, typed some code into the keypad above the door handle to his office, his fingers dancing clockwise in a square, four digits. It clicked; he opened the door and disappeared inside. The moment the door closed, Parvaneh ran, desperate for the kitchen and her chores, anything mindless, any escape from the jumbled mix of love and fear and yearning and disgust and desire and greed and defiance all tangled up inside her head.

CHAPTER TEN

Bend, Oregon
December 11, present day

Less than a mile into my run along the quiet streets of Bend at six in the morning, it feels like my shins are on fire. I try to stick to the asphalt surfaces instead of the concrete sidewalks, but it does little to help. The grass is wet from last night's rain, and I only have one pair of running shoes, so I don't risk soaking them.

I give up and jog home after less than a mile. Not nearly enough. I limp into the house, where I'm greeted by Hailey, who's got her wet hair in rollers and is holding a steaming cup of coffee. I can hear the shower going down the hall; Martin's getting ready for work. "How was your run?" she asks.

"I need a softer surface," I tell her. "Lots of aches and pains lately."

"They've really improved the River Trail over the last few years, and it's mostly packed dirt south of the Old Mill District. Rocky but really pretty."

I thank her, turn down her offer of breakfast, listen as she informs me that her cleaning lady is coming tomorrow and could I please leave my key—it's their extra one—under the mat if I'm not here when they arrive? I promise her I will. Then I start the edits on the stories Valentina sent as I wait for my turn in the shower. The sooner I get through them, the sooner I can get to the library, but if I rush and make mistakes, I'll be screwed. So I try to focus, but I'm restless and distracted.

It's four days until the anniversary. I feel it like a shadow stretching long at my side.

Someone decided to murder Tadeas. Arnie. Someone drew out their plan on his body and followed it through, sliding a knife through flesh and guts. Kidneys and lungs. Heart and liver.

They all have a different feel, a different give.

The memories shouldn't be this keen, this sharp and merciless, but there they are, where they've always been in my empty moments.

I pull myself together and edit the damn stories.

I make it to the library by one. The lady at the information desk tells me yes, they do have the *Bend Bulletin* in the microfilm archives, from 1903 to 2014. After that, it was entirely digital. Before that, the digital archives don't have image files because the photos were made using film, and they were never scanned in.

Just like Miles told me. I'm so glad I made it here before he did.

After thanking the info lady, I head down to the microfilm room, open the door, and freeze.

Noah's at the desk in front of one of the machines and grins when he sees me. "Hey!"

"Hey. What a coincidence." I scan his workspace. He's got a couple films out, dated March 2000–July 2000 and November 2000–December 2000. Shit. "What are you up to?"

He looks behind him, following my gaze. "Figured I'd peruse the archives, see what the local coverage was."

"Of the fire?"

He nods. "Did you know they used to come to town? People hired them to clean houses and stuff. I guess they made some of their money that way."

"Huh," I say. "That's interesting."

"I wonder if anyone around here remembers them," he says. "I'm trying to write a story on the anniversary and the Moore murder."

"What's your angle?"

He frowns. "I don't just want to rehash what happened. But after talking with Miles last night, it got me thinking about the survivors."

"The kids?"

"They're important. And I'm going to get their comments about this stuff. But I want to highlight the survivors who no one is talking about."

I laugh and shake my head. "You and Miles. Are you guys sure you want to plant your flags on that particular hill? I mean, if no one's talking about it, maybe there's a reason. Honestly, I'm just trying to help Miles keep his story on the rails—we can't go off into conspiracy-theory land. I talked to one possible source yesterday who thought there were people who escaped...because they were rescued by aliens."

He snorts. "Well, we both know *that* wasn't what happened."

"Right," I say, looking away from his gaze. "Are you done with your research session? Miles sent me over to make sure he has all the relevant local coverage."

"Oh. Yeah. I don't want to get in your way. I'm good for now." He looks down. Shuffles his feet. He looks so young. "Hey, would you be willing to read a draft of what I write? I'd be grateful to get feedback from an actual professional."

"I'm not a journalist."

"I know. Miles said you're his copy editor. His fact-checker. He said you keep him on the straight and narrow."

"That's me," I say quietly. "And sure. I'll read your piece. Send it over once you're done?"

He nods, eager like a child. I endure another few minutes of small talk with him. He tells me that he and Arman are going hiking this afternoon along the river trail, and I tell him I'm planning to go for a run there tomorrow. And then he's gone, and I can finally get to work.

I don't know the date, but I know it was June. I reach for the reel, then look around the room. Everything I want is already right here— Noah accessed the very reels I need, so I don't sign my name on the clipboard next to the archive.

I sit down at the scanner and pick up the March-through-July reel. I know because the info lady told me that the library's database includes a searchable index for the paper. I input the word *Oracles* just to see what led Noah to pull this particular reel, given that the fire didn't happen until December of that year. And sure enough, it's as I feared.

I remember the moment, remember thinking it wasn't what we were supposed to be doing, remember thinking Darius would be furious if he knew.

The Oracles Are Here, and They Want to Clean Your House

Such a stupid headline. But that's the one I want; I put the reel on its peg, thread it under the glass, and wind it onto the receiving peg. Once the film is loaded, I skim through for the date the index gave me—June 26. "They call themselves the Oracles of Innocence," the author, Joel Keeler, wrote. "You can call them a church, a cult, or a social club, but here's what they really want you to call them: your favorite new house cleaners."

I skim the article, just two columns and a picture—with a caption. Shit. *Pictured, right to left: Octavia, Fabia, Zana, Roshanak, Parvaneh, Eszter, Laleh, and Minu. They say they do not have last names, only the names given by their god.* My heart stops—I remember him checking the spelling of our names, and I remember Fabia's certainty. I didn't want to be caught like that, frozen. But there I am, among all those smiling faces, eight women in robes, looking sunny and carefree. I stare at myself from twenty years ago, so clueless, so in love with all of it, still blind to what was coming even though it had already started to tilt sideways, just a slight list, the kind that makes you seasick before you even realize the world is unsteady.

All but two of us are dead.

I look stupid in that picture—and I was. I can't believe I gave him my *name*. I close my eyes and breathe. That name is not my name anymore. It's just a few syllables, a chain of letters, completely unofficial. It links me to nothing.

It's the picture that freaks me out. Did Noah actually see this, or had he only just searched the archive when I walked in on him? And if he did see it, would he even recognize me? I look so different. My hair especially.

But he's noticed my hair.

Of course he did. Everyone does.

I stare at Fabia's face, as plain as I remember it. *Marie Heck-en-der.* She always looked peevish to me, like she'd just tasted something sour. I wonder if a decade in jail cured her of that. I wonder where she's hiding, how she's rebuilt her life, whether she still thinks about the moment she locked us all inside.

It was already burning. Just little fires, scattered about. But she knew what she was doing. Darius had known exactly whom to give that particular job to. Would anyone else have done it if he'd asked?

Probably most of them, now that I think about it.

I peruse the archive and find one other story before the fire, from September 2000. Something I didn't know about before. The article mentions concern voiced at a meeting of the Deschutes County council about the Oracles, with three property owners complaining that their proximity to the compound might lower property values and another woman expressing concern for the well-being of the children on the compound because she'd seen one little boy at the edge of her property, wandering alone. Darius himself showed up to explain that the children were all too young to attend formal schooling and that they were extremely loved and well cared for. He also stated to the council that the Oracles had improved the 210-acre property by drilling two wells and installing septic systems, by building structures that could be assessed and taxed, and by respecting all zoning laws. He questioned whether anything but prejudice could be at the heart of all these complaints. The article notes that the meeting ended without a recommendation of action.

When I was there, I never questioned the property, the buildings, the surplus of food. We never starved. We didn't live in luxury, but we had everything we needed. I hadn't always had that in my life to that point, so it made it harder to think of leaving. I was trapped.

No, I was a coward. What would my life have been like if I'd gotten out sooner?

I try not to wonder if I could have had something good and normal. I remind myself that nothing ever had been good or normal, that I was probably doomed either way.

Except for one critical thing: I wouldn't have had blood on my hands. His, hers. I didn't know what I was capable of until that night.

I load up the reel for December 2000 and brace myself. Numb and cold, I read through each story. A fire at the Oracle camp. Children unharmed, sent to foster care. I stare at the sentence, read it twice. It says there were twelve children, doesn't give their ages. I hate that. I hate not knowing.

Because really, there were thirteen.

I shiver. Reading these articles, looking at that picture of all of us—it's like shaking the hand of a ghost.

My phone buzzes, making me jump. It's Miles. "Hey," I say. "What are you up to?"

"Ransom is an asshole. I'm going to have to file a Freedom of Information request to get the autopsy reports and the crime scene report."

"What a pain." Thank god. It buys me time.

"Today I'm focusing on Portland and on tracking down Marie Heckender. Her and Shari Redmond. Fabia and Ladonna were their cult names."

"Any idea where they're hiding now that they're out of jail?"

"I'll get there. Did you make it to the library?"

"I'm here now. There aren't many stories about the cult before the fire."

"Any pictures? Do we have images of these people? That could really help," he says. "Because with facial recognition software—"

"I couldn't find any," I tell him. "I combed the entire 2000 archive. Do you want me to go back to 1999?"

He's quiet for a few seconds. "Sure, if you have time," he finally says. "I'm trying to track down a few leads in Portland, like family members of the ones who died. I'm building a running tally of who was on the compound at the time of the fire."

"I can do that," I say quickly. "It's no problem. But this is a lot, so if you're hoping to get it before the anniversary—"

"Don't worry about it. Just get whatever you can. This could be a series, multiple stories over the next month or two."

"I'll do my best to find them. And if I find Fabia and Ladonna, maybe I could even interview them for you?" Not that I'd actually talk to either of them...but he wouldn't know that.

He laughs. "Eager for a byline?"

"Just trying to help."

"If you can even find them, you're a lifesaver. This frees me up in the best way."

We end the call, and I go back to the archive, feeling more restless than ever, realizing I didn't ask what he intended to do with his freed-up time. I can't worry about it now, though—I've already taken the most dangerous bits from him. I'll be able to make sure he only finds what it's safe for him to find. I can do this.

But telling myself that doesn't make me feel better. Forget tomorrow; I need to go running this afternoon. This morning's little jog wasn't nearly enough, and I feel like I'm going to explode. Seeing that picture in the archives, knowing it's been there the entire time, like a screaming indictment for anyone who knows where to look, such a close call. If Miles had come in here and found this... I have to go. I have to move.

I need to run. More than I need to breathe.

I slip the reel containing the photo into my purse. I get up, find a reel box marked March–June 1992, and remove it, putting the empty box back on the shelf and slotting the 1992 reel into the March–June 2000 box. I put it away along with the other one Noah pulled.

I make one final check of the room, remove a white hair I've left on the chair cushion. I erase the cache on the browser and sign Noah out, realizing too late that I could have seen what he searched for before I arrived, which could have been interesting. There's something about him that's unsettling, but he's also young and naive and just wants a good story.

Like a less-experienced version of Miles, who takes more of my attention. With the reel in my purse, I feel safer than I have since he first mentioned Arnold Moore and going to Bend.

I zip the purse, wince as I turn to the door; everything aches. But it doesn't matter. I know what I need, and the only thing between me and the trail is an hour or so of searching for Marie Heckender and Shari Redmond. Fabia and Ladonna.

Those two could end everything for me.

CHAPTER ELEVEN

The Retreat
May 17, 2000

Parvaneh stood outside the closed bedroom door, the tray of pureed food cooling as she dawdled. She hadn't seen Shirin since the incident in the meeting hall, and she wouldn't be here now if it weren't for Basir. Stressed with the arrival of a delivery truck bringing their monthly supply of flour, sugar, rice, and all the things they couldn't grow or butcher themselves, he'd told Parvaneh to take care of the old woman, and she hadn't had a choice in the matter.

As nice as Darius had been the day Shirin's leg broke, as much as it seemed he'd forgiven her, the last week had made Parvaneh feel as invisible as she'd ever been on the streets of Portland. With the exception of sympathetic, kind looks from Eszter, no one else would even meet her eyes. Except for stern orders, even Basir wouldn't speak to her. Darius had told her this was by his instruction, so she could understand the importance of remaining on a journey even when you weren't being constantly praised for each step. She wasn't a dog, was she? Did she really need to be fed a treat every time she sat on command?

She'd promised herself she'd learn the lesson, and she knew it would be worth it. And as hard as this was, it was still a million times better here than the streets. No one took advantage of her. She never went hungry. She had a place to sleep each night. Even though no one was speaking to or looking at her, she knew they were doing it to help her. And she had a shot at something more if she could just get over herself, her greed and mistrust. Maybe that would start today, with Shirin. She let out a breath and, steadying the tray, opened Shirin's bedroom door.

Shirin lay beneath her blanket, with her splinted, wrapped leg propped on a special wooden platform that had probably been made by Tadeas, who seemed fairly handy. She peered at the ceiling, her lips moving but only hoarse whispers coming forth.

"Hi," Parvaneh said quietly, not wanting to startle the old woman, who hadn't seemed to notice her entrance. She shuffled forward with the tray, around the mattress, to the little table and chair next to the bed, the only other furniture in the room. "I brought you a meal." She smiled. "Made with love."

Shirin didn't respond. The ceiling held her interest.

Parvaneh sat down in the chair, picked up the spoon. Basir had said she'd probably need to feed Shirin. "Do you want an extra pillow under your head?"

"Tell him I won't," Shirin said, her voice weak and rustling. "He can try to get me, but I won't go."

"Shirin?"

"Don't tell Aunt Jewell. She crocheted that sweater for me last Christmas, and he threw it into the fire. That's how I burned them." Shirin splayed her skinny fingers wide.

"Shirin," said Parvaneh. "It's time to eat." She scooped up a small amount of the mush from the bowl. "Have a bite. It sure does smell good." She passed the spoon beneath Shirin's nose to give her a whiff.

"I think it was synthetic," Shirin whispered. "It melted. And then it burned, and he made me watch."

"Here you go." Parvaneh moved the spoon close to Shirin's papery lips.

"I won't," she said. "I won't." Tears glinted at the corners of her eyes.

"You need to eat," Parvaneh said gently. It seemed like Shirin was drifting between now and then, present and past. There was a strange energy in the faint pulse in the hollow of her throat. She poked the corner of Shirin's mouth, and a bit of food smeared on her upper lip.

Shirin flinched. "I already signed it," she said. "You can't do anything now."

"Please," Parvaneh said. "If you don't eat, I might get in trouble." She poked Shirin's mouth again, and just as she went to slip the spoon between her lips, Shirin turned her head, so this time, the food smeared across her cheek. "Come on!"

She scooped up another bite of food, sweat prickling on the back of her neck in the stuffy, dark room.

"Look at that," Shirin said, her eyes unfocused. "Yes, I'd love to dance." She smiled at the ceiling. "I haven't seen you here before." She began to hum a tune, off-key and grating.

Parvaneh shuddered. She leaned over and tried to part the old woman's lips. Shirin grimaced but didn't resist. She opened her mouth to say something, and Parvaneh slipped the spoon inside, depositing a lump of the congealed slop on the woman's tongue. Shirin's eyes went wide, and she gasped.

And then her eyes went wider. Her mouth hung open and her

body lurched. Her hands clawed at her throat. Parvaneh watched, paralyzed as a million thoughts spun inside her mind. How could someone choke on *porridge*?

"Come on, Shirin," she said, her voice oddly singsong. "I'll help you sit up."

Awkwardly, she pulled a pillow from the stack under the bed and tried to lift the rigid woman's head, but Shirin bucked and arched, in silent combat with herself. Her face had gone beet red. Parvaneh shoved her arm beneath the woman's sharp shoulder blades, yanked her up, and slapped her on the back. Saliva stretched from Shirin's mouth, a thin thread all the way to the covers in her lap.

"Help," Parvaneh shouted. "She's choking!" She kept slapping, pulling Shirin forward, hoping that wasn't a bone breaking beneath the frantic collisions of her palm with Shirin's spine. "Help," she screamed. "Someone help!"

Fabia and Ladonna appeared in the doorway. "What are you *doing* to her?" Fabia shrieked. "You're hurting her!"

"She's choking! I don't know what to do!"

Darius pushed between the two women. "Get her to the meeting room," he said tersely. Tadeas and Kazem entered and made for the bed.

Hands closed over Parvaneh's. Pulled her away from Shirin, who continued to writhe, her face purple. Eszter held her tight, providing safety and warmth. Parvaneh relaxed, feeling the hard lump of Eszter's meditation stone against her back.

"Hurry," Darius said. "The time is now."

"I didn't do anything," Parvaneh begged. "I was just trying to feed her!"

"Shh," said Eszter, her arms still tight around Parvaneh's body. "You're okay. It's going to be okay." She steered her through the door and guided her out of the building, across the clearing, toward the meeting hall. "You're going to be okay. Just stay quiet."

She was the opposite of okay. Everyone had been shunning her, and now she was going to be blamed for hurting Shirin again. They were going to kick her out—no money, no name, no shelter, no food. They were going to send her away and let her die.

She began to cry.

"No," whispered Eszter as they reached the door to the hall. "This isn't about you." She took Parvaneh's face in her hands. "Focus on the moment."

Parvaneh gritted her teeth, wanting to scream. Everything had gone wrong so fast.

Eszter let her go and pushed her inside and up the aisle, where everyone stood at the altar, surrounding Shirin. With little shoves and a constant stream of soothing words, Eszter propelled Parvaneh all the way up the steps.

"She should stand next to me," Darius said.

Eszter tugged on Parvaneh's hand, her expression a million messages at once—*stay calm, I'm here, it's okay, I'm terrified.* "Come on," she said aloud. "Do as he says."

Parvaneh hadn't even realized he was talking about her. Dazed, she let Darius clasp her hand and pull her toward him. Right next to Shirin's head, her open eyes, her lips turning purplish blue, her fingers scraping at her tongue.

Darius yanked Parvaneh against him, her belly pressed to the altar. He grabbed her wrists and moved her hands toward Shirin's body.

She pulled back instinctively. This woman was dying, and no one was talking about 911 or ambulances or hospitals. They were just letting her suffer.

"Stop fighting me," Darius murmured. He forced her palms to Shirin's throat. Parvaneh cried out, feeling the loose skin of the woman's neck, the trembling beneath her skin. "Feel it," he said. "Feel the consciousness reaching for her. For *us*."

Parvaneh didn't want to feel it. She didn't want to feel anything. She didn't want to exist. Darkness licked at the edges of her vision. Her whole body tingled. Darius pressed himself against her back while everyone else murmured words beyond her comprehension.

Parvaneh gagged. She couldn't breathe. Darius wedged his knee between her legs, holding her upright. The fog closed in, and her ears began to ring. The only things she could still feel were Shirin's twitching throat and Darius, his body a cage, forcing her fingers closed. The din in her head grew louder, the sound slicing through her brain, cutting her into pieces.

And then everything went silent and black.

She awoke to the sound of water dripping and gasped at the feel of a cool rag on her forehead.

"Be still," Darius said. "You're safe."

She opened her eyes. She was lying on her back in one of the private rooms like Shirin had—actually, this *was* Shirin's room. "Is Shirin—"

"The consciousness welcomed her soul back into its loving embrace, and as she began her journey, we all felt it."

"But you—you made me—"

"We all knew it was time for Shirin to return to the consciousness," he explained. "And you had the honor of witnessing her departure."

"We *caused* her departure," she whispered. "Why didn't we help her?"

"This was what she wanted. She was a true follower of the consciousness. We were lucky to have had her for as long as we did." His voice was somber but not sad.

"She looked scared," Parvaneh said, hoping she didn't sound accusatory. She was terrified that this would be blamed on her. At the thought, tears started in her eyes. "I was trying to feed her. I didn't want to hurt her!"

"No one said you hurt her."

"Fabia did."

He frowned. "It sounds like Fabia was the one who was scared. And not in touch with the movement of the consciousness through all of us." His eyes met hers. "But you felt it. You touched it, and you recognized it, didn't you?"

Parvaneh opened her mouth to argue, but wasn't this what she wanted? "I...think maybe?"

"You recognized the force of it even if you don't have words to describe it. The deep profoundness of all of it—it was too much for you to bear in that moment."

"I fainted," she murmured, realizing he must have carried her here, stupid and helpless.

"You were overwhelmed when it touched you." He stroked the backs of his fingers across her cheek. "You shuddered in my arms. You made me feel it too." His fingertips traced down the column of her throat.

It reminded her of Shirin's throat, twitching and pulsing as her soul fought its way out of her body. She shivered.

"See?" he whispered. "You feel it even now. And once again, you make me feel it too." He closed his eyes and drew in a deep breath.

Parvaneh didn't move. She squeezed her eyes shut, trying not to cry.

His lips descended on hers, his tongue jutting between her lips. His hand closed over her throat, holding her there. She froze with the shock, with the sharp, hot demand of it. He pulled back, breathing hard. "You make me taste it," he said roughly. "I can feel the consciousness calling to me from inside of you. It wants us to connect. Soul to soul. I knew you were special."

She stared up at him, uncertain, hopeful, terrified. Her entire self was a jumble of mismatched signals, memories, words. "I...I think I feel it," she said hesitantly.

He nodded, as if that was what he expected. He stroked her hair away from her face. "I know the last few weeks have been hard on you. I know you've wondered if this was the right place for you. You wondered if anyone cared and especially if I cared. I've seen it all. Even when you think I wasn't looking, wasn't seeing, I saw."

It hit her square in the chest. Tears streaked down her cheeks. She turned on her side, sobbed while he contained all of her in his arms.

She wasn't sure how long they stayed like that, with Darius whispering words of understanding in her ear, telling her that she was helping *him* on *his* journey. In her whole life, nothing had felt this safe and good. After the most frightening minutes of her life, here she was: held and accepted and seen. *Finally.* She nestled into him, greedy for every second and breath he was willing to share.

He pressed a kiss to her temple. "I hate to leave you, but I need to check on the others."

"It's okay," she whispered. "I understand."

His hand rested on her head. "I know an experience that profound leaves its mark on a person, and I am going to help you through it."

She nodded. Turned her head to find his face close to hers. This time, the kiss was slower but no less demanding. As before, confusion twisted with fear and hope inside her. Was this romantic, or was it spiritual? Was she supposed to want him in this kind of sexual way?

What she wanted was to be safe. To make sure this was her place, where no one could uproot her. She welcomed him, arching upward. He groaned and let her go. "I'm having trouble focusing," he said with a chuckle. "Your soul speaks to me so clearly."

"I feel it too."

He stood up. "Tonight, after our group meditation session, you and I will meet privately to continue your guidance." He reached into the pocket of his robe. When his hand emerged, it was curled into a fist.

"Each week, we send a group to town, to do some cleaning jobs and shopping for the things we don't purchase in bulk. Supplies for the children and such. Would you like to be assigned to this team next week?"

She nodded. She hadn't been off the compound for months. It felt like a huge reward.

"Close your eyes," he said.

She did without hesitation. Would he kiss her again? Did she want him to? Did it matter anymore?

The questions fell silent as she felt him take her hand. Turn her palm to the ceiling. A warm, hard-edged object was pressed into her hand. He curled her fingers around it. And then he left, closing the door with a soft click.

Parvaneh opened her eyes. Looked down at her hand, her fingers opening like the petals of a flower. Sitting on her palm was a meditation stone, blue with markings she'd only just begun to recognize.

She cradled it to her chest as she laughed and cried until her body relaxed into sleep.

CHAPTER TWELVE

Bend, Oregon
December 11, present day

The text from Gina, Arnie's alien-obsessed girlfriend, comes right as I pull up in front of Hailey and Martin's house.

> Found that list of people who were never IDed and
> might of made it out. Kyra Zana Parvaneh Ester Roya
> Lala Someone got out you can print that.

I stare at her words, cold prickles zapping across my skin. This is the list of six, the only ones left unidentified after the ashes cooled. I'm one of them. We were the strays. All young women, under twenty when our world caught fire. I remember their faces. I remember how they died. I remember what I did.

Thanks, I text back. Will vet this info and follow up.

Back in my room, aching and jittery, I settle onto the bed with my laptop. My heart is beating way too fast—121 beats per minute—considering that all I did was read a text and walk down the hall. It's because of what I have to do next.

I start with Shari Redmond. Ladonna. Great baker, practical, level-headed, utterly devoted to Darius until the end. I see that she served her time, but after that, there are no mentions of her, no obituaries, no marriage announcements, no residential listings, absolutely nothing. She's a freaking ghost.

I Google the only other survivor from that night: Fabia. I remember the look on her face, too flat to have contained such malevolence. Or maybe devotion. At that point, I didn't care what it was, only what it was doing.

Locking us in.

After *Fabia* yields no real results, I Google her other name. Not the one Darius gave her but the name she had before. I know better than anyone that it might not have stayed her name, but I remember the first time I met her, how strangely proud she was of it. She held out her hand to shake mine. "Marie," she said. "Heckender." There was a light in her eyes, an anticipation. Easy to read even though I've never considered myself particularly good at reading people. Her, though, I could always read. She was the most obvious person I've ever met.

Marie Heckender, she told me. *Heck-en-der*, she repeated when I shook her hand. I remember wondering if she wanted me to give her my last name, and I had no intention of doing that, not the one that had been strapped to me since birth; I hated it so much. Later, she told me she thought I might recognize her name. *My asshole father does his best to make sure people know it*, she said.

Sounds like you're pretty angry with him, I replied.

She looked disappointed. *He's CEO of Willamette Central Bank*, she told me, resentment seeping from every word. *Too busy making money to notice his family. So yeah.* Then her face turned, lifting in a sharp smile, the only sharp thing about her. *I pulled all my money out of the trust fund before I came here. Maybe he'll notice that.*

Before we left for the compound outside of Bend, Darius pulled me aside. Like he could see the doubt all over me. He could see straight through me, maybe even at the end. *Marie's loyalty will carry us through dark times,* he said. *This is what the consciousness communicated to me.*

I believed him then. I shoved down my instant suspicion and dislike of Marie, who became Fabia, who became a murderer because he wanted her to.

I suppose he wanted me to be one too. And he got his way.

I shift my legs, curling them to the side, and peer at my search results. If I want to survive, I have to know every fact, every minute shred of evidence. I have to know all of it better than Miles. *Before* Miles whenever possible.

The woman calling herself Fabia was taken into custody at three in the morning, along with Tadeas and Ladonna and over a dozen children under the age of four, after Deschutes County emergency personnel responded to a trucker's call to report a fire off Route 20 between Tumalo and Sisters, right on the edge of the Deschutes National Forest.

She was identified as Marie Heckender after her father, Jack Heckender of Portland, got her an expensive attorney who managed to get a judge to grant her bail—after she'd been charged by the Deschutes County DA with thirty-five counts of first-degree murder. *That* made headlines. And then she blamed everything on Darius, cooperated with authorities, and testified against Tadeas and Ladonna. She got off with less than a decade in prison.

In the article reporting her release from Coffee Creek Correctional

Facility just south of Portland, it is noted that her parents visited her every week. They asked that their privacy be respected during her parole. She's been free for almost a decade.

A chill runs through me. This world suddenly seems too small. With Arnie spending Thanksgiving with Hailey and Martin, with Miles connecting with Chief Ransom, it feels like anyone could link things up at any moment. I have to keep Miles away from Marie Heckender.

I shoot to my feet. I can't focus, can't think. I need to run *now*. If I don't, I'll start screaming, and I won't be able to stop.

I tear off my clothes and pull on my leggings and a running shirt. My socks and running shoes. I pop another four ibuprofen because I know this is going to hurt. I grab my earbuds and keys, head to my car, and make the quick drive to Riverbend Park. The trail's still cement here, but Hailey promised it was packed dirt farther south, so I turn up the music and take off, desperate for the release that comes with a heart rate running at least 80 percent of max.

I know what I'm going to do. I have to find Marie before Miles does and somehow scare her into not talking to the media while acting like I desperately want her to. I have to talk so she doesn't recognize my voice, but it's been twenty years since she heard it. And then I'll tell Miles I did everything I could to convince her to sit for an interview, and I'll say she threatened to sic her lawyers on us for harassment. Given what I've read about their effectiveness during the trial, for which her father spared no expense, it really could work. I could keep her away from this. From me.

That leaves Shari Redmond, a.k.a. Ladonna. She must have changed her name. I should have been monitoring all of this all along. But instead, I've had my head buried in the sand.

My fists clench even though they're supposed to be loose. My ankle turns as I land wrong on a rock, and I stumble but catch myself, sending spikes of agony lancing up my shins and into my knees. Anger is the heat in my chest, anger at myself for failing this test, anger at the world for making it so damn hard.

I dodge around two guys hiking along the trail, their backpacks and water bottles telling me they're planning to be out for a while, even though twilight is painting the sky pink and orange and steely gray. My back is throbbing and so is my head. But I want to run forever, follow this river to its end, over a cliff, down the falls, far away from the terror that's ridden me ever since Miles announced he was coming to Bend.

Who am I kidding? I've been terrified a lot longer than that. Now it's bloomed in my head like a carnivorous plant looking for sustenance, devouring all the scraps of peace I'd managed to gather to myself over the years. A degree. A name change. A knit-together past woven out of lies.

It happens so quickly that I barely have time to catch myself. My toe snags on a root, and the ground rushes up to meet me. I throw out my hands to keep my face from colliding with a cluster of rocks, and I succeed.

The cost, though: my left wrist. Like inserting my arm into a volcano, into a wood chipper, both at the same time. I let out an airless scream, my vision crimson. My heart beats in my throat, my fingertips. The ground shakes beneath me and I hear shouting, even though one of my earbuds is still in my ears, my music pounding. I look up at the stranger kneeling down, his arms outstretched, concern etched across his face.

He's not a stranger, though. Noah, his dark hair mussed, his friend

Arman on my other side, leans toward me, panting. "Dora! Are you all right?"

"My wrist." I hold it against my chest carefully, like a weapon, the pain so sharp I'm surprised it doesn't stab right into the rest of me. "It's broken."

"We should take her to the emergency room," says Arman, gently removing the earbud from my left ear. He and Noah exchange looks over me. "St. Charles is about fifteen minutes away, but that's from the car."

"Which is a few miles away." Noah curses as he gives me a once-over. "Can you walk? Anything else broken?"

"I don't know," I whisper. It feels like all of me just shattered. Nausea coils in my stomach.

"She doesn't look like she weighs much," says Arman. He has wide-set eyes and a heart-shaped face, a narrow chin for a man, and a ghosting of familiar features. Arman grimaces as he peers at my wrist. "I can carry her."

He slides his arms beneath me and rises with me held against him. Arman's stouter than Noah is, short and wide instead of tall and lean, as he picks his way down the path, back to the car with me like a child in his arms. I hold in a scream behind the wall of my teeth, clenched so tightly that no one could ever pry them open.

"Dora," says Noah. "Any chance you parked your car nearby? Ours is up at Sawyer Park."

"Riverbend," I tell him, gasping as Arman stumbles against a tree. His jacket smells like woodsmoke and weed. His body smells of sweat and beer. I've ruined their hike.

"Awesome," says Noah, full of shaky fake cheer. "We'll be there in a sec. Keys?"

"I have a pocket in my leggings..."

It might take Arman a minute to reach the lot, or maybe ten, or maybe thirty. I lose track, tumbling in the mouth of the beast that's chewing me up from the inside out. I overhear Noah tell a few people I'm going to be all right, that they're taking me to a hospital, like he wants to make sure people don't think they've mugged me on the trail and are taking me away to murder me. It would be easy enough to do if they wanted to. I'm in no shape to put up a fight.

I laugh at my own morbid thoughts as I'm carried across the parking lot, which causes Arman to give me a worried look.

Noah asks, "Are you delirious or just enjoying this experience?"

"Neither," I say with a gasp as Arman shifts my body so Noah can get at the back pocket of my leggings. I cry out as he pushes too hard against the exact spot on my spine that's been killing me for weeks.

Noah takes me from Arman and loads me into the back seat, somehow managing through it all to keep my arm pinned against my chest. Once I'm buckled in, he scoots in close and presses my hand to my shoulder, keeping it from flopping painfully. He, too, smells of beer and weed.

They talk to me constantly as we drive to the hospital, with Noah telling me about how he broke his leg skiing when he was eleven and Arman telling me that he fell out of a tree when he was a kid and broke his arm, but his mom didn't believe him about how badly it hurt and didn't take him to the hospital for almost a week.

Arman pulls into the emergency bay at the hospital. Noah flings open the door and carries me into the ER while Arman drives my car away to park it. There's a chaos of faces, a chaos of noise, the chaos inside me, with Noah telling the nurse I fell on the trail and might have multiple broken bones. I lift my head as he talks to the reception desk lady. Our eyes meet, mine and hers.

The memory of the first time we met explodes like a bomb in my skull. I can almost smell the cinnamon.

Spots ooze into my vision. Words lose their edges and become droning, buzzing nothing. I can't fight my way to the surface of this. I don't even know which way is up to safety. For all I know, I'm swimming deeper into darkness. Into danger. It's her, I know it's her, it can't be her.

Please don't let it be her.

My pleading thoughts fall silent as the darkness swallows me whole.

CHAPTER THIRTEEN

The Retreat
June 24, 2000

Parvaneh sat up, pulling the sheet around her body. Next to her, Darius breathed in slow pulls of air, his body relaxed in sleep. In the candlelight, she imagined him younger, before he'd become aware of the reality that lay beneath the trappings of the exterior world. He'd told her how he'd followed all the rules, obeyed Mommy and Daddy, gone to college, gotten a job, gotten rich...and the whole time, he'd felt like a fish on land, knowing he was in the wrong place and that his soul would die if he didn't figure out where he belonged and how to get there. And once he did, once he saw the world as it truly was, he was consumed with the desire to share it with people who could see it too.

Tonight, he'd told her that he believed she had it within her to see more clearly than any of his other followers. He'd told her that her soul had wings, that he could teach it to fly—it was why he'd named her Parvaneh. Like he'd *known*, right from the start, what they could do together. He'd told her that when she surrendered to him totally, she was blessing him, too, making it easier for his own soul to delve deeper into the mysteries of the consciousness.

He'd told her he needed her, especially now.

"You should get back to the dorm," he said. "It's better for the others, to see you there."

She turned to see him watching her. "What will they do, if they know we're—"

He reached for her hand. "It's important for you to remind them that I'm helping you to reach your potential as an Oracle, which will help all of us in our journey." He squeezed her fingers. "To protect them from weak thoughts and impulses. *How* I help you reach your potential should stay between us for the good of everyone else."

Parvaneh bit her lip. "I was wondering...before we started... doing *this*, you had a lot of evening meditation sessions with other Oracles."

He gave her a somber look. "See? Even you, who have come so far in the last few months—even you are vulnerable to that poison. You're jealous."

"No! I'm not," she said. "It's just, with all the pregnancies, all the babies—"

"Do you doubt my motives and decisions?"

"No."

"Do you doubt me when I tell you that you're special to me? Do you think I'm lying?"

She shook her head.

He kissed her fingertips. "Do you think you are ready for all my honesty? It's hard sometimes, being responsible for so many people." His eyes closed. "Sometimes it's very tiring."

She took his face in her hands. "I don't want to put more burden on you. Tell me whatever you want or need to tell me. I trust you completely."

He sighed. "There have been times that I have given of my body in order to advance the development of some of my Oracles. Some people need to be freed of their inhibitions, their past traumas. Some need to overwrite the pain of past relationships or abuse. Sometimes I make sacrifices for the good of others because I know that's what the consciousness requires of me. And sometimes it touches me, tells me to prepare a home for another soul it wants to give us. I've committed my life to its will—I have no choice."

"Is that what this is?" she whispered.

"*No.* This is different. And perhaps I'm being selfish, grasping this wonderful thing for myself. Has it harmed you?"

She laughed. "It's been the best thing that's ever happened to me."

He leaned against her, touched his forehead to hers. "For me too. But I want to protect our fellow Oracles from the envy that might result from our connection. Does that make sense?"

She nodded, though she couldn't help thinking about how badly she wanted to rub it in Fabia's stupid face. The thing that would stop her from doing that was Octavia. She could tell from the way Octavia and Darius interacted that they had been together, and now she, Parvaneh, had taken Octavia's place. But she liked Octavia. She didn't want her to feel jealous or sad.

"They know you're devoted to each and every person's unique path," she said. "That's obvious, right down to the meditation stones you make for all of us."

He pulled her toward him for a kiss. "Thank you for saying that. It helps keep my energy up. It sustains me. Now go, so you're in your bed before it gets too late."

She pulled her robe over her head. "Should I...?" She gestured at the door to the closet.

He nodded. "It would be distracting to the others to see you come out of my cabin."

She slid the closet door wide and turned on the light, revealing the ladder descending to the tunnel. He'd explained his design of the compound, to protect all its members and his own ability to lead them. The meeting hall, situated in the center, was flanked by the dining hall and the men's dorm on either side, with the women's dorm next to the men's and the children's dorm next to the dining hall. A three-mile-long gravel road connecting the compound to a county highway was located across the clearing and surrounded on either side by dense woods. The pastures and gardens where they raised their food were down the trail to the south of the dining hall. Darius's private quarters were nestled in the woods approximately fifty yards southeast of the meeting hall—and they were connected to his office in the meeting hall by an underground tunnel. It was a rickety thing, wooden bolsters holding back encroaching earth, fallen lumps of dirt and rocks littering the path, more each passing day, it seemed. Parvaneh had taken to jogging along, partially hunched over, to get back to the surface as quickly as she could. Whenever she was down there, it felt like the entire thing was about to collapse on her. But she never complained—Darius hadn't constructed it to be pretty. He'd constructed this system to allow him to focus entirely on his purpose without distraction.

And now, it allowed her to return to the others without emerging directly from Darius's cottage in full view of anyone who happened to be walking between the barns and gardens, a distraction none of them needed. She descended the stairs, using happy thoughts to beat back her fear of being buried alive. Darius wanted and needed her. The knowledge was a heady kind of drug running through her veins, healing all the wounds of the past.

She was grinning by the time she climbed the ladder to the meeting hall and emerged into the closet in the private office Darius had designed as the place where he spent most of his time. The safe, set into the wall across from the closet trapdoor, winked in the light from the office. He'd showed her what was in it—stacks of cash and a few gold bars. He'd told her he was planning to use the resources to build a special new retreat far from Bend, a place only for the most devoted Oracles. He'd promised they'd go there together someday, maybe soon.

She pressed her ear to the door to the meeting hall and heard a few murmured voices. But they grew fainter after a few minutes, and then she heard the door to the meeting hall shut. She emerged into the big room, letting the office door close and lock with a click. He'd told her the code, another sign of his trust in her. She hurried down the aisle and let herself out at the back. Within a few minutes, she was walking into the women's dorm and heading straight for the bathroom.

Ladonna was at the counter, brushing her teeth. Their eyes met in the mirror right before she spat into the sink, Ladonna's big and brown and impossible to read. Parvaneh ducked into a stall.

"Where have you been?" Ladonna asked.

"Meeting with Darius," she replied.

"Mm-hmm."

She came out of the stall to find Ladonna leaning against the counter. She looked tired since having her baby three months ago, and dark circles hung like weights beneath her eyes.

"What?" asked Parvaneh.

Ladonna shook her head. "I noticed you finally got your stone."

"I'm grateful to Darius for being willing to train me."

"He's generous that way," Ladonna said. "With all of us."

Parvaneh nodded eagerly; she had no intention of letting Ladonna know how Darius felt about her. "He loves all of us and wants us to meet our potential."

"He took me off the cleaning crew so you could take my place."

"Oh."

"Don't give me that pitying look. I've been dragging ever since I dropped the baby. You did me a favor." She gave Parvaneh's shoulder a squeeze. "You don't have to look so nervous." She arched an eyebrow. "But you should take a shower before you go to bed."

Parvaneh's cheeks burned as Ladonna trudged from the bathroom. She bowed her head and inhaled salt and sweat, the scent of Darius and what they'd done together. She stepped into a shower stall, rinsed off, and put her robe back on. Then she quickly brushed her teeth and headed back to the room she shared with Fabia, Eszter, and Zana, a girl about Parvaneh's age or maybe a few years older, with very short hair and a quiet, tentative manner. The lights were out as Parvaneh slipped inside and crawled up to the top bunk across from Eszter.

"You're late. Again," Fabia muttered in the dark.

"I was meditating," Parvaneh said.

"It's disgusting, seeing you throw yourself at him," Fabia said.

"Shut up," snapped Eszter, breaking out of her usual patient tone. "Stop picking on her. Stop sowing discord."

Fabia grunted. "I'm not the one constantly begging for special attention."

Anger flashed hot inside Parvaneh. "Why don't you focus on your own enlightenment instead of constantly sniping at everyone else?"

"I'm focused on the well-being of the *group*."

"If you care about the group," Zana said into the dark, "then please be quiet and let us sleep. Who cares where she was? She's here with us now, and if she was meeting with Darius before, then that's his decision, and we're supposed to be trusting him."

"Zana's right," said Eszter. "You trust him or you don't—"

"I do," Fabia said quickly.

"Then trust him to know how to treat each of us," Parvaneh said. "And let's get to sleep. It's a long day tomorrow." Then she lay in the silence that followed, grinning up at the ceiling as she remembered how Darius had treated her, knowing that she was finally exactly where she was supposed to be.

The eight of them exited the RE/MAX real estate office, mops and vacuum and spray bottles packed into their buckets, their gloves still on and their robes smelling of cleaning fluid. Parvaneh bustled over to Octavia to relieve her of a stack of sponges she'd been about to drop all over the strip mall's dirty sidewalk. "Do you really think we need so many people to clean a single office suite?" she asked. "What if we split up into two crews? We have enough people on the compound to do four, if you think about it. This could really be a business."

Octavia gave her a grateful look as she handed over the sponges and a spray bottle. "We'd need another van if we had more than eight."

"I can mention it to Darius."

"Oh, here we go," said Fabia. She rolled her eyes as the other women murmured their disapproval.

"I'm sorry," Parvaneh said to Fabia. "I didn't realize you wanted us to make as little money as possible to support our family."

"I wasn't—"

"Excuse me," said a man who had just parked his red Nissan outside the diner next to the real estate office. He had a bag slung across his chest and was wearing a backward baseball cap. "I saw you guys here last week. Do you mind if I ask if you're a religious group or something?" He gestured at them. "With the robes?"

"We're the Oracles of Innocence," Fabia said quickly, just as Octavia had opened her mouth to speak. "We're just normal people... but everybody's looking for peace and enlightenment, right? We're on that path."

"The Oracles...of Innocence? Is that some kind of cult?"

"We're a group of like-minded people," said Octavia. "But you can call us whatever you'd like if it makes you feel more comfortable to label us."

"Do you go to church?" Fabia said peevishly. "Are *you* a member of a cult?"

Eszter put her hand on Fabia's arm, murmuring for her to be quiet, but Fabia shook her off.

"I meant no offense," said the guy. "What's with the cleaning supplies?"

"We have agreements with several local businesses," Octavia said. "We provide cleaning services at a very low and fair price."

"And we're always looking for more business," Parvaneh told him, offering her prettiest smile.

The guy smiled back. "My name's Joel. I work for the *Bend Bulletin*. It's a pretty cool angle, a group like yours offering affordable cleaning. I could put a little item in the paper if you guys would like."

"That would be great!" Fabia announced.

"Fabia, I don't think—" Eszter began.

"It's perfect advertising, both for the Oracles and the business," said Fabia. "We can have him put the number in the article." They had one phone at the compound—it was in Darius's office.

"I can definitely do that," Joel said, opening his bag to reveal a camera inside. "Could I get a picture?"

"I don't know. I think we should ask Darius first," Parvaneh said, taking in the concerned expressions of Octavia and Eszter. "He should decide." The others—Zana, Roshanak, Laleh, and Minu—looked intrigued but unsure.

But Fabia was righteous in her certainty. "Don't you guys know anything about marketing? Step one, people have to know you exist." She turned to Parvaneh. "Weren't you *just* suggesting we could do more business if we split up?"

Parvaneh gritted her teeth. Eszter frowned. Octavia said, "I guess it couldn't hurt."

"Perfect," the guy said, pulling his camera from his bag. "Just get closer together. And smile!"

Fabia's smugness hadn't receded by the time they returned to the compound. She chattered about her father—who she hated, if her endless complaints could be believed—who had taught her all about marketing and business. As soon as they'd put their supplies away and cleaned up for dinner, Fabia paraded into the dining hall and sat down at one of the long tables, right next to Darius. "We had a very good day," she told him as the rest of them sat down.

Behind them, the children cavorted while they waited for their meal. Parvaneh heard Xerxes calling her name, and she turned and waved. Xerxes grinned, his blond hair falling over his eyes. Octavia walked over to give him a snuggle, and he greeted her with open arms. Parvaneh felt a stab of jealousy.

"What made the day so good?" Darius asked even as his eyes found Parvaneh's, sending a tingle down her back. "Maybe the best is yet to come," he added.

"We're going to have a lot more cleaning customers," Fabia said loudly, clearly trying to draw his attention back to her. Parvaneh fought the urge not to smirk.

"And why is that?" Darius asked.

Eszter and Parvaneh exchanged looks as Fabia chattered about their encounter with the reporter. Octavia returned to the table and sat next to Ladonna, who was breastfeeding her baby as others set plates of beef stew in front of them.

"...and with that kind of publicity, we'll probably need more people to be on the crew," Fabia finished.

"What *exactly* did you tell this reporter about us?"

"I—" Fabia paused. The flat, cold tone of Darius's voice had clearly given her a chill.

"He asked if we were a cult," Parvaneh said.

"*What?*"

Fabia flinched. Octavia explained what she'd told the reporter about who they were, but it only made his expression harden.

"You know the world doesn't understand us, don't you?" He looked around. "You realize that the more they know about us, the more envious they'll be, and the more they'll try to destroy us." His eyes narrowed as he turned back to Octavia. "You *agreed* to this?"

"Fabia thought it was important for us to do," Zana said.

"Oh, is Fabia your guide now?" Darius asked.

Parvaneh's heart was beating hard, but she wasn't sure if it was dread or excitement. Danger dripped from every one of Darius's words as he stood up and said, "Everyone, we'll be meeting as one group tonight after dinner. Fabia requires our support to remember why she's here."

Fabia had turned ashen. "But I—"

"Shh," said Octavia.

No one said much of anything as they ate. Parvaneh poked at her bowl while Eszter shoveled it in, apologizing even though she didn't have to. She was eating for two after all. When they'd finished, Darius marched them to the meeting hall. A strange sort of excitement pervaded, evident in the darting looks and curious expressions. Even the children had been invited to the meeting; the ones old enough to run around made good use of the aisles and rows of chairs as their playground of the moment. Xerxes barreled into Parvaneh and wrapped his arms around her legs. As she tried to peel him off of her, he only held on tighter.

Eszter came over to help. "Come on, Xerxes. It's time to go to the back," she said as she pulled his arms. "The adults are meeting now."

"I want to be an adult," said Xerxes. "I'm already four. How many years is it?"

Eszter smiled. "It might be higher than you can count."

Xerxes scowled as Parvaneh finally pried him loose. "I can count to a hundred!"

"Fabia, take off your robe and get up on the altar," Darius instructed from the front.

Pale and miserable-looking, Fabia complied, shedding her robe and trying to cover her breasts as she mounted the dais.

"Kazem," Darius said. "Pass out the switches."

Parvaneh turned to see Kazem marching up the aisle carrying a bucket full of sturdy sticks he appeared to have gathered from the woods. He held it out as he reached the knot of them standing near the front, and everyone took one, including Xerxes. Eszter began to take it from him, but Darius put a hand on her arm. "No," he said. "Let him have it. He's a part of this community too."

Parvaneh was nearly breathless as she took in the scene in front of her, each person with a stick. She moved closer to Darius, who was standing at the altar, looking down at Fabia's dimpled, trembling form. "Do you submit to the wisdom of this group and to my guidance?"

Fabia sobbed. "I was trying to do something good!"

"You substituted your will for mine, and you overruled the others—you failed to listen to their wisdom. You failed to protect this body. You failed the deep consciousness." He gestured around him, to everyone with sticks. "Do you accept that you failed, Fabia?"

"I'm sorry," she cried.

"Do you accept this lesson we're giving you?"

"I'll accept anything you want," she whimpered. "I won't do it again."

"Sometimes," said Darius, "the lesson has to be felt in the bones." He nodded at Kazem, who raised his stick and brought it down hard on Fabia's butt.

She screamed.

"Everyone," said Darius quietly. "Please show love to Fabia by offering her this lesson." He stepped back, and Parvaneh realized he didn't have a stick in his hand. He was depending on them to deliver the guidance.

Parvaneh was happy to.

She smacked Fabia across the back and noted the red mark it left.

Then she did it again. The others were smacking their sticks down with varying degrees of intensity. Eszter seemed hesitant to cause pain, but she obeyed just like the rest of them. Xerxes appeared at her side, in Darius's arms. "Go ahead," Darius instructed. "Help Fabia learn the lesson."

"I don't like how you play with me," Xerxes shouted, and he whapped her in the head with the stick. "And I don't like when you pull my hair and tell everyone you didn't!" He hit her again. "And I don't like the way your breath smells, and I don't like the way you sing!"

Darius caught the boy's hand before he struck again. "This isn't to punish Fabia for doing things you don't like," he said calmly. "We're helping her to learn humility and how to listen to others."

"But I want her to listen to me," Xerxes said loudly. "Because she always tells me to be quiet." He yanked his stick back and whacked her again.

Parvaneh hit Fabia again too, but no longer because she wanted to hurt her. What she wanted more than anything was for Fabia to quit screaming, to quit being so pathetic, to quit acting exactly like Mama had every time one of her boyfriends got mad and took a crack at her. Hunched in a corner, worthless and weeping, caring only about herself, expecting her tears to make other people care, but of course they didn't. Of course they didn't.

"Parvaneh, that's enough," Darius said, grabbing her wrist before she could take another shot.

The others had all stopped as well. They were all staring at her. Darius gently pulled the stick from her hand, a few flecks of blood clinging to its rough surface. Fabia had fainted, or maybe she was faking it, but either way, she was limp, eyes closed, bruised and bleeding and pink all over. Parvaneh turned away, feeling a twinge of nausea.

"Octavia, Eszter, take care of Fabia. Our meeting is over for tonight. Ladonna, Zana, Roshanak, take the children to bed." He gave everyone their orders, calmly instructing them as if it were any other night, but there was a strange, fevered light in his eyes. And then he turned to Parvaneh and said, "Come with me. You and I will meditate."

Parvaneh knew exactly what it meant, exactly what he wanted and needed. She fought a smile as she followed Darius to the door of his private room.

CHAPTER FOURTEEN

Bend, Oregon
December 11, present day

I lie in the hospital bed, the flowered curtain the only thing between me and the world. I'm hazy with pain, but the meds they gave me have dulled it a bit. I flinch when the doctor, the one who told me we'd decide what to do after the X-ray had come back, pulls back my fabric shield and rolls a laptop on a cart to the side of the bed. His badge identifies him as Malcolm Chikere, MD, attending physician. His voice is resonant and soothing, but what he has to say is not.

He turns the laptop to reveal my X-ray displayed on the screen. "A pretty clean break, radius and ulna, both of your arm bones, right at the base of your hand. See?"

"Yep," I say, exhaling a slow, nauseated breath. My head is swimming with horror. Did I really see her, or was that my delirious brain putting a face on all my terrified thoughts? "Are you going to cast it up so I can get out of here?"

"We need to talk about that, actually. How long have you been a runner?"

"About twenty years."

"Are you aware that you're underweight?"

I want to roll my eyes, but even the thought makes me dizzy. "I'm not anorexic, okay? I eat. I'm just a vegan. And I run. So I'm thin."

"You reported that your weight was 110 pounds, and your height is five five. That means your BMI is 18.3, which makes you underweight, technically speaking."

"*Technically* speaking. Okay..."

"Your film is suggestive of some bone loss, Ms. Rodriguez."

"What does that mean?"

"When I see a wrist film like this, it usually belongs to an eighty-year-old lady who's been smoking for fifty years."

"So...not good?"

He frowns at the image of my bones. "You'll need another test to confirm, but I can tell you right now that your bone density is abnormal, suggestive of osteoporosis. Has your doctor ever spoken to you about the possibility?"

I haven't been to the doctor in years. "What does this have to do with my weight?"

His smooth brow furrows. "Individuals with eating disorders are at higher risk for developing early onset osteoporosis. And this"—he points to my X-ray again—"is the kind of thing that happens to people who have early onset osteoporosis. You reported that you fell while running. That kind of incident shouldn't have snapped your wrist like this, not in a woman your age."

I stare at the film, a black-and-white tally of my own fragility, how easily I can break.

He closes his laptop. "Do you have back pain?"

I gesture at the middle of my back. "It just started a few months ago. It's worse when I run, but I don't want to stop doing it. It's good for me."

"It's another symptom. You'll need more imaging to confirm, but you may have some small fractures in your vertebrae, as your bones aren't quite strong enough to manage the stress you're putting on them."

"I'm only thirty-eight," I say quietly. "I know I have white hair, but I'm not old."

"Unfortunately, your body's acting like it is," he tells me. "Do you have regular periods?"

"Never really have."

"Ms. Rodriguez, I can cast your arm, but I think we're dealing with a larger problem here."

"Can it be reversed? The premature aging and bone loss?"

His gaze drops from my face to the floor. "You can arrest it, maybe. But you really need to talk to your GP. And you may have other health issues. Osteoporosis is silent until it's not. But I think your body is trying to tell you something. And I think you should listen to it." He clears his throat. "The nurses are prepping the room for the casting, so we'll get you in there soon so you can go home sometime tonight. Sound good?"

I nod, just to get him to leave. And after he does, I sit behind my curtain, staring at my splinted arm. Until recently, I was proud of myself. Of my own determination. Of my cleverness. Oh, I thought I was *so* clever. I thought no one could ever find me, figure it all out. I thought that if I covered enough miles, I could stay ahead of everything I left behind, the fires and bodies and blood and my own crimes, the way I killed people I once loved. But here I am, only a few miles from the place where I first started running, from the graves and ashes of my victims. And unless I really was hallucinating, only a few rooms away from the person, one of so very few, who could set my world on fire again.

I have to see her again. Maybe I'm wrong. I don't know what I'll do if I'm right.

But it turns out that I don't have to go find her. I don't have to move at all. She opens the curtain, dressed in her scrubs, her Crocs, her black hair short now, in waves against her skull, her brown skin lined with a few marks of age but still surprisingly smooth. She comes in with a clipboard, and I hold my breath as we lock gazes. "Ms. Rodriguez?" she asks. "I need to get some insurance verification, as we didn't get to do that when you first arrived. It won't take long."

I blink at her. The voice is the same. The face is the same. Does she recognize me? Maybe she doesn't. I look different. It's been twenty years.

And if the doctor is right, I've apparently aged a lot more than she has.

Her hand shakes as she puts pen to paper. It sends my heart rate into a zone that sets off the monitor, beeping madly. She turns to it with eyes that narrow as they read the numbers. "No need to be nervous," she says and punches a button that silences the sound.

With a dry mouth, I tell her my full name, my birth date, my employer, my insurance plan, but that my card is in my purse, which is at my parents' house, and she'll have to let me call it in later. She tells me that she should be able to find everything she needs with the information I've given her. She thanks me. Stands up. Puts her shaking hand in her pocket. Pauses before pulling the curtain back. "I can tell you recognize me," she says quietly. "But you... I thought you were dead. We all did."

"I'm sorry, I've never seen you before." I squint at her name tag. It says her name is Essie Green, but I know now that's not what it used to be. Just like she knows that my name isn't Dora Rodriguez.

"I don't want trouble," she says.

"I'm not here to make any," I tell her. My pain is amping up again, sharper with every word out of her mouth.

"Keep it that way. Or I'll tell them who *you* are."

I force out a laugh. "I'm sorry, but do you do this to all the patients who come in here with splintered bones?"

Her face smooths, but her big eyes are somber and seeing as ever. "You must have thought you were smart. You obviously still do."

"Honestly, right now, all I am is confused." I have no idea what the right move is—do I admit what we both know and ask for her help, or do I double down on my attempt to gaslight my way through this? I don't know enough about what she's like now to tell me the right answer. But I do remember what she said on that final night: *We all have a part to play, and I don't have a choice. Neither do you.*

I don't feel like I have much of a choice now, either. But it's not the time to match wits, because I have none. "I really need more pain meds. Assuming you have everything you need, Ms. Green, could you please ask the nurse when I could have another dose?" I stare at her face. I do not look away. I tell myself I have nothing to fear even though I am a liar of the worst sort.

But it works. She looks away. Nods. Leaves.

It's only after she's gone, after the swell of relief has subsided, and after the nurse administers another dose of morphine that it hits me, along with the opioid: Ladonna knows who I am—and I've just given her everything she needs to find out a whole lot more.

I've lost track of time in this windowless room in the ER, but the clock tells me it's after nine. It occurs to me that I should have called

Hailey to let her know, though I'm not sure how this works anymore. Twenty years ago, when they took me in, I fell into their rhythms easily, compliantly. I hid the burns on my legs, silently screamed as I cleaned and dressed them in the bathroom late at night, hid every trace of ooze and ick, did my laundry at three in the morning, scrubbed the insides of my pant legs until they wore thin, bit my tongue bloody, and smiled with gratitude that was real. They didn't ask much of me, just that I eat meals with them, help keep the house clean, and get my life back on track.

They thought I was a homeless runaway, drifted down from Portland in search of a better place. I was a monster in their midst, desperate to hide my true self. The first few months, as the smoke and ash settled and the cult catastrophe right up the road was the only thing people talked about, I was terrified that at any moment, Ben Ransom would come to the door and point the finger at me. I was convinced someone would realize who I was and that I'd escaped and that I'd done something terrible.

But here I sit, cast up to my elbow, aching and damned. My options tumble in my head: give up and confess, run and hide, stay and fight. The first is impossible and enraging. I've worked too hard for too long. The deaths I caused... I had convinced myself they would have happened anyway, or maybe they were deserved. It never quite fit, but it was enough to help me turn away, keep going. No confessing, then. No giving up.

I could run. I've changed my name before; I could do it again. I've been anonymous before, no friends, no relatives, on the move. I know how to survive. But it's exhausting to consider, especially because my body seems to be falling apart. I have a job now. Health insurance, which it suddenly seems like I desperately need. A few fragile friendships, like with Miles and Valentina. I've reconnected with Hailey and Martin, and that feels good too. No running, then. I'd be lucky if I didn't break my ankle on the way out the door.

That means I have to figure out how to make sure Miles never discovers that Shari Redmond, a.k.a. Ladonna, a.k.a. Essie Green, is right down the hall. She's here in Bend. *She* might have killed Tadeas. Marie could have as well. The thing that bothers me, though? It's how he was killed. Those knife wounds, planned out. X marked the spot. Stabbing by number.

I swing my legs over the side of the bed. They unhooked my IV a few minutes ago and told me I could go when I felt able to. Noah and Arman left a while ago—Arman told me where he parked the car and gave me back my key. Noah insisted he'd check in with me tomorrow, even when I said it wasn't necessary, and then he sheepishly informed me that his story is in my inbox already. I reach for my phone with my good arm. The battery died a few hours ago, so I slide it into the pocket of my leggings. I'm glad they didn't make me undress and wear a hospital gown—I hate questions about the scars.

"What the hell? I can't leave you alone for a minute," Miles says from outside the curtain.

I jump at the sound of his voice and crumple onto the bed. "You scared me," I say. "Come in."

He peeks his head around the curtain, then pulls it back. "Noah called me hours ago, but I was on the road. I got here as soon as I could."

"Where were you?"

He runs his hand through his hair. "I was headed up to Portland. I decided to try to find Marie Heckender. And I did."

My mouth goes dry. "Yeah?"

He nods. Bounces on his heels. "Six feet under. I think we're dealing with something big here, and I don't think the authorities even realize it."

"She's *dead*?" Cold prickles bloom across my chest.

"In a fire," Miles says.

One-handed, I brace myself on the side of the bed. Whether I hated her or not, it's still a shock to know she's gone. And that she died in a fire...

Miles eyes my left arm, which is in a sling. "Meanwhile, you were doing your best to damage yourself."

"I fell on my wrist the wrong way," I mumble. "Unfamiliar trail." And, apparently, a crumbling eggshell of a body. "Why wasn't Marie Heckender's death all over the news?"

"She'd gotten married. Changed her name. Was living quietly out on a ranch in the western part of the state. I found her new name listed among survivors in her dad's obituary from earlier this year. And I guess her husband was visiting his ailing mother down in Arizona three weeks ago, and their house here in Oregon burned down, which means she died before Arnie did. But although the fire is suspicious, the local authorities are still just saying it's under investigation."

"Why were you driving up to Portland?"

"You can't get autopsy reports in Oregon unless you're family, so I was going to try to convince her mom to give me access."

"Do you know if she was stabbed too?"

"Not without that autopsy. I'm sure they did one. Suspicious fire? Probably the husband's a suspect. I read the local report—no mention of the cult connection." He grins. "I'm gonna break this one wide-open. I think we've got a serial killer in our midst."

"Killing cult survivors," I whisper. And Ladonna—I guess her name is Essie now—she knows who I am. I'm not as hidden as I thought. Not as safe as I assumed.

"Mr. Connover?" comes a familiar voice from the hallway.

"Yeah?"

Essie Green pokes her head in and smiles, though it doesn't reach her eyes. "Oh, good. You found her."

Miles takes a step closer to me. "I certainly did—thanks for helping me negotiate this maze of a place. Can I take her home?"

She nods as I start to protest. "You shouldn't be driving with one hand, morphine still on board," she says. "You're a stubborn one," she adds, leaning forward. "I've met your kind *before*."

I don't know if it's her expression or the fact that Miles just told me about Marie, but it feels like a threat. "Let's go," I say to Miles.

"Excellent," he says, looking pleased. "Now I get to meet your folks."

"That's right, you *said* your parents were locals," Essie says. "It's a small town. Maybe I know them?"

"Probably not. Let's go, Miles," I choke out. This is the hospital where Hailey used to work, for god's sake. Not in the emergency department, but still. Panic claws at me.

Miles stays close to me as I wobble toward the doorway, past Essie's keen eyes. I'm going to have to deal with her, but it can't be now. It's all I can do to put one foot in front of the other, to string more than two words together. She could destroy me; I've handed her the sledgehammer, the bullets, the matches and blades. If I don't find a way to fix this, she's going to ruin everything.

"Thanks so much for taking care of her, Ms. Green," Miles says to Essie, turning his considerable charm in her direction yet again.

"My pleasure, Mr. Connover," she says. Then she pats my good arm. "You take care of yourself, Ms. Dora. But I know you're a *survivor*, so I'm sure you'll be fine."

Miles puts his arm around my back as I rock with a wave of nausea and dizziness. Murmuring supportive words, he guides me out of the emergency department, where he's parked his car illegally nearby, just far enough back not to block incoming ambulances. Still, a nurse who is standing outside smoking gives us a dirty look as we pass. I turn my face away; it suddenly feels like everyone can see me for exactly who and what I am.

Miles opens the passenger door of his Prius for me. "Let's get you home and I'll tell you about what else I've discovered."

I sink into the seat. "I guess there's only one survivor left, then. Now that Marie's dead."

"Well," he says, drawing out the last part of the word. "Yes and no."

"Oh. Right. Your wild-goose chase about the people you *think* escaped the fire—"

"That's a real possibility!"

"—and the kids. But there's no way to find out who they are if they don't want to be known."

"*Mostly* true, but get this: I did some research on Shari Redmond. Haven't tracked her down yet—looks like she changed her name and went underground, not that I blame her—but it turns out that Marie wasn't the only one with family. And Shari's family? Apparently, one of the kids rescued from that compound was Shari's, and her parents successfully petitioned the court for custody. I called them this afternoon on my drive up to Portland."

I'll be lucky if I make it home without throwing up. "What did they say?"

"Turns out they'd been trying to get Shari out of the cult for over a year when the fire happened. And they weren't the only ones—Shari's parents have made a few connections and formed a little community up there in Portland. Like the adult children of Lucy Bathhouse, who gave Darius control over her entire estate—she was a bit of an heiress, apparently—had also been trying to extricate her. Funnily enough, though, her name wasn't among the list of victims provided by Marie Heckender. She just claimed Lucy had left the compound a month or so earlier. They have no idea what happened to her."

"You think she's still alive?" I know for a fact she's not.

He shakes his head. "She was terminally ill when she joined up. That was one of Darius's MOs. He'd cozy up to wealthy women who'd been handed a death sentence by way of a support group he ran. Claimed to be a kind of spiritual adviser. He recruited right from the hospital, if you can believe it—had some social workers he'd conned into thinking he was legit, and they referred people to his group. He snagged at least three over the years, and each of them signed over power of attorney so he could spend their money however he saw fit. The families had to sue to recover assets from his estate. They each got only a fraction back—that compound was a money pit. He was nearly drained when the fire broke out, on the verge of foreclosure."

"So you talked to this Lucy person's family too?"

He nods. "Her daughter is in contact with someone who left the Oracles before they came to Bend. That person might be able to tell me who went unaccounted for, who didn't die."

My head is pounding. "Why are you so obsessed with this?"

"Because *someone* killed Arnie and Marie. With fire. And maybe stabbing. Like they're enraged about what happened that night."

"That doesn't mean it's a former cult member," I say quickly. "It could be a family member. It could be a sick psychopath with a cult obsession."

He gives me a rakish, sidelong smile. "I didn't get this far without trusting my intuition." He pulls up in front of Hailey and Martin's house. "Let's get you inside."

"I'm fine," I say, wincing as I pull the door handle.

"Bullshit." He gets out and pulls my door open, then carefully helps me onto the front walk.

Hailey appears on the porch before I can assure him I'm able to make it to the house alone. "Oh lord," she says as she rushes toward us. "What the hell happened?"

"I fell on my run," I say, trying to assure her.

"Dora's tougher than she looks," Miles adds.

It feels like all my blood has rushed to my feet, leaving the rest of me empty as I watch Hailey jerk back at the sound of my name.

I had forgotten. I never told them about the name.

The one I stole from her dead daughter.

CHAPTER FIFTEEN

The Retreat
August 26, 2000

They sat cross-legged and back to back. Parvaneh kept her eyes closed, focusing on Darius's voice as he chanted in the language of the deep consciousness. She forgot time during these moments, forgot who she'd been before Darius had given her a new version of herself.

Honk-honk. They both jerked as the sound blared from outside.

"Darius?" came a voice on the other side of the office door. "We've got a situation." It was Kazem; he sounded concerned.

Darius strode to the door, and Parvaneh followed close behind. The honking continued, and now she could hear someone shouting. They trailed Kazem down the aisle of the sweltering meeting hall and into the sunlit clearing, where a beige minivan had parked. Its front doors were open, and two people stood next to the van, in agitated conversation with Eszter, who had her hands up as if to show she was unarmed. One of the newcomers, a balding man with cheeks like deflated balloons, jabbed his finger at her. "Where is she?" he shouted.

Eszter said something Parvaneh couldn't hear, and the other

visitor, a woman with an auburn bob and a bright-red face, shoved Eszter, who stumbled back.

"Hey," shouted Parvaneh. She stalked past Darius. "What the hell is wrong with you? She's pregnant!"

The man frowned, looking Eszter over. "Hard to tell with those robes you people wear." He gave Darius and Kazem, the only men in sight, a look of thinly veiled disgust. "Dress-wearing freaks," he muttered before announcing, "We're here for our mother, Lucy Bathhouse."

Darius had a bland look on his face as he took in the red-faced couple. "Why would you think she's here?" he asked.

"Because she came down here with you," the man shouted. "She's due for another round of chemotherapy starting Monday—in Portland! You're endangering her life by keeping her here."

Eszter looked at Darius. "Is he talking about Ziba?"

Darius put his hands on Parvaneh's shoulders. "Eszter. Parvaneh. Extend some hospitality to our guests. Offer them a drink."

"Parvaneh and Eszter," said the woman, sneering. "What are your *real* names? My mother's name is *Lucy*."

"Those of us who choose to be here have accepted our true names," said Parvaneh.

"You're a child," said the woman. She glanced at Eszter. "Both of you. And I suppose that baby is yours?" She jabbed her finger at Darius.

Eszter blushed, and Parvaneh watched her with a dimly pulsing shock. She'd said it was Gil's. Had she *lied*?

The man's focus was still on Darius. "The guy at your house in Portland said you'd brought Mom here. She needs to come back with us."

Parvaneh felt a flash of annoyance. Why would Gil tell these people anything, let alone exactly where his fellow Oracles were?

"Everything Ziba needs is here," Darius said, his tone mild.

"We'll go to court," said the man. "You conned her into signing some power of attorney, but it's not going to stand. Not when we're done with you."

"Eszter," said Darius. "Please fetch Ziba. Let her know there are people here to see her."

Eszter, her eyes downcast, walked toward the women's dorm. Parvaneh stared after her, rage and jealousy leaving bruises on her heart. She'd been so blind. So naive. Eszter had slept with Darius and lied about it. Like she knew it was wrong.

Darius stood calmly while they waited for Eszter to return. Ziba's adult children gazed about with open contempt.

"Before the Oracles found me, I was homeless," Parvaneh blurted out, hoping for a smile from Darius. "And now I have everything I need, physically and spiritually. We all do."

"My guess is you don't have stage IV cancer, though," said the woman. "Our mother does."

Parvaneh turned as Eszter wheeled Ziba out of the women's dorm in a wheelchair, which didn't exactly look easy when it hit the gravel of the clearing.

Parvaneh jogged over to them. "I'll take it," she said to Eszter, who was breathing hard.

"I'm not going with them," Ziba said, wincing at every jolt of the wheelchair. "Why are you making me see them?"

"Mom," the woman cried, running toward them with tears in her eyes. "What have they done to you?"

"Don't call me that," Ziba said. "You should go." She looked away, tears visible in her eyes.

"You don't even want us to call you 'Mom'?" The man glared at Darius. "You've totally brainwashed her, you bastard."

"Ziba is a valued member of our community," Darius replied. "We take care of her."

"Mom, you're going to die if you don't come with us," pleaded the woman.

Ziba had covered her face with her hands. Parvaneh stomped over to the strangers. "She doesn't want to go with you! She might be ill, but she's not crazy, and she can do what she wants! Get the hell off our property!"

The two interlopers looked warily around at the growing number of Oracles surrounding them.

"Michelle," said the man. "Let's go."

"We're just going to leave her here?" Michelle asked. "But you said—"

"Let's *go*," he said firmly, his eyes flitting back and forth. Parvaneh glanced around—Tadeas had come up the trail from the barns and had a bloody knife in his hand. "You people are *insane*," the man hissed. "A crazy cult is what you are. You won't get away with this."

"Go," Ziba said faintly. Her hands fell away from her gaunt face, and Parvaneh saw that she was crying too. "Just go."

Michelle let out a sob as she climbed into the van. Her brother looked gutted as he got in the driver's side. "This isn't over," he said before slamming the door. The minivan's tires kicked up gravel as he zoomed back down the rutted drive that led to the road.

"Everyone, go back to your chores," Darius said.

Nearly everybody bustled away, but Darius motioned Tadeas and Kazem over to him. He spoke to them quietly while Parvaneh returned to Eszter's side. Together, they wheeled the older woman back to the dorm. Ziba kept her eyes closed as they tucked her back into her bed. When they exited to the hallway, Parvaneh caught Eszter's eye. "It's his, isn't it?"

Eszter looked away. "I didn't want you to be upset. And I knew you would be."

The truth was a gut punch, sharp and searing. She'd half expected Eszter to laugh, to reassure her, of *course* she hadn't slept with Darius. "You think so little of me, and so you lied. Nice."

"It was between me and him, Parvaneh." She put a hand on her belly. "He was helping me deepen my trust and commitment."

"Was. So you're not sleeping with him anymore?"

Their eyes met. "You don't need to be jealous," Eszter said.

"Do you have feelings for him?"

She grimaced. "Am *I* supposed to be jealous now that he's spending more time with you? Are you going to be jealous once he focuses on someone else?"

This time is different. He said it was. "I trust Darius. Definitely more than I trust you."

"Don't be distracted by petty stuff." Eszter moved her hand from her belly to Parvaneh's cheek. "And don't let it hurt our friendship. I know I won't."

He's mine, Parvaneh wanted to scream, even as she wondered—were *all* the children Darius's? Not a one belonged to Kazem or Tadeas or Basir? Darius had told her he'd had to obey the will of the consciousness when it needed another vessel for a soul, and she wanted to believe that. But what if he'd just been horny? And what if Eszter had been the one to pursue *him*?

She clenched her teeth. "The only thing that hurts our friendship are your *lies*," she hissed at Eszter.

"Am I interrupting something?"

They turned to see Darius standing in the building's entryway, his smile taut.

"We put Ziba to bed," Eszter said, then walked quickly down the hall toward her room.

Darius approached. "You look upset, Parvaneh."

She shook her head. "I just hated to see how much those two stressed Ziba out, you know?"

He nodded. "Feel sorry for them. They've never come close to what we have here. Instead, they'll do *everything* they can to destroy us. I'm going to speak with Ziba."

"Are we meditating again tonight?" she asked, moving closer, placing her hands on his waist.

He glanced up the hall and moved away from her. "Don't be greedy, little one." He pushed open Ziba's door, went inside, and shut it behind him, leaving Parvaneh alone and empty-handed in the hall.

Parvaneh trudged across the clearing to the meeting hall, her thoughts full of thunderclouds. Everyone was milling around, preparing for evening meditation while the kids darted about. Tadeas was standing with Kazem near the door, looking grim. "...told him we could do it, but we need to think about how to butcher it after. I wouldn't want any of them to go to waste. We need the meat for winter."

"Won't happen for a little while," said Kazem, lowering his voice as she walked by. "We'll figure it out."

She entered the hall, dim and candlelit, hazy and perfumed, close and stifling. A few people were sitting in the chairs lined up in rows in front of the altar, but most had gathered at the front and were already sitting cross-legged, their hands cupped around their meditation stones. Eszter had her eyes squeezed shut, her teeth clamped over her bottom lip, her fingers closed tightly over the rough edges of her stone. A surge of anger swelled inside Parvaneh.

She plopped down, pulled her meditation stone out of the pocket of her robe, and peered down at its markings. He'd told her the V-shaped thing was the beak of the ancient bird, Simurg. And the other, upside-down V was a mountain. Damavand. Powerful symbols. She needed that power now.

A crash at the back of the hall caused a collective gasp, and everyone turned to see that Darius himself had kicked the door open. It was obvious why—Ziba was in his arms, shaking against his chest, her fingers twitching.

"She is going to join the consciousness," he said brusquely as he came up the aisle. "Everyone, come. With her sacrifice, let Ziba allow us to touch the consciousness as she goes."

Everyone jumped to their feet and moved to the side so Darius could mount the steps to the altar and lay Ziba down. The old woman's jaw was clenched. Foam frothed between her lips.

"She can't be saved?" Octavia asked, looking horrified.

"It's too late," Darius replied.

"We could take her to the hospital," Parvaneh volunteered.

"Did she take something?" Eszter asked, using the sleeve of her robe to wipe some of the froth from Ziba's mouth. "She seemed fine earlier."

"Why are you all questioning me?" Darius shouted. "Don't waste this profound moment or you'll be wasting the gift she's offering us!" He put his hand on Ziba's head, stripping the scarf off her bald scalp. "Now, with all our enemies circling, this is our chance to listen to the divine wisdom of the universe, closer now and in this moment than you've ever felt."

He waved the scarf in the air like a battle flag while he stared daggers at Octavia and Eszter and Parvaneh. "You're willing to miss it all, just so you can take a dying woman on a pointless trip to the hospital?"

Her stomach quivering with nausea, Parvaneh moved in next to Darius, determined to get back in his good graces. "You heard him," Parvaneh said loudly as the others moved hesitantly to the altar. One by one, they laid hands on Ziba, who looked like she was in agony. Darius put his on her throat.

As they began to chant, Parvaneh watched him, wondering if she was imagining the increasing tension at his knuckles, the constriction, the pressure. She closed her eyes and focused on the consciousness as the voices around her merged into one.

CHAPTER SIXTEEN

Bend, Oregon
December 12, present day

I cannot deal with this tonight, but here we are. All the most dangerous people in my world have converged in the last few hours, bumping up against one another in potentially devastating ways, and I'm so riddled with pain that I can't keep them apart. Now, even though it's after midnight, Miles has invited himself into the house, and Hailey is casting gutted looks between the two of us, wincing each time he says my name.

If I don't get him out of here, he's going to start asking questions that begin my unraveling. He looks around the living room. "Not even a prom pic on the mantel?" He smiles when he notices the large, framed picture hanging between two bookcases. A dark-haired, round-cheeked toddler, her head thrown back in a laugh and her arms up, fingers spread as snow falls around her, an angel surrounded by white fluff. "Aw, you were cute!" He pushes his glasses up his nose and squints as he looks closer. "Um..."

"Thanks for driving me home," I say. "I'm exhausted and almost due for another Vicodin."

"It *is* late," Hailey says, her voice faint.

"I'll be heading out, then," Miles says. "Dora's mom, so nice to meet you. Dora, I'll see you tomorrow." His brow furrows as he looks back and forth between me and the picture on the wall.

Maybe he's noticed the child has striking brown eyes, while mine are blue. But I can tell he's not going to ask, and so I have time to make up a lie.

"I'll see you tomorrow," I say, backing toward the hallway as Hailey shows Miles out. She closes the door behind him and leans on it like she needs something to hold her up.

"Dora," she says quietly. "He kept calling you that."

If she took a look at my driver's license, she'd know it all, but I can't bear to tell her. For all intents and purposes, I've stolen their dead daughter's identity. "I took her name," I admit.

Hailey sinks into the couch. She looks anxiously down the hall, as if she's afraid Martin will come out and ask what's going on. "*Why?*"

"I needed a new start. But I wanted to stay connected to you." I swallow the lump in my throat. "Every time we talk, I've meant to tell you. You're the only real parents I ever had, and even though I needed to be on my own, I guess I wanted to pretend I was really your daughter."

Her eyes fill with tears. "But you are our daughter, Christy. You didn't need to change your name to make that real."

Christy was never my name anyway. It was just another lie, told to protect myself. My eyes are stinging now, but I'm too dehydrated to cry. Or maybe just too damn empty. "I never knew Dora, but I know how much you loved her." I glance at her picture, the one I stared at every day when I first arrived.

I remember wondering if my daughter would have looked that way, had she lived.

I lean forward, hunching like the old woman I'm already becoming. "I'd lost so much," I say breathlessly. "I wanted to keep this one thing close. I'm so sorry. I can leave. Go to a hotel."

Hailey moves to my side. Puts her hand on my back, so gently. "I won't pretend like this doesn't hurt me, and I also won't pretend like I completely understand, but I'm not angry. And you're not going anywhere."

I lean into her, and she holds my head against her belly, her hands in my hair, as I start to sob.

I barely sleep. Every time I drift into a drowsy haze, I remember a different sort of pain, the one that comes with crushing grief and despair. I remember Ladonna's eyes, her knowing gaze, her pity. I remember hating her because her pity made it all real. I remember the animal fear, the animal rage. And I wake with her face in my mind, knowing I have to go back to the hospital and find her. I have to make sure she doesn't tell anyone who I am. I also have to keep Miles from getting to her.

I open my eyes as I hear Martin lumber into the shower at the end of the hall. I wonder if Hailey told him. Dora, the first one, the real one, would be a year older than me now, had she survived the encounter with the drunk driver who smashed into the passenger side of the Rodriguezes' station wagon in 1986. She hadn't been properly secured in the back, so she was ejected from the car—and the driver got away with a citation for DUI and minimal jail time— leaving Hailey and Martin to bear the weight of guilt virtually alone.

Last night, I resurrected all that pain. I also reminded them that they don't know who I really am. It's the absolute worst time to have them thinking about that. I've made so many mistakes. Today, I have to try to fix them. I text Miles, using voice command.

> If you send me what you have for the interview with Michelle Bathhouse, I'll call her and get the fact-checking done.

It takes him several minutes to respond. You're not going back to Seattle?

> I'm fine. Send me what you have. Wouldn't want you to get scooped.

It turns out that's literally impossible.

Predictable. Miles is ambitious and aggressive to a fault when it comes to his stories, and though it feels like he's way ahead on this one, that can always change if the *New York Times* or the *Post* or even the *Daily Beast* decide to send someone to investigate. Probably the *Oregonian* is the biggest threat, though—I add checking their coverage, as well as the *Bulletin*'s, to my to-do list. And in this respect, I'm with Miles. If the story stays quiet for now, it's possible that I'll be able to steer it away from dangerous shoals and cover up any sharp edges before anyone notices. I've already got the picture, which is a start. And I took care of Arnie's crazy girlfriend and her list of possible unknown survivors. Now I need to get Ladonna—I mean *Essie*—on my side, and I need to make sure Michelle Bathhouse didn't tell Miles anything that could lead to me.

My inbox is slowly filling up, stories from Valentina to edit, along with Noah's story. His subject heading reads "Call me as soon as you read." I roll my eyes and archive the message; unless he's willing to focus Miles on the Children of Darius story, he's not much help to me, and I don't want to read another unknown-survivor-focused piece. Miles's new message appears—he's attached his interview notes for Michelle Bathhouse. I read through what she told him.

There's a description of the compound. Of Darius. Of Lucy refusing to leave, telling them not to call her *mother*. Of a man—a description Miles has linked to Arnold Moore—brandishing a bloody knife as they drove away.

And this:

Names remembered: Parvaneh. Ester. Two young girls, ~18, pushing L's wheelchair, one thin, light-brown hair, blue eyes, one overweight, pregnant, dark-blond hair, blue eyes. Cross-check with any known images, name lists, identities of the dead, call Maxwell.

My throat constricts, seeing the two names rubbing up against each other. I lived, she died, but my god, it was close. Her death was my fault. Tears sting my eyes, even as they focus on the only other name in the paragraph. Maxwell.

I text Miles. Who's Maxwell?

Michelle Bathhouse hooked me up! He was in the cult.

My brain spirals back in time, rummaging for names and faces, panic seeping in at the edges of my thoughts. I blow out a shaky breath and voice text: Want me to call him and do a screening interview?

Looking to flex those journalistic ambitions! You can get all that done from your sick bed?

What else have I got to do?

Rest? You broke your arm yesterday!

And don't I know it. The pain is gnawing at me, but I can't take anything that might dull my thoughts. It's a matter of survival. This'll keep my mind off of everything.

Okay. I'll check in later. I'm heading out to Marie's ranch to interview her husband and see if the sheriff and medical examiner out there will give me the time of day.

I'd be a lot more panicked about that if Marie were alive. As it stands, I have some breathing room. Miles trusts me to do some of his legwork, and it's the best news I've gotten in a while. We have a plan, I text him.

Great! This could be the info we've been waiting for.

He texts me the guy's contact info. Maxwell Jennings. The name isn't familiar, but a lot of people joined up and got their names before I even arrived in Portland. It's why I didn't know Ladonna's before name until after everything burned—she'd been with Darius for two years before I became an Oracle.

Sitting up in bed, I make my to-do list and lay out my grid of the facts I need to check. Cult names. Before names. Appearances. Quotes. Timetables and dates. Then I call Michelle Bathhouse, my heart hammering before she even picks up the phone.

"Ms. Bathhouse? I'm Dora Rodriguez from the *Hatchet*. I work with Miles Connover as his fact-checker, and I'm calling to confirm the details of the interview you two did yesterday. Is this a convenient time?"

"Oh," she says. "I told him everything I knew yesterday. It was nice that *someone* cared to ask."

"Have you had trouble getting others to listen?"

She sighs. "No one seemed to care much about my mom when it turned out her body wasn't one of the people they found in the fire. I think she was dead before that. They killed her, but no one cares because the ones who did it are dead now too."

"I'm so sorry for your loss. Miles let me know that you and your brother drove down to the compound to try to get your mom out of the group."

"The *cult*? Yes," she says, sounding impatient. "Like I said, I told him all this yesterday."

"I'm just verifying the facts, ma'am. It's an important part of the journalistic process." I check Miles's notes. "You estimate that your visit to the compound took place on August 26?"

"Yes," she says. "I remember it was a Saturday because I went to church the very next day to pray for her soul, and I just broke down. But the minister told me I couldn't give up on her, and the Lord never would either."

"You described the leader of the group, Darius—"

"Oh, those stupid names they gave themselves. Stephen Millsap was a psychopath, and I won't call him by that stupid name!"

"Fair enough. I understand."

"*Do* you?"

I close my eyes. "I just mean that your point of view makes sense."

"All those people," she says. "Those girls. It's so awful, what he did."

"The two young ladies you mentioned. I want to verify—"

"Parvaneh," she says. "And Eszter."

"You described Parvaneh and Eszter—one was pregnant and overweight, and the other was slender. Do you know which was which?"

"I'm not sure. I think maybe Eszter was the fat one."

I smile, bittersweet and pained. "And both girls had brown eyes?"

"I thought I told him they were blue."

"I'm looking at his notes. It says brown. Is that a mistake?"

"Let me think."

"If it helps," I offer, "I have a picture of a group of cult members, and the two women you've named are also identified in the picture. Their eyes look pretty dark."

"Oh," she says. "I guess it's been a long time. You're probably right. And I guess it doesn't matter much."

"One little truth can make all the difference. Facts always matter, Ms. Bathhouse."

"I guess you wouldn't have a job if they didn't."

"That's correct," I say, knowing I'll never have a job in the business again if I'm caught. I run through the rest of the details with her, the tension in my body slowly subsiding. We end the call after a few minutes, and I'm on to the next one: Maxwell Jennings. This one is trickier. I have to be careful. I dial the number and introduce myself when he answers.

"About time," he says. "Michelle said you guys were gonna be all over this."

"Mr. Jennings—"

"Max."

"Max—when did you join the Oracles?"

"1996. I was one of the first. I knew Steve before he got the idea to give us all those Persian names. Classic cult stuff, right? Change people's names, and you own their identities."

I shift as uneasiness takes hold. "You weren't mentioned in the 2005 book."

"Yeah. It was a little soon. I didn't want to out myself; I just wanted to get on with my life. But now—twenty years. God. I can't believe it's been twenty years."

"Do you mind if I ask you a couple questions? We're trying to get an accurate list of who all the cult members were so we can better understand exactly who died in the fire."

"Oh, I can do that," he says. "I was basically Steve's secretary for a while. He kept records—like, financial records and everything—for everyone who joined."

"I was given to understand that many who joined were..."

"Strays?"

"Struggling."

He laughs. "I guess they were both. He wanted whatever he could gather, though. As much as people were willing to tell him. Known family, any assets, whether they had access or could ask relatives for money, whether anyone might come looking for them."

"Do you still have these records?"

"Hell yeah. I got the receipts, as they say."

Shit. "Are you willing to provide them?"

"Depends on what you mean by *provide*."

"If you are willing to allow me to review your records so that I could verify them is what I meant," I babble. I have to get my hands on those records.

I can hear him shuffling papers. "Got 'em right here," he says.

"Would you be willing to mail them?" I ask.

"Are you crazy? They're my only copies!"

Even better. "I'd be happy to meet you somewhere," I suggest.

He sighs. "I guess it's time this stuff got out there. Where are you located?" he asks. "I can meet you this afternoon."

"I'm in Bend, actually," I say, giving my arm a doleful look. "But I can drive up—"

"I can meet you in Eugene," he says. "Not quite halfway, but I have friends down there. Been a while since I visited."

"If you don't mind my asking," I blurt out, "what was *your* Oracle name?"

"My name? Oh god. This is sort of embarrassing. It was Gilgamesh."

"Wow," I choke out, remembering the dark-haired, muscular guy who was one of the first Oracles I met. The one who always had his notebook with him. "That's a regal name." And if he recognizes me, I am in a world of trouble.

We arrange to meet at four and end the call. I am taking a massive risk, but now that I've locked down that damn photograph, Max is possibly the only person alive, apart from Essie, who could link me to the Oracles. And Essie might have good reason to stay quiet.

My phone buzzes with a text. It's Noah. How are you doing this morning? I don't suppose you read my story yet?

I'm fine, I reply. I'll try to get to your story today, but I've got a lot on my plate.

> I'll buy you lunch after you read it, and you can tell
> me your thoughts in person

This kid is nothing if not persistent. Will try to get back to you soon as I can.

I pull my stuff together for a shower, and my phone buzzes again. Rolling my eyes at this boy who can't take a hint, I look down at the screen. But it's not Noah. It's Gina, Arnie's girlfriend. *Again.*

> I told my friends you would be writing a big story about Arnie but nothings on that website and they said you might not be who you say you are I couldn't find anyone named Dora on the site

I read her message a few times, calculating my response. I'm a factchecker. I don't write the pieces, I finally voice-text back. Journalists do.

> Whats that persons name then

I can't put her in touch with Miles now. I don't have the energy to manage it, and it feels like the walls are closing in. I take a shower with my arm wrapped in a plastic bag, and I thank my lucky stars that both Hailey and Martin have left for work by the time I emerge. I take time to put on heavier makeup than usual, because when Max knew me, I didn't wear any. I style my white hair, thankful for the trick of genetics or whatever it was—maybe even osteoporosis for all I know—that made my natural color fade so quickly.

Essie Green recognized me, though. Even with all the years and trauma, she knew.

I contemplate calling Max and canceling. But unlike Ladonna, who I lived in the same dorm with for a year, who saw me every single day, Gil wasn't that close to me. And there's a lot to be gained if I can get ahold of his information, make sure it doesn't get out. My life. My freedom. And it's not as if I'm preventing Miles from writing the story; I'm just excising a small piece of it that no one will realize is even missing.

I type up my notes from the check of the Michelle Bathhouse interview, writing that the only detail he got wrong was the eye color on the two girls. Then I pace until he texts back: I love your attention to detail. I exhale with a smile.

I'm getting ready to leave for the meeting with Max when the doorbell rings. Was today the day the cleaners show up? I can't remember.

I grab my purse and keys, cursing as I bump my arm against the bedside table. Grimacing, I head down the hall and into the living room. I walk to the door and answer it.

There's no one there. I didn't think I'd taken that long; if Hailey was depending on me to open the house for the cleaners, it's just one more thing I've screwed up. I lean out the door and look up and down the street, but there's no one at the curb, no one on the sidewalk. A car is turning at the intersection a block away, an ancient-looking sedan, but there's no sign of anyone else out and about. I'm about to close the door when I glance down. My stomach drops.

There, on the welcome mat, is a blue stone. Markings carved into its rough face.

Etched in red.

CHAPTER SEVENTEEN

The Retreat
October 3, 2000

A drop of sweat clung to the end of Darius's nose as he bowed his head over the piglet. It lay on its side on the altar, eyes glazed as its blood ran down a funnel and into a bucket next to Kazem's feet. He, too, had his head down, expression hidden. Parvaneh had overheard him arguing with Darius about using the pigs as channeling vessels. Kazem hadn't thought it made any sense; he didn't see how an animal, even a smart one like a pig, could help them touch the deep consciousness. But Darius said it was life and death that brought them closer, and any life would help them, though human life was best.

Kazem had drugged the animal so it didn't struggle or suffer, but Parvaneh felt uneasy all the same—she'd seen the creature struggling to avoid the squirt of medicine into its mouth when she went to tell Kazem they were ready. He'd given her a *look*, silent and seething. She'd glared back, holding her ground. Then she'd asked him about his loyalty, his commitment. His face had gone smooth and cloudy, almost as if he had taken the sedative himself. He said his loyalty was strong as ever.

Parvaneh wanted to believe him, but as the weather had started to signal the slow but inevitable return of winter, a few people had begun to grumble, especially after Ziba, her pushy adult children with their threats, her death at the end of August. *Of course* it had affected Darius. Of course it had been stressful for him. And of course it had made him more short-tempered, more eager to help all of them tap that vein of the deep consciousness and drink from its wisdom. The millennium approached, bringing with it all kinds of danger. He was in charge of protecting them, and those people had just barged onto their compound and threatened to sic the authorities on them, even to have their children taken away.

Parvaneh had done her best to support him. To please him. She was terrified he was slipping away, but he explained that he'd *had* to meet in the evenings with Ladonna and Zana and Goli and Laleh—they needed more support than Parvaneh did. Their faith had been wavering, and he'd needed to reach out to them individually. She'd told him she understood, but she was eager to return to the times when he'd spend every evening with her alone. He'd promised that time was coming soon.

"Do you all feel that?" Darius asked, his hands on the animal's back.

Parvaneh looked down at a smear of blood on her hands, which had been gently stroking the dying pig's pale-pink skin. Her stomach burbled with nausea.

"Do you feel that throb?" he continued. "That's the consciousness, telling us to dig in instead of pulling away. The only path to real enlightenment is to keep searching with a hunger and thirst that's unquenchable save for one source: that thick vein of immortal wisdom that hides in all of us, dormant unless we focus. Unless we offer our utter commitment and sacrifice. As Ziba did. As Shirin did. As all of you might one day be called to do."

Parvaneh felt a tremor pass through the pig's body. She raised her head to see Octavia peering at Darius, her brow furrowed. Eszter was also looking at Darius with a quizzical expression. Maybe, like Parvaneh, wondering if she understood what she'd just heard.

Darius glanced around as if he felt the ripple of uncertainty shimmy up his arms. "You look fearful," he said to Octavia. "You love this life too much. You confuse your skin with your self. That is weakness."

Eszter lowered her head again, as if she was afraid of being called out. Parvaneh lowered hers for the same reason. But then Octavia said, "I'm not confused. I'm just asking for more wisdom about all of this."

"That's an excuse," said Darius. "You're wrapping your rank fear in all the right words, but I can see it all around you, hanging in the air like stench." He scowled. "Your doubt is poison, Octavia. Take it out of here before you hurt the rest of us. This isn't the first time, but it has to be the last. You've become a cancer, killing us from the inside."

"I'm not—!"

Parvaneh looked up in time to see Darius snap, "I know it was you."

Everyone had gone still and watchful, and the pig's final, labored breaths—a signal that the moment of closest intimacy with the consciousness was at hand—were slipping past unnoticed. Darius's face was ruddy.

Octavia's was slowly draining of color. "What are you talking about?"

"You told them where to find us. You want to ruin us!"

She shook her head. "I've never wavered."

"You told them!" he shouted. "You betrayed us! You wanted them to take Ziba away!"

"I didn't tell anyone anything! What about Gilgamesh? They'd been to the Portland house. He probably told them!"

"Ziba's son said he did," volunteered Eszter.

"*No one* asked you to speak," Darius barked. As Eszter clamped her mouth shut, her cheeks suffusing with red, Parvaneh felt a zing of grim satisfaction alongside a rush of sympathy. She hadn't forgiven Eszter for the lie. She still wondered what Eszter had been trying to conceal with the deception—was Eszter in love with Darius? Was she going to try to get him back? But at the same time, Parvaneh missed their closeness, their late-night talks. Especially now that things had gotten so strange.

Darius was shaking his head. "Someone's been giving people ideas, Octavia. About the children."

Octavia stepped back from the altar. "Why would I *ever* do anything to hurt our children?"

Darius stood up to his full height. "I get my answers straight from the consciousness." He stroked the flank of the pig. "Just now." He looked around. "Did the rest of you feel it? There are people among us who are pulling us away from our goal. Make no mistake: they are killing us more effectively than any knife." He glared at the top of Kazem's bowed head—he was the only person, in addition to Octavia, who wasn't eyeing all the others at the altar, all the rest gathered on the steps of the dais. There were thirty-nine of them now, not counting the children. Which of them was dragging everyone down?

Parvaneh had felt it growing over the last many weeks, as the animals had been sacrificed one by one. Comments about wasting meat, worries about having enough for winter, concern about causing pain unnecessarily. Stray words, seemingly harmless. But what they really meant was these people didn't trust Darius. They didn't have true faith in his vision. Anger surged inside her, crackling like a current. "I feel it. How that doubt is poisoning us," she blurted out. "If you don't have faith during times like this, do you really have it at all?"

"Wisdom from one of our youngest Oracles," Darius said, offering her an approving smile. "Faith is the tie that keeps us linked to one another and the consciousness. Without it, you can never hope to touch it, never hope to feel that liquid gold sizzling through your veins, that promise that when you shed this skin, you will be forever linked with it. You can't hope to feel one with the consciousness without faith. If this is how you feel, full of doubt, you are a cancer."

His eyes narrowed. "And we will root you out. Our trials are at hand. Our commitment will be tested. The attacks come from the outside, like the attackers Octavia invited in, but they also come from our very ranks. The two-faced. Those with hate in their hearts. Only the purest of us will pass that test, and to pass, some of us, and perhaps those who are closest to the consciousness, the ones who can save us all, will make the ultimate commitment."

Parvaneh felt a zing of excitement mixed with the buzzing drone of nausea as the smell of blood pervaded the room. He'd told her about the special retreat, the wonderful place just for a few of the most devoted. This had to be what he was talking about.

But Octavia said, "The ones closest to the consciousness. Are you talking about the children?"

"It is not for you to question me," he said loudly. Then he

grimaced and clutched at his head. "You've pulled me away from the consciousness, just as you'd hoped."

"I didn't hope to do anything like that!" she cried. "I'm trying to understand what you mean! You always said the babies were links to the consciousness, our purest way to connect—in creating their bodies with our own, in raising them in this place, closely linked to the source of all." Her expression went steely. "It's why you've worked *so* hard since we came here to father so many." She looked around at Zana, Minu, Laleh, Ladonna, Parvaneh, Eszter. "How many new babies should we be expecting?"

Parvaneh gritted her teeth. She didn't want to be tossed into the same category as the others. He'd told her she was special.

"You're selfish, Octavia," Darius snapped. "And *weak*. Get out of my sight." He glanced at Ladonna. "Go fetch Xerxes. It's time he understood."

"*No*. He's too young," Octavia said.

"Get out," Darius roared, even as Ladonna jogged down the aisle and out the door.

Octavia shook her head. She descended the steps unsteadily, tears flowing. She was halfway down the aisle when the door opened again and Ladonna appeared, holding Xerxes by the hand. When he saw Octavia, his face lit up, and he yanked himself away from Ladonna to run to her.

Darius's face transformed into a blank mask. Parvaneh reached out instinctively to touch him, connect with him, but he shrugged her off and descended the steps, approaching as Octavia enfolded her son in her arms. "Mommy, why are you crying?" Xerxes asked.

"Shh," Octavia whispered. "It's okay."

"Get away from him," Darius said quietly. "Don't poison him with your touch."

Octavia straightened. "You'll frighten him."

"He is a creation of the consciousness," Darius told her. "Any fear he feels comes from the venom you've pumped into him."

"Don't—" she began. Then her mouth snapped shut, and she glanced down at Xerxes, who was watching her carefully. "*Please.*"

Darius curled his fingers around Octavia's arm and pulled her away from the boy. Parvaneh could tell, even in profile, that it hurt, but Octavia didn't cry out. Xerxes, though... "Don't be mean!" he shouted.

"Ladonna," Darius said mildly. "Take Xerxes to the altar."

"No!" Octavia screamed.

Darius shoved her away. She stumbled into a row of chairs. He stalked back toward the altar, and Ladonna didn't have to take Xerxes because the boy was chasing after his father. "I told you not to be mean," he shouted, smacking at Darius's butt with his little fists.

Parvaneh's heart was beating so hard that it hurt. As Octavia ran from the meeting hall, sobbing, someone needed to make sure Xerxes wasn't scared, that he understood. But if she was the one, would Darius think she was being defiant? All she wanted to do was help.

Before she could move, Eszter descended the stairs. "Xerxes," she said sweetly. "We're all just trying to teach you. We want to answer all the questions you have."

"Why are you mean to my mommy?" Xerxes wailed.

"She was trying to hurt you," Parvaneh said, though even as the words flew from her mouth, her mind began to question them. "She was trying to make you scared. But you're never scared, are you?"

Xerxes blinked. "No."

"That means your mind is in the right place," Eszter said.

Darius gave them a small smile that lifted Parvaneh's spirits high.

He knew they were loyal. He knew they were trying to help. She caught Eszter's eye and offered a nod of appreciation. Eszter nodded back.

"Is my mind the same thing as my brain?" Xerxes asked, wiping a smear of snot from his nose. "And what's that?" He pointed up at the altar, where one of the pig's hooves protruded over the side.

"It's a pig," Kazem said.

"Is it sleeping?"

Discomfort flickered in Kazem's eyes, but then he said, "It was helping us connect with the most important thing in the universe."

"A pig?" Xerxes asked. "It just likes mud."

"Then I guess the pig is like you," Darius said, his smile growing, his shoulders relaxing now that no one was provoking him. "Which goes to show that perhaps the most innocent among us are the best conduits. I believe this is the lesson for tonight. You can all go back to your dorms."

Parvaneh felt a pang of misgiving as Darius guided the now-calm boy back down the steps and away from the altar. Xerxes couldn't see it, but the pig's throat had a small, deep wound. Its purpose had been fulfilled. But this was a pig. And Xerxes was a child. She hoped Darius only meant *conduit* in the way he'd meant it a month ago, before Shirin and Ziba had died on this altar, before they'd started to go through a few pigs a week, before *conduit* had meant *dying*.

Darius announced that he was going to the children's dorm to meditate there, and he led Xerxes away. Parvaneh frowned, her hopes for spending the evening with him dashed. Then she shook herself a bit. This, she realized, was the doubt. That destructive force each of them held inside. The one that tore them apart. She pushed it away, stomped it down. Flinched as Eszter put a hand on her arm. "Are you all right?" Eszter asked.

They walked together down the steps, ahead of the others. "I wish Octavia hadn't challenged him like that," Parvaneh said.

"She was worried about the children."

"We should all be." Parvaneh gestured at Eszter's baby bump. "If someone comes in here and tries to take the kids—"

"I know," said Eszter. She gave Parvaneh a pained look. "I just want things to be like they were before, you know?"

Parvaneh hugged her, resentment melting away. "Yeah," she whispered fiercely. "I know."

"Get up," Ladonna said tersely, shaking her awake in the darkness. "Darius needs us."

Parvaneh sat up, realizing Eszter and Zana were already dressed. "All of us?" she asked.

Eszter was tying her hair back with a cloth. She looked sleepy and worried. "I hope this isn't what I think it is," she whispered to Ladonna. Somehow Eszter already seemed to know what was happening, or at least suspect. The resentment prickled to life again in the basement of Parvaneh's heart.

"Darius asked for the four of us specifically," Ladonna said.

Because they were the most loyal. He knew they wouldn't let him down.

They pulled on their clogs and tromped out of the dorm, leaving the few dozen other women sleeping soundly.

Ladonna led them across the clearing, lit by a canopy of stars, to the door of the children's dorm, where Darius stood with Kazem and Tadeas, looking grim. He held his hand out, and Ladonna offered hers, palm up. He dropped the keys to the van onto it. "She won't be moving fast, and you can catch her before she makes it to the road. Bring all of them back."

"All of them?" Parvaneh asked.

"She took Xerxes and Parisa. She's going to kill them."

Eszter's mouth opened, but she seemed to think better of what she was going to say and shut it. But Zana blurted out, "I don't think Octavia would hurt the baby and—"

Darius grabbed her by the arms. "If she takes them away from us, she is killing them. If you don't understand that, you shouldn't go. And maybe you shouldn't be here at all."

"I understand," Zana said quickly. "Thank you for offering me that wisdom."

"Come on," Ladonna said. "She's been out there almost an hour. We have to get going."

They followed her to the van and piled inside. Parvaneh wondered if it was the wisest thing for Darius to choose Eszter, pregnant as she was, to be in the search party when Kazem and Tadeas would be faster and stronger. But then she remembered how Eszter had soothed the boy, almost getting him to forget what he'd just witnessed happening to his mother. And Parvaneh had helped. It made sense that they would go. They might even be able to sweet-talk the boy into coming back without a fuss.

"Why would she do this?" Zana asked, shaking her head. "She has no right."

"She thinks because she gave birth to them, they belong to her," said Ladonna. "Darius was right when he said she was selfish." She started the van. The headlights illuminated the gravel of the drive, rutted with puddles that had formed from a few days of late September rain. Octavia had delighted in the deluge; she'd spun around with her face to the sky, her mouth open, and she'd gotten a few of the toddlers and Xerxes to join her. Parvaneh had watched from the kitchen and laughed at the pure joy of it.

Now Octavia had run. Left them. And taken the child Darius had said would be an important conduit.

She peered through the windshield, trying to spot a flutter of robes, a glimpse of blond hair, the smear of a muddy footprint. Ladonna switched on the brights, widening their view of the dark forest on either side of the narrow road. "There they are," Ladonna announced after a few minutes, speeding up.

Sure enough, a few hundred yards ahead, two forms were jogging along the road. Xerxes and Octavia, who must have had the infant cradled against her body. When she realized they were coming, she knelt next to Xerxes and said something to him, then got up and started sprinting down the road.

Xerxes ran at a right angle to her, straight into the woods.

Ladonna cursed and slammed on the brakes. The van skidded to a halt. "Parvaneh and Eszter, go get him back. We'll get Octavia and the baby."

Parvaneh shoved the door wide and jumped out. Eszter lumbered out behind her and took off into the woods, leaving Parvaneh to slide the door shut. As soon as she did, the van shot forward. To her right, she could hear Xerxes shriek and the crash/crackle of Eszter running through the thick ground cover, the burst of sound as she called his name. Parvaneh lunged into the brush, worried that Eszter would never catch the boy.

Despite the chilly night air, anxious sweat prickled across her forehead and upper lip. She glanced to her left, down the road, in time to see the headlights illuminate a solitary, running figure before blocking it out. A thump and a terrible scream split the darkness.

Parvaneh froze. Octavia. The baby. Nausea and disbelief twisted hard inside her. Had Ladonna just...? She wouldn't have, would she? A shudder ran through Parvaneh's body.

But then she shook herself. That was doubt, trying to slow her down. Xerxes was still out there, and that was her mission. She forced her legs to move again, toward the sound of Eszter's voice, pushing everything else away.

CHAPTER EIGHTEEN

Bend, Oregon
December 12, present day

I sit there for a few minutes, staring down at the meditation stone. I know who left it—Essie figured out the address last night and decided to leave a message. A warning. As if I really needed one. She's threatening to out me. What she doesn't realize is that I'm just as eager to keep her out of this as she is.

I have to make her understand. If I don't, she's going to ruin everything.

I check my watch. Ladonna is going to have to wait. I have to get going if I want to be on time to meet Gil—it's quite the drive. And I'd better go ahead and see if I'm capable of actually managing my car with a cast up to my elbow and pain that's barely touched by ibuprofen, but there's no way I'm taking opioids right now, not when I need to operate a two-ton rolling metal capsule. I grab my stuff and check my makeup; it's weird and intense, and I barely look like myself, which lifts my mood. I head out to the car, happy at least that my right hand and arm are intact. I'm not going to think about the fact that my body is falling apart until I get myself through this mess.

I head to Eugene, settling in for the long drive as my arm starts to throb with every beat of my heart, sharp and hot and, in a way, mercifully distracting. I can barely think about being nervous because everything hurts too much.

I arrive at the bar where we've agreed to meet a few minutes early. Noah has texted me during the drive. **Did you read it yet? Want to meet?**

"Jesus, kid," I mutter, then voice text, biting out each word: **Noah, I'm trying to work. I'll get to your story as soon as I can!**

My phone buzzes almost immediately after I send, and I curse. But it's Max Jennings, a.k.a. Gil, a.k.a. the man with all the receipts. **I'm at a table.**

My watch tells me that my heart rate is 105. I check myself in the rearview mirror. I am not the same person I was in so many ways. This is going to be fine.

Awkwardly, I get out of my car, toting my laptop bag. The cold knifes through me; I didn't wear a coat because it's too awkward getting it on and off. I head into the bar, inhaling the funk of beer and french fries.

The hostess greets me as I crane my neck and spot a bald, heavyset guy sitting alone in one of the booths. I tell her I'm meeting a friend, and she gestures in his direction and asks if that's him. I tell her it is, even though I'm not sure, and it actually calms me down. If that is him, it goes to show how much someone can change in twenty years. He's a universe away from the lean, muscular, dark-haired guy in his thirties that I remember.

"Max?" I ask as I reach his table.

He looks up from his almost-empty beer and grins. "Dora?" He rises and offers his hand to shake, even as he realizes my left arm is in a cast. "Ouch," he says as I maneuver myself into the booth. "Did that happen recently?"

"Yesterday," I say with a wince.

His bloodshot brown eyes go wide. "And you're working today?"

"This story is important, and with the anniversary of the fire coming up—"

"Tell me about it. I'm dreading it." Though he almost looks excited.

"Can you tell me about the dread?" I ask as I pull out my notebook and pen. "You weren't there, were you?"

He shakes his head. The waitress comes to the table, and I order a Diet Coke. I ask if Max wants another beer, and he eagerly accepts.

"I'm in contact with a few of the family members," he says once the waitress walks away. "Like the Bathhouses. I know their mom didn't die in the actual fire, but since she's never been accounted for, they consider the fifteenth to be the anniversary of her death. Michelle—that's Lucy's daughter—is the one who put me in touch with you people."

There's something weirdly intense about him; it's coming across the table in spiky waves. "The anniversary is in a few days," I say. "I know it's a difficult time to be revisiting this stuff."

He's shaking his head. "The murders," he tells me. "It's going to get huge once everything comes out."

"Murders." As in, more than one. "Apart from Arnold Moore?"

"Marie Heckender," he says. "Suspicious fire."

"How did you know that?"

He gives me a quizzical look. "Google?" He pats the messenger bag sitting next to him. "I'm a guy who likes information. I like having it. I like finding it. In another life, I could have been a..." He rubs his chin. "I don't know. Some respectable professional who does something with information." He finishes his beer. "Anyway. You were asking me about Lucy Bathhouse."

I wasn't, but okay. "I've read a little about the compound," I tell him. "If she died on the property, do you have any idea why authorities didn't dig up the place, searching for bodies?" I know where a few lie, buried and unknown.

Max snorts. "There was no way Steve would have left any bodies there. If anything, he probably fed corpses to the pigs."

In response to my obvious queasiness, Max makes a pained face that doesn't quite cut through his jittery vibe. "Quite a thing, am I right?" He tilts his head. "Hey, have you ever spent any time in Portland?"

My mind goes into hyperdrive, trying to figure out what to disclose and what to hide. "Not really. I'm originally from Bend, but I live up in Seattle now. I just moved there from St. Louis. So I've been all over."

He shrugs. "You just look familiar. I wondered if we'd run into each other." With a small smile, he adds, "But I'd probably remember your hair. Pretty cool."

"Thanks," I say. "And I don't think we've met, but it's always possible. Small world and all."

"For sure." He shakes his head and pulls a thick notebook stuffed with loose papers from his bag. "Anyway, two down, one left," he says as he thumbs through, landing on one dog-eared page. "Shari Redmond's the one left standing. Ladonna. She's the third who went to jail."

I shrug. "We haven't yet tracked her down. I'm starting to think she's unfindable."

The waitress brings our drinks. Max takes a healthy swig of his.

"Shari probably changed her name when she got out," he says, wiping his mouth with his sleeve. "Can you blame her? Shit, I knew things were going south even before everything came to a head. I told Steve: I have to get away from this. I couldn't follow where he was going."

"You never lived on the compound."

He shakes his head. "Before Steve moved the entire cult down there, we would all spend weekends in the woods and stuff. Like, while he was building the place." He sits up, sticks his chest out. "I helped him design it. You'll never see this mentioned—I guess with the collapse of the big meeting house building, they never found it—but there were tunnels. Did you know that?"

I turn my head to sip from my drink. My skin is tingling with cold prickles as a memory hits: the decision I made, the death I guaranteed. And the reason no one ever found her body. "I had no idea," I say hoarsely. If he tells anyone about the tunnel or writes about it, people might go looking. And they'll find her there, one more mystery solved.

"Probably long since caved in," he says, chuckling. "We weren't exactly professionals, and he wanted it to be secret. Only a few knew about them."

"And you never gave police a heads-up?"

His face falls. "Look. If they'd actually wanted to do more than move on as quickly as damn possible, they coulda found 'em." He glances toward the exit.

"I get it: you weren't even there," I say quickly.

He nods. "That's right. Hadn't been there in about a year, actually. Steve needed someone to mind the Portland house where we'd been based. We'd totally outgrown it by the time everyone moved to Bend, but he was hoping to keep recruiting. I was the obvious choice, I guess. He trusted me, and I was a good record keeper." He gives me a crooked smile and holds up the notebook. A few pages fall out, and he laughs. "Or I was compared to everyone else."

"And when did you leave the group?"

"I got word from Lisa Donald—her Oracle name was Octavia— that things were getting superweird. She asked me what to do, and I told her to leave. Just take her babies and go." His brow furrows. "I don't know if she ever did. I never heard from her again. But when *she* wanted out, I knew it was time for me too. Because Lisa and me? We were with him from the beginning. It started out good, you know? I'm not some nut."

"Of course you aren't," I mumble. "I've read that these groups… They just pull people in. People in need. It seems like the Oracles did that."

"Better than most, I'd say. And it really was good at first, for a lot of years." He's almost done with his second beer, so I offer to buy him another. When he accepts, I wave the waitress over and place the order.

Then I gesture at the notebook. "How many members were there in all?"

"Lots of people came and went. I have records of everyone we brought in, even the ones who didn't stay long. I'd interview people, names, birth dates, hometowns, education, their families. Steve wanted all that as soon as possible. He'd memorize that shit." Max's jaw clenches. "And then he'd use it to find their weak spots—anyone with mommy or daddy issues, especially the girls? He'd move right in. Be the daddy. Preach abstinence to all the guys until our balls were blue as the fucking sky above, while he was busy 'implanting the seeds of the consciousness' in all the pretty young things." He groans and runs a hand through his hair. "And the older ones? Those were the cash cows. He'd sweet-talk them all the way to the bank and drain all their funds. I can't believe I helped him. But then again, I wasn't the only one. And some people, let's be honest, Arnie and Marie and Shari? What they did was *a lot* worse than what I did."

My eyes are riveted to that notebook. "Can I take a peek?"

"It's all for real." He slides it over to me. "I told you I was serious."

I flip through the pages, noting a few familiar names—Ladonna, Roshanak, Kazem, Basir—and several I don't know. The people who left before I joined. He's got their real names followed by the names Darius gave them. It's enough to make my mouth go dry. "And you didn't give this to the police after the fire?"

He shakes his head. "I didn't want to be anywhere *close* to this. Soon as the fire happened, I took my shit and got out of town. Lived down in Mexico for a bunch of years, just trying to drink the pain away. Did you see how they treated the people who survived? They were pretty eager to punish everyone involved. I only moved back earlier this year." He rubs his hands over his face. "What a world."

"Some of the bodies in the fire were never identified," I say, staring down at Kazem's information, so many things I didn't know. His birth name was Isaac Meyerson. He was born in Tallahassee and had a college degree from Florida A&M, majored in veterinary technology. What it doesn't say: how he made his way to Oregon and to the Oracles. Why he stayed. How he died.

I remember the look on his face.

"You could have helped the police figure stuff out," I say to Max, "if you'd stuck around." He looks as if he wants to snatch his notebook back, so I add, "But I understand your viewpoint. You must have been traumatized when you heard what had happened."

"Oh god." He gratefully accepts his third beer—a double IPA—from the waitress. He moans after his first gulp. "It was such a fucking nightmare. I couldn't believe Steve had gone that far. But as I thought about it, it didn't seem that crazy."

"What do you mean?"

"He was always full of himself. Looking back, I can see the narcissism. But man, when he talked, for a long time, it just made sense, you know? It was all about finding a deeper meaning and purpose, something I needed badly at that point. And the meditation? That was good. It got us all vibing together. But when he started bringing in these old ladies with cancer and having us meditate through them, it started getting a little strange."

"Meditate through them?" I ask, determined to sound as clueless as possible.

He gets through most of his beer as he explains all the things I already knew. "I still hung on after that," he says, "but I started pulling back a little, questioning things. Not out loud, though. Just to myself." He sighs. "Honestly? I wonder if some of this is my fault."

"Why?"

He finishes his beer and raises his head. He frowns. "Wait. Is this all on the record? Are you going to print everything I say? I don't want to incriminate myself or anything." He reaches for the notebook.

I pull it back. "I'm not a reporter, and this is all off the record. But you know what my colleague is looking for, right?"

He nods. "Michelle said he was trying to get all the names because he thinks one of them might be looking for some payback. Like some sort of horror movie." His eyes are shiny as he adds, "Don't think all of this doesn't have me double locking my doors at night and stashing a gun in the glove compartment."

"You really think someone might come after *you?*"

"With two survivors dead and only one left?" A shrug. "You never know. Hey, I'll be right back. Need a pit stop." He slides out of the booth and heads for the bathrooms, walking carefully and leaning on tables as he goes.

I watch him enter the men's and then frantically flip through his notes, realizing that they're organized by the date of first contact. I find myself all the way in the back, on the final page of recruits. My blood turns cold as I review the handwritten details of seven lives.

Paired with Gina's information, in the hands of an investigative reporter like Miles, this information could be the end for me:

Anna Wilbur (ESZTER 1/12/99)—from Champaign-Urbana, IL, DOB 3/10/82, finished tenth grade, left abusive home, not in touch with parents, younger brother, no assets, no contacts.

Arnold Moore (TADEUS 12/24/99)—from Des Moines, IA, DOB 12/4/61, high school GED, parents deceased, older married sister, has done farm/manufacturing work, major meth addiction (note: Darius says will have to be clean before initiated), no assets, no contacts with family.

Kareem Simons (did not commit)—from Oakland, CA, DOB 2/15/74, finished high school, currently employed at PDX as gate agent, parents divorced, no contact with dad, close with mom who is office worker, has one sister who may move to Portland, will not give account info.

Lucy Bathhouse (ZIBA 1/12/99)—from Eugene, BA in English, widowed 1992, two adult children, Dave and Michelle (both independent, employed, practicing Episcopal, possible pushback), diagnosed stage IV breast cancer 12/98. Available account First Republic, acct#9000001056978991, balance as of 1/3/99 $56,003.25, is willing to close out Schwab portfolio, balance as of 1/3/99 $1,342,990.45, will initiate transfers.

Dana Logan (ZANA 9/25/99)—from Sacramento, CA, DOB 10/11/81, *grad high school, two semesters Oregon State, parents (mom is real estate agent, dad is plant manager) send $300/mo and more on request, will follow up.*

Marie Heckender (FABIA 12/24/99)—from Portland, OR, DOB 4/22/80, high school grad, one semester University of Oregon, dad is Harold Heckender (Willamette bank CEO). Available account Oregon Pacific, new checking acct#4718592519180484, balance as of 11/19/99 $19,433.47, available for transfer to BoA acct, will initiate.

Karen Turley (PARVANEH 12/24/99)—from Battle Creek, MI, DOB 8/3/83, finished eleventh grade ("barely"), younger brother, abusive home, no assets, no contacts.

It's enough to devastate—a name, a birth date, a place of birth. Why did I feel like I had to give him my actual name and date of birth, for God's sake? I'd been so cautious. Not wanting to give anyone a doorway to all of me. The only other Oracle I ever told my birth name to besides Gil? Dead because of me.

But I remember why I confessed. I was so glad to be in a safe place, with nice people and abundant food, so desperate to finally be accepted that I would have given them my account number, too, if I'd had one. On impulse, I pull the sheet of paper from his notebook and tuck it into my bag not a moment too soon. Max lumbers out of the restroom and plops down again. I offer to buy him another beer, and he declines. The alcohol seems to be catching up with him, and our conversation lags. I ask him if I can take the notebook to review, but he shakes his head and tugs it back across the table, telling me it's his to protect. I pay the bill, thank him for sharing, and ask him if he has a ride home, since he's clearly not in any condition to drive.

"Sorry," he says blearily. "I'll call my friend for a ride. We've all got our issues, you know?"

"Yes," I tell him. "I get it."

We say our goodbyes and I offer vague promises about following up. I tell him that if Miles is interested in pursuing his information, I'll put them in touch. Then I drive back to Bend with the silver bullet in my bag. It's only one page of almost a hundred, and none of them were numbered; he might never know it was missing. And it's the only additional link I can think of that connects me to the Oracles.

Which means I'm safe. It's almost enough to numb the pain in my arm. But as I pull up to Hailey and Martin's house, everything comes roaring back, and I realize I've forgotten one very important detail.

She's standing on the porch with Hailey, waiting for me.

CHAPTER NINETEEN

The Retreat
October 3, 2000

've got him," Eszter shouted. Parvaneh saw a rush of movement up ahead and to her left. She sprinted toward it.

"Let go!" shrieked Xerxes. "Let go, you big pig!"

"We have to take you back," Eszter huffed, trying to control the boy as he smacked at her face and kicked at her belly. "Parvaneh, help me!"

Parvaneh rushed up to them and grabbed Xerxes around the middle, wrenching him away from Eszter. But the boy's legs pinwheeled wildly, landing a few hard kicks to Eszter's body. She moaned and sank to her knees. Parvaneh wrapped her arms around Xerxes, holding him so tight that he began to scream that he couldn't breathe even as he continued to kick wildly. Angry now, she clamped her hand over his mouth and twisted around to hike back to the van. "Are you okay?" she called back to Eszter.

"Right behind you," Eszter said weakly.

Parvaneh picked her way back to the road, ignoring the struggling bundle in her arms. *Be numb*, she told herself. *Do your job. No doubt.*

Darius needs you. She chanted these things in her mind, one word for each step, over and over, feeling the poke of the meditation rock in the pocket of her robe with each lurching movement from her captive.

The crunch of footsteps behind her told her Eszter wasn't trailing that much. Up ahead, she could hear moans, choked sobs, and... arguing?

"Did they catch her?" Eszter asked as she caught up. She was holding her distended belly with both hands, breathing hard.

"You guys there?" Ladonna called. "We need some help." Her voice sounded odd. Flat.

Parvaneh paused about ten feet behind the van. Xerxes wasn't struggling much now, just whimpering. He had probably completely exhausted himself over the last few hours. His warm weight was oddly comforting. "Can you go up there and help them?" she asked Eszter.

"I'm not...sure," Eszter said, grimacing as she rubbed her side.

"Fine." Parvaneh marched up to the van. "Get in. He's calmer now. Just hold him. I'll help Ladonna."

Eszter climbed in, and Parvaneh handed over the limp boy. She watched the two for a moment, taking in the misery on each of their faces. Then she faced front and marched around the van, steeling herself.

It didn't help.

Octavia lay in the gravel perhaps fifteen feet away, blood matted in her long, blond hair. Ladonna stood over her, arms slack at her sides.

"The baby," said Parvaneh.

"I've got her," Zana said from the other side of the van. She moved forward into the light, cradling a bundle in her arms.

"What happened?" asked Parvaneh.

Ladonna glanced at Zana. "Octavia threw the baby onto the road."

"No she didn—" Zana began but snapped her mouth shut as Ladonna took a quick step toward her.

"And then she stepped right in front of the van," Ladonna continued. "I didn't want to hit her, but I also didn't want to hit Parisa. It was like she made me..."

Zana shifted her weight. She looked uncomfortable, unable to meet Ladonna's gaze.

"You're saying she forced you to run over her," Parvaneh said.

Ladonna's big, brown eyes were flinty. "That's what I'm saying."

"What are we going to do with the body?"

Just as she asked, Octavia made a retching sound. "Oh my god," Parvaneh said, walking toward the sprawled body. "She's still *alive?*"

Parvaneh squatted next to Octavia and murmured her name. Octavia groaned, and her fingers spread over the gravel, like she was reaching for something. "We have to get her to a hospital," said Parvaneh.

"What?" Ladonna stalked over to them. "No. That is *not* the plan."

Parvaneh stood up. "She's hurt, but she's not dead. She might live if we get her to a hospital."

"You don't think the cops'll be asking questions once we get there?"

"You just said she stepped in front of the van. So that's what we tell them."

"They won't believe us. And if you tell them *I* was driving? You think anyone's gonna give a Black lady the benefit of the doubt in this situation? You realize this is Oregon, right?"

"Fine! We'll tell them I was driving," Parvaneh said. "But we should take her."

Ladonna's eyes narrowed. "What do you think Darius would say about that?"

"You think he'd want her to *die*?"

"You heard what he said—she was trying to destroy us from both the outside and the inside." She gestured down at Octavia. "If we take her to a hospital and get everyone in town wrapped up in our business, how is that *not* destroying us from the outside? Besides, if she survives and decides to tell everyone we're the bad guys, how's that going to go for us? So now we bring her back. Pick up her legs."

Parvaneh's stomach turned, and she took a step back, shaking her head. "I can't," she whispered, looking down at Octavia, remembering her kindness, the way she enfolded her children in her arms. She looked back at the van. "Xerxes..."

"You think this is easy for Darius?" snapped Ladonna. "Didn't you see how much it hurt him to have her turn on us like this? Don't make it harder."

She was right. She'd held him in the night as he lay racked with the pain of betrayal and the stress of leading all of them through the darkness. "Okay," she muttered. "But we can't let Xerxes see—"

"We can put her in the back." Ladonna pointed at Zana. "Go open up the rear doors, and then get in the van. And stop whimpering, for God's sake. You'd think someone hit *you* with the damn van."

Zana did as Ladonna asked.

Octavia's body seemed irreparably broken. Twisted in impossible ways. Parvaneh whispered her apology and promised to take care as she positioned herself behind Octavia's legs and slid her arms under the woman's knees. Ladonna did the same with Octavia's upper body, cradling her bleeding head in the crook of her elbow. "All right," said Ladonna. "Up on three."

She counted. They rose, Octavia sagging in the middle, blood dripping from her head wound. Tears stung Parvaneh's eyes as they hustled their fellow Oracle to the back of the van. In the middle seats, she could hear Xerxes sleepily asking where his mother was and Eszter murmuring that she had gone to bed and that was where they were taking him too.

"She said we were going to a new place," he replied.

"She changed her mind," Eszter said quietly. "She wants us to take care of you."

The ride back to the compound was silent. Xerxes and baby Parisa had fallen asleep. Only Zana's sniffling breaths cut the quiet, along with the occasional muffled gurgle from the back, but Parvaneh told herself it was her imagination, brewing up a living nightmare. The air was heavy with a dreamy sort of shock.

As Ladonna pulled into the clearing, the headlights revealed a small crowd waiting for them, milling around outside the meeting and dining halls. Darius strode forward as soon as the van stopped, frowning at its grill. He plucked a lock of long, blond hair from the front. His eyes met Ladonna's through the windshield.

"Eszter and Zana," said Ladonna, not taking her eyes off Darius, "take the babies to bed and then join us in the meeting hall. Parvaneh, you're with me."

Parvaneh reminded herself to breathe. When she heard Ladonna's door slam, she willed herself into action, climbing out of the van and heading to the back again, where Ladonna was already telling Darius what had happened. "I don't know if she wanted to die or what. Certainly seemed like it."

Parvaneh wasn't sure she believed the story, but Darius didn't question it. "Maybe the consciousness moved inside of her. This was supposed to happen, as sad as it makes me." He looked over his shoulder at Kazem and Tadeas. "Take Octavia to the altar. We all need the wisdom she can channel."

Kazem looked uncertain. "But if she was destroying us, how can you be sure what we channel is—"

"Death is when the consciousness reaches up to reclaim its essence," Darius said loudly. "And Octavia is offering us this gift."

He was saying he knew she was going to die, and they weren't going to help her. Instead, they were going to use her. Parvaneh stepped back as Tadeas and Kazem approached. Darius caught her eye. "You're upset about all of this."

"Of course I am."

"Ladonna told me you wanted to take her to a hospital."

She looked away. "We're here, aren't we?"

"Are you?" he asked, drawing near. "I'm not sure you're here at all."

"I just think we should help her," she murmured.

"Even if it hurts all your fellow Oracles?" he asked. "Even if it hurts *me*?" His fingers caressed her cheek.

She met his gaze.

He stared at her for a long moment. "Stand with me as we channel her energy. This is the price of her rebellion but also the payment of a debt. We can't waste that."

She followed Darius to the meeting hall, where everyone else had already gathered. The candles were lit; the air was perfumed and dense, like a second skin.

As Darius approached, the group moved like one organism, reaching out to touch him, even while peering skittishly at Octavia, who lay, partially untwisted now, on the altar. Her bloody hair covered her face. Parvaneh wondered if Kazem or Tadeas had done that on purpose, unable to look at what had happened to a woman they'd known so well. Octavia had seemed like the mother of them all, just as Darius had been their leader, their father.

Darius mounted the stairs, and Parvaneh joined him. Hesitantly, she put a hand on Octavia's back. She looked up at Darius, hoping he would quicken the process, just as she suspected he'd done with Ziba, just as he'd guided her to do with Shirin. In this moment, Parvaneh realized it was a mercy, helping them along. He was doing something beautiful, in a way, even with all the ugliness he'd been handed.

And now it was *really* ugly. Blood seeped from Octavia's head wound, skin peeled back and torn, bone chips mixed with a few white flecks in the red mess of her hair. No hospital could fix this. Ladonna had made the right call, and Parvaneh's instincts had been all wrong. She only wished Ladonna hadn't told Darius about her moment of doubt.

Parvaneh glanced at the back of the meeting hall to see Eszter slowly making her way to the front. She looked exhausted, holding her belly like it had become heavier than she could bear.

Parvaneh closed her eyes, knowing she should focus and meditate, unable to think anything except *Please, please, let this be over soon.* She hoped Octavia was moving toward a vast golden light, one that didn't judge every mistake but instead offered a forever home, a forever oneness. Time seemed suspended, hanging over them like the blade of one of those guillotines that chopped off a head cleanly. She craved a neat break, a sharp moment of before and after when they knew Octavia was gone, but this was more like a slow leak.

The sound of a stifled sob finally drew Parvaneh's head up. Beneath her palm, Octavia's skin had grown cooler. But it was Eszter who looked cold, pale as a ghost, sheen of sweat on her brow. For a second, Parvaneh thought she might be having an experience, a soul-shaking encounter with the presence that had given all of them life.

But then she realized: Eszter was not okay. She was leaning on the altar as if she couldn't stand on her own. Her eyes were open, bulging out of her round face while her fingers grasped at the hem of Octavia's torn, muddy robe. Parvaneh touched Darius, nodding toward Eszter as soon as he looked at her.

Concern darkened his eyes. "Eszter?"

She shook her head and began to sink to the floor. Kazem, standing next to her, felt her movement and turned to catch her. When he looked down, he barked, "Darius."

Darius and Parvaneh rushed around the altar, and Parvaneh went cold. Blood had pooled between Eszter's feet. She was clutching at her belly.

At the baby who wasn't due for another two months.

CHAPTER TWENTY

Bend, Oregon
December 12, present day

Making sure my bag is zipped, I carefully get out of my car. The faster my heart beats, the more my wrist hurts, and seeing Ladonna and Hailey together sends it over 130 per minute. I approach cautiously, noting Hailey's smile and Ladonna's—*Essie's*—lack thereof.

"Hi, Hailey," I say as I reach the porch. "And hi, Essie. Didn't expect to see you here."

"Essie and I have known each other for a few years," Hailey says. "I was still working at the hospital when they hired her." She pats Essie's arm. "She's the first face hurting patients see when they come to the ED. Always a smile, but she also knows exactly how to triage and get people where they need to go."

My eyes meet Essie's. I know full well what she's capable of. But I'm not supposed to know her at all, so I smile and say, "That was certainly the case last night."

"I figured you'd be tucked into your bed and resting, Ms. Dora, but I see you're on your feet today," says Essie, focusing on my bag. "Busy, busy."

"It's just my wrist," I reply as it throbs. "I can do my job with a cast."

"And what is your job exactly, if you don't mind my asking?"

"She's a copy editor and fact-checker for an online news magazine," Hailey says. Her proud and hopeful expression makes my chest ache.

"News magazine?" Essie's eyes go just a bit wider. "Is that what brought you back to Bend after so many years of giving your mom the silent treatment? Because I didn't realize that Hailey's daughter named Christy was actually you last night!" Her tone is pleasant enough, but the words make me want to scream.

"Yeah," I say, staring her down. "Name changes can *really* be confusing, am I right?"

Her smirk dissolves. "And you're in town for work?"

"She's working on a story about the Oracles of Innocence anniversary," Hailey says. "Almost twenty years. Can you believe it, Essie? Were you in the area at the time?"

"Hadn't moved down from Portland yet," Essie says, shifting her weight from foot to foot. Finally on the defensive.

I tilt my head. "Nice of you to stop by, but did you want something in particular?"

"I was on my way to work, but I wanted to see how you were doing," Essie says. Her hand is in the pocket of her scrubs, fisted. "Just checking in." Her eyes narrow. "You're looking a lot more energetic than anyone expected."

"No rest for the wicked," I say.

"That's what I'm afraid of," Essie says, glancing at Hailey. "Would you mind if I spoke to Dora privately? I actually had a question about her insurance. You know how strict everyone is these days about confidentiality! I wouldn't want to get in trouble."

Hailey waves her off. "No problem at all. But don't be a stranger,

Essie. I've missed hearing your laugh. We should get together sometime soon for coffee or lunch."

"I'd love that," says Essie, waving as Hailey goes back in the house. As soon as the door shuts, Essie rounds on me, nostrils flared. "What the hell kind of stupid game are you playing?"

I take an instinctive step back, eyeing the windows and wondering if Hailey is watching. "I could ask you the same question. Any chance you've been out to visit Marie in the last month or so?"

"I haven't gone any damn place. I'm trying to live my life and do my job," she says in a low voice. "And suddenly you show up like a rat that's been hiding underground for twenty years while the rest of us faced the consequences."

"You faced consequences because of what you did, *Ladonna*," I snap. "And we both know you did a hell of a lot more than you were charged with."

"And you? I've seen reports about what they found after the fire. And now I'm wondering what exactly you had to do with that."

"Because I'm not conveniently dead?"

"No, because you *pretended* to be dead for the last two decades. And if you did nothing wrong and had nothing to hide, I wonder why that is."

"I'm not here to hurt you, Essie," I tell her. "So stop threatening me."

She blinks. "Threatening you?"

"The veiled comments in front of my colleague Miles, and now Hailey? Coming to the *house*?"

"Poor Hailey has no idea who she's dealing with, does she?"

My watch chirps to inform me of an irregular heart rhythm, and we both flinch.

Essie pulls her hand out of her pocket. Fingers fisted. Like she wants to hit me. "How can you be trying to paint *me* as the threat here?" She holds out her hand. On her palm sits a meditation stone, blue with red letters. "I found *this* on my windshield early this morning as I left work," she says.

I stare at the rock, suddenly dizzy. I can't tell if she's playing me or not. The rock that was sitting on this doorstep this morning and is now hidden in my suitcase—the stone I was so sure *she* left for me—looks almost exactly like the one in her hand. "I didn't leave that for you," I say slowly.

"Uh-huh. That's why it showed up the day after I see you again for the first time in twenty years." She steps off the porch, shaking her head. "You were always a two-faced snake, you know that?"

I move closer to the door. My good hand shakes as I reach for the knob. "You've been threatening me since the moment you recognized me. Don't come here and suddenly claim you're the victim."

"I heard a rumor," Essie says as she puts the stone back in her pocket. "Arnold Moore—he was found with one of these in his mouth."

"It's true," I tell her. "And I was up in Seattle at the time. But *you* were here. And I'm wondering if it happened on your night off."

"Why would I want to hurt him?" she asks.

"You've hurt people before, and you didn't seem to feel a stitch of remorse." I lower my voice, my gaze darting around to make sure no one's within earshot. "I know you hit Octavia with the van, and I've never believed for a second that she stepped in front of you. You might not have gone to jail for murder, *Ladonna*, but you deserve to." And with that, I open the door and head inside, where I go back to my room. The bed has been made, the area rug vacuumed, my suitcase closed with everything tucked inside. I guess the cleaning crew was here... I kneel in front of my case and rummage through it until I find the stone exactly where I hid it. I climb onto the bed and collapse. I'm sick with pain and terror, sick with memories of blood and carnage and fire. I can't tell if Essie's just a bystander in all of this or the perpetrator.

Or another target.

But if she is, then I am too. Somehow, someone found us both. And either that person has a sick sense of humor or they're the killer, and this is the warning.

I have to get out of here. I can't put Hailey and Martin at risk. I drag myself off the bed and start to pack.

I whirl around when Hailey knocks on the door. "Yeah?"

She pokes her head in. "Can we talk?"

I jolt with a memory. "I forgot to leave the key under the mat for the cleaners."

"They called me this morning. I gave them a key—I shouldn't have been just leaving it under the mat anyway. But that's not what I want to talk about."

"I'm checking into a hotel, Hailey. I...need to concentrate on my work."

"I need you to be straight with me," she says. "And we both know you don't have the best record on that front."

"I'm sorry again about the name."

"I think you know that's not what I'm talking about."

My mouth is so dry, even though the rest of me feels like it's about to melt down. "Have a seat," I say hoarsely.

She sits on the end of the bed. "Funny you'd come to town to report on the Oracles."

"It happened here, Hailey. And I didn't choose the story. Miles did."

"But you said you didn't travel for work. Yet you traveled for this. And please don't claim it was to see me and Martin. I don't think I could bear you lying about that."

I slump, realizing what a shitty person I am. "I might not have come here just to see you, but I'm glad I did. You both saved my life, and I'll always be grateful."

"Were you one of them?" she blurts out.

"What?"

"I've always wondered." Her eyes are glazed with tears.

"You never let on," I murmur.

"We cared about you," she said. "We wanted to protect you."

Maybe they shouldn't have. I've been so selfish. That rock in my suitcase, so similar to the one found in Arnie's mouth—it was left on Hailey and Martin's doorstep, not mine. Whoever did it knows I'm here.

"I need to finish packing," I whisper, moving to get up.

"You're not going anywhere," she says.

I edge off the bed. "I'm in a crap-ton of pain, and I don't need to be interrogated, okay? I'll be out of here in a bit."

Tears slip from her eyes. "Martin told me I shouldn't ask," she says quietly. "I don't mean to chase you away."

"You're not," I say wearily. "I just have so much work to do right now." I don't know if this was a real threat or if someone—like Ladonna—is just playing mind games, trying to scare me off while making me believe she's a victim too. But I can't put Hailey and Martin in danger. I can't risk losing them.

With a muffled sob, Hailey leaves the room, and I pull out my phone and make a reservation at the Doubletree. I ignore another text from Noah about meeting later this evening; at least this one includes an inquiry about how I'm feeling, but it's still annoying. And as I'm zipping the bag, my phone pings with yet another text, this one from Max.

> I'm missing some of my notes. Any chance you tucked them in your bag by mistake?

I can't deal with this right now. I put my phone away, drag my bag down the hallway, and wrestle it out the door. Once in the car, I text Hailey, thanking her for her patience and promising I'll explain when my work in Bend is done. I owe her a lot more than a shitty electronic goodbye, but it's all I can manage right now.

I drive to the hotel in a daze, check in, and gratefully accept help getting my bag to my room. I close the door and lock every lock, leaning against it and telling myself I'm safe for the moment. I have the space to think. This is going to be okay.

I trudge down to the ice machine, fill my ice bucket, and use the plastic bag that lines the bucket to create an ice pack for my wrist, holding it right where the searing pain makes it hard to think. I haven't eaten all day, so I scrounge a protein bar from my suitcase, from the box of twelve I brought with me.

My food for the week. I know I have an issue, and I know why. But right now, I just have to push forward. I text Miles. How's it going? You coming back tonight?

His response comes after a few minutes. Staying over in La Grande tonight. Meeting with sheriff in the morning. Marie's husband told me she was found with a rock in her mouth. Still waiting for the rest of the autopsy, but I was right—serial killer. I'm gonna get a Pulitzer for this.

I can barely breathe as I reply, so I have to dictate it more than once. You earned it. Then I toss my phone onto the bed.

Arnie and Marie, killed and burned, left to be found with meditation rocks in their mouths. The same kind that was left for me and Essie.

I didn't really warn her. I was so convinced she was the one who'd left it for me. As much as I don't trust her, the anger and fear in her voice when she showed me that rock seemed genuine. And if it wasn't her, she's in danger.

For a half second, I consider leaving it alone. I remember her willingness to kill in Darius's name. I remember how she backed him to the very end. And she's the one person who can out me now, the *one* person who knows for sure. Hailey and Miles just suspect, but Essie? Max's receipts have nothing on her.

But then I realize what a hypocrite I am, telling myself I've changed while not considering that maybe she has too. How her friendship with Hailey seemed sincere and how truly rattled she seemed by the rock.

I grab the phone, dial the hospital ED, and ask for Essie Green. When they tell me she's not in, I ask for a call back and tell them it's urgent. After I end the call, I take a Vicodin for the pain, brush my teeth, and slide between the sheets. My phone is charging on the nightstand, the ringer turned up to max volume. When Essie calls, I want it to wake me up. I need to warn her. And maybe talk straight with her. Maybe, just maybe, she could be an ally. We weren't always enemies. We used to be sisters.

On that strangely hopeful note, I drift into a deep, hollow sleep.

CHAPTER TWENTY-ONE

The Retreat
October 4, 2000

Parvaneh sat at Eszter's bedside, holding the now-cold bowl of soup she'd brought from the kitchen. Basir had made Eszter's favorite, split pea with ham, but Eszter had taken one look at it and turned over again.

She still held the tiny infant in her arms. Darius had told them all that she should be allowed to cradle it for as long as she needed to.

It was a girl.

Eszter had seemed in shock when Darius announced she would be placed on the altar. This time, it was Kazem who suggested a hospital, but Darius had been confident Eszter could birth the child right there, with all of them to witness the miracle. Kazem had argued that it was dangerous for Eszter, that all the blood meant something was wrong, that the baby might not live if it didn't have medical support; it was too fragile, born too soon. Eszter hadn't been able to speak for herself, had only been able to groan and cry as the pain stretched beyond her ability to bear it. But Darius had been so certain. He'd said it was all a sign—the consciousness had taken

Octavia back to the source, but it was offering them an exchange. The new baby would be a powerful symbol of how close they'd come to enlightenment, because of their commitment to the journey.

Instead, after twelve long hours and too much blood, the tiny creature had been born without life, blue and still but perfect in every other way. Ladonna had cut the cord and placed the little body on Eszter's chest.

Eszter had tried to nurse her, and Parvaneh had wanted to cry. The only thing that had stopped her was an exhaustion that had hammered at her until she'd become numb. First Octavia, now Eszter and her baby. Even Darius had seemed in shock. He'd told them to clean up the meeting hall to get it ready for the night session. Then he'd trudged to the front, gone into his office alone, and hadn't emerged.

Parvaneh needed to sleep, but she hadn't wanted to leave Eszter, who hadn't said a word since the birth. They'd spent weeks barely speaking, and that was Parvaneh's fault. She'd allowed her insecurity to suffocate the best friendship she'd ever had. Pathetic. And now her friend needed her, and she was determined not to let her down.

Eszter had lost so much blood; her skin was frighteningly, sickeningly white. *Make sure she eats*, Kazem had told Parvaneh. *She needs food and fluids, or she may die too.*

And then he'd said, very quietly, *She might die anyway. We won't know about infection for another day or two.*

Parvaneh looked Eszter over, a big slug wrapped in blankets, the body of the baby, the size and weight of a footlong bun, pressed to her chest. "Kazem said he'd be in soon to check your pad," she said to Eszter, if only to remind her that she wasn't alone. "He wants to make sure you're not bleeding too much."

"You don't need to be here," Eszter muttered. "I'm sure you need some sleep." She turned onto her back, gazing at the ceiling. The brown fuzz of the baby's hair tickling her chin.

"I'm not leaving you in here alone," Parvaneh said.

"I'm not alone. She's here too."

Parvaneh let her head hang back, taking in the same view as Eszter, the drop ceiling, the squares neat, perfect, predictable. The opposite of the last twenty-four hours. "I'm so sorry," she murmured.

"Do you think she would have lived if they'd taken me to a hospital?"

It was said flatly, blandly. But every phrase felt like a trap. "I'm not a doctor," Parvaneh said. "Kazem said it was too early."

"Premature babies survive all the time. When they're in the hospital."

This conversation was dangerous, not just for the questions but for its path. If they followed it all the way, it led straight to who they were, what they were doing. "We can't know," Parvaneh said.

"Darius used me. He used her. And that was more important to him than we were."

"Don't say that," Parvaneh pleaded. "He loves all of us."

"Did he love Octavia?"

"You know he did."

"So that's what he does to people he loves."

The nausea that had been nagging Parvaneh lately reawakened. "He didn't do it. And Ladonna said what happened with Octavia was an accident."

"You don't really believe that."

She didn't. But admitting that wouldn't help anyone, including Eszter. Did she want to end up like Octavia? Even if Eszter simply got whipped like Fabia had, it was more than Parvaneh could bear. Parvaneh reached for Eszter's hand. Cold and clammy and limp. She squeezed Eszter's fingers. "You're my best friend here," Parvaneh said. "And you always seemed so wise. You've helped me so much."

"Or maybe I hurt you."

Parvaneh shook her head. "I'd rather be here than anywhere else because we're together, and we're seeking something wonderful."

Eszter turned her head. "Is this wonderful?" she whispered, then looked down at her baby. "Do you want to hold her?"

No, Parvaneh wanted to shout. But Eszter hadn't let the baby go for hours, and this was the first indication she might be willing to. "Can I?"

Eszter carefully handed the child over: terrifyingly tiny, unspeakably perfect, closed eyes with eyelashes, the shells of her ears, the bow of her mouth. The moment Parvaneh took in all those features, she felt it, the possibility of this little person, the hope and potential, the thoughts she'd never think, the mother she'd never lay eyes on. Parvaneh had thought she was too numb to cry, but now the tears came. She grimaced trying to hold in the pain and held the child to her chest, rocking it gently. She'd have to reel it all in, convince herself that it was all for the best, all the intention of the consciousness. But she couldn't do that with Eszter's dead child in her arms.

Eszter began to hum a lullaby, singing words to a song no one had ever sung to Parvaneh, at least not that she knew. Maybe, long before memories could take root, her mother had been able to love her. Maybe she'd looked at Parvaneh the way that Parvaneh could see this child now, as a precious but fragile gift. Or maybe, as she'd told Parvaneh so many times, she'd simply been a mistake, a broken condom and way too much booze, and there had been no lullabies, only Hank Williams Jr. and Sawyer Brown on in the background while her mom entertained her latest loser, while Parvaneh scrounged what she could from the pizza boxes on the table, the chips her mother left out so she wouldn't have to cook her kids a meal.

This baby's life would have been different. Eszter would have been a wonderful mother; she was softer and sweeter than anyone Parvaneh had ever met, except for maybe Octavia. She could maybe still have kids. She could move on from this, like they all would. Parvaneh would stay by her side and help her with every step, just like Eszter had helped her at the beginning.

"Thank you," Eszter said when she finished. "Will you help me with something?"

"Anything."

"I want to bury her."

The nausea rose again, but Parvaneh swallowed it back. "Do you want to have a little more time with her while I get what we need?"

Eszter nodded, and Parvaneh rose and kissed her on the forehead. "I'll be back in a little bit." She cupped the baby's head in her palm for a moment, then left. Pulling her numbness around her like a cloak, she walked out into a breezy, sunlit world, bright and warm and wrong. She skirted the dining hall and followed the path to the barns and pastures. The round, earthy smell of manure and the deep grunts of the pigs reached her after a few minutes, and when the barns came into view, Kazem was already striding toward her. "How is she?" he asked.

"She wants to bury the baby," Parvaneh replied. "Can you give me a shovel? And maybe...I don't know, a box? It feels wrong to just put a body in the ground."

"Tadeas," he called over his shoulder. "I need the shovel." He turned back to Parvaneh. "We can wrap her in cloth, like a shroud. She'll...return to the earth more easily that way. Better than a box."

"Is that what you did with the others?" Parvaneh asked. "Octavia and Shirin and Ziba."

Kazem couldn't meet her eyes. "No." He glanced at the large pigsty next to the barn. "But for this little one, it seems right."

Tadeas came running out of the barn with a shovel. Kazem explained its purpose as Parvaneh took it from him. "Does she want us to be there?" Tadeas asked.

Parvaneh thought back to what Eszter had said, the way she'd begun to question everything. "She asked that it just be her and me." Until Eszter's mind was in the right place, she shouldn't be speaking to anyone except someone who'd protect her, who wouldn't let those doubts be known.

Tadeas nodded. "Tell her we love her, and we're here."

"Tell her to drink and eat too," said Kazem. His nostrils flared. "Or she'll be on that altar again soon."

The urge to vomit was rising again. Shovel in hand, Parvaneh ran to the shed next to the dining hall where they stored fabric Beetah used to make the robes. She cut a big square from one of the big rolls of cloth and then returned to the dorm. Eszter had combed her hair and tied a scrap of fabric torn from her robe around the baby's head, making a little bow. It was one of the saddest things Parvaneh had ever seen, but she smiled and said, "That's so nice." She gave Eszter a once-over. "Are you sure you're up for this? I could—"

"I need to be there when she goes into the ground," Eszter said. "I want her to know I was there."

Parvaneh led them out to the woods. "Should I run back and ask someone where we should—"

"Over there," Eszter said dreamily. She looked ghoulish in the sunlight, like the beams avoided her round, white face instead of caressing it with warmth. She was pointing to the base of a slender pine surrounded by golden needles. "It's a nice spot. Last summer, I liked to sit there when I had a break, just to meditate in the quiet."

"That sounds like the place." Parvaneh marched over to it and began to dig, her thoughts on the slice and whisper of the shovel through needles and earth, the stark smell of the dirt, the hole that grew bigger with each passing moment. Eszter stood next to her, humming as she gazed down at her daughter. After a few minutes, Parvaneh was panting and aching and worried she was going to throw up right into the hole she'd worked so hard to dig. Eszter was busy wrapping the baby in the cloth, still singing. She looked broken and clumsy and beautiful, all at the same time.

"Do you think that's enough?" she finally asked Eszter. The hole was about two feet wide and just as deep, and she knew it wasn't good enough for a grave, but she wasn't sure she could do much more without falling over in exhaustion.

"It's fine," Eszter whispered. She hugged her daughter to her chest one more time, which was when Parvaneh noticed the wet blotches on Eszter's chest. Milk, she realized. She leaned against the tree as the raw pain and the scent of it sunk in, as Eszter laid her baby in the ground and whispered words that Parvaneh knew she'd never forget for as long as she lived, in such contrast to her own childhood, her own mother. Eszter murmured about the adventures they could have had together, the way they would have loved each other, the secrets they could have shared. After a long moment, Eszter sat back. "Go ahead," she said, folding her arms over her damp chest.

"Kazem told me you were burying it" came a voice from behind them.

Darius was standing near a tree maybe twenty feet away. Parvaneh had no idea how long he'd been there. A shiver ran through her; he looked drawn and sad and eerily still. Fear tingled in her chest; she hadn't told him they were doing this, and she had no idea what he was thinking.

Eszter turned to him. "She's gone now," she said simply.

Darius watched them for a moment, his gaze flitting between them. Then he opened his arms wide, offering a hug. Parvaneh stepped toward him, relieved to have the comfort, but he shook his head. "Eszter needs me." He focused on her. "Come here. You've been so brave. So committed. You are a treasure to us. And to me."

Eszter looked down at the milk blotches on her chest. Then she raised her head and stared at Darius with a blank, unreadable expression.

Darius made a sorrowful, comforting sound and closed the distance between them. He pulled her against him, letting the wetness reach him. "I feel it too," he whispered. "We made her, and she would have held a beautiful soul. I feel it too."

Eszter pressed her face to his chest and sobbed. Darius dismissed Parvaneh with a jerk of his head, and so she left them there next to the open grave, shovel lying next to the pile of dirt she'd pulled from the ground. Dizzy now, unable to hold on to a single coherent thought, she trudged back to the women's dorm, one feeling finally rising above the rest.

She lurched into the bathroom and dove into a stall just in time. It felt like someone had reached inside her and clenched a fist around her stomach, squeezing until there was nothing left. When she finally got to her feet, flushed, hoping for the stars floating in front of her to fade, she heard running water in the sink beyond the stall. She emerged, feeling like a trapped animal.

Ladonna stood by a sink, holding a cup of water. She offered it to Parvaneh, who accepted it gratefully. After she'd rinsed out her mouth, she straightened and met Ladonna's piercing gaze. "You're sick?" Ladonna asked.

Parvaneh shrugged. "It's been a stressful few days."

Ladonna tilted her head. "When was the last time you had a period?"

Another shrug. "They've never been regular. A few months, I guess."

"And now you're feeling nauseated."

Parvaneh leaned on the sink. "A little?"

Ladonna walked from the room, leaving Parvaneh to refill her water glass. Ladonna came back a second later carrying a small rectangular box, which she handed to Parvaneh.

"A pregnancy test?"

"We keep some on hand." Ladonna's mouth twisted. "You didn't think you were special, did you? It was only a matter of time."

Her head buzzing, Parvaneh went back into a stall. Read the instructions on the package. Peed on the stick. Waited, snatches of worry and hope tangling in her skull like a nest of snakes. She had wondered if this might happen, had known it could; it wasn't as if Darius ever used a condom. But for some reason, she hadn't spent much time thinking about it—there had been too many other things to think about lately, so much work, so many chores, so much meditation. And as she watched the little lines form on the test wand, first one, then another, all she could think about was Eszter and her baby. The awful vulnerability, the soggy, aching sorrow.

She was going to have a child, and all she could feel was terror.

CHAPTER TWENTY-TWO

Bend, Oregon
December 13, present day

M y buzzing phone yanks me from a dream of tiny graves, small holes and huge mounds of earth next to them, row after row and a shovel in my hand. My throat is tight with grief. Blinking back tears, I check my screen. It's almost nine, and Miles is calling, which is good. I forgot what I was supposed to tell him last night.

"Hey," I say.

"Did I wake you up?"

"I don't usually sleep this late."

"You're usually out running, right? Did the doctor say when you'd be able to get at it again?"

"Hopefully soon." Maybe never again. Depressed at the thought, I sit up. "What are you up to?"

"Headed into my meeting with the sheriff. But I wanted to tell you—I heard from Noah Perry. He said you were editing a story for him? He said it's taking you a while to get to it and asked if I was willing to read it. Claims it's big. The balls on this kid, right?"

"He's persistent, I'll give him that. Honestly, I thought that child-survivor angle was unique—are you sure that's not where you want to focus?"

From the rush of background noise, I can tell he's driving. "They've formed this little club, which is great. But two of three known adult survivors have been murdered, and if I'm right, it's this ritualistic thing, you know? Driven by resentment a mile deep. I don't see how those kids would be real suspects." He makes an annoyed sound. "Honestly, I'm not sure authorities have any idea what they're dealing with here. But if I'm right, they need to find Shari Redmond and warn her, because she's next."

A chill runs down my spine. She might be next...but I seem to be on the killer's list too. And I can't tell anyone unless I want to out myself. Suddenly I feel trapped, at the bottom of one of those graves with dirt pouring down.

"You still there?" Miles asks.

"Yeah," I breathe.

"Have you tried to locate Shari Redmond?"

"No luck so far." Because she'd tell him. I know she would. Unless I can convince her not to, and maybe we could protect ourselves together. "I'll keep trying. But in the meantime, the child survivors—"

"Valentina said I need to drill down, not cast a wider net. That guy Maxwell Jennings—I finally got around to calling him. And it's the funniest thing. I spoke to him just now, and he told me he met with you in person *yesterday*."

"I meant to mention that," I babble. "He had some written records, and I wanted to vet the stuff for you first."

"You could have told me he had contemporaneous records—that's huge."

"You know, with my wrist and everything—"

"I get it," he says. "I'm just under some pressure here, and we know there are two missing bodies that could well be missing survivors, and Max told me he has records for *all* of them. Stuff he never shared with authorities. If we can convince him to make this stuff public, it's huge. I've got a videoconference with him later today."

And Max has figured out that I've got some of his records. "Are you sure he's legit, Miles? I mean, why would he have held on to this stuff for so long?"

"Dora...you literally just met with him."

"And he's a total drunk. Went through three double IPAs in about an hour, and—"

"I hit that mark a few days ago at Deschutes Brewery," he says with a laugh. "I already like this guy."

"But he'd probably been at it for a while before I even got there," I continue. "He's got a stack of old papers with a bunch of scribbles on them, and for all I know, half of it is made up. He seemed a little...I don't know. Shady."

"Like Arnie's girlfriend, Gina?"

I hear the suspicion in his voice, and it scares me to death. "Different flavor of crazy," I mutter.

"I guess I'll see for myself in a few hours. I'll check in later. Let me know if you find Shari."

He ends the call, and I sit there, gazing down at my phone. Something's different, and it's my own stupid fault. I've been careless.

I pull Max's page of notes from my bag. The page that could end me. Handwritten more than twenty years ago, lying dormant and deadly this entire time. Slowly, I tear the page into strips, separating flesh from bone, numbers from words, before names from after names, the living and the dead. Like a zombie, I shuffle over to the bathroom, still ripping the page into smaller pieces. Then I stand over the toilet and let the fragments of my past flutter into the water. I flush it, watch the ink and paper swirl, and know I've done something unforgivable.

But it's just one more unforgivable thing in a mountain of them.

Still in a trance, I take a shower, thinking about Noah. Miles has shut down the child-survivor angle, but I have my own reasons for wanting to know more. I recall those children, some more than others. One in particular. I remember what I did to him, in those final hours, in that final moment. It's something I've tried not to think about for twenty years, but now it's coming back. Maybe, out of this horrific mess, I can get a tiny serving of peace. Maybe Noah can give me answers he doesn't even realize he has. I text him and tell him I'll meet him for lunch. His response is lightning fast. Awesome! Root Down in half an hour?

After showering, popping a small handful of vitamin I, and checking my email and texts—nothing from Hailey or Martin; maybe they've finally given up on me, which is exactly what I deserve—I drive to the café to meet Noah.

To my surprise, he's not alone. As I slowly get out of my car, he and Arman are standing in the parking lot, waiting for me.

"Hey," says Noah. "Did you read my story yet?"

"Sorry. I've been superbusy."

A flash of anger crosses his face and is gone so quickly that I almost wonder if I imagined it. He smiles. Glances at Arman. "I guess you'll get to it when you get to it. But I'm serious, it's big. Anyway, I'm starving. How about you?"

"I could eat," I say cautiously, giving Arman a questioning look.

He gives me a baby-faced smile. "I asked Noah if I could tag along."

Noah leads us inside, snags us a table, and flirts with the young woman behind the counter while Arman and I peruse the menu. I order a chickpea salad, and Noah orders a bulgogi tofu sandwich. Arman orders the tofu yakisoba. The young woman, beaming at Noah, gives us our order number, and we sit down to wait. "Arman's actually the reason I'm in Bend," Noah says. "One guess why."

Arman blushes. I peer at him, realizing once again there is something strangely familiar in the shape of his eyes, the narrow bridge of his nose. My heart lurches. "On my god," I whisper. "Are you...?"

"A child of Darius," Noah says, even as Arman opens his mouth to answer for himself. He lowers his voice as the young woman sets our food in front of us; this time, Noah is oblivious to her charms. "Arman's my contact for the group."

Which one is he? Which one? I focus on Arman. "How long have you known?"

Arman glances at Noah, who nods. As if giving permission. "My mother told me when I was twelve maybe?"

"Whoa," I say, still looking at him greedily, still trying to imagine which tiny kid he might have been. "That's young to discover that kind of heritage."

His smooth forehead puckers as his brows draw together. "It just came up one day, and I guess I asked the right questions. She adopted me when I was about two."

"Do you have any idea who your birth mother was?" My brain is churning as I try to place him. Could he be Kyra's baby? Or maybe Roya's? The longer I look at him, the more familiar he seems.

He shakes his head, focusing on his noodles.

I poke at my chickpea salad. "How did you find the Children of Darius group?" I ask.

Noah is practically bouncing in his seat. "Oh, he didn't find the group. He *created* it."

Arman nods, looking shy but gratified. "It was a few years ago. For a while, I was all alone," he says. "I felt like a loser."

My heart goes out to him. "How did you find others?"

He fidgets with his napkin, tearing off a strip. "Just on some genealogy sites. Not an advertisement, but I put out a notification for anyone who might be part of my extended genetic family."

"Which sites?" I ask. "I didn't know you could do something like that."

"I mentioned one in my story," Noah says. He's polished off his sandwich and still looks hungry. Then again, he always looks a little like that.

"Do any of the other children of Darius live in Bend?" I ask.

Arman shakes his head. "They're all over now."

Memories of those babies and toddlers are rushing back, their chubby cheeks and soft hair, their shrieks of delight when Basir would blow soap bubbles for them outside the dining hall on summer days. "They're all grown up," I murmur.

"We're still trying to get them all together, maybe next month," Noah says.

"How did you two meet?" I ask. Because it suddenly occurs to me that they've never said. Their relationship seems more than journalist-source. Noah's clearly the boss, and Arman seems like the puppy dog, tagging along. "You're said you're not in school together."

"We met as I was researching the story," Noah says. "He's on the custodial crew over at Mount Bachelor. A local, born and raised. You too, right, Dora? Miles said something about you staying with your folks."

"I'm at a hotel," I say. "It's actually really close to this place. You picked the perfect spot."

"Bend's not very big," says Arman.

"It's amazing how such a small place can be home to such a grisly history, right?" Noah's eyes meet mine, bright blue and intense. "And I'm constantly finding new angles to this story, like this anniversary. It's drawing people out of the woodwork, you know?" He looks over at Arman. "Wouldn't you say? I mean, this is *your* past."

Arman smiles. "You're right," he says, turning to me. "Would you like to come with us to get ice cream?" He glances at my cast. "We can all drive together."

"Great idea," says Noah, slapping Arman on the back. "We can take this conversation on the road. A moveable feast. Where's the best place in town to get the creamy goodness?"

"Lots of good places," says Arman, ripping another strip from his napkin. His meal is only half-eaten, but he's still done better than I have.

"Yeah, but which is your favorite?" Noah asks.

"I don't know," says Arman. "I don't really have one. Excuse me. I have to go to the bathroom." He gets up and heads for the unisex at the back.

"Alone at last," says Noah. "Any idea when you'll get to the new story?"

I force down a bite of my chickpea salad. It tastes okay; I'm just not hungry, even though I know I need to eat. "This afternoon, I promise," I say. "It's been a lot." I lift my casted arm.

Noah looks a little crestfallen. "I thought you might *really* want to read it." Another piercing gaze. "Or that Miles might if you didn't."

"I know it feels really urgent," I tell him. "But if it's as good as you think, it's going to be big no matter when we read it. This anniversary isn't the deadline, Noah. Good material is timeless.

"I really should go," I add. Essie might be at the hospital by now, assuming she's working today.

"You don't want to get ice cream with us?"

"I have to get back to work," I tell him. "Maybe even squeeze in a few minutes to read your story. I'll get back to you soon, okay?"

My phone pings. It's Miles, and the message turns me as cold as the open graves from my nightmare.

> I found Shari—actually, she found me. She's in Bend, and she's willing to talk! I'll have a new interview for you to fact-check tomorrow night!

CHAPTER TWENTY-THREE

The Retreat
November 17, 2000

Parvaneh pulled herself to her feet when she heard the pop of tires on the gravel outside. The children's dorm was chilly despite the space heater in the corner, but the kids didn't seem to notice, most of them toddling around in the playroom, full of pillows made from the same material as their robes and wooden toys Tadeas had made over the last year. A few other Oracles sat on the floor, cuddling or nursing the babies, playing with the children. Parvaneh had taken to coming in here between her duties to play. She was going to be a mother after all. She hoped she wouldn't be awful at it.

Xerxes scowled up at her, surrounded by an assortment of blocks. "I'm not done playing with you!"

"I heard something." She went to the window, and her skin rippled with goose bumps. A police cruiser had parked in the clearing, and a cop was getting out.

Xerxes stood on his tiptoes and held on to the sill to pull himself high enough to peek. "That car is painted all over," he said. "Who are they?" He sounded awed. And very curious, as usual. He'd coped with Octavia's disappearance from his life through fits of screaming and crying and being more bossy than usual. He'd seemed to blame Darius and refused to speak in his presence, the only time he kept silent for more than a few seconds apart from when he slept.

"It's a police car. Those are police. They make sure people obey the laws."

"What are laws?"

"They're like rules. And there are a lot of them."

"Oh. Like how we have to close our eyes when we talk to the deep consciousness."

"Sort of." Parvaneh watched Basir come out of the dining hall, saw the cop eyeing his long robe and the smears of blood on the apron he always wore. He was obviously asking what the cop wanted, but whatever it was caused Basir to head straight to the meeting hall. "Laws are like big rules. Like, you're not supposed to kill...anyone." Her voice faded as she thought about Shirin. Ziba. Octavia. Eszter's tiny baby. "You're not supposed to take things that don't belong to you. Stuff like that. If you break those laws, they could put you in jail."

"What's that?"

"They lock you in a room and don't let you out."

He frowned. "Fabia does that to me when I make her mad."

"What did you say to make her mad?"

"I told her Mommy was going to come take me away and Fabia couldn't come with us."

Parvaneh stroked the top of his head. "You miss your mom."

He directed his attention out the window. "Are they going to take Darius to jail?"

Parvaneh turned to see Darius stride out of the meeting hall with Eszter at his side—where she'd been glued for *weeks*. At first,

Parvaneh had tried to be glad; Darius had brought her back from the edge, calmed her down. He'd put a smile back on her face after she'd looked like she wanted to dive into the grave with her little girl. Out of everybody on this compound, apart from Darius himself, Eszter was the person Parvaneh cared about the most. The one person she'd be willing to step aside for when it came to Darius. But at this point, did Eszter really need all that? He hadn't wanted to have any special meditation sessions with Parvaneh in weeks. It made her wonder if he'd just been trying to get her pregnant, and now that she was, he was done with her. It took every bit of strength and commitment she had every day to push that resentment away, but it was a persistent creature, and it kept coming back.

And coming back.

Darius and Eszter stopped several feet from the cop. She looked up at Darius adoringly while he spoke to the officer. "I don't think Darius is going anywhere," Parvaneh said.

"But he pushed Mommy. He made her cry."

Parvaneh's throat felt way too tight. "He didn't want to hurt her." She hoped.

"I think the police should take him to jail."

"You shouldn't hope that. And you shouldn't say that."

"I can say anything I want. I remember the bad word. Do you want me to say it?"

"No." The cop was gesturing at the dorms, and Darius shook his head. After a few more seconds, the cop got back into the cruiser and pulled away. The tension Parvaneh had been holding inside drained away as soon as the car was out of sight. "See? It's fine. I have to go."

"No," Xerxes shouted. He launched himself at Parvaneh, his head colliding with her belly and his hands grabbing at her sides.

Instinctively, she shoved him away, flashes of memory flickering, the way he'd kicked at Eszter's belly. Xerxes staggered, hit his head on the windowsill, and began to cry.

"Oh, honey, I'm sorry," Parvaneh said, dropping to her knees and reaching for him, but he shrank from her touch.

"You're mean too," he screamed, slapping at her face. Red-faced, he collapsed on the floor, clutching at his head and wailing.

Ladonna came around the corner and saw them there. "What on earth is going on in here?"

"I need to get to the kitchen," Parvaneh said. Half of her wanted to stay, to bring Xerxes around, and half of her wanted to scream in his face. She knew he'd been through things he couldn't understand. But she'd also seen him lash out at Eszter, and she knew he didn't always care who he hurt. Just now, he'd crashed into her belly like he *wanted* to hurt her. So she left him with Ladonna and headed out to help Basir make dinner. They'd gone through all their pigs in the last few months, so it had been mostly potatoes and other root vegetables lately. Bread and soup. Night and day. After so many nights and days filled with dead meat, it had almost been a relief.

Her hands hurt, and she was nursing a cut from the potato peeler by the time she sat at her assigned table for the meal. Tadeas, Zana, and Kazem were already starting on their soup, and they greeted her with quick nods between bites. Most meals were eaten in silence these days, and it set her teeth on edge. She missed the easy conversation of months past, the gentle teasing, the bursts of carefree laughter as they passed the food. Even the children had grown more subdued as the days grew crisp and dreary; maybe they could sense the weight of fear and uncertainty the adults carried on their shoulders. And Parvaneh's body wasn't helping her mood much—lately her hunger had become vicious, turning her desperate and cranky as nausea nibbled at her edges. Because she was pregnant, she was given an extra portion of bread for every meal, but it never seemed like enough.

Tonight, though, it wasn't just silent. The tension in the room was a scent, metallic and sharp. People flinched at the scrape of spoons against bowls, the slam of the door after each Oracle entered for their dinner. By their anxious glances and stiff postures, she could tell nearly everyone had noticed or heard about the cop by now. She wondered how many of them knew what he'd wanted and if they would tell her if she asked.

She was halfway through her potato soup when Darius entered the dining room from the kitchen. The sight of him was a held breath, more painful as the seconds passed. He stood there and let his eyes rest on each table, on each Oracle in turn, all of them staring back, questions hanging in the air. When his unreadable gaze touched hers, icy prickles bloomed in her chest.

After a moment, he came over to their table. Eszter was at his side and holding a tray containing four cups of milk. She looked placid and blank and secure, but slight tremors from her hands sent little ripples through the liquid in the plastic cups. His movements clipped, Darius placed the cups in front of the four of them, each one hitting the table with a sharp *click*. Then he raised his arms to draw everyone's attention, which was unnecessary. Every pair of eyes in the room was riveted to him already. "The consciousness has given me a message," he said, more loudly than necessary given the hush in the air. "Our time of testing has begun, and all of us will need to prove our commitment to this journey." He gestured at the milk.

Nobody moved. Parvaneh met the gaze of each of her tablemates.

Kazem's gaze was veiled, his face unreadable as usual. Tadeas and Zana looked nervous.

"Drink!" Darius barked, making Parvaneh twitch in her seat. He softened his tone, but it still held the sting of impatience. "Go ahead." Then he shook his head, looking sad. "I'm starting to see why the consciousness is so far out of our reach."

Tadeas cursed softly and drank the milk in three big gulps before slapping his cup back on the table. Zana's hand was shaking as she reached for hers. Kazem downed his like a shot of whiskey. And Parvaneh knew she had no choice. She didn't know what was going on, and she couldn't allow herself to think about it—there was a faint sheen of sweat on Darius's brow. His jaw ticked with tension. He needed commitment in this moment, not defiance or questions. The milk was heavy and smooth on her tongue, faintly sweet, and she swallowed quickly.

Darius closed his eyes and drew in a deep breath, steeped in relief. He looked pleased. Parvaneh's heart soared as his lips parted to speak.

"You have all just ingested a fatal poison, and you will be dead in about thirty minutes."

Surprised gasps hissed through the room. Parvaneh blinked, uncertain she'd heard him right. Across from her, the color drained from Kazem's face. But Eszter still stood at Darius's side as if he'd just announced they were going to have a picnic. "Everyone, please finish your meal quickly and go to the meeting hall," Darius instructed, his tone brisk. "These four will be our channelers for tonight." He put his arm around Eszter and steered her away from the table while Kazem, Tadeas, Zana, and Parvaneh sat in a gutted silence.

The other Oracles didn't meet their eyes as they filed out of the dining hall, but hands trembled and whispered questions carried. This was real, Parvaneh realized. This was happening. When they were mostly alone, Kazem chuckled as he met Zana's gaze. "I never thought this was how it would go."

Zana burst into tears. Tadeas put his arm around her and whispered, "Think about where you're going. No more pain. No more struggle."

Parvaneh stared at him, baffled. Everything he was saying proved his commitment, but she felt none of it. No peace, no eagerness.

All she felt was rage. Nestled in her belly, the baby moved. She put her hands on her barely rounded abdomen as chills rolled through her. It was a girl—she knew it somehow, knew it to her bones. A girl like Eszter's, perfect like Eszter's had been. And now Darius had killed her too.

With a clenched jaw, she rose. "What's the point?" she asked. "Is there *any* point?"

"He's helping us find enlightenment and become one with the consciousness," said Tadeas, rising and helping Zana, who was still sniffling, get to her feet.

"I'm *pregnant*," said Parvaneh. "He kills me, he kills my baby."

"It's not a baby yet," said Zana, swiping tears off her face with the sleeve of her robe. "The consciousness hasn't delivered its soul. Maybe you'll meet it tonight."

Parvaneh's lip curled. She'd said things like this before. It was supposed to make sense. Except suddenly it didn't. Something vital had been ripped from her. She reached into her pocket and wrapped her fingers around her meditation stone, needing something to steady her. Her heart was beating like the blades of a ceiling fan, racing but taking her nowhere. Was that the poison working in her body?

Would the baby feel it? Would it hurt her as it did its damage? She squeezed the rock even harder, until it felt like her bones would poke from her skin. The baby kicked again, a flutter deep inside.

Her ears ringing, her lips growing numb, she followed Kazem, Tadeas, and Zana out of the dining hall. She peered up at the sky; this was the last time she'd ever see it. She looked down at the ground to keep from crying. As they entered the meeting hall, no one spoke. Darius awaited them at the front, but instead of directing them to the altar, he had arranged four chairs in a square, facing inward. "Sit."

Parvaneh chose a seat that allowed her to keep her back to everyone. She would never make it to the retreat he was building for his most committed. Of the forty Oracles, he'd chosen her to die. Had he chosen to kill their child—and her—as a punishment for her doubt, her questioning?

Or maybe she'd done this to herself—and her baby.

Parvaneh raised her head. Instead of calling the others to put their hands on them, to begin to meditate and channel, Darius simply watched them. Waiting. Fury burned in her chest. It was a new feeling, at least when it came to him. It felt wrong, like a crime.

Kazem cleared his throat and winced. "I think I feel it," he whispered hoarsely, rubbing at his neck.

"I do too." Tadeas's face had turned ruddy, and his eyes were glassy.

Zana began to sob again.

"Zana, why are you crying?" Darius asked. "You should be overjoyed. The consciousness chose you. It's reaching for you now."

Zana covered her face and pitched forward, almost sliding from her folding chair. Kazem caught her, held her in place, his arms around her and his voice a low murmur, promising peace and wonder and joy forever if they could only get through this moment.

Parvaneh could tell from his tone that he was trying to convince himself too.

Darius turned his attention to Parvaneh. "You're not scared, are you?"

"No." She was a ball of anger, wrapped in a gauzy mist of disbelief. If she thought about what was happening to her baby, she wouldn't be able to stay calm. "I'm not scared at all."

Darius grinned. "And do you feel the poison working like the others do?"

Her heart continued to pound, but as she searched her senses for some other indication of her rapidly approaching death by poison... she felt nothing. She shook her head.

He didn't stop smiling. "Everyone, come lay hands on them. These precious Oracles, chosen for this sacrifice. Hurry. We only have fifteen minutes to reach for the consciousness before it claims them."

Everyone gathered around. Hands rested on Parvaneh's shoulders and arms. When she felt a hand on her belly, she flinched. But it was Eszter, kneeling at her side. "Don't be afraid," she said quietly.

Parvaneh felt the sudden urge to pull Eszter's hair. *She* didn't have anything to be afraid of; she'd become Darius's favorite. She probably knew all the secrets Parvaneh had thought lay only between her and the man who had changed her world. And now he was sending her away *forever*. She gritted her teeth as hands squeezed and rubbed and patted, as voices murmured all around, as she waited for the dying to begin.

Except it didn't. After several long minutes, Darius said, "Everyone, step away from them."

Parvaneh opened her eyes to see Kazem, Zana, and Tadeas still breathing, still living. And Darius grinning. "You have proven your loyalty and commitment," he said to them. "You passed one of the tests the consciousness set before you." He began to clap, and after a few stunned seconds, the other Oracles joined him.

Relief and confusion crashed over Parvaneh, one then another, over and over. Tadeas began to laugh, big and braying, his shoulders shaking and feet stomping. After a few minutes, Kazem joined him, tears sparkling in his eyes, his hand reaching for Zana's. Zana still looked shaken, but then Darius grabbed her and spun her around, yanking her away from Kazem's side before pulling her into a bear hug and kissing her on the forehead, stamping her with his pride. Everyone was laughing and cheering now, all able to breathe again, the air sweeter because of what they'd all experienced together. Parvaneh floated through the rest of the night in the haze of it, as Darius offered himself to his Oracles, as they laid hands on him and meditated well into the night. It almost felt like it used to. At the end of it, Darius told them they had all done well, and he disappeared into his office alone.

Parvaneh walked back to the women's dorm with the others, and she smiled when Ladonna offered her and Zana thick slices of bread and butter Basir had sent over from the kitchen. She ate it slowly, savoring every bite. Then she went outside to look at stars she never thought she'd see again. They winked, flinty and far, in a darkness as deep as the consciousness.

"Are you coming to bed?" It was Eszter. She had a blanket folded over her arm.

"Are you joining Darius tonight?" She knew she sounded peevish—and that she shouldn't. But she had no energy left to push everything down.

Eszter took the blanket off her arm and wrapped it over Parvaneh's shoulders. "You handled that *really* well. Darius was so proud of you."

Parvaneh stayed quiet. In months past, she might have told Eszter exactly what she was thinking and feeling, confided all her fears. But of all the Oracles, Eszter, who'd been sewn to Darius's side for weeks, was *not* the person to confess her doubts to. Not anymore. "Why were the police here?"

Eszter bit her lip. Glanced toward the meeting hall. "A welfare check. I guess Ziba's children called them. They wanted to know if she was okay. Still alive."

Parvaneh turned to Eszter, the blanket pulled tight around her body. "What did he tell them?"

"That she left the compound of her own accord."

"I guess that's sort of true." But it didn't ease her mind. "Did the cop believe him?"

"He said he might get a search warrant if Ziba doesn't turn up."

"Was Darius upset?"

Eszter looked out at the meeting hall. "He says we're being tested. We have to prove ourselves worthy."

"Well, I guess I did. And tomorrow, I bet I have to prove myself worthy again."

Eszter's smile was ghostly. "You could leave," she murmured. "Tomorrow, when we're cleaning in town."

Maybe she should. Maybe it was the only way to save herself—and her child. But...where could she go? She had no education, no skills, no job. No car, no license. No money, no accounts, no insurance. No name, no family. No community, not if she left the Oracles. Parvaneh turned to Eszter. In the faint glow from the dorm's windows, the shadows were not kind to her round, heavy face. "Why would you even suggest that?" It felt like a trick, just like the poisoned milk. Or...a test. "Are you trying to get me to leave?"

Eszter's face was unreadable. "Only if you want to."

"I'm fully committed."

Eszter nodded. "I guess we all are." She turned and went back inside, leaving the stars to Parvaneh.

CHAPTER TWENTY-FOUR

Bend, Oregon
December 13, present day

After reading Miles's text a few more times, I call the hospital. I need to warn Essie, but I also need to get myself on the same page with her. It's not too late to get this thing back on the rails. I know she works in the evening and it's only early afternoon, but I have to take the chance. She knows I work at the *Hatchet*. And she'd already met Miles, for god's sake, even if he doesn't realize it. She called him "Mr. Connover," so he'd given her his name, made himself easy to find. I'm such a fool. I could have made her my ally, and instead I've pushed her toward the enemy. And not for the first time.

Essie's not at work. I do my best to weasel contact information out of the attendant who is, but she just tells me she'll give Essie a message.

Then I text Miles, choosing every word carefully.

> If you give me Shari Redmond's contact info, I'll be all set to fact-check tomorrow. Streamlining so you can get it to Valentina ASAP.

Laptop on my thighs, aggravated as hell at the stiff, itchy cast on my left arm, I edit one of Kieran's stories and wait for the ping of Miles's response. The pain is slightly better today, but it makes me feel vulnerable. Not as vulnerable as this, though: I can't figure out how the person who left the meditation stone on Hailey and Martin's doorstep found me. Who would even know who I am besides Essie? Did she tell someone? Did Hailey voice her suspicions to one of her friends in town?

For a moment, I consider Max, a.k.a. Gil. He thought we'd met before. Did he make the connection? But the rocks were left for me and Essie *before* I met him. Michelle Bathhouse has a motive, as do other family members of people killed in that fire. Could one of them have tracked me down before I even remembered they existed?

Then there's Arman and Noah. Arman is just a kid, though, and Noah seems totally in charge. Does he have some game going that I haven't yet figured out? I open my laptop and Google Noah Perry. Not much apart from his bylines at the *Quest*. I sign into my fake Facebook account and try to find him there, even as I wonder if people his age are even on Facebook anymore.

They might be, but he's not. So I look on Twitter and then Instagram, and there he is. A few hundred followers. Posts dating back to 2017. He's a bit of an adventurer. There are pics of him in Patagonia and Nepal. Pics of him in NYC with a pretty young woman with long, shiny, brown hair. It turns out those light roots I saw are blond, and he's just dyed it in the last few months. His profile is the Robert Frost quote: *Two roads diverged in a wood and I—I took the one less traveled by, and that has made all the difference.* After that, it just says: *Fully. Committed.*

I shiver. To me, that phrase means something very specific.

On the one hand, Noah seems like a normal young guy. Attractive, outgoing, from a wealthy enough family that he's been able to travel all over the world.

On the other, he makes me nervous. He's too eager. Does he know about the meditation stones? Would Arman have told him?

How could Arman have known, though? He was barely a toddler when the Retreat burned. His mustache is still peach fuzz. There's no way he'd remember details about life on the compound.

I go to Google Arman, but I realize I don't know his last name. I dictate a note into my phone to find out. Next, I search for Children of Darius. Nothing relevant to the Oracles in the results. That doesn't mean it's not somewhere on the dark web or in some shadowed corner I can't find. But it does make me wonder if Noah isn't being honest. It doesn't make him a killer, though. Why would a kid his age, obviously from a rich family, stalk and murder a bunch of cult survivors? Just for the thrill? It doesn't make sense.

My phone buzzes. It's Miles. Still buzzing with a jumble of questions, I answer. "Hey. What's up?"

"I'm driving back," he says. "Should be there around ten."

"Do you have Es—Shari's number?" I squeeze my eyes shut, hoping he doesn't notice my mistake.

"Her name's Essie Green," he says. "I'll get you the info when I'm not driving. Did you know you've already met her?"

"I did?"

"At the hospital. Lady who was collecting your insurance info."

"You're kidding. Really?"

"Mm-hmm. Before she found me, I had contacted her mother in Portland. Michelle Bathhouse had given me her info. Bernice Redmond didn't want to give me any information about her daughter; I guess they've had a falling out, but she also said Shari wanted to start her life over and Bernice wasn't going to get in the way of that. But nineteen years ago, Bernice got custody of a little boy who was on the compound the night of the fire. He's Shari's son, but Bernice raised him while Shari was in prison. His name is Jamal Redmond, and he's a junior at Oregon State."

His tone is strange. Flat and sharp. It's making my heart rate spike. "And?"

"He said he'd been looking for his half siblings for years. Even put his genetic info on all the sites to put himself out there. And guess what."

"What?"

"Nada. Nothing."

"As in, he hasn't been contacted?"

"Exactly, Dora, but isn't this how the Children of Darius supposedly finds people?"

I reach for the glass of water by the nightstand, suddenly parched. Wondering if Noah Perry has constructed a massive prank and the joke's on all of us.

"I should have dug into this before pushing the story on you." I can't believe I let this stupid story distract me. I tell Miles about the results of my internet scavenger hunt. "At this point," I conclude, "I'm wondering if Noah just found this kid Arman and paid him to go along." Arman, who Noah tells me was born and raised in Bend, couldn't even give Noah the name of *one* place to get ice cream in town. And Noah kept speaking for him. Covering for him. I probably just fooled myself into thinking he looked familiar.

"You don't think he's the one doing all of this, do you?" I ask.

"Not really," he says. "But I do think you should be careful. He seems like the kind of guy who doesn't realize who he's stepping on as he goes for the prize. Anyway, I'll be back tonight, and we need to talk this through. I'm about to call Ben Ransom and suggest that he do some extra patrols in Essie's neighborhood. I already told her about Marie—I wasn't going to let someone get killed just so I could get a story."

"Because you've confirmed that Marie Heckender was murdered the same way Arnold Moore was," I guess.

"Like I said, we'll have a sit-down when I get back. Gotta go make some calls. Talk to you soon." And he's gone.

But his mention of Essie Green's neighborhood gives me an idea, one I can't believe I didn't think of before. It takes me only a few minutes of online digging to come up with the Bend address for Essie Green. Car key in hand, I head out. A cold rain has begun to fall, chilling me from head to foot as I cross the parking lot. It's late afternoon, but the light has faded quickly, any scraps of sun swallowed by thick thunderheads. I program Essie's address into my GPS and hit the road, cursing at the awkwardness of my left arm.

Essie lives in southeast Bend, just off Wilson Avenue, in a neighborhood of little ranch homes, scrubby lawns, and abundant trailers and old pickups in the driveways. I turn onto her road and slow to a crawl. I'm trying to make out the number on a rusty mailbox when flashing police lights fill my rearview mirror.

I pull over immediately, my heart rate approaching 150. With a shaking hand, I dig through my glove compartment for the registration and proof of insurance. By the time I come up with it, there's a cop at my window. I roll it down. "Hi, Officer." His name tag says Montenaro. I can't make out his face because he's shining a flashlight into mine.

"License and registration," he says.

I hand everything over. "Can I ask why you stopped me?"

He peers at my documents. "Dora Rodriguez," he says. "From Seattle."

"I'm down here for work," I babble. "My folks live here."

"We've been warned of some suspicious activity in this area, Ms. Rodriguez." He looks my car over. "One of the homeowners reported seeing an old blue Corolla like this one cruising the streets slowly. Your family lives in this neighborhood?"

I shake my head and grasp the steering wheel with my left hand, making sure the cast is visible. "They live in the Old Mill District," I tell him. "I've actually never been in this neighborhood before. I'm just here..." My voice trails off as everything slides into place like the tumblers on a lock. Suspicious activity in the area. Him noting my out-of-state status and probably my plates. Miles telling me only an hour ago that he was about to call the police chief and ask them to do more patrols. I'm making myself look guilty as hell. At this point, if Essie knew I was here, she'd probably tell them all about me. I swallow hard and grin. "Honestly? I got turned around in the dark and the rain. I haven't been to Bend in a while, and it's changed a lot!"

He glances toward the passenger seat, where my phone screen has gone mercifully dark. A moment ago, Google Maps would have betrayed me. "You need some directions?"

"Yes! I'm headed to Root Down? I don't even think it was here when I last visited!"

He gives me cursory directions to the café before telling me I'm free to go. Shaken to the core, I slowly drive away, knowing there's no way I'll even get close to Essie this evening. And I don't think I can go back to the hospital again; it would raise too much suspicion.

By the time I pull into the hotel parking lot, I've got a text from

Hailey. Half expecting it to be about my ill-timed visit to Essie's neighborhood, I read it immediately.

> Got a call from Gina today. Complaining about a reporter named Dora from the Hatchet. Says she's going to contact the management because you stole her information.

I *so* do not need this. I didn't steal anything, I dictate. She wanted to tell me all about little green men, and it wasn't usable information.

> She said she gave you names of cult members who were never accounted for and might still be alive. She thinks one of them killed Arnie. Is there something you want to tell me?

I want to scream. Are you suggesting that I'm a murderer? I am, but that's not the point.

> No, Christy. But I do think you're a liar.

Her words hit me like a blow to the chest. It doesn't matter that she's right. She was one of the only people in the world who really seemed to care about me. Now I've ruined it. Because that's what I do, I guess. Telling myself it was the only way to be safe, when really it just left me isolated. The rain washes tears off my face as I trudge through the downpour back to my room. I strip off my wet clothes, take a Vicodin, and fall onto the bed, exhausted and aching.

When the phone rips me from sleep, I register the time, 6:07

a.m., a second before I answer. It's Valentina. "Dora," she says when I answer. "Where are you?"

"At my hotel," I say blearily, shaking myself out of the opioid haze. "What's wrong?"

"It's Miles," she says. "He's been in an accident."

"Oh my god," I whisper. "Is he okay?"

"No," she says. "He's at the hospital in Bend. They called me from his phone. I've got to break a story before we get scooped, so I can't get down there until tonight. I was hoping—"

I'm already on my feet. "I'll go right now."

CHAPTER TWENTY-FIVE

Bend, Oregon
December 14, 2000

Parvaneh climbed into the van and leaned back against the seat. The air smelled of bleach as Eszter slid the door shut. She clumsily fell onto the seat next to Parvaneh and clutched at her belly, looking stricken. Parvaneh raised her head. "Are you okay?"

"Oh," she said in a squeaky voice. "I just felt a...pang."

Ladonna glanced back from the driver's seat. "As in, you might be pregnant again?"

Eszter shot Parvaneh an anxious look and shook her head. "As in, I might need the bathroom soon." She continued to hold on to her belly as she fastened her seat belt with her other hand.

Ladonna snorted. "I'll get us on the road as soon as Fabia gets our stuff loaded."

The rear doors of the van slammed, and a moment later, Fabia got into the front passenger seat. She rubbed her hands together. "I hate winter. My hands are like hamburger."

Parvaneh shuddered and gazed out the window as they rolled through the parking lot, taking in the stares of a few locals, the bright colors of their coats and hats, the strange, superficial film of ordinary that clung to all of it, the cars, the shopping carts, the grocery bags brimming with cartons of orange juice and cans of Diet Coke and bags of Lay's potato chips and round heads of lettuce. She watched a mother taking her child out of a car seat and cooing to it as she strapped the kid into a cart. It all seemed unreal. Like scenes from a movie.

She ran her hand over the swell of her belly. She'd lain awake so many nights recently, wondering if she needed to rejoin that world for the sake of her daughter. Fearing that if she didn't, it wouldn't only be her on that altar someday—these days it felt like anything could happen at any moment. She was supposed to think of the little one inside her as a shell, a body waiting for a soul, but that was harder each time she felt a kick. Somehow, it only made things outside of her body more confusing.

"Did you hear what Kazem was saying this morning at breakfast?" she said to no one in particular. "The cow we sacrificed last week?" They'd had to meditate over it in the freezing barn while it bled out, and afterward, Parvaneh had thrown up behind a tree. "He didn't have enough refrigerator and freezer space to save all the meat. Some of it went bad."

"The hogs are having litters of piglets, though," said Fabia. "He said that too." She cast a narrow-eyed glance at Parvaneh. "You doubt Darius's decisions?"

Parvaneh clenched her jaw and shook her head. "It was just a statement of fact," she said when she could speak without screaming.

"But your tone," said Eszter. "Your tone is so hostile."

Parvaneh's entire body flushed with a poisonous heat. Eszter had been saying things like this for the past two weeks, commenting every single time Parvaneh didn't look appropriately serene and content. Like she wanted to get Parvaneh in trouble.

Her hand froze over her abdomen as the baby kicked. Eszter was watching, and suddenly it all made sense. She was jealous. She'd lost her baby.

Fabia, too, was greedily eyeing Parvaneh's swollen belly. "You'll be off cleaning duty soon," she said.

"I worked it until the very end," Eszter said.

"Yeah, but your baby came before it should have," said Ladonna. "I shouldn't have sent you to run after that boy."

"It wasn't your fault," Eszter said quickly. "It all happened according to the will of the consciousness. Just like everything that's happening now. I'm moving forward." Her eyes had gone unfocused, peering through the windshield at the road ahead, the van carrying them closer to the compound, their secluded society of blood and death.

That was what it had become. After Octavia, after Eszter's tragedy, after the visit from the cops and the looming threat of a search warrant, Darius had shown flashes of joy and confidence, but he hadn't been the same. He was worried. Looking for something to save them all as the new millennium began. Parvaneh just wanted things to go back to the way they'd been in the spring and summer, when everyone was happy, when Darius had thought she was special, when he'd whispered wonderful secrets into her ear, when she'd known she belonged, finally. But it seemed like he'd turned to Eszter for comfort—and as much as Parvaneh didn't want to blame someone who had lost so much, it seemed like Eszter had only made things worse. What killed Parvaneh was that she had been in Eszter's position only a few short months ago. Things had been peaceful, then. Better. With one terrible event, though, Eszter had replaced her. Everything had changed.

Now, as the days grew shorter and the nights had turned frigid, the current on the air crackled with danger. One word out of line, and you could be whipped until you bled to help you back to the path. It had happened to Parvaneh last week, after Eszter had expressed concern about Parvaneh's commitment in front of Darius, simply because she'd been caught playing with Xerxes near the barns and had been late to help Basir with dinner. For some reason, Eszter had been snooping around in the woods, spying, and had seen them there and tattled. And because Eszter had so much influence with Darius now, so much *power*, it seemed, her tattling had instant and painful results.

Darius had made Xerxes watch while everyone whipped Parvaneh, while she buried her face against her arm and clamped her hand over her mouth to keep from screaming. He'd wanted to teach the boy a lesson: when even one of them strayed, they all suffered. Xerxes had cried until he was exhausted, and he had refused to even look at Parvaneh ever since. Because of Eszter. Or because Parvaneh really had strayed.

The battle between resentment and obedience, between running away and staying put, between defending herself and staying faithful to everyone and everything she'd been working toward, was constant. And crushing. What had once seemed the only safe place in the world was now a minefield, and as Ladonna turned onto the gravel road that would take them the last few miles to the compound, dread rose inside Parvaneh's throat, threatening to choke her.

She had to leave. Had to get out. She just didn't know how.

Fabia yawned and rubbed at her face. "I wonder what will happen tonight."

"It was amazing, wasn't it? Last night?" Ladonna sighed. "I really thought I was dying, and I swear I saw the consciousness, like this big, old golden hand, all warm light."

Darius had passed out milk again at dinner last night, to all of them this time. He'd said that a few cups were what he'd taken to calling "vehicles," ready to carry the drinker to the shores of the deep consciousness. They were to drink and wait. To have faith—and to hope that the consciousness had chosen them for the journey. Half an hour later, a few of them, Fabia and Ladonna included, had slumped in their seats. Parvaneh had thought they were really dying. All of them had. They'd carried the four unconscious Oracles to the meeting hall, laid them on the floor, and meditated as a hushed awe filled the room, thick as the perfume of incense. Parvaneh could have sworn she'd felt the power of it, her meditation stone vibrating in her palm as Fabia had taken a deep, snoring breath. She waited for the moment of death, unable to untangle the feelings of shock and horror and thrill at the idea.

It could have been any of them. It could have been her. It hadn't seemed painful, and she was supposed to *want* to rejoin the consciousness. That was what Darius had been telling them through the fall, that this world was imperfect, that they would be tested and some of them would be taken as sacrifices, as bridges to help the rest of them cross over and at least touch, for a moment, that divine presence. She'd tried so hard to feel excited. But all she could feel was exhaustion and dread.

She didn't want to die. She knew she wasn't supposed to be afraid of it, but she couldn't help it. And she couldn't show her fear, or everyone would interpret it as doubt, and no one else seemed to be feeling doubt these days. So the problem was with her. That was what Darius had told her last week, as he'd concluded the whipping. That he hoped they'd beaten the doubt out of her. But all they had done was drive it underground.

"What the hell?" Ladonna muttered. "Who's that?"

A car approached from the other direction, coming from the compound. Ladonna pulled over to the side to let it pass. From her seat behind Ladonna, Parvaneh could see the driver, a middle-aged woman with graying brown hair. Their eyes met for a moment as the woman maneuvered past the van, just briefly, but the look in her eye sent a chill riding along Parvaneh's skin.

"Government plates on the car," Eszter said, squinting out the back.

Fabia cursed. "More harassment. When we live more peacefully than everyone else."

Ladonna pulled into the clearing a few minutes later, where a crowd of Oracles and the children were milling around. As they got out, Darius came to meet them.

"Who was that?" Eszter asked him. "Did they want to execute a search warrant?"

Darius looked grim. "They're going to take our children. They have no idea what they're doing."

"Where do they get off?" Ladonna asked. "They don't have the right to do that."

Darius's sharp gaze scanned the women who had just returned from town. "*Someone* called Child Protective Services," he said. "They wouldn't tell me who. But they're going to come back. And I wouldn't be surprised if the police are with them."

"They just showed up," said Zana, coming forward with Ladonna's chubby, rosy-cheeked baby boy. "They said there had been a call about us *hitting* the kids."

"But we don't," said Fabia.

Xerxes, who had been examining the right front tire of the van, trying to pry a stone from its grooves, looked up at her. "You hit me all the time."

Fabia laughed. "You big fibber. Of course I don't."

Xerxes scowled. "You did yesterday when I called you a cow face."

Parvaneh walked quickly to the back of the van to keep anyone from seeing her smirk. As she unloaded the mops and brooms, she heard Darius tell Xerxes that it was wrong to lie.

"You're the liar," Xerxes shouted.

Darius instructed Fabia to help Zana take the children back to the dorm. Then he told everyone to convene in the meeting hall for an important announcement. Eszter said she urgently needed to go to the bathroom but that she would join them as soon as she could. Parvaneh peeked around the van to see her rushing off, still holding her belly, leaving Parvaneh to do all the unloading by herself.

By the time she got to the meeting hall a few minutes later, nearly all the Oracles had gathered. Darius stood on the altar steps. His hands were clasped in front of him. His eyes lit on each person as they walked down the aisle. When his gaze landed on Parvaneh, she remembered how wonderful it had felt when he'd looked on her with approval, when she'd felt like he loved her. She would have done anything for him. Their eyes met, and a faint smile pulled at his lips. She put her hand on her belly, to remind him what they had created together, something worth saving.

Eszter blundered in a minute later, panting but no longer clutching at her middle. She plopped into the seat next to Parvaneh, which instantly put her on guard. The last thing she needed was to be beaten again for some perceived doubt, not when the tension was this high. She could see it in the darting glances of her fellow Oracles, the way they were sitting so straight. They felt what she did: a tightening of their senses, the breeze of threat raising the fine hairs on their arms.

"Oracles," Darius said, "we are under attack." His head dropped back, as if the enemy had just landed a blow. "My only goal in creating this place was to enable us to journey to enlightenment together, away from all the selfish, sabotaging, degrading evil of this world. I spent every cent I had to make this world for you, so that we could share in a journey toward the ultimate...together. Now we move forward on faith alone."

He descended the stairs to pace near the front row, the hem of his robe brushing Parvaneh's clogs as he passed. "This last year has brought us miracles. All of us, I believe, have moved closer to our goal. And I had hoped we'd have the time we needed to achieve it, but now I know. *Our* time, I'm afraid, is up. This world isn't going to leave us in peace."

"They have no right to come onto our private property and tell us how to live," said Basir.

Hamzi, a guy in his thirties who spent most of his time in the gardens near the animal pastures, nodded. "We can protect ourselves. Arm ourselves. I was in the military before. We could—"

"You're not gonna win a fight with the police," said Ladonna, sounding annoyed. "They have guns too—and a lot of backup."

"And they'll bring them the next time they come," said Darius. "I have received wisdom from the consciousness—we're entering the new millennium, but we won't be allowed to see it, not unless we devote every fiber of our beings to this test. If we go on as we have, they'll come." He jabbed his finger toward the back, toward the world. "The only thing we can do is deny them the victory they're so hungry for."

"How do we do that?" Kazem asked. "They can't do much to us. We haven't done anything wrong."

"They'll twist everything," Darius said. "They'll say we killed Shirin and Ziba and Octavia. They'll accuse us of child abuse and murder, things they do all the time, the things we'd never do in a million years. Can't you understand that? This world won't allow us to go on existing!"

"So we'll leave," suggested Kazem. "We don't have to sit here and wait for them to come get us."

"Exactly!" Darius paused at the center of the room. "We'll leave. I've made a plan."

Parvaneh's hope surged—this was what he'd told her about. *Finally.* The special place he'd been preparing. Even if she wasn't his favorite anymore, maybe he'd still take her along, if he thought she was devoted enough. And if Eszter didn't block the way. It was such a relief: they weren't trapped here on the compound—there was somewhere else they could go. She grinned.

Darius nodded at her. The confidence in her expression seemed to reach him, strengthen him, hopefully remind him what they'd once shared. He squared his shoulders. "Tomorrow night, we'll begin. Some of you will make the journey first, and you will be guides for the rest of us. Some of you will be sentinels, chosen to assist the guides in the journey. Whatever role you're given, I know each of you will fulfill it with the whole measure of your dedication. You know only good things await us."

A few people shifted in their seats. Parvaneh felt a trickle of anxiety.

"Every journey requires bravery," he continued. "We came here because we were committed, and we'll leave here because that commitment has only grown stronger with adversity. Are you all with me? Are you fully committed?"

Several people said, "Yes!"

Darius's eyes narrowed. "Are you *all* with me?"

"Yes," Parvaneh said, along with all the others. Next to her, Eszter murmured her agreement. Parvaneh turned to her. "You don't sound certain, Eszter. Is that doubt?"

Eszter smiled. "If I shout it or whisper it, the answer is the same."

"Eszter's right," Darius said. "Tomorrow, as we embark, she'll be a sentinel. Parvaneh, you as well." He walked around the room, designating nine guides, twenty sentinels. Kazem, guide. Zana, guide. Hamzi, sentinel. Basir, sentinel. And so on. Next, he assigned each guide to two sentinels—Kazem was paired with Hamzi and Basir. Zana with Kyra and Laleh. Vahid with Parsa and Izad. Goli with Beetah and Roya.

Finally, only Fabia, Ladonna, and Tadeas sat silent, looking worried and disappointed that their names hadn't been called.

"Darius," Fabia finally said. "What about us?"

"You have another purpose," Darius assured them.

Parvaneh raised her hand. "You didn't assign a guide to me and Eszter."

Darius smiled. "That's not true. I have." He knelt in front of them. "I'm assigning you the most important guide of all."

Parvaneh felt a rush of satisfaction—he meant himself. It was exactly the reassurance she'd needed. "We'll be honored to help you."

He kissed her forehead. "I know, my butterfly." He stood up and addressed the group. "Tomorrow night, we will all meet here, one final time in this place. And then we will set out. I will provide you with all the tools you need for the journey. I've already prepared, as I knew this was coming, only waiting for the consciousness to give me the signal. Tonight, we'll have a big feast. Basir, go begin the preparations. All the meat." He turned to Kazem. "I wouldn't want to waste a single scrap of it, right?"

Kazem smiled, but there was uncertainty in his eyes.

As people began to file out, Parvaneh rushed over to Darius. She wanted to touch him, to pull up the memories of their closeness, to show him that she was all there, all in. "I'm so happy to be your sentinel, Darius. I know we'll—"

"You're not *my* sentinel, Parvaneh."

The smile melted from her face. "But—"

"I said your guide was important, but you should never have assumed it would be me."

Parvaneh looked around at everyone still remaining in the meeting hall. "Then who?"

He grinned as Eszter approached them. "The two of you are assigned to Xerxes."

CHAPTER TWENTY-SIX

Bend, Oregon
December 14, present day

I'm so panicked that it takes me several seconds to find my laptop bag, my purse, my car in the parking lot. I'm so disjointed that I have to adjust the seat twice; I must have scooted it back to give my broken arm more room as I got out of the car. Miles was supposed to be back by ten last night, and who knows when he was in the accident, but it must have been hours ago. I'm terrified of what I might find.

I drive straight to the hospital and get shunted into the emergency department because the main doors are still locked. The attendant behind the desk isn't Essie; it's the woman I spoke to yesterday, who seemed uneasy with the urgency of my request to speak with her colleague. This morning, she looks haggard, her graying hair pulling loose from her ponytail. She greets me with a haunted, wary gaze. What with the terrible weather, especially in an area that doesn't see a ton of rain, there have probably been more than a few accidents in the last several hours.

She looks Miles up and tells me he's been admitted to a general floor, which is a relief: he's not in the ICU. She reminds me that it's not visiting hours yet, but she calls up to the unit, and the nurse says he's awake and had just asked if anyone had come to see him overnight. With a churning stomach, I ride up in the elevator and get out on the fourth floor. The place is still mostly dark, save for dim lights over the charge nurse's desk. When I approach, a nurse tells me that Miles is in room 409.

It's a small single room, and the curtain is pulled around the bed. "Miles?"

"Hey," he says, sounding thrashed.

I pull the curtain back. His leg is casted up over his thigh, held up with what looks to be some sort of medieval torture contraption, and his face is swollen and bruised. "Oh god."

"Broken femur," he says. "And internal bruising, apparently. A few broken ribs." He turns his head, revealing that the left side of it is plastered with bandages, his curly hair sticking up, shaven in places just outside the bandaged spot. His glasses are nowhere in sight. "Twenty stitches. Mild concussion." He gives me a sloppy grin. "*Lots of pain meds.*"

"What happened?"

He lets out a shaky breath as he repositions his head on the pillow. "You remember what I just said about the concussion?"

"You can't remember?"

"I remember getting off the phone with Valentina, who tore me a new asshole because I hadn't sent her the story yet. And that's it until I was being unloaded in the ambulance bay in the worst pain I've ever felt."

"Is your car...?"

"Apparently, the police carted it off."

"What? Why?"

"They said it was a hit-and-run. My car flipped. It was upside down in a ditch. Luckily a trucker drove by and saw the wheels sticking up."

"I'm so glad you're okay."

"Yeah?" he asks. His tone is flat. Weary. But he sounded like that even before this accident. "I have a story for you to fact-check and copyedit."

"Didn't you tell me that Valentina—"

"I told her I didn't have it ready. I didn't say I hadn't written it. I wanted you to read it and make sure everything is accurate before I send it on."

My heart picks up the terrified rhythm it's maintained almost since Miles's first mention of Bend. "I'd be happy to take care of it."

He glances at his phone, charging on his bedside cart. "Promise me one thing."

"Anything." I'm craving his smile, his easy, confident manner. But it seems to have been smashed out of him last night.

"Work on it here, not at your hotel." He nods toward the laptop bag hanging off my shoulder.

"How did you know I was at a hotel?"

"I talked with Hailey yesterday." His eyes are closed, and his voice is weak.

I quietly begin to set up at the plastic chair by the window. As upsetting as this is, selfishly, it *could* be good for me. From his hospital bed, Miles can't traipse around the state, picking up all the evidence of my connection with this mess. So whatever story he's written? For a while, that might be it. And that would be fine with me. Except it means that I care more about myself than him, which is shitty. I promise myself I'll make it up to him somehow, someday.

I've just sat down when Noah texts. I roll my eyes—it's only seven in the morning, and he's back at it. Whether you've read my story or not, we need to talk.

I'm considering a sharp reply when Miles yanks me from my thoughts. "I sent the file to you just now. My computer was destroyed in the accident. Good thing I always have a backup."

"I'm on it," I say. I pull out my notebook to build my fact-checking grid. But a few seconds after opening the file on my laptop, I've forgotten all about checking any facts.

It's called: Running for Her Life: How Far Will One Woman Go to Escape Her Past?

It feels like my throat is closing.

Getting out of a cult isn't easy, and the psychological aftermath can be just as difficult and treacherous. Therapists who specialize in work with former cultists describe the recovery process as long, complicated, and often painful, with anxiety, panic, dissociation, and depression relatively common. Former cult members are often embarrassed, and stigma in the general public—including the belief that those who join cults are gullible and weak— abounds. As a result, it shouldn't be a surprise to anyone that many former cult members keep that information to themselves, preferring not to discuss what happened to them and others during their time in the cult.

But what if "what happened" involved multiple deaths? Maybe even murder?

On December 15, 2000, a fire at the Oracles of Innocence compound in Bend, Oregon, claimed the lives of 33 of its members. Three cult members, all of whom were outside the main building affected by the fire, none of whom attempted to save their fellow Oracles, and one of whom actually barred the door of the building, effectively condemning dozens of people to death, were until recently thought to be the only adult survivors of this tragedy. All of them served time for their actions that night. Today is the twentieth anniversary of the blaze. And it turns out there is another story to tell. One that has become, for this reporter, very personal.

"Miles..."

"Read to the end," he says, his tone clipped.

My eyes sting as I read on.

On the morning of December 8, I got a tip, a Twitter DM. It was from an anonymous account with the handle @Darius1: "Arnold Moore, Oracles of Innocence, almost 20 years. You are closer to this than you think." I kept my skepticism holstered and Googled it, and with the first hit, I knew I'd struck gold. I had no idea at the time how deep the vein went.

What I discovered: one of the adult survivors of the Oracles of Innocence catastrophe, Arnold Moore, had been murdered in a very strange way. A rock, very similar to dozens of painted rocks found all over the compound after the fire, reported to be channeling talismans, had been shoved into his mouth. He'd been stabbed multiple times, but according to an anonymous source at the county medical examiner's office, each wound was outlined in permanent marker, as if the killer had planned in advance where to strike. A review of the autopsy of Stephen Millsap, a former stockbroker and cult leader who went by the name "Darius," reveals matching wounds. To me, it looked as if someone had tried to stage a copycat killing, maybe to send a message. I wanted to investigate and report.

When I first pitched the story to the editorial team at Hatchet, *our newest fact-checker, Dora Rodriguez, looked ashen. But the next thing I knew, she volunteered to travel to Bend in order to help me research the story. She had told me she was from Bend, in fact, and informed me she'd be staying with her parents, Hailey and Martin Rodriguez.*

They aren't her parents as it turns out. On December 16, 2000, the day after the fire, Martin Rodriguez was driving back to his home in Bend after visiting his ailing mother in his native Eugene. He discovered a young woman in mismatched, ill-fitting clothes, running along the side of the road approximately two miles outside of Bend, less than ten miles from the still-smoking ruins of the Oracles of Innocence compound. A Good Samaritan at heart, Mr. Rodriguez offered the young woman a ride and ended up giving her a place to stay. She told him her name was Christy. It was only the first of many lies.

"You spoke to them without telling me," I murmur, a tear slipping down my cheek.

"Because I couldn't trust you."

"You don't understand," I choke out.

"You're going to have to make me. Because this? It's the only story I've got."

Mr. and Mrs. Rodriguez reported that even then, they suspected "Christy" might have escaped the Oracles cult. According to Mrs. Rodriguez, "I had always hoped she would open up if we gave her enough time, but all that happened was we got more attached. I didn't want to ruin things. I was afraid she would run, and that had become the last thing I wanted. I kept telling myself I could ask her about it the next day. But I never did."

Mr. and Mrs. Rodriguez felt they knew Christy well enough to trust she could never hurt a fly, and they had their own reasons for keeping their suspicions to themselves. They lost their only child, Dora, to a drunk driver in 1986, and Christy became like a daughter to them. They didn't want to lose another. A few days ago, Christy admitted to them that she had changed her name to Dora Rodriguez, claiming it was a kind of tribute. She's been going by that name for the last ten years at least, according to a check with a previous employer. She has covered her tracks well.

It took me a few days to realize she was trying to sabotage my story.

I skim the rest. He knows almost everything. He spoke with Gina, Arnie's girlfriend. Hailey gave him her contact information. And he's talked to Max Jennings. He reports that at least one page from Max's records of cult members went missing after he showed me the file. And Miles describes how, on his very first afternoon in Bend, he went to the library and searched the archives of the *Bend Bulletin*, startled to find a picture of several female cult members, one of whom looked extremely familiar. Suddenly that part of the Twitter message made sense: *You are closer to this than you think.* He explains that he returned to the archives after his suspicions about me had grown—and discovered that the microfiche reel containing the only known copy of the photo had disappeared...after I had told him I couldn't find any photos of the cult members.

"It was Noah," I stammer. "Didn't you see his name in the log?"

"Apparently, you did too, which means you were there after him, which Noah confirmed. And he swore up and down it wasn't him. Honestly, on that one? Not sure which one of you to trust."

I close my laptop. I can't read anymore. I know it's all over.

"You could have been honest," he says. "But instead, you put both of our careers at risk. You were perfectly willing to take me down with you. You could have ruined me, Dora."

I push myself out of the chair to approach the bed. I freeze when Miles flinches. "I left the cult before the fire," I tell him. "I swear."

"Which is why you were found running down the road the day *after*."

"I—" Shit. "You don't understand."

"You keep saying that. And then you tell another lie."

I glance back at my laptop. "Have you sent this to Valentina?"

His eyes flick toward the door. His hand edges toward his call button. "Remember what I said about always having a backup?"

"I'm no threat to you, Miles." I hold up my casted arm. "If I tried to do anything to you, not that I ever would, it would probably break more of my bones than yours."

His brow furrows. "Are you sick?"

"Would it matter?"

"I don't know." But then his expression hardens. "You know what? I don't believe a single word that comes out of your mouth, so no, actually."

"I never wanted to put your career in jeopardy. I only wanted to protect myself."

"From *what*, Dora?"

I look out the window as an ambulance, sirens wailing, turns off the road and races toward the entrance to the ED. "You saw what happened to the others."

"But you were *inside* the building that night, weren't you? Not outside, refusing to rescue anyone."

"How do you know?"

"Those three were on trial for murder," he reminds me. "I have zero doubt at least one of them would have mentioned the presence or involvement of another cult member in their own defense. I called Marie Heckender's trial lawyer. He told me that she never mentioned any other survivors except Arnold Moore and Shari Redmond."

"I wasn't there when it happened, Miles. I was—"

"Hailey recalls finding crusty bandages in the garbage more than once. She thinks you were burned that night."

"*That's* what you're going on?"

He grimaces. "Stop lying, Dora. *Please*."

I grab my bag. "What do you want me to do, Miles?"

"All I want is the truth. Let's start with your real name."

"My real name," I say from between clenched teeth, "is Dora Rodriguez."

"But it's not the name you were born with, and we both know that."

"I'm leaving," I snap. My panic has shorted me out, sizzled my nerves. "I'm really sorry you got hurt, Miles, but this ambush? Totally uncalled for."

He laughs. "It's totally called for. The only question is whether you'll take the steps necessary to make things right."

"You want an exclusive interview?" My voice is pure acid. "You want all the slimy details just so you can win some award?"

His gaze is steady. "I really did like you," he informs me. "I really hate that I still do."

"I liked you too," I tell him, determined not to cry. "Please don't do this."

He opens his mouth to speak, but a knock at the door interrupts. "Come in," he says.

I turn to see another specter from my past. The chief of the Bend police department strides in, his midsection rounder and his head balder than twenty years ago. Ben Ransom looks at Miles and then at me. "Christy," he says. "Been a while. Long enough that you became an entirely different person, I hear."

With a guilty glance at Miles, I say, "Hi, Ben."

Ben is stone-faced. "I talked to Martin last night. He didn't let on, but you tore them up with that name change, *Dora*."

Miles clears his throat. "To what do we owe this pleasure, Chief Ransom?"

"I'm here to try to understand better some of the details of the accident." He looks over at Miles. "It sure as hell has the look of something suspicious." He turns back to me. "But I was looking for you too, so it's nice that you're here."

"What about?" I ask.

"Essie Green died in a suspicious fire last night." His eyes are cold and so is his tone. "And I'd like to bring you down to the station and talk to you about that."

In shock, I head down to the lobby with Ben, realizing I didn't even say goodbye to Miles. Essie's gone. Killed. My thoughts are nothing but a buzz of confusion.

When we reach the main entrance, I turn to Ben. "Should I just meet you there?"

He shakes his head. "We're impounding your car. I got the order last night."

"Last night? When... Why..."

He gestures to a police car parked in a spot reserved for first responders. "Let's talk on the way."

"Are you arresting me?"

"Do you want to give me a reason?" He's got his fingers in his belt loops. All fake friendly as he walks to the car and opens the rear passenger door. "It'll be better if you cooperate."

It doesn't feel like I have a choice. Ben settles himself in the front seat, buckles in, tells dispatch that he has the person of interest and is on his way to the station. Asks if someone will set up room 2A for him.

"What's that—an interrogation room?"

"It's a conference room. Chill out."

"I'm in the back seat of a police car, Ben."

"You know, I always did wonder about you. Showing up all of

a sudden, right after the fire. But Hailey and Martin, oh, did you know they lied for you? Martin said he picked you up on 97 up near Terrebonne, coming from the other direction. He said you had a bad family situation up in Portland, that you'd hitched down here and hit a dead end."

I cover my face with my hands. They were so much more than I deserved. Then I raise my head. "Wait. *Why* are you impounding my car?"

"There were some streaks of paint on Mr. Connover's car. Looked like someone ran him off the road. Blue paint, it was. Turns out Officer Montenaro filed a report saying he stopped a Dora Rodriguez in a blue Corolla yesterday afternoon. I couldn't believe it when I saw the name. I was a senior in high school when she died, you know. Big news all over town. At first I thought it might be a coincidence, but then I called Martin, just on a hunch. He'd mentioned you were in town, and Montenaro's report said it was a woman visiting her folks."

"I got lost, Ben," I say wearily. "I haven't been to Bend in a while."

He grunts. "Funnily enough, you were only a block away from Essie Green's house when you were stopped. And your car matches the description of a vehicle seen in the neighborhood before too. Essie's got a nosy neighbor who *loves* to call us." He rolls his eyes.

"I'd never been in her neighborhood before last night," I snap. "And I have no idea where Essie Green even lives or why I'd be interested."

"I figured you'd care, since you know her from way back when." Stopped at a light, he turns and gives me a grim look. "Don't make the mistake of thinking I'm stupid."

I bonk my head on the seat cushion a few times, barely able to contain my frustration. "I'm just trying to figure out what's happening," I say. "My friend's in the hospital, and now you're suggesting that I'm the one who put him there? Why would I do that?"

"I dunno. Why would you?"

I open my mouth to scoff, but then, I *do* have a reason to hurt Miles. And he knows it. A simple conversation with him would give Ben all the ammo he needs.

"You can check the location tracker on my phone. It would show that I was at my hotel all night."

"No, it would show that *your phone* was right there. Occasionally, people do venture out without those things, especially when they're smart enough to know it's a way to track them. I'll speak with the front desk staff about whether anyone saw you."

"I didn't attack Miles! Or Essie, if that's what you're thinking."

"I saw your car in the hospital parking lot over an hour ago, *Dora*. I'm the one who called it in. There were scrapes of silver paint along the side. Guess what color Mr. Connover's car is?"

I squeeze my eyes shut, trying to focus through the whir of my panic. I never hit anything that would have left silver streaks on my car. I never... Wait. I had to readjust my seat to drive to the hospital.

Almost as if someone taller than me had been driving it.

"Noah Perry," I blurt out. "He had my key. He and his friend Arman drove me to the hospital the other day when I broke my arm. He could have copied it before he gave it back. And he could have stolen my car to go after Miles! I swear, it was in a different spot in the parking lot when I tried to find it last night, and it was clear someone else had been driving it!"

"Uh-huh," says Ben, pulling into the police station lot. "We'll check on it, though it's funny that these details are only coming to you now. Noah Perry you say?"

I nod frantically. "You have to bring him in. He's also really interested in the cult. He's practically stalking me, trying to get me to read this story he wrote about it. He must have gone after Essie Green."

"Funny, that. Almost no one knew Essie Green used to be in that cult. It wasn't public information. I know her from church and recognized her from coverage of the trial. We'd talked about it a few times. Nice lady. Did her time. She didn't deserve what happened to her last night." He parks the cruiser and turns to look at me. "I just decided to throw her involvement with the cult out at you a few minutes ago, and you didn't skip a beat. Because you already knew."

"I didn't kill her, Ben!"

"You've worked hard to cover up your past. And here's your colleague, Mr. Connover, doing his damnedest to uncover all the secrets of that goddamn cult. And here's Essie Green, who probably recognized you, am I right? Seems to me like you've got a passel of reasons to silence them. Now. Would you like to come inside and tell me your side of things, just to clear everything up?"

He unbuckles his seat belt as his cell phone rings. He answers, asks short, sharp questions: *When? How bad?* I lean forward, trying to catch what's being said. The back of his neck is slowly turning bright red. He ends the call and says, "You can go. We'll have to talk later. Maybe you should head back to the hospital."

"Something wrong?"

"Yeah," he tells me, looking the slightest bit hesitant. Almost apologetic. "It's Hailey and Martin. Their house just burned down."

CHAPTER TWENTY-SEVEN

The Retreat

December 15, 2000

The children had been eerily quiet all day, and a blanket of heavy silence hung over the clearing. Darius had told everyone they would journey on in stages, and he hadn't said how long it would be—a day, a week, a year. But he'd been clear on one point: it started tonight. They had to be ready because this test was the true opportunity to demonstrate their commitment. Parvaneh was determined to prove herself worthy and to see what came next. If Darius offered her a better place for her and her baby, she would jump at the chance.

But if things got ugly, she'd have to leave for the sake of her daughter. She'd have to break her own heart into a million pieces and walk away from the man who'd changed her world and her mind. She'd have to walk away from everyone and everything she'd come to love over the past year and the place she'd been sure she'd live for the rest of her days.

At the thought, tears sprang to her eyes and doubt flowed through her. Should she stay and fight for what she loved instead of just running away again? Her little brother's face rose in her memory, him splashing in the old kiddie pool she'd found by the side of the road and set up in the yard. It had a slow leak and needed constant refilling, but his joy had made her feel real, important, necessary. Then she'd left him there, run away to save herself. What if she'd protected him? What if she'd tried? Could she have made things better for both of them if she'd stayed?

Inside her belly, the baby kicked. Darius had shown her the long list of names he chose from when he initiated new Oracles. They were all Persian, names of victory and ancient mystery, he said, wisdom sent to him by the consciousness. She wanted to name her baby girl Fairuza; it meant "woman of triumph," exactly what she wanted her daughter to be. But why would she want to bring a child into this world, where forces of pure evil stalked them, eager to rip away everything that was precious? Why would she want to have her baby only to lose her to some artificial, earthly authority who would turn the child into a thoughtless pawn, yet another sheep? Could Darius protect her from all that?

Parvaneh stood in the woods as the sun set and the timed lights of the barns burst to life in the distance, pinpricks of brilliance through the trees. From here, she could make out the smoothed mound of the tiny grave she'd dug for Eszter's baby a few months ago. She wondered if Eszter had chosen a name for the child, a hopeful signal fire to draw the soul to the right place. She wondered if Eszter was eager to rejoin her baby. They hadn't spoken much since Darius had selected them as sentinels for Xerxes, and for good reason. Eszter took every chance lately to question—in front of Darius—whether Parvaneh was actually ready for such an important job. And if Parvaneh showed any annoyance at all, Eszter commented on that too. It had become hard to look her in the eye.

She squatted, covering her face with her hands. Those were not worthy thoughts. If she indulged them, Eszter would be right about her.

"What are you doing?" asked Ladonna, walking back from the barns with a few bottles of milk. Her look was cautious. Like she expected Parvaneh to explode.

Parvaneh smiled. "I felt moved by the consciousness, like it had a message for me."

"About tonight?" Ladonna asked.

Parvaneh nodded. "This is our moment to prove ourselves. And Darius trusts me enough to place me in the center of the action. I'm honored to have been chosen."

"Everybody's buzzing all about this today. Zana. Eszter. You and Fabia and Beetah." Ladonna arched one eyebrow. "We all have a part to play. No one part is more important than any other."

"What's your part exactly?" She couldn't keep the acid from her tone.

"Okay, little miss high horse." Ladonna's expression turned stony, and she resumed her walk up the trail. "Keep telling yourself how important you are if that's what you need. Darius said he wanted to start soon."

Parvaneh watched her go, irritation fizzing inside her, mixing with fear. In a way, they'd been practicing for this moment for weeks. Darius was too wise to leave them unprepared. They'd grown in trust and faith one glass of milk at a time. All of them had done it, and all of them knew how it felt. Painless and peaceful. Like slipping beneath the surface of lapping warm waters, vast and welcoming. And on the other side, eternity.

Despite all that, Parvaneh was incredibly relieved she hadn't been chosen for that particular journey.

She tromped back to the dorm, reaching it as Eszter did, having come from wherever she wandered off to these days. Parvaneh still couldn't understand why Darius trusted her so much. She'd turned out to be a such a backstabber. Right now, her round face was flushed, her eyes shiny. "What's wrong?" Parvaneh asked, her voice syrupy sweet. "You look troubled."

"What if I was?" she asked quietly, wiping her face with the sleeve of her robe.

"I thought you were never troubled. Isn't that what you want Darius to believe?"

Eszter shook her head. "I think it's what you would like Darius to believe about you, but it's so obviously *not* true that it troubles us all."

Parvaneh was astounded by the way Eszter could twist everything. "You probably just came from his cabin—where you probably tried to convince him, yet again, that I don't deserve to be in there with the rest of you."

In the past, Eszter would have had the decency to look embarrassed, but not now. Her gaze was direct. And hard. "What if I did?"

"Why do you hate me so much?" Parvaneh tugged at her robe. "You chose me to be part of all of this, remember?" She jabbed her finger at Eszter. "You approached *me* on that curb in Portland. You could have left me alone, but instead, you drew me in."

Now Eszter did look away. "I did," she murmured. "And now I know that was a mistake."

The pain was a physical one, knifing through Parvaneh's body, piercing the thin skin of her control and sinking into the well of rage it contained. "Picking me was a *mistake*? What the hell did I do to make you hate me this much? We were friends!" she shouted. "And

I helped you. I cared about you. But suddenly, you do your best to make me look bad in front of Darius." Her entire body shook with the betrayal. "I still have bruises from the beating I got because of *you*."

"I didn't want you to get hurt," said Eszter so miserably that Parvaneh wanted to believe her. But then she added, "I didn't know that would happen."

With a burst of bitter laughter, Parvaneh said, "You're a liar. Either that or you're stupid."

"I'm neither," Eszter said quietly.

"Then what is it? Are you jealous?"

Eszter's head snapped up. "Jealous of what?"

Glaring at Eszter, Parvaneh slowly and deliberately put her hands on her belly.

Eszter's expression twisted with something Parvaneh couldn't quite read, maybe pain, maybe just simple irritation. "I don't understand why you haven't just left," she blurted out. "No one wants you here! I've been trying to tell you that for weeks. It would be better for you if you quit. Just go! I'll make sure no one notices until it's too late to stop you."

Parvaneh stepped close to Eszter, her hands curling into fists. "I'm more committed now than ever. And if you try to mess this up for me—"

"You'll what?" Eszter sighed. "Just know that I tried, and I love you."

From the clearing, a whistle rose, high and sharp. "It's time," Parvaneh said.

Eszter began to trudge toward the meeting hall. Parvaneh fell into step beside her. They were all supposed to be helping one another remain committed, but Eszter had done nothing but prod Parvaneh to quit for a long time now. And at this moment, when everything was on the line, it was the last thing she should have been doing. They should be standing shoulder to shoulder, trying to figure out how best to get back to where they'd been, when everything was good.

In the clearing, everyone was assembling. The guides, including Kazem and Zana, looked nervous, Zana pulling at a loose thread at the shoulder of her robe, Kazem pacing like a caged tiger. The sentinels, including Basir and Beetah, looked more relaxed. Fabia came out of the children's dorm dragging Xerxes by the hand. "I don't want to go to the boring meeting," he shouted as she yanked him across the gravel.

"You're going to meet the consciousness," Fabia said. "Don't you want it to like you?"

Eszter rushed over to them, wearing a smile. "Xerxes, guess what. Parvaneh and I are taking care of you tonight!"

Xerxes pushed a heavy lock of blond hair out of his eyes. "You'll play with me?"

"I'm sure there will be time for that," said Eszter, "but we need to do our work first."

Xerxes narrowed his eyes. "What kind of work?"

Fabia groaned. "Your work is to stop asking questions for five minutes! Can you do that?"

He stuck his tongue out at her. Parvaneh would have laughed, but the sight of his childish antics wrenched her into the hard now of things. Doubt was like wind, prying up hastily nailed boards, seeping in through all the cracks, rattling her bones. What she really needed now was courage—and the knowledge of where to direct it. Thoughts awhirl, she walked forward and joined Eszter, barely restraining the urge to shove her to the side. She offered Xerxes a bright smile. "Let's go into the meeting hall to find out what activity we're doing next!"

Xerxes offered up a tentative, intrigued look and allowed Parvaneh to take his hand. Together, they walked toward the meeting hall, Fabia keeping pace. "Shouldn't you go back to the children's dorms?" Parvaneh asked. "Isn't that your job tonight? Babysitting?"

Fabia lifted her chin. "My job is between me, Darius, and the consciousness. It's no more or less important than anyone else's."

"You sound like Ladonna," said Eszter, speaking Parvaneh's thoughts aloud. "And you're right. But is it a secret?"

"All is revealed in the right time," Fabia said breezily, pulling the door open by its big metal handle. "Your journey is only beginning," she said as the rest of them filed past.

Parvaneh walked away from the cold and into a stifling, candlelit world. Darius must have had the incense burning for hours, and hundreds of candles had been arranged around the room, on the chairs, on saucers right on the carpeted areas, on the steps of the dais. They glowed and wavered in the breeze as the door opened, harboring a hypnotic kind of beauty. She spotted Darius in front of those dais steps, his arms folded, hands cupping his elbows. Once the door closed, he turned to them, his blue eyes bright.

He lifted his arms. "Come forward! This is the moment we begin our ascent to the path we've been seeking with such devotion over the last year."

Still clutching Xerxes's sweaty hand, Parvaneh marched up the aisle. Ten milk glasses had been assembled on the altar. Some sort of leather-bound object had been lined up behind each, but she couldn't make out what it was. Heart hammering, she pulled Xerxes to the side as they reached the front, to make room for everyone else.

"Sentinels, flank your guides. They will be your meditation channel tonight, and you will be their anchor."

Parvaneh shifted so that Eszter could squeeze in on Xerxes's other side. The rest of the groups spread out around the room. Darius waited for them to find their places. He seemed agitated and shaky, not excited and joyful like she'd expected.

"I brought you all here to share this journey with me," he said. "Now we continue it together. I will be the last to leave; I hope by that time you'll all be waiting for me in that beautiful, shining place."

Alarm spiked in her chest. It didn't sound like he was taking any of them to a new, special retreat.

"Guides, line up. Each of you gets a vehicle for your journey." He gestured at the milk glasses, then strode up the steps of the dais and handed out the glasses one by one, saying, "Take it back to your sentinels and drink."

Parvaneh knelt next to Xerxes. "Do you want..." She paused, her voice trailing off. She was about to ask an innocent child to drink something that would silence his mind and might stop his heart. What would Octavia say if she were here? What if this were Parvaneh's child? She looked up at Eszter. "I can't," she whispered.

Darius looked over as if she'd shouted it. As all the other guides shuffled back to their sentinels, glasses in hand, Darius grabbed a cup from the altar and brought it over to them. "Xerxes," he said. "Drink."

From behind them came a sob. "Don't make me do this," Zana wailed.

Darius turned toward the back. "Kyra and Laleh, help Zana fulfill her purpose."

Parvaneh watched, wide eyed, as Laleh grabbed Zana from behind, holding her fast, while Kyra took the milk and pressed the cup to Zana's lips. "Kazem," Zana sobbed. "Help me."

From a few feet away, Kazem stood, empty glass in hand, tears on his face. "Zana, let it go," he said, sounding weary. "It's all right. We'll all be together again soon."

Zana sputtered and coughed as Kyra poured the milk down her throat.

"Everyone, follow Kazem's example," said Darius. "He understands what is expected of him and how the rest of us suffer if he is a coward."

Kazem's wrecked expression revealed nothing but marrow-deep sorrow. Parvaneh's throat went tight. She looked at the cup in Darius's hand and then down at Xerxes, who seemed rapt and frozen as he watched what was happening to Zana. He looked up at Darius. "I don't want milk."

"You don't have a choice, Xerxes. You were chosen for this."

"I. Don't. Want. Milk!" He tore his hand from Parvaneh's, ducked Darius's grasp, and dodged Eszter's clumsy, too-slow lunge. He raced down the aisle toward the back doors with Parvaneh on his tail. At the sight, Goli screamed and tried to follow, but her sentinels grabbed her. Both murmured reassurance as they grappled with her. Parvaneh reached the back doors only a second after Xerxes, but not quickly enough to keep him from pushing them open.

Fabia stood just outside. Holding a crowbar.

"I should have known you'd try to get out of it," she sneered at Parvaneh. Then she rushed forward and shoved Xerxes back. He collided with Parvaneh, knocking her off balance and into Eszter, who'd been a few steps behind. Parvaneh heard the sound of metal scraping against metal, and when Xerxes threw himself at the doors again, they barely budged.

Fabia had barred the door. They were trapped. *She* was trapped.

"Parvaneh and Eszter, bring him forward," Darius called. "Doubt and fear are the enemy. Faith and love are our only allies now."

Tears stinging her eyes, panic slithering up her spine, Parvaneh grabbed Xerxes around the middle and carried him kicking and screaming up the aisle. His clogs batted a few candles to the floor, but Parvaneh didn't have the strength or wherewithal to right them.

When they reached the front, Darius tried to hand Parvaneh the glass, but it was almost as if she'd gone numb. She couldn't make herself reach for it.

He tilted his head. "Will you take his place?" His voice was level. Calm. Wise. "I'm depending on you, Parvaneh. I need you now. I've always needed you. You know I'm only trying to protect us." He reached out and stroked her cheek.

While Parvaneh hesitated, Eszter squatted next to the struggling boy. Tears stained his reddened cheeks. "This is going to make you feel better," she explained to him. She took the cup from Darius, wrapped her arms around Xerxes, and tried to bring it to his lips, but her shaking hands caused her to spill most of it down the front of his robe.

Darius made an annoyed sound and grabbed Xerxes by the hair. "Get it into him," he said tersely.

Parvaneh watched, dazed, as Eszter poured what little remained in the cup down Xerxes's throat.

Darius smiled and patted the boy's head while Eszter held him. "It's enough," he said to her. "It'll keep him calm."

Parvaneh looked around the room. Most of the guides were sitting now. The air smelled faintly of smoke. The whole meeting hall had turned hazy, dusky tendrils swirling overhead.

Darius walked back to the dais. "Tonight is the real test, the thing we've been training for all along." He reached over and grabbed one of the leather-bound objects. He held it up.

It was a hunting knife with a leather-bound hilt. There were nine more still on the altar.

Zana was still weakly struggling as Darius took the knife down the aisle and handed it to Kyra. "There is nothing more powerful than blood," Darius said as he walked back. He passed out the knives to the sentinels. "This is the moment we channel that power. You all know what to do."

From the back of the room came a gurgling scream. And then another. Blood blossomed from Zana's stomach and chest as Kyra drove the knife into her. As Parvaneh turned back to the front, she saw Eszter hunched over Xerxes, whispering in his ear. But the boy had gone glassy eyed and didn't seem fully aware. Which was for the better, because Darius had drawn near, offering Parvaneh a knife of her own.

"This is when your wings open and you fly," he said to her. "Prove your loyalty. Prove your commitment." He moved close to her. Put a hand on the mound of her belly. The tiny life inside her kicked. "You are my butterfly. I need you now." He stroked her abdomen. "We *both* do."

Another scream. And another. There was a crash as several chairs were overturned, as someone, probably a guide, struggled and fought to stay alive, to keep breathing.

This was the moment. She'd come so far. It was her or the boy. The boy or her *daughter*.

And there was no way out.

Her ears ringing, her nose filling with the scent of smoke, she reached for the knife.

CHAPTER TWENTY-EIGHT

Bend, Oregon
December 14, present day

Standing outside the Bend police station as it starts to rain, I request an Uber. I scowl at the drops hitting the asphalt, pinging off windshields. I feel like a boxer, punch-drunk from all the hits, barely able to stay upright. Before I get in my ride, Ben yells from the window of his squad car, tells me not to leave Bend or he'll get a warrant for my arrest. And then he tells me Hailey and Martin were being transported, and they don't have any relatives in the area, so I'd better get a move on.

I'm back at St. Charles in less than ten minutes. By the time I arrive, Noah's sent me another text:

> Stop ignoring me.

I put my phone away, glad I brought his name to Ben's attention.

It's a different attendant at the front desk of the ED this time, but she looks as hollow eyed as the one last night, maybe because at that point, the woman already knew her colleague Essie was dead. Maybe she even recognized my voice and wondered if I had anything to do with it, since I'd been practically stalking Essie for the previous two days.

I've walked into so many traps of my own making that I've lost count.

The attendant tells me that Hailey and Martin Rodriguez were admitted an hour ago, and both are being treated for smoke inhalation. She said Hailey is in fair condition but Martin's more serious. When I ask if I can see them, she calls the attending and confers with her, casting cautious glances in my direction. Finally, she tells me that she'll take me to Hailey's room.

When I walk in and peek around the curtain, Hailey's seemingly asleep, her face streaked with soot, an oxygen mask strapped to her face. My eyes fill with tears, and I step back out into the hallway. This is my fault. Whoever's been setting these fires, they probably were trying to get to me. I have no idea who could be after me, so I don't even know how to protect myself, let alone the only two people in the world who care whether I live or die.

Essie was my number one suspect. Ladonna was capable of killing. Back then, she had a hard streak and a clear head in moments that made other people panic. It's probably why Darius assigned her to stay outside; he knew she would make sure Fabia did what she'd been told and see that Tadeas didn't lose his head. Now she's at the morgue, and she was right to be scared. I wonder if she recognized her killer when he came for her.

It could be Max—he had all the information. He lives in Portland and was in Eugene, a few hours from all the murder sites, but with the exception of this fire, which apparently started only an hour or two ago, all the murders took place at night, which gave him time to drive back home. It's after ten now, not too late. On impulse, I pick up my phone and call him.

"Hello?" From the background noise, I can tell he's in the car.

My fingers go tight around my phone. "Max?"

"Yeah? Dora? You found my notes?"

"I looked through all my stuff and didn't find them. Was it a lot of pages?"

He clears his throat. "Only one. The last one, if my dates are correct. It was the page listing the final group of people who joined before everyone moved to Bend. I've been trying to recreate it, but you know."

"It's been twenty years."

"Yeah. Fortunately, I was at that last initiation ceremony. Those people, I remember. I sent Miles the list. And after I talked with him, I checked—two of them were never accounted for after the fire: Parvaneh and Eszter. I emailed him everything I could remember last night."

I'm screwed. He's given Miles the last pieces of the puzzle. Once Miles realizes that and outs me publicly, the questions will come, and the fact that I've worked so hard to keep hidden only makes me look guiltier. I've done this to myself. But the one thing I'm not guilty of? Trying to murder Hailey and Martin. "Max, where are you right now?"

"Why?"

"If you're in the area, we could meet again. I'm going to look through my papers again, to see if I can find your missing page. Maybe we—"

"I'm going to communicate directly with Miles from now on. Thanks." He ends the call.

He refused to say if he was in the area. It means virtually nothing and makes it impossible to rule him in or out. There's a reason why I'm a fact-checker and not a detective.

Of course, I'm probably not even a fact-checker anymore. I'm a liar, I've committed countless breaches of professional ethics, and I'm not only going to lose my job, but I'll never be employable in this field again. And that's if I can manage to stay out of jail, which is becoming more doubtful by the day.

My thoughts turn back to Noah and Arman. Noah's the one writing stories about children of Darius, but for all I know, Arman isn't one. Or he is, and Noah is manipulating him. He's so domineering, so clearly in control of that relationship. It doesn't mean Arman isn't helping him, though. I can't trust either of them. But maybe, if I can get Arman alone, I could wheedle a few answers out of him.

If only I had his contact info. I do have Noah's, but at this point, with my car potentially used to commit a crime and maybe even to stalk Essie, it seems like my best course of action is to avoid him like the plague. Even if he didn't attack Miles, and I'm not sure why he would except to get some crazy revenge after Miles refused to indulge the Children of Darius story, he still might have committed the murders.

Maybe Noah is a child of Darius himself. Or maybe he's just a psychopath.

Only one thing makes me question everything: he knew I was at a hotel. And if he did, why would he set fire to Hailey and Martin's house?

A nurse enters Hailey's room. Amid the beeps and the droning intercom, I can hear the faint rasp of Hailey's voice. My eyes fall shut. It could have been so much worse.

The nurse pops her head out. "Are you Dora?"

Though it's been my name for years, right now, it's a relief to hear. "Yes."

"Your mother is awake. She'd like to see you."

My mother. The words make my throat constrict. I enter the room again, carried by those syllables. "Hi."

She gives me a weary smile and moves her mask aside. "Glad you're here," she whispers.

"What happened?"

She shrugs. "It started in a closet. Not sure how. But Martin found it, and I found him. I barely got him out before everything went up."

In a closet? "Was there a fuse box in there?"

She shakes her head. "That utility closet between the kitchen and the garage, where we keep our cleaning supplies."

Cleaning supplies. It sticks in my brain like a strawberry seed in my tooth. But I can't dig it out or make sense of it. "I'm glad you're okay."

"Martin will be fine too. His throat and lungs were seared a bit, I guess." Her eyes close.

"I'm sorry. About everything. I know you talked to Miles."

"My way of doing a sort of intervention. You don't need to do all this, kiddo. You don't need to lie all the time." She tucks her face back into her mask, takes a few more breaths, and lifts it again to continue. "We started loving you after we suspected, and the more we knew you, the more we loved you."

I sink onto the chair next to the bed. "I don't deserve it."

She reaches out, and I give her my hand. "You were always the sweetest, gentlest thing. You hadn't been with us more than two days when you went out and got us Christmas presents."

"It was the first real Christmas I'd had since I was little," I murmur. I let go of her hand. "But Martin gave me the money, so I don't deserve any credit."

"You're determined to get me to push you away, aren't you? And back then, you were afraid of letting us know anything about you."

"Because I was terrified you *would* push me away."

"Either way, you're convinced that if we all knew who you were—or now that we're starting to figure it out—we'll all see you're unlovable. But that's bullshit. Everybody deserves to be loved."

"That's why you're a social worker," I say with a sniffly laugh. "I've ruined my whole life."

"You've made mistakes. But you can fix them."

I shake my head. "You don't know what I've done. But now, that's going to be the question. And no one's going to believe anything I say, because I'm a liar."

"I know you didn't do this to me and Martin. You'd never hurt anyone on purpose."

I stare at the floor, remembering exactly how I hurt other people on purpose. "I didn't kill Arnold Moore. And I didn't kill Essie Green. I swear." I shake my head. "I don't think Ben believes me."

"Ben's a good man. He'll follow the evidence and the law."

I'm still shaking my head. "Miles is going to publish that story about me. You're quoted in it. You might have seen it as an intervention, but he sees it as a Pulitzer."

She frowns. "I got the sense he really cares about you."

"Doesn't matter. I care about him, but look at what I've done. Nothing but lies. If any of them had made their way to print, he would've been the one blamed—it's his byline." For all I know, he's already sent the piece to Valentina, and I can't blame him.

The problem is, it makes me look guilty as hell, and the whole world is about to know. Panic shakes me from the chair. "I'll let you rest." I move toward the door. "I love you, Hailey. I know I haven't shown it, and I've caused you and Martin nothing but grief, but I still love you. I'm so grateful for everything you've done for me." I can barely get the words out; it hurts too much. "Just know that, all right?" I turn to go.

"Dora?" Her voice is weak, but the word is powerful. I turn to look at her. "Don't run."

I press my lips together and flee, striding down the hall, through the emergency department, out the sliding doors. I call another Uber, assessing my options. Because running? Right now, it feels like the only thing I can do. I can't sit by and let them pull me apart, detail by detail, crime by crime.

I *have* to run. The only question is where. And how.

During the ride back to the hotel, I narrow it down. I can go to a Rite Aid, buy some hair dye, empty my bank accounts, and do my best to disappear...or I can swallow back my bottle of Vicodin and get it all over with.

I'm still churning as I unlock my hotel room door and sit on the bed. I pull out the bottle and read the label. Ten-milligram pills. I look it up—it takes nine or ten to kill a person.

I have fourteen.

I lie back on the bed. I've fought so hard, for so long, to survive. I've *killed* to survive. I've put myself ahead of everyone else, not caring about the damage I've done. Maybe it's time to stop running, like Hailey said. Maybe it's time to stop everything.

Or maybe it's time to stop being such a coward.

I sit up, shoving away the weight of my own self-disgust. I can't believe I'm doing this again. After a lifetime of running and finding nothing but pain and loneliness at the finish line, I'm *still* sitting here, thinking that's better than facing the truth. How pathetic and stupid.

Tomorrow is the twentieth anniversary. It's time to face this and take what comes.

I pull out my phone and voice text Miles. I'm sorry for lying, for putting your career at risk, for being a shitty fact-checker and friend. I'll set it right if you'll let me. Send the story to Valentina whenever you're ready. I'll verify the details if either of you guys trust me enough to let me near it, and if you don't, I'll work with whoever else you assign to it so they can independently verify. I'm done hiding.

I hit Send before I can think too much about it, diving off that high board without hesitation. It feels like I've just finished the longest, hardest run of my life.

A knock at my door brings my head up. It could be Ben, tracking me down. It could be the room cleaners. They knock again. I walk over to the door and peek out the peephole. No one's there. Curious, I open the door.

He looms over me, flattening his palm on the door even as I rear back to try to shut it. "Dora," says Noah. "I told you we needed to talk."

Then he pushes his way inside.

CHAPTER TWENTY-NINE

The Retreat
December 15, 2000

Before Parvaneh could grasp the handle of the knife, another hand batted hers away. Eszter's fingers closed around its hilt, and she claimed it for her own.

"Eszter, don't be greedy," Darius chided, his hands slipping away from Parvaneh's body.

"This," Eszter said, blowing out a shaky breath. "This is the most important thing I've ever done."

Parvaneh reached for the knife again, but Eszter whipped around, nearly slicing Parvaneh's fingers. "*Don't*," Eszter snapped.

Parvaneh edged back. Xerxes had sunk to the floor. Eszter stepped around him. She gazed up at Darius. "I've loved you since the day we met."

Darius smiled. "As I love you."

Eszter opened her arms. "I need your strength now."

Jealousy pulled so tight around Parvaneh that she could barely breathe. As people died all around her, Eszter was making this a romantic moment with Darius—and making Parvaneh watch, overwriting everything Darius had said to Parvaneh a moment ago. She almost gagged on her hatred.

Darius leaned into Eszter's embrace. She threw her arms around him. For a moment, all the sounds seemed to fade away. Darius's eyes closed.

Then he screamed.

The muscles of his neck went taut, and he shoved Eszter away and clawed at his back. His hand came away coated in his own blood. Before Parvaneh could understand what she was seeing, Eszter lunged. He wasn't even able to raise his arms to defend himself. Her arm whipped down again, and again, and again. His back, his belly, his throat. Parvaneh shrieked as she watched Darius collide with the dais, his blood-smeared hands knocking candles this way and that, one catching on his robe.

"Let's go, Parvaneh," Eszter screamed, hurling the knife away and scrambling over to Xerxes. She yanked him up and cradled the woozy boy's body. "I know the code!" She limped toward the door to Darius's office.

In a detached daze, Parvaneh took in the scene around her, Kazem sprawled on the floor, bleeding, Basir and Hamzi crouched over him, meditating as sweat and tears streamed down their cheeks. Zana was lying on the steps of the dais, flames from an errant candle licking at the hem of her robes, even as Kyra approached her from behind, hesitant but determined looking, hunting knife raised.

Darius was on the other side of the dais, inching forward on his stomach, his robe stained with blood. He reached out, desperately grasping...for Eszter, who was punching in the code to his private office.

Rage exploded through Parvaneh as she watched Eszter, the stupid, fat, homely, useless traitor, punch at the combination. She'd stabbed Darius. *Darius.* The only man who'd ever loved Parvaneh. She ran for him, reaching him as Eszter disappeared into the office.

"Darius," she cried.

He was bleeding from everywhere, it seemed. His lips dripped red as he turned to her, panting wetly. "Get her," he whispered hoarsely. "Three eight two one. Get her." He coughed.

Then Parvaneh coughed. The room was filling with smoke, bitter and stinging. On the other side of the altar danced a lick of flame. She tried to pick Darius up off the floor, desperate to pull him to safety, but he screamed in pain and was far too heavy to lift. Eszter had ruined him.

She'd ruined everything.

"Three eight two one," said Darius, his voice halting. Agonized. Their eyes met. "Go."

This was her test. She ran for the door and had it open a few seconds later. A thump from the closet told her where the traitor was—trying to escape through the tunnel to Darius's cabin. She moved toward the sound, even as she heard someone banging on the other side of the door to the meeting hall. "Let us out," Kyra screamed. "Fire!"

But Darius had given his orders. He'd offered her the chance to prove herself worthy, finally. She'd get Eszter, bring her back, and then she'd help the others. She drew in a deep breath and immediately fell to her knees, coughing. Smoke curled its fingers under the door, reaching for her. She crawled to the closet, pulled back the carpet square over the tunnel's trapdoor, and flung it open to find Eszter on the rungs, descending.

With all her strength, she grabbed Eszter by the hair. Eszter shrieked and clawed at her hands, but hatred and fury gave Parvaneh a power she'd never felt. Xerxes landed in a boneless sprawl at the bottom of the ladder, a foot caught in one of the lower rungs, but he wasn't going anywhere. Parvaneh wrenched the traitor upward and dragged her back into the office.

"Come with me," begged Eszter as she struggled to free herself from Parvaneh's merciless grasp. The smoke was getting thicker by the second. Holding a huge handful of Eszter's hair, Parvaneh yanked her toward the door to the meeting hall. From outside, she could hear staccato chirps; someone was trying to punch in the code. Her heart leapt. She grabbed the door handle, registering its incredible, searing heat only a second before it burst inward, bringing with it a wall of flames.

She brought her hands up as Darius fell on her, his robe on fire, his movements disjointed, the only sounds coming from him animal grunts. Nearby, Eszter let out a pained yelp; as Darius tumbled to the floor, the flames spread to the bottom of her robes as well, and she batted at them furiously.

Parvaneh dove for Eszter as she began to crawl back toward the closet. It felt like someone had wrapped a length of barbwire around her chest; breathing was a chore. But adrenaline fueled her. She jumped on Eszter, who screamed. A lancing pain brought new awareness—Parvaneh's robes were on fire too. But she wasn't going to let it stop her. She ripped the garment off. Naked and free, she grabbed Eszter just as the traitor reached the open trapdoor.

"Come with me," Eszter said again. "Think of your baby!"

"You ruined *everything*," Parvaneh shrieked, slamming her fists into Eszter's back. Her head. Any place she could reach. Her thoughts were a rending wail as everything she'd ever wanted and needed burned all around her, as the past stretched its skeletal fingers long and gashed her heart. She'd thought she'd broken free, but it was all she felt, all she had left, this black, hard misery and the realization that the one good thing she'd ever had was now ash and cinders. "You killed us!" She bunched her fingers in Eszter's robe and pulled her backward with all her remaining strength.

Eszter's hand plunged into her own robes, and she whirled around and up. Parvaneh registered a flash of blue before her vision exploded with fire and stars. Everything went inside out, bright red and all wrong. She collided with something hard—the corner of the safe—and went down. She found herself facing Darius, the man who had changed her world. But she couldn't make out his features anymore. *Everything* was engulfed in flames. Dizzy and confused, she looked around. Her thoughts had gone dark and sluggish like the smoke coiling and dancing above her. Everything hurt.

Eszter. That bitch had hit her in the head with a meditation stone. And she'd gotten away.

Parvaneh dragged herself toward the trapdoor. If she didn't get out of this room, she was going to die here, like Darius, like all of them. She would die, and it would be for nothing. Her baby girl would die for nothing.

With a lurching heave, she pulled the trapdoor open again. The flames bit at her ankles, her calves. She threw herself down headfirst and slammed into the dirt floor below, loose soil raining down from above, grit crunching in her teeth.

Her vision blurred with blood and tears, Parvaneh could just make out a limping, hunched figure ahead. Moving slowly. Weak and fragile. The traitor. The destroyer.

With every movement bringing a fresh agony, every breath telling her she didn't have many left, Parvaneh began to crawl after her, already knowing it was far too late.

CHAPTER THIRTY

Bend, Oregon
December 14, present day

I dart to the side, but he easily blocks my way and shuts the door. "I'll scream," I say.

"No, you won't," he says as he fastens the door's latch lock. "Have a seat."

I glare up at him, my thoughts spinning. He's so much bigger than I am. Unquestionably stronger. And I'm like a hollowed-out eggshell, ready to break.

When I don't move, he takes my arms and steers me toward the bed. The he looks down at me, those blue eyes intense. "Don't scream, okay? I only want to talk. I swear."

He's between me and the door. It won't be difficult for him to stop me if I run. I sit down on the edge of the bed. "Is this really necessary, Noah? You could have just called me."

"You didn't reply to my texts, so I knew you wouldn't answer if I called." He lets out a bark of laughter. "This isn't really a phone conversation anyway."

"I'm sorry I didn't read your story," I tell him. "And Miles didn't really want to—"

He holds up a hand. "It's not about that. Well, not about Miles."

"It *is* about the story, though," I say. "I know your first one was fake—the Children of Darius message board isn't real. You made it up."

His brow furrows. "It's totally real."

"Miles met another child of Darius. The kid's been looking for his half siblings for years, putting up his genetic info on all the sites, including the one you mentioned in your story. And he's had no luck."

"That doesn't make sense." He's pacing in front of me, his palms cupping his elbows. "I've read all the posts." He whirls on me. "You think I made it up? That's why you won't give me the time of day?"

"If the group is real, then how did you really find it, Noah?" I watch his intense pacing—I've seen it before. In times of stress, in times of concentration, *he* would do the exact same thing. That night at the altar, moments before everything burned, this is how he looked. Because he knew what he was about to do. Because he craved the power of life and death, and he knew how to make it happen. My stomach drops. "You're one of them. You're his son. That's how."

He drops to his knees in front of me. "You recognize me?"

"How old are you?" I whisper. I'm so blind. I never once considered...

"You probably could figure it out if you spent two seconds on it."

"Xerxes," I breathe, swiping at my tears with my sleeves. I should have known. A laugh escapes me. "So many questions." And so many demands. "You haven't changed."

"You have," he says. "You used to be a lot bigger."

"You used to look up at me," I say as memories consume me. My gaze darts back to his face. "I thought you might be dead because of what I did."

"You would have read it on the news if there had been a child victim."

I shake my head. I'm afraid to say why it might not have been. I'm afraid he remembers.

"Well, here I am," he says in a hard voice. "Did you ever wonder what happened to me? Or did you just give up on me and get on with your own life?"

I shoot to my feet, my limbs shaking so much that I almost crumple to the bed again. "You have no idea—" My voice breaks. "You have *no* idea how badly I wanted to save you."

He looks confused. "But you did. Didn't you?"

I watch him warily. He was so young, and he was drugged. Does he actually know what happened? And if he does... "Why are you here?"

"I recognized you that first night we met at the bar, but I wasn't sure," he tells me. "I went to the library, checked the archives. I found that picture—Miles told me it was gone. I swear I didn't steal it."

"I know," I whisper. "I did."

He blinks at me. As if he's surprised I told the truth. "You looked really different but not different enough. And the way you hold yourself—that's the same. Like you're expecting someone to hurt you or yell at you." He gets to his feet. "I remember that night. Some of it, at least."

I close my eyes. I can almost smell the smoke. I can almost feel that soft, blond hair tickling under my chin. "I wish I didn't."

"He was going to kill me."

I nod. "He didn't like it when people defied him. And you..." I smile in spite of the ache in my chest. "You were *always* defiant."

He chuckles. "Yeah, my parents—they adopted me out of the

foster care system, didn't mind having an older kid because they were older themselves—they had to deal with how messed up I was. I'm therapized from head to foot. You'd think I'd be the most mentally healthy person in the fucking world, but..." He gives me a rueful look.

"You went through so much before you were even five years old."

"My mom," he says. "My *birth* mom. What kills me most is I never really knew... I remember her telling me to run. I remember being so scared. And then I never saw her again, and everybody said she left me."

"Octavia died that night, Noah. The night she tried to escape with you. It kills *me* that I helped bring you back."

"You didn't kill her, though," he says. "But I know who did." His voice has taken on the hard edge of long-suppressed rage. "Ladonna."

I feel like a rabbit, cornered by a fox. Afraid to move and draw his attention. I nod slowly. He was always smart, aggressive, and sharp. He could have killed Essie, exacting a final revenge on the woman who killed his mother. He could have killed Marie Heckender too. He hated Fabia even then. And she's the one who pushed him back into the building that night. The one who wouldn't let him escape his own death. Horror rises inside me. "Noah..." My voice shrivels to nothing. If he thinks I'm not an ally, he could literally snap my neck easy as breathing.

"Your mother was one of the nicest people I ever met," I say. "All she was trying to do that night was protect you and your little sister. She deserved so much better." I'm glad he doesn't know everything. His fury would be endless. And so would his pain.

"My sister," he murmurs. "I'll have to ask Arman... There aren't any girls on the board." He runs his knuckles along his stubbly jawline. "I was hoping the article would draw her out. She's the only full sibling I've got."

"Does Arman know you're his half brother?"

"No. I...I wasn't going to tell anyone. Ever. That asshole was my father." He grimaces. "I think I'm a lot like him."

It's probably why Darius disliked him. Xerxes always wanted to be the one in charge, even as a child. And while some men, some leaders, would be gratified by that similarity, it had all gone sour by the end, and Darius couldn't handle the boy's willfulness. "You're not like him, Noah. Don't think like that." Then I remember how he got in here. And what he might have done. Three people are dead. And Miles...

Noah's eyes narrow. "Why are you looking at me like that?"

"Did you copy my car key?"

He rears back. "No. Why would I even want to?"

"Do you happen to drive a blue car?"

"Yeah? So?"

My mouth has gone dry. His tone is like a blade, but I have to know. "Did you run Miles Connover off the road last night?"

His eyes go wide. "What the fuck? Is Miles okay?"

I can't tell if he's being genuine. "Pretty banged up, but alive and alert."

"Why would you think I'd do something like that?"

I shrug. "Honestly, I can't figure out what's happening. I only know that my entire life has crumbled around me, and it's my fault."

"You want to go take a look at my car? See if there are any dents or scratches? Would that help?"

I'm not sure. He and Arman still might have copied my key. But if we go out to the parking lot, it gives me a little room to call attention to myself, to get away. I still don't know what he remembers or whether he blames me for what happened or whether he's murdered three people in the last few weeks. "Okay."

"Let's go." He strides toward the door, opens it, and waits for me. I follow cautiously, waiting for the trick. He pulls his car key from his pocket as we reach the lobby. My eyes search for the hotel clerk as I pass, but no one's behind the front desk at the moment.

The air is thick with mist and drizzle as Noah and I exit the building. I look up at him, his hair dripping, water streaking down the harsh plains of his cheeks, and I can almost see the little boy with bright-blue eyes. The one who missed his mother so badly. The one who wanted to understand the world and all its mysteries. The one who had a question for everything. Now that I know who he was, my question is: Who has he become?

He points to a blue Honda parked next to the dumpster, in the shadow of a big pine. "Not a scratch on her," he says over the hiss of rain. He looks down at me. "You look nervous as hell, Dora. Let's go somewhere and get something to eat."

I look up at him warily.

He rolls his eyes and offers me his key. "Do you want to drive? Would that make you feel better?"

I shake my head. "I appreciate the offer, though."

Noah squints through the car's rear window. "What the..." He strides faster toward his vehicle, with me a few steps behind. The rear passenger door opens as I reach his side, revealing Arman inside.

He's holding a gun tucked close to his flank, aimed up at Noah. "When you said you were coming here to talk to her, I knew I had another chance. I was going to do it when we got ice cream yesterday, but *she* ran off." His gaze flicks to me. "Get in or I'm going to shoot him."

Noah goes stiff. "What the fuck are you doing, man?"

Arman's finger is curled around the trigger. "You can drive," he says to Noah. "But keep both hands in sight, or I'll shoot *her*."

Ashen, Noah drops into place and puts his hands on the steering wheel.

Arman keeps the gun pressed to the back of Noah's seat. "Get in, Dora. Now."

I obey. Something about the eerie, friendly calm of his voice chills me from the inside out. I had thought Noah reminded me of Darius, but Arman... I flinch as the door slams. "You stole my key," I say, guessing.

He snorts. "I knew I could get it copied the moment I saw how old your car is. It was easy." He glances to the front. "I put the address into your GPS. Just follow it. Oh! Hand me your phone first. You too, Dora."

Noah curses under his breath but does as he says. I do too.

As Noah pulls out of the parking lot, Arman hurls our phones out the window, and they land in a puddle at the side of the road.

I thought he was the follower. The weak one in Noah's sway. But now... "Is the Children of Darius board real?"

"Nah. It's just me and a lot of aliases."

"You asshole," Noah says. "*Why?*"

"We were looking for you," he says. "You...and *her*." He inclines his head in my direction. "And we thought if we found one of you, we might find the other."

"We," I say.

Arman smiles. "We're going to see Mother. She was so happy when she figured out who you were."

My heart is a fist, clenched tight. "Your mother," I whisper. Because it's not only Darius he resembles, and now I know why it struck me as so familiar. The shape of his eyes, the bridge of his nose—

His smile has gone now. "She said everything is your fault. You left us to die."

My lips shake as I murmur her name, one I haven't spoken aloud in twenty years. "Parvaneh."

CHAPTER THIRTY-ONE

The Retreat
December 15, 2000

Eszter burst into the dark of Darius's cabin, her limbs shaking, muscles ready to give out. The child in her arms felt like he weighed a thousand pounds.

She'd been training for something like this for the last several weeks, but even the short runs she'd tried to take in the woods had left her winded. Still, she didn't have a choice now.

Outside, the fire raged, but in here, she could only see the orange outline of it through the trees. And she could smell the smoke, but it was drifting up from below, from the passage she'd just dragged herself down, step by agonizing step.

She laid Xerxes on the bed. He stirred, whimpering. She'd wanted to only give him a little of the drug to keep him calm, to keep him from trying to escape by himself. She'd known he might try, and she'd been certain it would result in his death. Now, his ankle swollen a lurid purple and clearly broken, even if he woke up, he wouldn't be able to run.

She'd have to carry him. A desperate moan unfurled from her throat. It felt like her legs were still wrapped in the flames. A quick glance told her the skin of her calves was ripe with blisters and ash, red and black and gray. But she was still breathing, still alive. With a long way to go before she and Xerxes were safe.

A shout from outside made her flinch. If anyone else knew about the passage, they might check in here. And if she stayed here, the smoke would get too thick, and soon. Already it was wafting up from below. They had to go.

Eszter drew in a breath and coughed. "I can do this," she whispered, rolling her shoulders. She pulled the woolen blanket up from the corners of the bed, wrapping Xerxes like a burrito. He let out a high-pitched cry as she folded it around his feet, and she murmured an apology. Then she looked down at him.

What would Octavia think if she knew? Was she somewhere in the deep consciousness, hungering to see her boy again? Eszter shook herself. She wasn't sure any of it was real anymore. She hadn't been since the night they'd all let her baby girl die. She'd allowed Darius close, needing the comfort, expecting things to start making sense again, only to discover there was no going back. His words had sounded hollow. Cruel, even. He hadn't believed their child had a soul, not until it could be born alive. But Eszter had felt the vigorous kicks, the twists, the stretches. She'd known there was a real person inside her, needing protection until she was ready to emerge. No way it was just a soulless body.

Now she had another child to protect. And she felt more vulnerable than ever.

She moved to the door, opened it, and listened. Voices droned in the distance, but from the other side of the dorms. They were occupied with the fire, their voices rising in alarm. Hopefully they wouldn't notice or hear the two of them escaping.

She returned to the bed. With a groan, she lifted Xerxes and turned for the door. She froze when she heard another sound. One she herself hadn't made.

It had filtered up through the open trapdoor leading to the crumbling tunnel, just a scrape and a rasp. *Parvaneh.* Terror jolted her bones, guilt and sorrow hard on its heels. The last year flashed through her mind, the decision to approach the pale, skinny girl on the curb, the way that girl had become the best friend she'd ever had. It was Darius who'd ruined it, Darius who'd been the wedge between them. She'd been so sure Parvaneh would come with her, so sure they'd be allies. And she knew it was her fault they weren't—she'd let her fear suffocate her honesty. And just now, she'd felt Parvaneh's determination. She'd really been trying to kill, and Eszter and Xerxes would both be doomed by now if Eszter hadn't remembered the stone in her pocket.

She looked down at the little boy in her arms. She had no choice. She'd already decided who to save, and he would die if she didn't protect him.

She kicked the door to the passageway closed, squeezing her eyes shut as she whirled away from it. Forcing herself not to think about what she'd just done. Shouldering the cabin door open, she burst into the night air, gritting her teeth as the cold wind slapped her burned, bare legs. Her robe hung to her knees before ending in burned, frayed bits, and her feet squished and slid in her clogs. The boy in her arms was leaden, dragging her to the ground. She weaved her way through the trees, heading for the spot far behind the barns, almost at the edge of the property. Everything she needed was there.

But within a few hundred yards, every step was a determined effort. A wrenching stomp, an agonized rasp of breath through her singed throat, a readjustment of the fifty-pound bundle in her arms. Stomp, rasp, clutch. Over and over. She'd meant to run, but now even walking was becoming impossible. The thick adrenaline fog that had propelled her through the last hour was fading to fumes, pulling back the curtain on the pain, the terror.

The guilt.

She shook her head. If she thought too much about it, she'd drop to the forest floor and never get up. Instead, she pressed forward. Stomp, rasp, clutch. The cache, her treasures, were waiting.

She'd collected them slowly, week after week, from the homes they'd cleaned. Saved them for the moment she became sure. She hadn't wanted to be sure. She'd wanted to be convinced everything was good and right and getting better every day. She'd wanted to know she'd made the right decision, becoming an Oracle. Instead, each day had brought a touch more horror, and each night brought a touch more certainty, as Darius whispered his bloody fantasies in her ear. But each passing hour had also brought worry—these were people she cared about. People she didn't want to leave behind.

But now all of them were dead. Except for one. And it might all be worth it if she could save him.

When she reached the mound of pine needles that marked the spot, with the hulking barn, ebony and dense in the distance, she dropped to her knees and finally allowed herself to put Xerxes down. Her arms felt as if they were sleeved with stinging hornets, branded with the fiery pain of her own weakness. Shaking, she crawled over to the pine needle mound and thrust her hands into it, even as the spiny golden sprigs coated her bare, blistered legs. She pulled free an old sneaker, gray and purple. A size too big, but she'd hoped it would be close enough. She'd shoved it under her robe after finding it in a box marked *Goodwill* in the homeowner's garage, but she hadn't been able to dig through long enough to find its mate—Ladonna had noticed she was missing and come to find her. And then, a week later, she'd found another shoe, this one a dingy, white Converse, at the bottom of another homeowner's closet, piled with other shoes. Surely she wouldn't miss it?

Weeks, it had taken. She rummaged through the pine needles, pulling free a pair of woolen socks, a pair of old sweats, a man's flannel shirt, a hideous pink parka, a pair of holey tighty-whities she'd found in a bathroom wastebasket. Ordinary clothes. Ones that didn't mark her as a fool. A freak.

She looked down at Xerxes. Shook him by the shoulders before realizing that even if he was awake, she'd still have to carry him. Tears stung her eyes. She ripped the robe over her head, wrapped herself in the flannel, realized she should have stolen a bra. She leaned against the puzzle-piece bark of a ponderosa to remain upright while she pulled on the underwear and slowly inched the sweats up her legs, silently screaming in her head. She shoved her arms into the parka's sleeves, then pulled the small wad of cash from its inner pocket. Almost thirty dollars. She'd swiped it dollar by dollar so no one would notice, from spare cash in desk drawers, the tip jar in a salon, an emergency stash under someone's mattress. That one had been a five, but she prided herself on the fact that she hadn't taken more. She didn't want to hurt anyone. Didn't want to steal. But she'd been desperate.

She was desperate now. She'd begun to shiver, even in the parka. She needed to be moving again, to put distance between herself and Ladonna and Fabia and Tadeas. If they found her, they'd almost certainly kill her. Her crimes would be obvious.

She'd committed so many. In the end, her survival had mattered most. Hers and that of the boy at her feet. She didn't know why he'd become so important. She'd forgiven him for kicking her that night. It wasn't his fault. It might not have been the cause of the stillbirth. His spirit had reminded her that she could be brave. His defiance had reminded her that disobedience was an option. She knelt beside him, eyes burning, throat burning, everything alight. She slid her arms beneath him once more and heaved.

But she couldn't lift him. Somewhere in the last few minutes, her strength had left her, the fuel that had gotten her this far burned away. A strangled cry slipped between her lips as she tried again. It was freezing out here. He might die of hypothermia. He couldn't even walk. Her tears flecked his cheeks as she tried yet again.

She wasn't strong enough to save him. Just like she hadn't been able to save her little girl. After all that, she still wasn't enough.

Her chest bucked with a sob she was too scared to let out. She pressed her lips to his cold cheek, leaned her forehead against his. "I'm so sorry. I tried *so* hard," she whispered to him. "You deserve to live."

She shucked off the parka and wrapped it around his little body, over the blanket. He was breathing steadily, though soot blackened his nostrils and the corners of his mouth. His little heart beat furiously beneath her palm, defiant as ever. She'd imagined the two of them finding a new path in the world. She'd been ready to make sure he had a chance.

Now she had to abandon him. Like his mother had, neither of them strong enough to shield him from the world. Was it better for him to die in his sleep, out here in the woods, no more pain?

That was the basest, most pathetic lie she'd ever tried to tell herself. Of course it wouldn't be better. It would be yet another death on her bloodstained hands. Yet another abandonment. Like she'd abandoned Eric two years ago, whispering to him in the night that she had to go, no he couldn't come with her, he was too young, their stepfather wasn't interested in him so he'd be fine. She'd told him to be strong. She'd promised she'd be back for Christmas just to get him to stop crying. He probably hated her now.

Like Xerxes might if he lived.

After one more sad, wrenching heave, she gave up. Her face soaked with snot and tears, she tucked the corners of the pink parka tight around him, then got to her feet. On impulse, she piled pine needles around his body, hoping to trap his heat, hoping it would be enough. As she stepped back, a pop of color caught her eye; her meditation stone, which she'd used to hit Parvaneh, lay on the ground next to her discarded robe. In the end, it had saved her, just not how she'd expected. Amid all the unreality and sorrow of the moment, it was the one thing she could take with her to remind herself all of it had happened, that she wasn't insane, that she had escaped something real. She stuffed it in the pocket of the flannel shirt.

Walking away was harder than murder as it turned out. It wasn't a sharp, shocking pain, like the moment the blade of that hunting knife sank into Darius's body. This was an agony that rose with every step that carried her away from Xerxes. A searing certainty.

She bore the agony, plotted her way through the tree-studded darkness using the white markers she'd painstakingly laid down for herself to guide her to the state road...and she began to navigate toward freedom. Behind her, the fire glowed orange and evil. With every shift of the wind, she could smell death in the air. She wondered what people would find when it was all over. Would they know what she'd done, or would the flames cover the evidence of her crimes?

By the time she neared the county road, four miles through the woods, with sirens screaming and the sun laying the truth bare, she was on her hands and knees. Crawling, too exhausted to carry her hideous, weak body any farther. Defeated, sobbing, she dragged herself to a culvert near the road. She edged herself inside, soaking her sweats but finding a dry spot where the slender trickle of water diverted. A place to rest, finally. Wondering if this was her last morning on earth, praying that something out there would reach for her if she fell, carrying her to some golden vein of peace and light, she let her eyes fall shut and found nothing but darkness waiting.

CHAPTER THIRTY-TWO

Bend, Oregon
December 14, present day

Noah slows as his GPS tells him his destination is on the right. He turns into a gravel driveway rutted with mud and puddles. In front of us is a tiny cabin, smoke puffing from its chimney. The windows are lit with a cheery glow. It looks almost quaint. Noah pulls in behind an ancient-looking Ford Fairmount that I swear I've seen before—turning at an intersection on Hailey and Martin's street the morning the meditation stone was left on their doorstep.

"Get out," Arman snaps. He pokes Noah with the muzzle of the gun again.

Noah curses and shoves his door open, emerging with Arman close behind him. Arman keeps the weapon aimed at Noah. He seems to sense I'm no threat at all. Together, we make for the rotting front porch, our shoes sloshing in the mud.

As if she senses our approach, she opens the door. I haven't seen her in two decades, and I of all people know how time can warp and squeeze and twist a body. But still I am shocked by what I see.

She used to be so slender. I couldn't help but be jealous. I'd been slow and fat and hapless my whole life, something my mother harped about nonstop, hiding food and shaming me, something my stepfather used to make me think we were on the same side, slipping me treats, making me believe he cared so he could use me how he liked and keep me quiet. I'd dream of being tiny, lovely, certain everyone who saw me approved. And Parvaneh *was* lovely. Big eyes, silky hair, lips that formed a perfect little bow. Darius's gaze always turned hungry as he watched her. Only in the moments near the end, when those eyes would roll, when that mouth would twist with bitterness or suspicion, was her prettiness marred.

The woman before me bears little resemblance to that person. Her straw-like brown hair hangs to her chin. Her face sags with the weight of jowls and is pitted and slashed by scars, as if meth has been a close friend for years. Her body is swathed in a black tracksuit that clings to every roll and pucker. Her hands are encased in blue gloves. She sees me looking at them. "Burned," she says in a flat voice. Then she steps aside.

Arman wraps his fingers around my upper arm and pushes me inside after Noah. Parvaneh has pulled two chairs away from a table that takes up a good portion of the space. On one side of the room is a bunk bed, sheets rumpled and blankets tossed back. On the other is a square of counter space littered with crusty dishes, a small stove, a window with dingy beige curtains. At the back is a closed door, maybe one that leads to a bathroom. And set into the wall a few feet from the bed is a fireplace where cheerful flames dance.

Arman positions himself on one side of it, the gun still aimed at Noah. "Do as she says," he instructs. He glares at Noah. "I could shoot you."

"Because you've killed before, am I right?" Noah asks.

"He hasn't killed anyone," Parvaneh says. "He only sets the fires."

I stare at her. So casual about the lives she's taken. "You murdered all of them."

"They deserved it. You of all people know that."

"Are you the one who ran Miles off the road?" I ask.

"That was me," Arman announces, looking proud of himself. "He was about to draw too much attention to things, and Mother wanted a little more time to bring you in. So I took care of it. And I used your car, so people might think it was you." He looks at his mother.

"The reporter survived," she says, sounding irritated. "And framing her was stupid. What if she'd been arrested? How would we have gotten her?"

Arman clenches his jaw and stares at the floor.

Parvaneh leans against the counter. "You lost the weight," she says to me. "Looks like you went a little too far if you ask me."

"I didn't," I say quietly.

She grunts. "I've been looking for you for ages. Imagine my happiness when I figured out your little game."

I look over at Noah, whose eyes streak left and right like he's trying to find a way out. But Arman has that barrel aimed straight at his head. I pray he doesn't move.

"How did you find me?" I ask.

She laughs. "It wasn't easy—until it was. I looked for Anna Wilbur for years, along with Eszter Wilbur. Hell, Eszter anything. I even found your brother on Facebook and stalked him for a while, but after he posted about his long-lost sister a few years ago, I realized you were enough of a coward that I'd have to work a little harder." She gives me a stiff smile. "So I decided to come back to Bend. Because you know the only person who wasn't too chicken to go by his birth name? Tadeas. Arnold Moore."

"You forgot that Marie lady," says Arman.

"No, I didn't," Parvaneh snaps. "She changed her name when she got married. She wasn't hard to find. A pain in the ass to kill, though." She looks down at me. "You probably didn't feel so bad when you heard she was dead, am I right? You and I both hated that one."

"Jesus, you're evil," Noah mutters.

Parvaneh rolls her eyes. "She was always a bitch. But Arnie, he was just stupid. And talkative, with the right lubricant." She mimes lifting a bottle to her lips and gulping down its contents, then staggers a little. "It made him easy to kill too. But before I did, he told me how to find Ladonna. He'd seen her at the hospital when he had to take his girlfriend for some infection or something."

"But he couldn't have known about me," I say.

Her smile is eerie, her eyes faraway. "He didn't know what he knew. But because he was so helpful with Ladonna, I asked if he knew more. You know what he said? He knew some folks who'd taken in a girl just after the night we burned. And they'd always wondered if she had been part of the Oracles."

I shake my head, unable to wrap my head around what she's saying. "But they didn't even know—"

"It almost didn't work," she tells me. "Hailey didn't want to hire a cleaning lady at first, but I've got experience, and I don't charge much." She smiles at me. "Remember how we did that? And they've got the sweetest picture hanging in their living room. The one of their dead little girl. All it took was a question about her to get the story, and a few more questions after that to get her talking about *you*."

"She didn't know I changed my name," I said.

"Then maybe she never knew you as well as I do," Parvaneh says.

"I know how sneaky and greedy you are, how you like to take what isn't yours. Hell, you stole *my* fake name and made it your own, *Christy*. And it worked, so why wouldn't you do it again? Hailey had told me you worked for an online news magazine, and when I Googled Dora Rodriguez, sure enough, LinkedIn told me exactly where you worked. It all matched up." She tugs at her gloves. "I thought I'd have to go up to Seattle to get you," she says. "I wanted to scare you first, though. I wanted you to know what was coming. So I tipped off your friend Miles." She grins, shaking her head. "I never thought you'd have the balls to come down here yourself. But I'm so glad you did."

"You didn't have to go after Hailey and Martin." My fingers curl around the edges of my seat. "They're completely innocent."

She shrugs. "I didn't do much, really. Arman snuck in and put that candle in the closet. Hung the oily rag over it. But I'm the one who got Hailey to give me the keys to the castle, so to speak."

"Why hurt them, though?"

Her expression twists. "You murdered the most important person in the world to me. You ruined my son. I needed you to feel that. Too bad the fire took too long to catch." She gives Arman a scathing look.

It takes every shred of self-control I have not to scream with rage. "You didn't have to do that! You knew I was at a hotel. You even figured out which one."

"Actually, I did," Noah says with a sigh. "The mistake I made was telling Arman. Not to mention falling for his whole Children of Darius message-board scam." He turns to Arman, looking hopeful. "You really had me going, buddy. It's all fake, right?"

Arman nods. "She wanted to find you too."

"And I totally fell for it." Noah leans forward. "But you hear what she's saying about you? What she really thinks?" he asks, though Arman won't meet his eyes. "She said you're *ruined*. She's dragged you into this, and now she's blaming you."

"The only one to blame is *her*," Parvaneh says loudly, pointing at me. "*She* recruited me into the Oracles. We're only here because of her. Everything we've suffered is because of her." Her voice rises. "Arman was born *damaged* because of her." Her palm collides with the side of my face, twisting it to the side.

My ears ring and my cheek burns. I keep my eyes on the floor while I catch my breath.

"Arman told me what happened to your wrist," she says. "You're easier to break than you used to be. You used to have all that fat protecting you."

I slowly raise my head but keep my gaze trained straight ahead. "Did you bring me here just to insult me?"

"I brought you here," she says loudly, "to make sure you understood what you'd done."

I meet her eyes. "I know I hurt you. I know you being in the Oracles was my fault. I've never forgiven myself for that. But I tried to get you to come with me. You have to remember that. I tried to get both of us out."

"You tried to get me in trouble!" yells Parvaneh, her eyes suddenly sheened with tears. "You *tried* to turn everyone against me!"

"I *tried* to get you to see how insane it all was," I shout. "It wasn't safe to be open with anyone, remember? I dropped as many hints as I could!"

Her lips peel away from her teeth. She's missing her top left canine. "All while you were glued to his side, sucking up all his attention. You expect me to believe you were somehow trying to help?"

My nostrils flare. "You know what I was actually trying to do? Darius would have killed more people a lot sooner. That's what he wanted to do after Octavia. He was acting like a cornered animal. He wanted to sacrifice one Oracle each night, just like the pigs."

"I remember the pigs," Noah says, staring into the fire. "I could hear them squealing when Kazem tried to give them that medicine."

"You think you were saving people?" Parvaneh hisses. "What if that had been the key to our salvation—did you ever think of that? You stopped Darius from acting out the wisdom of the consciousness."

"Apparently, I didn't." I remember the tightrope every night, as he brought me to his bed, as he proclaimed that he'd heal my sorrow with a new baby, a new vessel for a soul. I swallowed down my growing disgust, and I tried, in any quiet, nonchallenging way I could think of, to steer that man away from killing us all, all while slowly plotting an escape. "I'm sorry. I never knew where you stood. I was afraid you'd give me away. And you're right about me—I was too much of a coward to admit I had doubts."

Parvaneh's eyes are lit with hatred. "But you let me get beaten for them. You told everyone it was *me* who doubted."

"I know you did. You were too smart not to."

"I loved Darius," she says, her voice rising again. "I loved him more than all of them did, and he was the only person who ever really loved me. And you killed him for no reason."

"No *reason*?" I whisper. "Darius wanted us to slaughter a child. All around us, people were being murdered—people we loved and cared about! Darius wasn't going to let Xerxes out of there alive."

"Maybe that was for the best," Parvaneh says.

Noah glares at her with a chilling kind of disdain. "You were made for him," he says. "So why didn't you stay by his side instead of running to safety?"

"Because of you!" howls Parvaneh. "You were meant to be the sacrifice. And you," she says, her manic gaze falling on me, "murdered the most amazing man in the world—I burned my hands trying to save him, but it was too late." She's holding them up, evidence of my crime.

"I know what I did," I say wearily.

"And he wasn't going to kill *you*," she adds. "So it wasn't self-defense. He trusted you, and you used it against him. For some horrible reason, he liked you best."

"He thought I was weak," I tell her. "He thought he had complete control over me, and he fed off it." Like my stepfather had. It hurt so much when I finally realized that. "And for a while, he *did* have control. I lived for him, and I lived for the journey. I believed in it until it stopped making sense. And once it did, I couldn't get things to fall into place anymore."

"Because you *are* weak," she says.

"I didn't want you to be hurt," I say. "I wanted you and your baby girl to get out." I glance at Arman. "She was so sure you were a girl." Then I turn back to Parvaneh. "I wanted to save you both."

"I saved myself," she says with a smile, raising her arms from her sides. "But only barely." Then she takes off her gloves and turns her palms to me, her hands braided with shiny scars. "Second- and third-degree burns. Nerve damage. Because unlike you, I tried to save him."

I won't give her the satisfaction of looking away. "None of us got out without damage."

"I barely made it out of that tunnel before it collapsed because you shut the door on me! I got lost in the woods and didn't find the road for two days. I was nearly dead, but I had to walk to that gas station on 20, which was miles away. I hid in the bed of a pickup and ended up in Salem, which is where I collapsed." Her face morphs into a caustic smile. "A pregnant Jane Doe. Weeks in the hospital. A few lies, a new start." Her eyes narrow. "And a new purpose."

I incline my head toward Arman. "You saved your baby. You did the right thing."

"Still saying whatever you think will save your skin," Parvaneh says, "no matter who it hurts in the end. Sweet, bland, weak Eszter." Her expression goes sour. "The face of a marshmallow, hiding the soul of a snake." She strides over to the fireplace and picks up a piece of kindling wood, a crooked, dry stick about two-fingers thick. She dips it into the flames. "I put fire retardant on Arnie. I wanted it to be obvious, what it was all about. I wanted to show the world what you put Darius through, how merciless you were. Didn't have time with Marie. She actually put up a fight. And Essie I didn't bother to stab. Just let her burn instead."

"I did that one. And I used your car to get there." Arman pulls a key from his pocket and holds it up.

"This isn't you, Arman," says Noah, trying to catch his eye. "You don't have to do any of this. You could end it here. Because you and me? We're friends. We can all just walk out of here right now," Noah suggests. His voice has turned soft. Rhythmic.

"Stop trying to twist me up!" yells Arman, slamming the butt of the handgun down on Noah's temple. Noah gags, like the pain is making him sick.

Parvaneh looks pleased. "I learned a few things from Darius," she says, still dragging her kindling stick through the fire. "The consciousness is pleased with you, baby," she says to him.

He gives her a wavering smile. She's done to her child what Darius did to us: invited our minds into little cages and danced away with the keys. "Why now?" I ask. "Why not let it lie?"

"Twenty years," she says. "With all of them finally out of jail and Arman old enough to be helpful. It seemed right." Kindling stick aflame, she walks over to me, trembling with what looks like excitement. "You're the reason we all burned, aren't you? All your struggling and fighting. That's when all the candles got knocked over."

"If it was me, then I'm sorry. I only wanted to save Xerxes."

She shoves the flame in my face, and I lean back as heat sears my nostrils. "You wanted to save one annoying kid, and you condemned the rest of us to die."

She's so warped that trying to convince her otherwise is pointless. I turn my head, leaning back so far that my chair tips back. Parvaneh lurches it back onto all four legs, shoving the flames close to my face again.

Panicked, I draw back my foot and jam it against her shin. It knocks her back and sends shooting pains up my lower right leg.

I think I might have just broken my ankle.

"Hey!" shouts Arman, stepping around Noah with the gun. But as Parvaneh pushes off the rusted refrigerator, flame still in hand, Arman looks over at her—and Noah jumps up, grabbing at Arman's arms. Knocking him against the back door, grunting and struggling.

With a screech, Parvaneh lunges for me, fiery stick leading the way, but I dive under the table, landing on hands and knees, my broken wrist screaming. Searing heat blooms on my left leg—Parvaneh has set it on fire. I shriek and bat at it while she tries to light the rest of me. As she thrusts the flaming stick under the table again, Noah knocks Arman off balance, and he goes staggering into his mother, flinging her against the counter.

Her flailing arm drags the stick across the window's curtains, setting them aflame just as I extinguish the pant leg that she'd set alight. My whole body is a ball of pain and terror while Noah and Arman punch at each other and Parvaneh, rubbing her side, comes for me again. She seems oblivious to the fact that the flames are now stretching toward the wooden ceiling. She only has eyes for me.

There's a sharp bang above me, followed immediately by another, thinner snap, and then a scream from Arman, who goes down clutching his leg. Ricochet.

As Noah dives for him, Arman fires from the floor. Noah falls back, blood spotting his shoulder, but somehow manages to kick the weapon out of the stunned boy's hands. Arman looks stricken as the gun spins across the floor toward his mother. She's only a few feet away from the table I'm under.

"Shoot him," Arman screeches as Noah collapses against the wall.

The heat from the flaming curtains is burning in my throat. Cinders descend in spirals from the ceiling. Parvaneh glares at Noah and bends down to pick up the gun. He's struggling to get to his feet again. He can't protect himself or get out of the way. Like that night twenty years ago, he's mine to protect.

I lunge from under the table and throw myself toward Parvaneh, bringing my casted wrist up with all the strength I have left. It collides with her face, and everything buckles. A shocking, icy numbness bleeds up my arm, which falls lifeless to my side. No pain, all pain. As she drops to her knees, cupping her hands around her bloody, gushing nose, I scoot back using only my left leg and right hand.

Arman crawls toward his mother, bawling, groping for the gun. I know what happens when he gets to it. My only chance is to get out.

But I can't leave Noah behind again. I wasn't strong enough twenty years ago. I'm not strong enough now. I have to try, though. I turn and peer through the smoke, but I can't see him anymore. "Noah," I call, sucking in a lungful of the acrid smoke. My body heaves; I can't breathe. Dimly, behind me, I hear Parvaneh and Arman coughing too, and I hear him talking to her, begging her to tell him what to do.

She tells him to kill me. My left arm hanging limp, my right ankle unable to support my weight, my lungs burning, I turn to look for Noah one more time. A dark shape looms on the other side of the table, and he reaches for me. His arms slide under my back, my knees. His arms pull me up. Hold me against him. In three long strides, he's out the door, just as the roof begins to crumble and fall in. He staggers a few steps before falling to his knees. "He's coming," Noah gasps. "He'll—"

There's a ravenous crack and groan, and the roof of the cabin caves in. Through the open door, I see a shower of fiery, orange sparks before Parvaneh and Arman disappear beneath the avalanche of brittle boards covered in a layer of wet shingles. Noah and I watch it burn for a moment, and then he says, "We need to get farther away."

"I can't walk," I say hoarsely.

He looks down at his bleeding shoulder, his jaw clenched. "I can carry you."

And he does, just twenty feet down the drive, but it's far enough. He sets me down under a ponderosa pine, on a thick layer of needles. I shake my head. "We need to get you to a hospital."

"You too," he says.

"Someone will see the fire and call it in."

He nods. I watch his profile, the blood crusting at his temple. "I was so worried you'd die of hypothermia," I murmur over the rush of flames. The little cabin is engulfed. Parvaneh and Arman are still inside. I'm too numb to feel anything.

"I woke up in the morning," he says, staring at the flames. "Pine needles all around me, like a cocoon. Someone had wrapped me so tight I could barely get out. And my ankle was broken. But I crawled back to the dorms, and there was yellow tape everywhere, and a police lady found me."

"I wanted to take you with me, but I wasn't strong enough," I choke out. "I left you there to save myself."

"You saved me," he says. "You don't think I remember?" He jerks his head toward the cabin. "*She* would have killed me. So when I woke up out there in the woods, in that pink coat—it was pink, right?"

I nod.

"I knew you had put me there. And I didn't know where you'd gone." He looks lost now, even as the wail of a siren tells us help— and a reckoning—is on its way. "I've been looking for you for years too. That's what the story was about, the one I wanted so badly for you to read." His Adam's apple bobs. "My therapist said I needed to reconcile myself to the fact that I'd never see you again, but I couldn't. All I wanted to do was see you. And to say thank you for saving my life."

I turn back to the flames. "I guess we're even."

CHAPTER THIRTY-THREE

Bend, Oregon
December 16, 2000

S he dragged herself out of the culvert, bringing herself into the frigid light of day, her eyes stinging with the brightness. Rebirth. She was new in this world, new to herself. She could become anything. Choose a new name. Become a new person.

Assuming she could make it to safety. Bend lay a few miles up the road, but she had heard the sirens, so many screaming sirens. The authorities might be on the lookout for anyone who had been in the fire...especially a murderer. She looked down at her legs, trembling with the burden of her body. Her black sweats were wet and stained, but you couldn't see any blood. Maybe she could find a shelter, a place that might give her a spare set of clothes, a meal, some water. God, she was so thirsty. Her head pounded with it. Her mind was a desert.

She squatted at the sound of an approaching car. She had to get out of this ditch and up onto the road. She had to get as far from this place as possible. She could still pick up a whiff of ash and smoke in the air.

She groaned with the effort as she pulled her way up to the road. She grimaced and brought herself to her feet. She breathed in freedom and exhaled hope. She wasn't dead yet. And until she was, she'd put as many miles between her and this place as she possibly could. She couldn't bear to think of what she'd left behind. What she'd abandoned. She could only look forward.

She gritted her teeth and began to run, each footfall a new agony, her thoughts bound up in hope and determination. She'd worked so hard to survive, no way could she give up now. Dreams of the new future she'd build for herself were so loud in her mind that she didn't hear the growl of the pickup truck's engine until it was just behind her, slowing to a crawl and then to a stop. Eszter didn't stop, though. She kept her eyes forward and her feet moving, her heart thundering with the presence of this new threat. When the truck didn't speed past her, she glanced over her shoulder at it and immediately stumbled with dizziness. The truck moved forward, once again pulling to a stop next to her. Its passenger-side window was already rolled down.

The driver, a man in coveralls, his messy, black hair held in place by a baseball cap, gave her a quizzical look. "You look like you're running from a ghost," he said. "You okay? Need a ride?"

Eszter looked up the road. She was so tired. Everything hurt. Nothing felt safe. She peered at the man, taking in his gentle smile and stubbly face. "I'm going to Bend," she said.

"Me too," he said, shoving open the passenger door. "Hop on in if you want. It's only a few miles."

Only a few miles to a brand-new world. Of course, she had no idea what she'd do once she got there, but right now, it barely mattered, as long as she was away from here. She carefully climbed into the truck, all her mental energy focused on not crying with the pain of the burns and the scream of her overtaxed muscles. "Thanks."

He held out his hand. "Martin Rodriguez."

She shook it. "Es—" She paused, clearing her throat. That wasn't her name, not anymore. But it didn't feel safe or right to use her birth name, either, and now the man was looking concerned, perhaps wondering if this bedraggled person he'd just picked up didn't even know her own name. The solution came to her as if murmured in her ear, a familiar voice lilting in her memory. A voice she'd never hear again, a friend gone forever.

She smiled at the man even as tears stung her eyes. "My name is Christy."

EPILOGUE

I sit in my wheelchair behind the partition, listening to the news crews setting up their cameras. According to my watch, my heart rate is 123. I'm surprised it's not higher.

Valentina pokes her head around the room divider. "You ready?" She steps around the temporary wall. "Here." She smooths my hair on the right side. "You look great."

I laugh, looking down at myself, my left arm and shoulder casted. My right foot's in a boot; I got away with just a stress fracture. I'm on an injectable med for the osteoporosis; I'm in therapy for the anorexia. And the trauma. I'm a mess, but I'm working on it—and probably will be for the rest of my life. "Is Miles out there?"

She nods. "This is his big moment too."

It's all part of our agreement, one we hammered out from our respective hospital beds, invalid to invalid. After he got my text, he didn't send the story to Valentina, deciding to talk to me one more time before he pulled the trigger. And twenty-four hours later, he realized he had a much bigger story on his hands. So he offered me a deal:

He won't tell Valentina what I did to sabotage him as long as I never divert from journalistic ethics again—if I do, it's all bets off, and he swore he would show no mercy. I believe him. I can only hope that with time, I can rebuild the trust he had in me before I ruined it. And maybe even win him back as a friend.

In exchange for this reprieve, he gets exclusive rights to tell my story, after this one press conference to satisfy the baying hounds of the media. It's meant to garner interest for the book deal. All Valentina knows is that I hid my past, and now I'm coming out in the open after being targeted by—and miraculously taking out—a serial revenge killer, with the help of a boy whose life I saved twenty years ago.

I'm being painted as a hero. A somewhat broken and complicated one, which makes me perfect for the times we live in.

It's more than I deserve. Another second chance in a life built from them.

Kieran leans around the partition and says, "All set."

"Okay," says Valentina, smiling down at me. "Ready to roll?"

"Ha-ha," I say as she moves behind me and pushes my wheelchair forward, around the partition and into the banquet room of the hotel. A veritable sea of cameras click and whir and glide around to track my progress toward the table at the front, a single microphone waiting. Valentina adjusts it so it's right in front of my face. Then she gives me a thumbs-up and goes to sit next to Miles, who is also in a wheelchair even though he's already able to maneuver on crutches.

I look out at the crowd—it's not only reporters here. Noah sits in the second row, a photographer friend from Reed next to him. He gives me a solemn nod. He's got a story of his own to tell and plenty of interest to build on. Plus, he's a lot more photogenic than I am.

Hailey and Martin are also here—they've been staying with me in my apartment, taking care of me now that I'm out of the hospital and while their Bend home is rebuilt, being the family I need right now.

I reached out to Eric, but I expect that to be more complicated. I only worked up the courage this morning to reintroduce myself, and I haven't checked my messages yet to see if he's replied. He might hate me for what I did, what I've become, and for not reaching out to him for so many years. But that's his choice—I won't make it for him, and I'm brave enough to face whatever he might want to say. I owe him at least that much.

I catch Miles's eye. The story has been building for three weeks, the murders of Arnie and Essie and Marie, the attempted murder of a reporter, a fact-checker, and a student journalist, the lurid revelation of my past and Noah's. I've spent hours being questioned by Ben Ransom, explaining what happened so he can resolve the fiery deaths of a serial killer and her accomplice son.

All my worry about my actions twenty years ago has dwindled to a low hum. Noah met with Ben and explained everything he remembered. Apparently, his therapist has notes that corroborate his memories. He remembers that I fought for him and that I risked my life to save him. Twice.

Somehow, the way it comes out...I'm not going to be charged with anything. Ben told me that there wouldn't be enough evidence to convict me and that it seems like a case of justifiable homicide anyway, because of Noah's witness statement. I still can't believe it.

I squint into the lights and offer a smile. The buzz of voices fades. This is my fourth new beginning, and I need it as desperately as I needed the first three. There are so many things I want to do over. So many mistakes to avoid. And it starts here, now. With the truth.

No more running. This time, I'm standing my ground.

"I want to start by introducing myself," I say. My voice quavers but gets steadier with every syllable. "My birth name was Anna Wilbur. My name when I was a member of the Oracles of Innocence was Eszter. The name I gave when I escaped the cult was Christy, a stolen, fake name for the shell I was back then." I look over at Hailey and Martin, and they each nod. I smile. "The name I chose for my new beginning was Dora Rodriguez, and that's the one I'm keeping. Now I'm ready for your questions."

READ ON FOR AN EXCERPT FROM S. F. KOSA'S

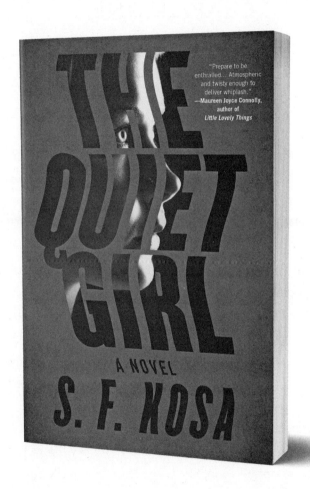

"Prepare to be enthralled... Atmospheric and twisty enough to deliver whiplash."
—Maureen Joyce Connolly, author of *Little Lovely Things*

THE QUIET GIRL

A NOVEL

S. F. KOSA

AVAILABLE NOW FROM SOURCEBOOKS LANDMARK

CHAPTER ONE

She hummed quietly as she watched the churning waves. It was a song with words she couldn't quite remember, though surely she had known them at some point—the tune came to her as easily as breathing. The ocean folded over on itself, again and again, and she felt the relentless movement inside her. She swayed, her bare feet embedded in the sand, while the salty wind whipped her hair across her face. Sandpipers sprinted by on their toothpick legs. A gull cried out as it swooped overhead.

She hummed a little louder. The tune had been looping through her mind ever since she'd gotten up this morning, but she couldn't dredge up the name of the song or recall who sang it. Annoyance pricked at her once, twice, then faded to a dull twinge as she let the sight of the waves lull her again.

She'd stay here all day if she could. Race Point was the very edge of Cape Cod, surrounded by infinite water and sky. From here, she could drift away on the wind. She turned her face to the sun, closing her eyes and spreading her arms. The tune had fallen silent in her throat; she was a wisp of smoke, a silky ribbon spiraling in the breeze.

Somewhere to her left, a man shouted. She spun around, arms winding instinctively over her middle before falling to her sides. Just two guys playing Frisbee. They didn't even seem aware of her. She turned back to the ocean and stared as a wave deposited a swath of foam a yard from where she stood. She could float away. She could fly. She was a song on the breeze. Her mind was empty. Empty.

As the waves spread themselves thin along the sand, she tried to reclaim the soaring freedom that had seemed within her grasp only moments before.

After a few minutes, she gave up.

Her hair had coiled around her throat; strands were caught in her eyelashes and had wormed their way between her lips. Her cheeks felt warm; she'd been so eager to get here that she hadn't bothered to slather on the sunblock. Her bare calves stung with the scrape of sand. Suddenly, she felt it all a little *too* much—her body, her skin, her hair. The tune she'd just been humming was gone, crowded out by tiny shocks of irritation.

She had no idea what time it was, and Lou had warned her about being late. His words scrolled through her mind: *Easy hire, easy fire. Under the table works both ways.*

She took a step backward, trying to shed the sight of the ocean, until finally it let her go like an egg white slipping free from its yolk. She felt her brain quivering in her skull, a delicate membrane holding everything in place. One prick and all her thoughts might come dribbling out her ears.

Her shift started at five. When had she left the boardinghouse? As she slogged through the shifting sand toward the parking lot, past the Frisbee boys, shovel-and-pail-wielding kids hunched over mounds of sand, and their exhausted parents floppy as seals in their loungers, she tried to remember the morning. It was like fishing through the grease trap at Haverman's, coming up with a few chicken bones and a lot of sludge. She recalled the musky scent of Esteban's skin as she crawled from the bed. Rough granules of sand sticking to the bottoms of her feet as she headed for the bathroom. Frigid spray from the shower hitting her shoulder blades. Hanging the towel on the wobbly hook behind the door. Buttoning her shorts, feeling them sag down to her hips. Sliding her feet into flip-flops, the strap between her toes. Blinking in the sun as she stepped outside into the already-sweltering day.

She fiddled with her bike lock, her fingers automatically poking the numbers into place. One-two-zero-four. She maneuvered the bike away from the crowded rack as more riders rolled off the trail and came toward the railing. One of them, a middle-aged man in blue spandex, halted his bike right next to her and reached for his helmet. His gold watch glinted in the sunlight.

"Excuse me," she said, and then she pressed her lips together, startled by the sound of her voice. Was that what she always sounded like? Was that her actual voice?

The man was looking at her, expecting something. What did he want? Oh.

She smiled. "Do you know what time it is?"

He checked. "About four thirty."

She swung her leg over the seat and steered the bike onto the trail. Can't. Be. Late. One word per heartbeat, thumping against the inside of her skull. She pedaled up the hills and leaned into the curves, weaving around families with wriggling toddlers, older women in wide-brimmed hats, and a few cyclists struggling to figure out the gears on their rented bikes.

She didn't have time to shower or change for her shift, but it didn't really matter. She would be spending the next eight or so hours in a steamy kitchen, loading and unloading the dishwasher, her hair curling along her temples and sticking to her face, trying to avoid Amber, who always made her uneasy. Amber's days off were her favorite days to work. Hopefully today would be one of them.

She nearly rolled through the red light on Route 6 as she pondered what day it was. She'd lost track again, maybe because she'd been working seven days a week lately, five to closing, five to closing, five to closing. The only thing she really had to keep track of was the five part, and she could barely manage that.

She picked up speed as she pedaled along Conwell, nearly got winged by a pickup as she hooked left onto Bradford, and swerved to miss a lady with a stroller as she bumped up onto the sidewalk on Commercial, right out front of Haverman's. The restaurant consisted of a covered beer garden patio snugged up against a narrow old house that used to belong to some fishing captain but was now taken up entirely by the kitchen, storage room, and Lou's upstairs office and apartment. The high-tops and bar seats were already full, and several folks were standing at the vine-covered arch marking the entrance to the patio, giving their names and numbers to Jenn, the hostess for tonight. As she chained her bike to the rack on the sidewalk, she gave Jenn a quick wave and was rewarded with a blank, stone-faced look.

She ducked her head as she went around the other side of the house and opened the employees only door in the alley. It might be hot and humid outside, but the climate inside was positively tropical. She closed her eyes as the familiar steamy funk enveloped her.

"Hey, Layla! I was just asking Jaliesa if you were working today!"

It wasn't one of Amber's days off.

Layla hung her bag on one of the hooks along the wall, noting the other purses and backpacks and registering who each belonged to. Purple pack—Jaliesa, the nice bartender. Pink hobo bag—Amber, the nosy waitress. Worn leather pack with the little hole that always tempted Layla to stick her finger in it—Arthur, the cute line cook. Her tongue itched as she considered his bag for the thousandth time. The material was so thin, so ragged, that it didn't stand a chance if she decided to jab her finger right through.

"Hey there, space cadet."

She flinched and turned her head. Amber was right next to her. Her mascara was smudged. Layla glanced at the wall clock above the hooks. "I'm not late," she said and smiled with relief. Her voice no longer sounded like that of a stranger.

Amber returned her smile, probably thinking it had been meant to be friendly. "We're short-staffed. Reese is out tonight. Lou wants you out front."

The words splashed over her like a bucket of ice water. "Whoa. No. I d-don't think—I mean, I'm not—" She looked down at her flip-flops, her too-loose shorts, her secondhand T-shirt with a whale surrounded by plastic bottles. There was a faded brown stain on the blue fabric, right over her left boob. She raked her fingers through her hair, but they got caught in the tangles.

Amber gave her an appraising once-over. "No worries. I got you." Amber grabbed her by the elbow and snagged the pink hobo bag as they sailed toward the employees' bathroom.

Layla's skin had gone goose bumpy. "I'm a dishwasher," she mumbled. "I wash dishes."

"Honey, it's Friday night, and you're about to make ten times more an hour than you ever could loading greasy plates into the monster machine."

"Why can't Arthur or Serge—?"

"Lou wanted another female server. Lesbians deserve eye candy, too, ya know." She whipped a T-shirt out of her bag, *Haverman's Helles House* emblazoned across the chest, and motioned for Layla to strip off her shirt.

She crossed her arms over her middle. "I'm not a waitress."

"You are now." Amber held up the shirt. "And if you're not, you can go tell Lou yourself."

She took off her shirt and yanked the other over her head. She wished she'd stopped to put on a bra this morning. Her eyes and nose burned. A droning buzz filled the space between her ears. Her vision flashed with blotches of red and black. She braced her palm against the wall.

Amber slapped lightly at her cheeks. "Hey. Hey. Layla. Stop having a panic attack. Jenn and Wanny and Oscar and me'll all be out there, and we'll look out for you. We need the help tonight."

Help. "Is—is Esteban—?"

"Your guard dog ain't here tonight, though I expect you know his schedule better than I do these days." Amber took her by the shoulders and gave her a brisk shake. "Come on. You're a big girl. Act like it."

Layla blinked. Amber had a sinewy neck and yellow hair with black roots. Amber had big dangly earrings that bobbled and swayed and clinked. Amber had a narrow nose and a triangle face and eyes that were murky green. Amber had a voice that sounded like barbecue and corn bread, not lobster and quahogs.

"If I screw up—" Layla began.

"Then don't."

Amber turned her around, and a moment later, Layla felt a brush run through her hair. She clasped her hands together and squeezed, fingernails digging into skin. She swore she could feel every single bristle slicing across her scalp, but somehow, with each stroke, she relaxed a little. The sensation was like a weight pressing down, down, down, submerging the words and thoughts that had been crowding to the surface a moment before. By the time Amber yanked Layla's hair back into a ponytail, her cold sweat had gone warm.

Amber handed her an apron. She pointed to the pocket. "Tablet's already in there. Just tap on the right table number, then the menu items. Keep an eye out for your table numbers at the counter and the bar so you can get stuff to the diners quickly. Lou hates it when stuff sits for longer than a minute, and I swear he times us. Check in on your tables just before they've got an empty glass, always offer another round, always offer dessert, and pretend like the sea scallop crudo has given you multiple orgasms. Lou wants us to push that one."

Layla cringed at the thought of putting scallops, or any other seafood for that matter, in her mouth. She couldn't imagine ever having liked it, but the nights she'd spent scraping the half-chewed and picked-over remainders off customers' plates had only deepened her aversion.

Amber scowled as she read Layla's expression. "I don't care if the slimy little things give you hives, for heaven's sake—*pretend*. It's all about selling, okay?"

Layla tied on the apron over her shorts and pulled out the tablet as Amber continued to rattle off instructions. Her mouth moved a lot as she spoke, but her eyes and cheeks and brow were completely still somehow. Layla stared until a clatter from the kitchen startled her back to attention. The tablet was in her hands. The one she would use to punch in the orders. This would be fine. Just fine.

"Of course it will," Amber said, making her realize she'd spoken aloud.

———

It was fine until it wasn't. The hours whooshed by as she concentrated on making it through each individual minute. She mixed up a few orders and spilled a drink at the bar, but the patrons were mostly sweet. It was better than dishwashing, because there were no blank times. Every second demanded her complete focus, and it was all she could think about. Nothing else. Nothing but pressing the right button, picking up the right glass, saying the right words, and smiling the proper smile, even as she handed over plates of raw oysters and scallop crudo that made her stomach turn.

She had no idea how many tables she had turned over, and the faces of the customers were all a blur. The air had gone cooler as the night progressed, as the lanterns drooping over the space came on, the sky beyond went dark, revelers strolled past, and drag queens stalked by, waving regally and pausing for photos with admiring patrons. She liked watching them—there was no telling what the face beneath all that makeup really looked like. It was as if they came out of nowhere and disappeared just as easily.

The crowd thinned out as midnight approached, and she paused at the bar to sip a glass of water Jaliesa had set there for her. Her shirt and shorts were damp with sweat, and her ponytail had slipped down to the base of her neck, where her hair stuck to her nape.

"Almost there, girl, and then it's time to count tips over a double G&T." Jaliesa shook a silver cocktail shaker in each hand while her ebony curls jiggled around her face. "My favorite part of the night."

Layla smiled into her water glass, enjoying the feel of ice on her tongue. Her mind was a quiet hum of white noise.

"Hey," said Jenn, tapping her on the shoulder. "I just seated three at six."

She took a final gulp of her water. "Okay." She tucked a stray lock of hair behind her ear. Table six was in the back corner of the narrow patio. Seated there were one woman and two guys who looked about Layla's age. One of the guys had his muscular, tattooed arm around the woman, whose curly black hair hung loose around her shoulders. The other guy, whose back was to her, had short red hair. They were dressed casually—shorts and T-shirts—not for clubbing.

She threaded her way across the patio and approached the table where the three of them were absorbed in conversation.

"—don't really want to go back until Saturday, but my parents leave for Paris on Thursday, and there's no way they're taking Mr. Drillby to a kennel," the redhead was telling his friends. He was talking fast, but his words were a little slurred, his voice a little loud.

"Hi there, and welcome to Haverman's. My name's Layla, and I'll be taking care of you tonight," she said to his companions, who had seen her standing there. "Can I start you guys off with something other than water?"

"I'll have the house margarita," said the woman.

"I'd love a Cape Cod *Blonde*," said her partner, grinning at Layla while his companion rolled her eyes.

As his friend spoke, the redhead turned his head and looked up at her. The loose smile he'd been wearing dropped away. "Maggie?"

"Nope. Can I—"

"Maggie Wallace," said the redhead. His eyes were bloodshot. He smelled like pot and whiskey. He grabbed her wrist.

The tablet in her hand clattered to the ground, and she let out a cry. She pulled her arm free of the guy's sweaty grasp. People's heads were turning. Eyes were on them. She scooped the tablet up, peering at the screen. It hadn't cracked, thank God. "A margarita and a Blonde," she said, breathless. "Anything else?"

The guy had turned back to his friends, who were giving him concerned looks. The tattooed guy had put his hand on the redhead's arm.

"I swear it's her," the redhead was saying. "I was telling you. Remember?"

"He'll stick with water," the woman said.

"I'll get those orders in right now," she replied, but her voice had gone weird again. Strange and unfamiliar. It made her wish she didn't have a mouth at all.

The redhead turned in his chair again. "You look exactly like her," he said. "My girlfriend was talking about you the other day. Come *on*. Reina Ramirez. You know her, right?"

She realized she'd been shaking her head vigorously. She stopped when the tattooed guy said, "Let it go, dude." He hadn't released his friend's arm. "Let the lady do her job."

Before the redhead could free himself, she headed for the kitchen. Jaliesa's mouth was moving as she walked by, but she couldn't hear what the bartender was saying. Inside her head, there was a low buzz and snatches of a song that seemed familiar yet impossible to place.

"Layla?" called out Amber, poking her head into the back as Layla reached for her bag. "Wait—you're *leaving*?" She pushed through the swinging door and dropped her tablet into the pocket of her apron. "What the hell happened?" She looked over her shoulder. "Did one of those guys grope you or something? Because—"

"No." She tugged the Haverman's shirt over her head, which was buzzing, buzzing, buzzing. She could make out Amber's words, but only barely. The shirt fell from her loose fingers, where it landed crumpled at their feet.

"You're kinda pale," the waitress said. "Are you sick?"

"Yeah," she replied. "I'm...done."

"Oh, honey." Amber sounded sympathetic as she watched Layla tug her stained blue shirt over her head. "I know it's been a long night." Amber sighed. "You really did great. We'll set aside your—"

But she was already out the door, down the alleyway, unlocking her bike—one-two-zero-four—and pedaling down the road. She didn't even know where she was going. All she knew was that she needed to get away.

READING GROUP GUIDE

1. Why do you think "Christy" first goes with Eszter that day in Portland? Imagine if you were in Christy's shoes. What would you do if presented with this kind of friendship, kindness, and opportunity?

2. How would you describe Dora? Why do you think she is well suited to her job as a fact-checker?

3. Miles tells the team at the *Hatchet* that the Oracles of Innocence story was huge news at the time. Why do you think audiences are fascinated by cult stories? What comes to mind when you think of cults?

4. Compare and contrast Eszter and Parvaneh. What do you think draws them together? What separates them? How would you describe their roles in the Oracles of Innocence?

5. Describe Darius. What character traits does he have that push him to hold this leadership role? How do you picture him?

6. What part of the Oracles of Innocence lifestyle did you find most intriguing? Most outlandish? Where do you think the dangerous turning point was?

7. If you had an Oracles of Innocence name, what would it be? Imagine you could take on a new identity and new way of life. How do you think that would feel? Why do you believe people choose that route?

8. Describe Miles and Dora's partnership. Do you think of them as allies or adversaries? How do their goals align?

9. Trauma plays a large role in the story. How do each of these characters manifest or work through their respective traumas?

10. What do you make of Xerxes's journey? Do you think his past defines him? If you were in his shoes, what would you make of your tumultuous early years?

11. What do you think happens to Dora once the story closes? Do you think she finds the peace she's been seeking?

A CONVERSATION
WITH THE AUTHOR

The Night We Burned **is a fascinating look at cults and cult psychology. What inspired you to write this thriller?**

As a psychologist, I'm always trying to understand why people behave and think how they do, and cults (also called "high-control groups") provide a fascinating challenge in that respect: Why do typical, intelligent people "allow" themselves to be manipulated and controlled in such strange, weird ways? I think most of us are fascinated with that question. My focus in this book was to show one (very extreme) example of how someone gets drawn in and why they stay *long* after things go bad.

Did you model the Oracles of Innocence after any real-life group? A mix of different groups?

The Oracles of Innocence grew from my understanding of several existing or past groups, including Heaven's Gate, the Branch Davidians, and the followers of Charles Manson. More prominent in my mind than any other, though, was the Peoples Temple and its notorious leader, Jim Jones. Several times before the Jonestown mass suicide event, Jones essentially had his followers "practice" by asking them to drink substances and then telling them they'd ingested lethal poison. He got them used to that kind of obedience before the tragic finale. He also exploited female followers by telling them that sex with the leader would help purge or heal them of their various trauma histories and issues (this is not an uncommon behavior among cult leaders). Jones also became obsessed with persecution, and the mass suicide came when he became convinced that the government was going to invade the compound and kill them all, including the children. In *The Night We Burned*, Darius uses all these strategies to control his followers.

What character did you connect with the most?

Dora, I think. She's painfully imperfect but wants to do better. She's terrified but wants to be brave. She knows the stakes and doesn't want to give up what she's built for herself over the years, but she also grows to understand that she's missed a few key ingredients. She comes to realize she's not trusting or prioritizing her relationships as much as she should, in part because of what she went through when she was a member of the Oracles.

Talk a bit about Dora and the way she has dealt with her trauma. What research did you do to bring Dora's character to life?

In terms of a formal psychology text, I relied on Alexandra Stein's *Terror, Love and Brainwashing: Attachment in Cults and Totalitarian Systems*, which explains how, under the right conditions, almost anyone can be manipulated in unexpected and surprising ways. Also helpful was Steven Hassan's BITE model (behavior, information, thought, and emotional control), which outlines how groups draw in and maintain control over members. A lot of people think only weak-minded or gullible individuals can be lured into high-control groups, which results in a lot of shame and self-condemnation for people who have survived them. Dora is an example of such a person—twenty years later, and even though she can *intellectually* understand why she joined and why she stayed, *emotionally* she's still fragile, in part because she's avoided seeking treatment and still bears the internalized stigma from her past. To portray her mindset, I not only read books like *Waco* by David Thibodeau and two books by Jeff Guinn (*Manson* and *The Road to Jonestown*), but I also watched several documentaries that included interviews with former high-control group members, including *The Vow* (about NXIVM), *Wild Wild Country* (about the Rajneeshpuram), *Holy Hell* (about Buddhafield), and *Going Clear* (about Scientology). These former group members provided a range of perspectives but also showed how intelligent, accomplished people can be drawn into these groups—and often experience trauma that requires long-term treatment to heal.

Talk a bit about the relationship between Eszter and Parvaneh. Why is their friendship so crucial to the story?

The relationship between Eszter and Parvaneh grounds and humanizes a story in which frankly crazy stuff is going on. I think their connection, forged from similar pasts and mutual need, helps carry readers through the difficult and hair-raising sequence of events that leads to the fire. Eszter doesn't lure or manipulate Parvaneh into the group so much as she wants to share this wonderful thing she's experiencing with someone who might need it as much as she does. It's only later that she realizes it was a terrible mistake, but at that point, it's too late to save both of them.

This novel has such an amazing twist to it. When you begin writing a thriller, what comes first, the hook or the twist? Do you always know the twists before you begin?

It depends. Sometimes the twist comes first, but in this case, the hook did. I knew I wanted to tell a story about a fact-checker who needed to conceal details of her past, and only later did I decide *how* I wanted to tell that story. At first, I considered including several additional perspectives (e.g., Miles, Ben Ransom), but after I churned on it a bit, I decided it would be best to distill it down to the two most important voices: Parvaneh and Dora.

What's been on your reading pile lately?

In the realm of fiction, I am currently riveted by *On Earth We're Briefly Gorgeous* by Ocean Vuong. In terms of nonfiction, I recently finished *Culture Warlords* by Talia Lavin and *Caste* by Isabel Wilkerson, both of which I highly, highly recommend.

What do you ultimately want readers to take away from *The Night We Burned*?

One extraordinarily common mistake we *all* make as humans is called "fundamental attribution error." It's our tendency to blame a person's character or personality when things go wrong. But when we do that, we lose all sympathy, and it's often because we don't think deeply enough about how the pressures and pulls of the situation shape human beings' decisions and behaviors. I'd love for readers to come away from *The Night We Burned* with more appreciation for how people's contexts, the behavior of others around them, and the dynamics of their present circumstances can lead them to do things we can't necessarily predict if we focus only on what's "wrong" with them personally.

ACKNOWLEDGMENTS

Like all my books, this one was a true team effort and collaboration. Many thanks to everyone at Sourcebooks Landmark, including Dominique Raccah, Kirsten Wenum, Heather Hall, Gretchen Stelter, and Sabrina Baskey, for their enthusiasm, support, and commitment to all the details that made *The Night We Burned* what it is. Much gratitude to my editor, MJ Johnston, for believing in this book and pushing me to make it better and especially for recognizing the power of the relationship between Eszter and Parvaneh from the beginning. Huge thanks also go to James Iacobelli for designing a cover that made me gasp the first time I saw it—and that made me keep going back to look again.

Thank you to the team at Irene Goodman Literary Agency and, in particular, to my fierce agent, Victoria Marini, for all your coaching, strategy, and honesty. I'm grateful for our partnership. Thanks also to Olivia Fanaro at United Talent Agency for your advocacy and enthusiasm. And to Jena Gregoire at Pure Textuality PR for your organization, creativity, reliability, and patience.

To my wonderful friends, including Lydia Kang, Jayne Tan, Natasha Goldman, and Paul Block, thank you for tolerating me no matter what emotional state I happen to be in and for feasts and merriment and conversation, even when virtual. And to Claudine Fitzgerald—I hope you realize how much I profoundly appreciate your cheerleading and belief in me, lady. Thank you.

I would not be able to dwell in the darkest places of the human psyche without the counterbalance of joy and light that comes from my family, particularly my children. Thank you to Taylor for mutual accountability and the sprints that carried me through the end of the first draft, and to Erin, Asher, Alma, and Evelyn for providing delight and comic relief when I emerged from the writing cave. Thank you to my parents and sisters, nieces and nephews, who love me unconditionally and generously. And of course, I could not have done any of this without the rock-steady support of my partner in crime. Peter, thank you for believing in me and my books, even in the moments when I can't quite manage it. And thank you for letting me spoil all the twists before you have a chance to read them.

ABOUT THE AUTHOR

S. F. Kosa is a clinical psychologist with a fascination for the seedy underbelly of the human psyche. *The Quiet Girl* was her debut psychological suspense novel. She also writes as Sarah Fine and is the author of more than two dozen fantasy, urban fantasy, sci-fi, and romance novels, several of which have been translated into multiple languages. She lives in Massachusetts with her husband and their (blended) brood of five young humans.

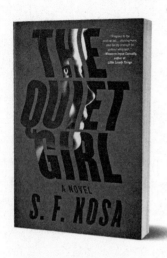